CW01082126

THE BROKEN KINGDOMS OF OSVOLTA

Book Cover by David Gardias / Best Selling Covers

Edited by E.J. Lounsbury / EJL Editing

Proofread by Brandee Paschall Books LLC

Chapter headers created with CanvaPro

Map designed with Inkarnate

Logo by Jessica Bretherton

First edition 2024

Contents

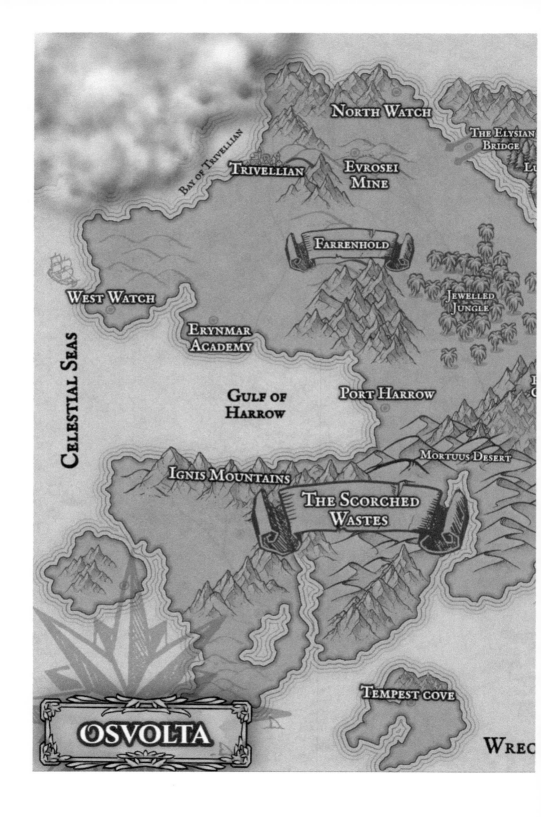

Dedication

For my mum who raised me on fairy tales and Disney stories, allowing me to believe in magic.
For my dad who always believed in me and pushed me forward when things felt hard and scary.
For my sister who's always there when I need her, forever in my corner.
I love you all, endlessly.

And to you, dear reader, thank you for taking a chance on MY story, every page you read is a dream come true for me. I hope one day you get to live your dreams too.

Pronunciation Guide

People:

Solveig Aila Maleen
  sool-vay / eye-la / mal-een

Emmerich Ryker Anders
  em-er-rick / rye-kur / an-ders

Adira Everette Etana
  a-dee-ra / ever-ret / eh-tah-na

Malik Etana
  mal-ick / eh-tah-na

Jasper Ade Etana
  jasper/ aid / eh-tah-na

Eleric Etana
  el-er-rick / eh-tah-na

Wrenn Bleeker
  like wrench without the ch / bleak-er

Teris
  Teh-ris

Dissin Sellen

diss-in / sell-en

Asta Cyrene Maleen
  like pasta if the p was silent / serene / mal-een

Xanthe Enya Whitlock
  zan-th-ee / en-yah / wit-lock

Aldrik Torrin Whitlock
  all-drik / torr-in / wit-lock

Renit Teria
  ren-it / teh-ria

<u>Things:</u>

The Valdrych
  the / vaul-d-rick

Gabos Leaf
  gab-oss / leaf

Nyteberry
  night-berry

Nexun Weed
  nex-uhn / weed

<u>Places:</u>

Torrelin
  t(o)-rel-in (the 'o' sounds like of without the f)

Marrelin City
  ma-rel-in / city

Luxenal Mine
  lux-in-all / mine

Cuprum Forest
  cue-prum / forest

Rialtus Keep / Mountains
  ree-al-tuss / keep /mountains
Solist Port / Cove
  sol-isst / port / cove
Farrenhold
  fah-ren-hold
Trivellian
  Tr-iv-el-e-an
Evrosei Mine
  ev-row-sea / mine
Erynmar Academy
  eh-rin-marr /academy
Estrellyn (The Scorched Wastes)
  eh-strel-in
Ignis Mountains
  ig-nuhs / mountains
Mortuus Desert
  mor-toos / desert
Elithiend
  eh-lith-ee-end
Vhallakyr
  val-la-key-er
Valelinn
  va-leh-lin
Miram Meadows
  mih-ram / meadows
Elysian Caldera / Bridge

uh-li-zee-uhn / caldera / bridge

Osvolta

oz-volt-ah

Author's Note

Dear Reader,

The Broken Kingdoms of Osvolta contains mature themes and is intended for ages 18+. Reader discretion is advised.

Themes include:

Abusive relationship, Assault, Blood, Bodily Fluids, Bones, Burns/ Burning, Classism (those with powers and those without), Death (including death of loved ones), Emotional Abuse, Experimentation, Family Conflict, Fighting, Forced Labour (prison camp), Gore, Incarceration, Injury, Misogyny, Murder, Physical Abuse, Poisoning, Profanity, Religion (not real world), Scars, Sexism, Torture, Violence.

CHAPTER ONE

The Reaper of Luxenal

The sharp metallic crack of the prisoners' chains created a deafening echo. A building orchestra, backed up by scratching pickaxes in craggy earth, as the rain poured in a deluge. There were few incidents that could halt operations at Luxenal Copper Mine. The weather was not one of them.

High above the open cast, figures cloaked in shadow observed the prisoners suffering, safe in their warm alcoves. Behind one of the reinforced windows was a woman dressed in all black. She sipped from a glass of whiskey. Fresh, non-melting ice shards clinked a soft melody against the crystal. Her eyes drifted from the melee below, to the cloud drenched sky where the weak sun edged closer to the horizon.

She'd kept them waiting long enough.

Straightening the copper cuffs at her wrists, she tied her hair into a knot to keep it safely out of the way. She'd made the mistake of leaving it loose only once before, and nearly lost her own life to her vanity in the process. She still bore a thin raised scar on her neck as a reminder to never be so foolish again.

Slowly, she rose from her perch by the window, reaching for the hip holster laying on the edge of her desk. Buckling it tight as she crossed the room to wrench the door open. It stuck for a moment, becoming trapped in its frame that had swollen with perpetual damp, before finally releasing, allowing her to exit into the hall.

She'd spent two long years in the claustrophobic dark of Luxenal Mine, growing familiar with all its twists, turns and horrors. With one last right turn, she sauntered into the dank, open space of the entryway.

"They were expecting you a while ago." A small voice squeaked from the corner.

She froze. Lip curling as she turned, taking slow, purposeful steps toward the meek, brown-haired girl.

"Repeat that," she snarled, slamming a hand down on the desk, leaning in close. The girl jumped as the sound reverberated around the room, the papers she clutched scattered to the floor, her gaze falling with them.

"Fetch my cloak." She flicked her chin toward the closest behind the girl.

"Of course, right away," she stammered, flying from her chair with such panicked speed, it clattered to the ground behind her. When she returned, her eyes were glassy, chest heaving as her hand shook where she held the cloak. And the woman thought she saw the nervous flutter of the girl's heartbeat at her neck as she snatched it from her grasp.

"Next time you want to test giving out orders, don't choose someone with the authority to have you in chains before sundown." She flung the cloak around her shoulders in one swift movement, narrowly missing the girl's face, as she strode for the doorway. The tarnished copper handles were cool against the warmth of her palm as she flung the doors wide open to stride out into the downpour.

The great open cast lay before her, like the charred maw of an ancient beast of legend. To the left was a stage. Dissin Sellen, the Commander of Luxenal Mine, stood atop it, surrounded by a hoard of guards. He grimaced at the sight of her.

"All rise for Her Royal Highness, Solveig Aila of House Maleen. Princess of Torrelin, High Inquisitor of Luxenal Copper Mine, Master of Hydromancy."

Mud splashed Solveig's boots, leaving a pattern of russet speckles in its wake as she strode up to the makeshift stage.

"Commander Sellen." She spoke in a monotone, over the din of the prisoners' tools.

Two guards came up the steps behind her, dragging a prisoner with them. She faced the inmate as they chained him to a set of hooks on the stage, before her gaze slid back to the commander's.

"Charges?"

"Dereliction of duty and conspiring against the crown." Solveig's eyes gleamed. The wind blew slick tendrils of hair across her face as she spoke. "Connall of House Kano, you heard the charges. How do you plead?"

He didn't speak, only turned his gaze to meet hers.

"Your charges carry the penalty of death, Mr Kano. Should you choose not to speak in your own defence, I will have to judge you based solely on the information available to me."

Silence.

Time stretched.

Solveig's impatience grew thinner as she flexed her hands, and the blue gems set in her cuffs glowed. "Have you lost your ability to speak, Mr Kano? Nod your head and I'll send for ink and paper for you to scribe your defence instead."

Stillness, and with it the last thread of her patience snapped. The gems in her cuffs became blinding as her hand collided with his body. Pain akin to a whipping lanced across his chest. His screams reverberated around the mine.

"So, you do still have a voice," she sneered, eyes glittering as she travelled down deep to that roiling part of her soul where her power lived.

The lines about the man's face crumpled in agony, his screams grew louder, desperate. His cheeks hollowed, lips chapped and bleeding as his skin pulled tight. The wooden panels beneath them grew slick with a liquid that came not from the heavens above, but from within him.

Solveig's eyes opened, pupils dilated, sweat beading on her forehead despite the rain as she withdrew her hand.

"I don't want to hurt you, Mr Kano." She sighed, head shaking. "But if you leave me no choice, then I will do what I must."

Connall gasped, chest rattling with every exhale as he spoke in a cracked voice from his arid throat. "Horseshit, you thrive off it." He coughed, grimacing from the pain of his skin and muscles stretched tight over bone. The agony of his internal organs slowly desiccating. "The screams feed your power." His eyes narrowed as venom dripped with every word. "You and your kin deserve to rot in the deepest, darkest pit. I pray death befalls the elementals, the Crown and all else who enable your reign of terror."

Solveig remained stoic, for she had been called far worse, but she couldn't let the slight go unpunished. "An impassioned speech, Mr Kano, but I'm afraid you have merely signed your own death warrant."

A mask of indifference slid firmly over Solveig's face. No one spoke, no one moved, no one tried to stop her. "I Solveig Maleen, High Inquisitor of Luxenal Copper Mine, hereby sentence you, Connall of House Kano, to death. But I want everyone to see." She gripped his hair tight. "That when I could have tortured you, drawn every drop of liquid from you, instead I showed you mercy."

Yanking his head back, allowing their eyes to meet once more, she gripped a jewelled dagger. Releasing it in a single fluid movement, to draw the sharp-edged blade across his exposed neck. Watching as his blood spilled. Impassive, as the life slowly drained from his eyes. Until she threw his still body to the ground at her feet, wiping his blood from her dagger on the rags of his clothes.

CHAPTER TWO

The Perfect Weapon

O rnate mahogany doors swung open. The golden handles crashed into the grey stone walls as Asta Maleen, Queen of Torrelin, stalked into the dining hall of High Tower Castle. The papers in her hand crushed beneath the weight of her anger induced grip.

"You never should have indulged her with those ridiculous daggers." She raged, ice-blue eyes fierce as they zeroed in on her husband, the king, sat at the head of the table. His golden hair, turning white with age, glimmered under the light of the morning sun, grip tightening on the utensils in his hands as Asta spoke. He didn't even spare her a glance as she strode across the room to him. Leaving her seething as he lazily returned his utensils to the table. Her foot tapping as he patted at his mouth with a silk napkin.

"Lower your tone, dear wife," King Emerson warned. "It is unbecoming of a lady of your stature to screech to the heavens."

Asta only glared at him as she spoke. "Your daughter has defied our orders. Again."

"*Our* daughter, Asta. She is as much yours as she is mine."

"That girl is no daughter of mine," she spat. "She's a beast. Wild, untameable."

King Emerson sat back in his plush velvet chair; hands folded before him as he regarded his wife. "Then she is exactly what we trained her to be."

"She's little more than a dangerous liability." Asta cried, words choking in her throat as she fought to control her tone under the king's gaze that burned as though he'd encased her in flame. Only the doors opening across the room broke his hold as his gaze flicked to his son, Prince Killian, as he sauntered in, tossing an apple between his hands.

"What's dear old sister done this time?" The prince laughed as he bit into the apple's shining green flesh. Both king and queen watched as their eldest child took a seat at the table between them. He crossed one leg over the other, taking a second bite of the apple; its juices coating his thin lips as his gaze flitted between his parents.

"Your sister," Asta stated, turning back to King Emerson now, "has disobeyed orders once again. Dispatching the latest prisoner with a slice to the throat instead of her magic."

"And?" Killian shrugged, glancing at his father. "At least she still killed him. I'd say she's still under your control enough to keep killing them without question. What does it matter how she did it?"

Asta sighed, rubbing at her eyes as she placed the crumpled letter from Luxenal Mine on the table. "It matters because we didn't spend years transforming her into the perfect weapon, training her magic to be useful, for her to slash their throats and end it quickly."

"Last I heard, she still uses it. Tortures information out of them before killing them quickly. Mercy, I suppose," Killian said, taking another bite of his apple, the edges browning slightly now.

"The man is dead, Asta," Emerson agreed. "What more do you want?"

"I want what we trained her to be. The sword in our hand, at our beck and call. Something has changed. She's been away too long and forgotten who's in charge."

"You worry too much, Mother." Killian smiled, tossing his half-eaten apple on to the table as he stood to wrap an arm around her shoulders. "Solveig is still desperately loyal. If she weren't, you'd be short an executioner. You wanted a weapon, someone to carry the stain of your enemies' blood for you. Bring Solveig back to Marrelin City now and you risk tainting us alongside her." His gaze flew to his father's, then, "People will talk. The deaths haven't stopped, not amongst the rabble. How many has it been this year? Fifty?"

King Emerson nodded, the only sign that he had been listening at all.

"You're already being scrutinised by the court for their heirs being born with weakened powers. Do you want the stain of the executioner princess lingering, too? It's best to keep Solveig out of sight and mind."

The king thought for a second before ringing the bell next to his breakfast tray. Within seconds, a harried servant raced into the room. Emerson beckoned him closer, whispering so neither Asta nor Killian could hear, before waving them off to fetch what he had requested.

"Have a message delivered to Luxenal that Solveig is to return within the next month." Emerson ordered, turning to his son again. "After she has dealt with this."

The servant practically ran back into the room, a file clutched in his hands. He placed it on the table before the three royals, bowing shakily as he exited the room.

Killian's eyes gleamed as they darted to the file. "Another job?" he asked, brow quirked with interest.

"This one is personal to Solveig."

Killian reached across the table to flip the file open. A wide smile cut across his face as he read the name of the prisoner.

"Tensions are high at Luxenal. You could cause more than one death with this one." His gaze lifted to meet his fathers, "or is that your intention?"

Asta paled as she too caught sight of the identity of the prisoner. "You'll risk everything we've built over this."

"You wanted to know if Solveig remains loyal to us, my dear." Emerson shrugged. "What better way than this?"

CHAPTER THREE

Target Practice

Solveig sensed a shift in the air that wasn't from the change of seasons. Something was different; it had been quiet. Too quiet. Two years at Luxenal. Fifty executions, and Solveig hadn't known it to be this quiet in the months before winter. It was unsettling.

Throwing back the covers of her bed, she dressed quickly, in supple, deep brown pants, and a forest green cotton shirt. Lacing her leather boots by the flickering candlelight, she packed a small bag of supplies and headed out to the dark halls of the officials' residences.

The cavernous open cast lurked to her right as she exited into the fresh air, an endless pit of deep black mystery in the still dark morning. Further she went, past sorting houses, guard stations and, finally, the crematorium. The chimney was mercifully smoke free for once. Head down, she exited through the main entrance block. The guards stood on the perimeter wall didn't even glance her way as she headed straight off to the left into the western edge of the Cuprum Forest. A small river lay roughly a half morning's walk away. It was a place Solveig frequented often; the mine offered little in the way of training grounds, and she needed to keep her skills sharp.

Solveig had learned from an early age that she couldn't solely rely on her hydromancy and had to foster a talent for fighting instead. Skills she had paid for with her own blood and sweat. A currency of bruises, lacerations, and broken bones. She couldn't afford to lose her edge.

The sun rose before her as she approached the shadowed edge of the forest, colouring the sky in shades of blood orange and warm yellow. Hidden within the leaves, she paused, listening for the rush of the river through the birds' dawn chorus.

Torrelin was her home. Solveig often felt the power lurking beneath the surface, dance and play with that which lay in her veins. It was as though it recognised her. But magic could be a trickster, and the ley lines that ran deep within the earth, though tempting with the promise of unbridled power, were dangerous to play with. Often used to magnify someone's power, they could also drain it completely, something she couldn't risk falling victim to. She resolved to ignore its call, preferring her own eyes and ears over unknown, ancient magic in the dirt.

Autumn wasn't the best time of year for fishing in these waters. Most species had already swum down river toward warmer climates, but she hoped a few still lingered. There were limited options for target practice in the mine, moving targets were even fewer. Since they frowned on torture outside of her regularly scheduled executions, and she had no desire to end up in the crematorium herself, the fish were her best option.

The river gushed down the mountains thanks to the night's heavy rainfall; dangerously close to bursting its moss laden banks. Solveig watched, waiting until the first flash of brightly coloured scales appeared. No sooner had she spotted the rainbows arching off it, she released a dagger, slicing clean through the fish's belly. The foam collecting on the river turned pink as blood seeped from the wound. A direct hit on the first attempt.

Solveig repeated the move over and over for most of the morning, from various vantage points. Testing her speed, endurance, and accuracy. When the fish failed to appear, she would settle for non-moving targets. Practice was practice in the end.

Soon morning fled to midday, and Solveig took a seat against a tree, lighting a small fire to cook lunch. She gutted her kills with practiced ease, inhaling the cooling air as she went through the motions.

The weather was turning. This far north, the roads that led home would become thick with snow and ice, within a month or two, impassable until spring. With every passing year, Solveig wished the snow would come sooner and stick longer. She'd avoided Marrelin City for two years and often feared what it and its inhabitants may have become in her absence. It held nothing for her now anyway, except the prospect of a cage, and a lifetime chained to a power-hungry fool, her betrothed, Gabriel Orson. Her parents and his had signed the deal before they'd even buried her previous intended. They hadn't even allowed her to say goodbye, nor the time to mourn the man she had loved beyond reason. Not wanting to risk the chance that she would fall for someone they deemed unworthy a second time.

Torrelin was for her brother to inherit. She preferred to live out her days in the damp confines of the mine. There, at least, she had some semblance of freedom.

She chewed on the last of the salty white flesh of her catch, summoning a spurt of water from the river to douse the fire. Washing away any evidence of her meal before moving to pack her things. But the sound of a cracking branch saw her head snapping up. Moving quickly, she hid her pack beneath a dense Nyteberry bush and scaled the nearest tree to keep watch. The sounds of snapping branches and crushed leaves grew closer. Louder. Until eventually hushed voices accompanied it.

"Getting close now," a voice muttered.

"Yea, how d'ya figure that one?" came another.

"Grounds all orangey; means we're nearing the copper," the first insisted.

"Who put you in charge?" the third exclaimed.

"What ya bitching about, huh?"

"It's iron that makes the ground orange, rot brain, not copper."

"I'm in charge cos *they* said I am. How many of you have been in the Reaper's presence?" The group stilled. "Gotta have ya wits about ya in this place. Never know when she might creep out of the shadows to steal ya soul."

Solveig rolled her eyes at that. If only they knew the ghost of their nightmares was spying from above.

"How'd we get roped into this, anyway?" the second stranger grumbled.

"The prince said a message needed delivering, offered twice the pay. Don't know about you, but my roof needs fixing before the snow arrives," the first replied.

Solveig stilled this time. Even as children, she and Killian hadn't been close. If she were the recipient of his message, she knew the news wouldn't be pleasant.

Still, she remained on her perch. Hidden within the lush green foliage of the treetops until she could no longer hear even the faintest crack of a twig from the passing messengers. One step at a time, she scaled her way back down, careful to avoid scrapes from the rough bark. She fished her bag out from underneath the Nyteberry bush, surprised to find its branches still laden with berries, and made the long walk back to Luxenal.

Nyteberry was a popular poison favoured by the guards, when ingested in high quantities it resulted in agonising stomach pain. They'd often dose up anyone they deemed insubordinate before forcing them to work, day and night. Over and over until the message sank in.

Obey or suffer.

Solveig had executed countless guards who had caused a prisoner's death. Whether accidental or intentional, unless the prisoner died of natural causes, the only people with the authority to order their deaths, were her parents. King Emerson and Queen Asta. But it wasn't a deterrent for the sickest amongst them, those who enjoyed creating their own *enter-*

*tainmen*t. As long as they met their quotas, and no one ended up in the crematorium, the Commander, turned a blind eye to their *games.*

The sun drifted low in the western sky as Solveig passed through the creaking wrought-iron fence. The air surrounding the mine was chill, its proximity to the mountains often the cause. Clouds would build up against the perpetually snow-capped peaks, obscuring the sun from view, stealing its precious warmth.

The orchestra of chains and exhausted grunts echoed still as she skirted the edge of the complex, avoiding the open cast. Instead, she walked round the back of the sorting houses where the women, children and the elderly sorted rocks into designated piles for their ores and minerals. One young woman had her arm in a sling, held tight to her chest, bruises marring her neck and cheek. Unease crawled down Solveig's spine, and she wished she knew which guard had marred the woman's face so she could repay the favour.

She dropped her gaze quickly to avoid drawing attention to herself and made her way to the operations base that housed all the officials' offices. Somehow, the air inside the building was infinitely more humid. It reeked of rotting wood and rug fibres. Her gaze rose to the girl beyond the desk and froze. Because the girl Solveig had become accustomed to was missing. In her place sat a woman, with deep brown skin, her dark hair flecked with silver, secured back in an array of braids.

Solveig was about to clear her throat to gain the mysterious woman's attention, when she glanced up, churning silver eyes beheld her impassively.

"Your Highness, how may I assist you?" The woman's voice sounded smooth as honey. Her accent differed from anything Solveig had heard before.

"You have me at a disadvantage. Clearly, you know me and yet, I have never set eyes on you."

"Surely, it's not surprising for people to know who you are? A princess of the realm can hardly remain anonymous, and your exploits make it even less likely."

"Have any messages arrived for me?" Solveig asked, changing tack.

"A few messages arrived today, Your Highness."

"Solveig is fine."

"Solveig," the woman murmured, eyes falling to the papers in front of her, "but none addressed to you. Only the usual correspondence for the commander, a waste, honestly." She tucked a stray braid behind her ear, the sleeve of her sweater slipping slightly to reveal wrists silvered with old scars. "They labelled one as urgent. Alas, the commander is away this evening inspecting the new sleeping quarters in the expanded eastern sector." A single brow raised above burning eyes. "Was there anything else I could help you with, Solveig?"

"I don't believe I caught your name."

"I didn't offer it."

Silence yawned between the two women, coiling tight, waiting for either of them to break it. When neither did, the woman sighed, meeting Solveig's gaze once more.

"If a name is all you require to cease disturbing me, then you may have Viana and take your leave. I'm sure you've better mysteries to break into tonight."

"Viana is reminiscent of Farrenhold. Is that where you call home?"

"Am I on trial? I don't recall being dragged here in chains."

"Don't tempt me," Solveig whispered, taking a step forward. "It's been a few days since I scented blood in the air. I find I'm growing to miss it."

"Judging by the commander's correspondence, your blood lust will be sated soon enough. Shame though," she mused, eyeing the cuffs at Solveig's wrists.

"What is?"

"Magic fails around us every day and you decided it was wise to test the boundaries of nature with the capabilities of your own."

"How I choose to use my magic is none of your concern," Solveig said, sliding a dagger free, slamming it on the desk with a heavy thud. "How I use this, however, should be. I'll be speaking with the commander regarding your continued employment here. I've been itching for some extra target practice."

Viana didn't drop the princess's gaze as she spoke. "We will meet again, Solveig Maleen. Of that, I'm sure. The level of your blindness when that happens remains to be seen."

CHAPTER FOUR

Breaking and Entering

T hunder rumbled through the darkness, loud enough to shake the foundations of buildings. Yet it wasn't nature's rage that pulled the High Inquisitor of Luxenal Copper Mine from her dreamless sleep. Rather something softer, gentler. A whisper intent on being heard above the storm. It rang clear in her mind, as though someone had sat right by her ear as they spoke. She bolted upright, a chill clinging to her spine, for there was no one to be found in the shadows. What they'd said she couldn't recall. Her waking mind instead turned over the words the woman had spouted. What was she supposed to break into? Why was the commander staying away?

It had to be a trap. A game of the commander's own making. But she was awake now and with the tempest rattling the windows; it was unlikely that sleep would reclaim her.

She dressed quickly in black leathers, easier to skulk around in the shadows without being seen that way. Slowly, she edged her door open, searching for any signs of a patrol unit. Though her status as a princess of the realm protected her, it wouldn't do much if they caught her in the commander's office without authorisation.

As she approached his door, there wasn't a soul in sight. She pulled out her lock picking tools and set to work. The cacophony of the storm hampered her speed, forcing her to move slower, lest she lose a click of the lock barrel to the roaring call of nature. It felt like hours had passed when the door handle finally released.

She found the messages sitting in the centre of his desk atop discarded plans for the new buildings and shafts out east. Five lay there, but she was only interested in one. It was easy to spot, with the wax seal royal emblem on the reverse. Using the tip of a dagger, Solveig pried it open, pulling the heavy stack of paper out.

It was an execution summons, except the inmate's name was missing from the front of the file. Luxenal hadn't received a new prisoner in over a month. Whoever they were, they had to be important. Perhaps a high-ranking member of the anti-magicists, a group who had grown in popularity as more unexplained deaths occurred.

She flipped the cover over and the papers almost slid from her frozen grip as she stared at the name. She hadn't thought of him in years, but clearly, *he* had.

For the King of Torrelin had decreed that the next prisoner to be executed was Prince Malik Etana. The youngest brother of Solveig's childhood best friend Adira Etana, the future Sovereign of Farrenhold. A gamut of emotions raced through her mind before settling on bone searing anger.

She'd foolishly allowed herself to hope that in the years she'd been away, her parents would have softened toward her. Recognised how she had bowed and broken each piece of her soul to answer their every whim, but it still wasn't enough. It never was. They were playing games with lives to test her loyalty, and Solveig refused to play. It didn't matter how desperately she wanted her family to see her as one of them. She wouldn't be responsible for the end of a centuries-old alliance. Leaving her with no other choice.

The High Inquisitor of Luxenal Copper Mine was going to help a prisoner marked for execution to escape.

CHAPTER FIVE

Don't Look Back

S olveig had planned to return the documents to their envelope, but there was little point in trying to cover her tracks when she was absconding with a prisoner. Instead, she grabbed a scrap piece of paper and scrawled,

For the attention of Commander Dissin Sellen,

I am withdrawing my services from Luxenal's operations, with immediate effect.

HRH Solveig Aila of House Maleen

She left the note and the prince's execution summons atop the commander's desk before slinking back out of the room as a plan of attack formed in her mind.

Solveig knew it was unlikely they would escape Luxenal alive, never mind unscathed, but she knew every crevice of this place, even under storm covered darkness. They would have to be quiet, swift, and if they were lucky, they would reach the Elysian Bridge with enough air in their lungs to claim asylum in Farrenhold.

If they allowed her to set foot in their country at all.

Returning to her cramped quarters, Solveig rushed to gather any supplies that would fit in her bag. She wished there was time to rifle through the infirmary for bandages and medicine, but she couldn't afford to waste a single second.

Outside in the sheeting rain, the thunder was louder. The air felt close, as though the storm had finally moved into position above them. She dodged puddles of surface water, trying to avoid alerting any patrolling guards, as she made her way toward the men's living quarters. The last thing she needed was to go toe to toe with one of Commander Sellen's lackeys.

They had brought Malik to the mine four years ago. By now, he would be housed on subsection three. It was where all those who survived longer than a year wound up. The further down you dug, the more stifling the air became, the damper the conditions. Your belongings, your bedding, anything you had scrounged together would never be dry again. Most who moved to that level passed to the Netherworld within six months, but Malik, he carried on. A thorn in their side, thwarting best laid plans to ensure there was always room for more prisoners.

Solveig slunk through the room, dodging wayward shoes, puddles of water and dangling chains. With no small amount of luck, in the darkest, dampest depths, she found the prince's cot. With no time for subtleties, she covered his mouth with one hand. Before raising a finger from the other to her scarf covered mouth in a shushing motion as the prince's eyes flew wide in the dark.

It took forever for his eyes to adjust, but slowly Malik nodded in uncertain, jerky movements. Solveig unpicked the locks of his chains, and he sat deathly still, careful to avoid rattling them. Once he was free, she handed him a dagger. Even as a small voice echoed in the back of her mind that it was a stupid move. For he was as likely to kill her with it as he was any other guard.

But Solveig knew she couldn't leave him unarmed and vulnerable. If they were discovered, he wouldn't stand a chance without it. His body was weak. In a fight, he could never hope to win. But if he could incapacitate an attacker. With a dagger to the neck, eye, or somewhere lower and infinitely more tender. Then he could buy himself enough time to run.

Together, they made their way out into the storming maw of the mine. Solveig went ahead, ensuring the coast was clear, before beckoning Malik out. Leading him to a secluded outhouse a few paces away before turning on him. She covered his mouth once more, her dagger held tight to his throat as she hissed in his ear.

"You're marked. Do *everything* I say, and we might make it out of here alive. Use that dagger against me and you're on your own. You can't get out of here without my help and I will not have your death on my hands."

Malik only nodded. Staring in shocked silence as she removed her dagger from his throat.

"We head northwest for the Elysian Bridge. If we're pursued, you run for your life. Don't try to protect me. I can take care of myself. You run, and you don't look back. Understood?"

Malik nodded again, and Solveig did the same. Before moving off into the night. They had barely made it to the fence at the far edge. Wire cut and wrenched back, the tree line within reach. When the first blue tinged watch light ignited, one after another in quick succession. Until Luxenal Copper Mine was lit as bright as midday.

CHAPTER SIX

The Hope That Kills

Sirens conjured by Aire Wenders echoed through the night. Solveig broke into a run, hoping that Malik could keep up with her. The rain was relentless, falling akin to unbreakable sheets of ice. Their hurried footsteps splashed and slipped through slick reddish-brown mud, coating their shoes and clothes in a thick layer.

Further into the trees, they delved; the foliage growing thick with every step into woods that rarely saw passage. Solveig's leather suit protected her from the sharp scratch of branches, but Malik struggled. With every draw of blood, from the scrape of Nyteberry bushes and every splash of mud on his sodden clothes, he lagged Solveig's punishing pace.

The years in the mines had taken its toll. Malik was closer to knocking on death's door than ever before. With every second, minute, hour and day that passed, he welcomed it as an old friend. He'd lost all hope of rescue mere months after his arrival, having witnessed untold numbers of prisoners executed for the smallest infractions, the lucky ones at least. The less fortunate became test subjects for all the new methods of torture that the royal family could conjure up.

Solveig had got them further in their escape than he'd ever seen anyone manage. That had to count for something, but he knew it was the hope that killed the most. Still, he couldn't stop that small glimmer etching its way into his heart. The same hope that had abandoned him many years ago. He no longer dared to dream of seeing his siblings' faces again; nor of smelling the salty air of Farrenhold. In the early months of his incarceration, the memories had kept him alive. Made him long for simpler days, strolling through the cobbled streets of Trivellian. Recalling the sights and smells, the smiling faces of their citizens. Years later, he had forgotten even the warmth brought by a caring smile.

Bone deep weakness soon snapped him out of his daydreams, ripping that last glimmer of hope clean from his heart as he crashed on to all fours in the dirt. Solveig spun on her feet as though she had heard him fall above the crashing sounds of chasing guards and rolling thunder. She tried desperately to pull him to his feet, but he had become a dead weight in the mud.

"You have to move, Malik," she heaved, straining as she tried to pull him up, her boots slipping in the slick mud. She ripped the sodden scarf from her face. What use was hiding her identity when she desperately needed air to carry on?

"My time is done." Malik groaned, "take your dagger and get out of here before they catch you." He reached for the weapon he'd stowed in the waistband of his trousers, but even that was too much effort as he slipped further into the mud.

Anger flashed across Solveig's face, her jaw tense. "You are a Sun Prince of Farrenhold. I did not set you free to have you die in the rain-soaked mud of Torrelin. Now stand."

Malik hesitated before reaching to take her hand. He pushed himself to his feet as Solveig pulled with all her strength to help drag his weary bones out of the mud.

A branch snapped behind them. Blood curdling fear traversed Malik's spine as he and Solveig spun in search of their unseen attacker. Another quieter step had Solveig's head swivelling a second too late, as a shot fired, and a dagger gleamed as it arched toward them. She threw herself in front of Malik. The dagger lacerated her arm, a flesh wound. Nothing compared to the fiery pain that raged from where the pointed iron tip of a crossbow bolt lodged in her shoulder.

"Run, Malik," she rasped through gritted teeth, as she snapped the bolt in half, ensuring it would stay in place until healers were on hand to stem the blood flow.

"You can't hold them off on your own."

"There is no fighting, Malik. Not for you. Head for the bridge. Your brother's men will spot you as you cross." She tried to push him away, but he held his ground, a tortured expression on his face.

"Don't die, Solveig," he whispered, before turning heel and running for his life.

Solveig ripped the scarf from where it hung at the edge of her hood. Tying it around her shoulder to staunch the flow of blood as she spat.

"Come out and play, cowards." Her fingers twitched at her sides, poised to grasp her dagger. "I promise I don't bite."

As the years passed and Solveig's hydromancy failed to grow beyond simple manipulation, her family had instead transformed her into a merciless killer. A hunter with keen senses, so when the sound of rustling foliage resumed, she was ready. Letting her dagger fly. Aim true, she heard the unmistakable splash of a body falling into the waterlogged dirt.

One down.

The bolt had come from her left. Next was the dagger thrower. Her patience a keenly refined being, she could wait them out all night if she had to.

A blast of searing fire came at her suddenly. Solveig whipped a hand to her soaked leathers, drawing out some of the water that lingered there and used it to deflect the fire ball before it even got close. She let the attacker's own dagger fly back at them, hitting home once more with a second splash and squelch of a fallen man.

But the distraction allowed for a third attack to come from behind. One Solveig hadn't expected. The surrounding air became heavy, her arms constricted to her sides by the whim of an Aire Wender. They sauntered over to her now, confident that he had her trapped.

"Not quite formidable now, are you, Reaper?" he whispered as she struggled against the invisible bonds. She couldn't reach for the sword at her back, her last remaining weapon. Had no way of distracting the guard to force his concentration to slip.

"If I remember right, you always preferred daggers to death by magic, right, Princess?" He laughed as he plunged a dagger into her stomach. Pain lanced through her as she bit into her lower lip to silence her scream, waiting for the pain to settle.

It would be his first and last mistake.

"The reason I prefer daggers," she spat. "Is because it's more personal this way. You need to be close to your target for a killing blow if you lack experience. Close enough to leave yourself open." Quick as lightning, her hand gripped his arm, and she channelled all her power into pulling the nourishing, life-giving water from every inch of his body.

His muscles atrophied.

His skin pulling tight over his bones was enough for him to drop his hold, and Solveig took her chance. Disarming him quickly, careful to keep the dagger in her body, to staunch her blood.

With the invisible bonds gone, she made direct contact with his skin with both hands. Could sense every drop of liquid churning in and around him as she connected with it.

The blood loss from the bolt and dagger strikes hampered her strength, but still she pressed on. Wrenching the fluid from him, letting it seep into the ground at their feet. In her weakness, it was taking too long. His screams echoing and endless.

"How many of you followed us?" she demanded. But he couldn't respond, teeth clenched, veins in his neck bulging as agony racked through him. Solveig removed her hands, letting him catch his breath for a moment, before asking again.

"Tell me how many of you were on our trail and perhaps I will show you mercy."

"Go to the pit, Witch Bitch," he spat in her face.

"Only if you come with me." She smiled, eyes glittering in the dark, as she brought her hand down on his exposed neck to begin again.

"Give me a number and your family will have something more than a husk of a man left to bury."

The guard tried desperately to breathe through the pain. All the soldiers had gone through extensive torture training in case they ever found themselves held hostage by a prisoner. But no one alive today had ever heard of the type of power that the princess could wield. Any books that would have contained the knowledge were long since destroyed. So they never prepared for how it would feel to be desiccated alive in mere minutes. To live through your organs shrinking, muscles shrivelling, bones splintering. The pain eventually broke him, and he fell helplessly to his knees in the mud, as though bowing before a vengeful goddess.

"Three of us," he managed. "We spread out in teams. All we knew was that the prince was gone. We didn't know where or when."

Solveig sighed, drawing her sword from down her back, before skewering him through the heart, killing him instantly. Barely a drop of blood seeped from the wound as she wrenched the sword free.

Bending to retrieve her fallen weapons, Solveig felt weakness wash over her. Already depleted from her injuries, and the magic she wrought to deflect the fire without proper summoning. The added strain of drawing the fluid from the guard's body had pushed her to the edge. She fell beside the dried-out corpse. Slick mud seeped into her clothes as blood dripped from her nose.

The last thing she heard as her eyes fell shut was splashing mud and crunching branches before her consciousness abandoned her completely.

CHAPTER SEVEN

Dead Woman Walking

Solveig danced through memories tinged with the soft, glowing rays of past happiness. A solitary moment where everything was perfect. In a dress of shimmering ice-blue to match a handsome lord's eyes. They had danced the night away. Troubles forgotten. They sipped sparkling wine, laughed with their friend Adira Etana and, for once, Solveig and Killian had been civil to each other. It was a perfect glittering dream. But dreams end, and not all end happily.

Solveig woke from her involuntary slumber lying on her side in the dirt. Her shoulder screamed in silent agony where the bolt had pierced her. Blood covered her hands from where she tried to staunch the flow around the dagger.

"You've been out all night," a grim voice sounded behind her.

Solveig twisted, eyes flashing as they narrowed. "You were supposed to keep running." She struggled through gritted teeth as she forced herself to sit. Agony sliced through her; vision blurring as the meagre contents of her stomach roiled, threatening a return journey.

"The immediate danger was gone; you saw to that," Malik said with a morbid smile. Her face was ashen. The skin beneath her eyes bruised, a sheen of sickly sweat covered her.

"You don't know the way, do you, Malik?" she whispered, and the prince grimaced.

"I spent four years in the dark pit of that mine, Solveig. Do you have any idea what that does to a person? There are countless memories that I can no longer differentiate between which are real and which were dreams. There is more than physical torture going on in that place. I pray you weren't aware of the full extent." He walked toward her, feet crushing leaves into the dirt. "The girl I knew back then would be horrified by you now."

Solveig's eyes burned beneath the sickness. Her whole body tensed. "Then it's a good thing I buried her alongside her lover four years ago." She made to stand, using the rock he had propped her against to stabilise herself through the roaring pain in her stomach. Biting back a hiss as she twisted, causing the blade to shift. It bit into her already tender flesh as more blood oozed from the wound. She wiped a shaking finger beneath it to catch a few droplets, gaze hard at the confirmation of what her senses screamed at her. It was darker than normal; the wound was infected.

"Sit down Solveig, you're going to hurt yourself," Malik warned, placing a hand on her uninjured shoulder.

"It's either endure the pain or die here," she snapped, pulling away from his grasp. "You don't know what I can handle, Malik, and besides, you need me to get home."

Solveig spun on the spot trying to gather her bearings but there were no landmarks in sight, "how far from where I fell did you take us?"

"A mile or two northwest."

Solveig shook her head. "You're a fool. Do you think they're not out there right now searching for us? We must keep moving."

"You're in no condition to go anywhere. You need to heal."

"There's no time for that." She sighed. "Rip off your sleeve."

"What?"

"I need to pack around the wound, or I'll bleed out before sundown."

Malik did as she asked, all whilst eyeing the cuffs at her wrists. Her gaze followed his as she covered them with her hands. "My magic has always been weak, Malik. You know that."

"You're a Hydromancer, healer's magic. Why won't you use it?"

"Drop it," she warned, twisting the fabric around the blade as tight as possible. Bile rose in her throat as she bit back the pain.

"There's a river close by. You can use that to sustain your power. I've seen other manipulators do it."

"Other manipulators didn't poison their gift," she scoffed, shaking her head. "A walking instrument of torture doesn't need healing abilities."

"What happened in the last four years?" Malik asked, approaching her again with slow, steady steps, palms outward.

"What use would it be? You cannot change the past any more than I can. Do something useful and climb one of these trees and find any landmarks that could give an indicator of our position."

He followed her orders without complaint. Solveig was still royalty in these parts, and her word was as good as law. She tried to forage for nuts and berries, but the wound in her stomach smarted with every bend to pluck the supplies from their branches.

If they were lucky, they were a full day's hike from the Elysian Bridge. A dangerous amount of time to spend walking through the woods, caked in mud, with a trail of highly trained guards behind you. All with a festering wound. She was lucky she could even walk.

The sound of rustling leaves and scraping bark signalled Malik's descent. Solveig leaned against another nearby tree, a wave of weakness washing over her.

"What did you see?" She swallowed, trying to combat the dryness in her throat, a warning sign of the worsening infection.

"The mountains are to the northeast. Luxenal is behind us. I couldn't see much else. It was too dark still."

"If the mountains are to the northeast, then we're still on the right track. We keep heading northwest for another day or so, and we should be close."

"Can you even take another step?"

"If I don't; I'll die."

"How bad is it?" She averted her gaze.

"Solveig?" he pressed.

"There's an infection in my blood. I'm a dead woman walking at this point either way. North is my only chance."

"I could carry you."

"You lay one finger on me intending to carry Malik Etana, and I'll give you a wound to match."

"Fine, but if you black out on me again. I won't be held responsible for anything I have to do to keep you alive."

As the day wore on, the thick trees that bordered the mountains mercifully shaded them from the still lingering heat of the autumnal sun. Exhaustion leeched their bones, hunger ravaged their stomachs, and thirst tore at their throats. By the time the sun fell in the sky once more, turning the clouds a warm burnished orange that faded to pink, then purple as night-time once again drew close. Solveig had no choice but to lean on the prince for support as the infection rapidly spread and stole more of her strength. It was a miracle she was on her feet at all.

When at last she glimpsed flickering blue lights through the trees; Solveig thought she had succumbed to hallucinations. It wasn't until they drew closer that she realised it was real. They'd made it. The flickering blue lights were eternal flame beacons that lit the passage across the Elysian Bridge.

Malik shouldered most of Solveig's weight as they passed through the last of the trees to the small clearing at the edge of the bridge. Bringing the prince mere steps away from home soil for the first time in four years.

CHAPTER EIGHT

A Danger to Us All

"Take one more step and it will be your last."

A guard across the bridge levelled a gleaming, iron-tipped arrow at Solveig's heart, causing Malik to bring them to an immediate stop. Solveig fell to her knees, energy finally spent. As footsteps echoed along the wood panels, she raised her head. Her vision blurred as she took in flawless, brown skin and long, braided black hair, shaved on one side; each individual braid adorned with jewelled golden accents. They dressed in brown leather trousers and boots, a light cotton shirt, and a green leather vest. A sword hung from their hip and a quiver of arrows across their chest, the bow already notched.

But it was the face that stared down at her that shocked Solveig the most. It was older now, more mature, but unmistakably that of Adira Etana, the future Sovereign of Farrenhold, her childhood best friend. Behind them stood their surly brother Jasper, commander of the nearby North Watch.

"Lower your weapons. There is no danger." Malik said, palms raised. Adira's eyes narrowed as they flicked from Solveig's slumped form to the man before them. Malik was thinner, taller, his hair long and unkempt. The scruff of a beard covered his chin.

"Adira," Malik said, slower now, "lower your bow." Tension coiled in his muscles.

"There will be a time for reunions, Malik." Adira grimaced, "once the traitor at your feet no longer poses a threat. Now step aside."

Solveig laughed in resignation. "Did you think there would be a happy ending for me, Malik?"

The prince glanced at the dying woman beside him. She who had put her life on the line for him. He knew then that he could not let her die at the hand of his siblings. Whatever punishment awaited her, they could deliver it once she'd healed. Malik stepped in front of her, leaving Adira's arrow aimed at his own heart.

"Step aside," they ordered once more. "That woman is a danger to us all. I cannot allow her to enter Farrenhold."

"That woman," Malik snapped, "was your friend once, Adira, and now she's dying. She needs medicine."

Adira glanced at Solveig again with a shrug. "Why not show her some mercy and end it quickly?"

"You do this, Adira, and you're no better than them."

"You've been gone for four years. Things change. People change." Adira grimaced.

"Enough," a gruff voice called from behind Adira, as Jasper Etana finally entered the fray. "Adira, no one is defying your orders, but as commander of North Watch, passage across the Elysian Bridge is mine alone to give."

"We cannot trust her, Jasper. Let her into Farrenhold, and you risk everything we've built these last few years."

"She saved my life," Malik interrupted. His siblings' eyes swung toward him.

"You lie." Adira's eyes narrowed, venom on their tongue.

"What reason would I have to lie?"

"You always had a soft spot for her. You're blinded by the past. That"—they paused, flinging a hand toward the barely conscious woman before them—"is not the woman you once knew."

"Maybe, but that doesn't change the fact that she saved my life." Malik took a step forward, keeping Solveig behind him. "She put everything on the line to bring me home. Has our custom in that regard changed also? If you go back on those ancient laws now, what others will you make excuses for later?"

Adira remained still; arrow pointed at their brother as they weighed their options. Malik was right, Farrenhold law required payment in kind. They could not break it. Their eyes closed on a sigh before lowering the bow.

"She can enter North Watch, but no further. Have the healers see to her wounds." Adira turned to Jasper. "I want her guarded day and night," they ordered, before turning back toward North Watch alone, gripping the bow tight as though they fought every second against turning back.

Jasper faced Solveig. "Can you stand, Your Highness?"

Solveig tried. Willed her body to respond for the sake of her own dignity but couldn't summon the strength to raise higher than her knees. Jasper's gaze moved to Malik. "She's a Hydromancer. Why hasn't she treated her own injuries?"

"You know she would if she could," Malik said, looking down at the ashen woman.

"Princess Solveig, I, Prince Jasper Ade Etana; Commander of North Watch, Guardian of the Elysian Bridge; grant you asylum within the Sovereignty of Farrenhold. Under the agreement that you answer all questions that we, the royal family, may have for you."

Solveig raised her darkening gaze to Jasper one final time. She spoke through cracked lips, tasting her own blood on her tongue. "I, Princess Solveig Aila Maleen, accept your terms."

Jasper raised a horn to his mouth, blowing a signal that Solveig was not familiar with. Within minutes, a team of healers raced across the bridge with a stretcher and supplies in hand just as she blacked out completely.

CHAPTER NINE

Lack of Control

"Your plan failed." Asta Maleen, Queen of Torrelin, stated as she stood before her husband's ornate desk, and he did his best to ignore her.

"You should have dealt with her when you had the chance," she continued, undeterred by her husband's lack of interest, but her persistence paid off. King Emerson threw the documents he had been reading to his desk, the edges blackened and smoking.

"To what exactly are you referring, dear?"

"Solveig, of course, she failed to kill that boy." Asta's hands shook as she tossed a note on his desk. Her cheeks flushed with rising anger as she continued, "Better still, she helped him to escape, killing three guards, *three elemental guards,* in the process." Emerson rubbed at his eyes, leaning back in his chair, disregarding the note completely.

"And where is she now? I'm assuming you know, since you appear to be well versed in our daughters' dealings." He eyed her expectantly.

"Where do you think?" Asta spat, "with those untrustworthy, unfit rulers in Farrenhold. They've permitted her to claim asylum there. According to Commander Sellen, they're refusing to hand her over. Even with the offer of a full pardon for their brother on the table."

That was when the king finally took note of his wife's words, his eyes flashing to hers in less than a heartbeat. "You. Did. What," he seethed.

"I did what I judged to be necessary."

Emerson stood from his chair, bracing his hands on his desk, staring his wife down. "You have no authority to grant pardons. Remember your place in this court, *wife.*"

Asta ignored his thinly veiled threat as she continued haughtily, "Solveig must be recalled. It was foolish to have her stay away for this long. How will it look if this gets out?"

"Solveig will return to us. I have no doubt of that." Wisps of smoke drifted around the king's arms as the papers beneath his hands burned. Asta shook her head at yet another display of his failing control.

"You were wrong last time. What makes you sure now?" She placed her own hands atop the desk, water pooling around their hands as she smothered his flames. She leaned into his space. "Perhaps it's time that Killian took over. You're losing your grip, my love." Emerson's hand shot out, grasping her neck. He yanked her towards him as she clawed at his hands, desperate to draw in air. Only fear lay in the queen's eyes now, as she realised how easily she'd fallen into his trap.

"That boy knows nothing of making difficult choices, never mind leading a country." He loosened his grip just enough to allow Asta the opportunity to speak, her voice coarse from her swollen throat.

"Neither do you." She gasped, "The difficult choice was to have Solveig dealt with months ago and you allowed her to live. You chose wrong." She refused to back down, even in the face of her erratic husband.

A sneer grew across his face as his grip tightened around her throat again. "Solveig will return to Torrelin. She will come back to the fold, and she will re-enter the roll we planned for her. You needn't worry about such things. It is not your place." Flame licked across her neck from where his hand gripped her, though he kept the temperature bearable. For now. "I am sure there are better things you could be doing than trying to play king through me."

Emerson released his hold on her neck suddenly and she fell to the ground before his desk, landing atop the glass table in the centre of an old rug. It shattered around her; the shards slicing her exposed skin. A hand flew to her throat as she desperately sucked in precious air. Hatred leaked from every pore.

"You forget who I am," she croaked, moving to stand. "Who I was before I married you."

"I haven't forgotten." Emerson mused, retaking his seat. "Who you were simply ceased to be of consequence once you married a king. To be clear, your place was to be a pretty feature at my side. To provide me with a suitable heir, and right now, I'm not convinced that you have succeeded in either of those jobs."

"How dare—"

"How dare I!" the king roared, sending the papers before him scattering across the room fully alight with blue flame now. "I AM KING! You were the daughter of a penniless lord, with questionable parentage of the female line. I was merely too distracted by your other *assets* to worry about it, as I should have. An oversight that will not be repeated, I assure you. Learn your place in this court, my queen." He drew a scorching ring of fire around his wife's form. One that threatened to singe her clothes, burn her skin and suffocate her lungs if he dared draw it tighter around her. "Or I will find you a place outside of it. How would you like to be an acolyte of the temple? I hear the most devout amongst them take their vow of silence so seriously that they ensure its permanence, through slitting their tongues and sewing their mouths. Whatever it takes to shut you up for good."

The ring of flame extinguished, Asta was dismissed. Rage burned in her blood; she was not the type of woman to take orders from men. She was born to be a ruler amongst women. Bloodthirsty and power-hungry, she had eyed a marriage with the king for all the opportunities it could afford her. But she had failed to understand how difficult it would be to ensure he would do her bidding.

"Of course, Your Majesty," she said saccharinely as she bowed before him, appearing every inch the subservient queen. "Might I suggest a cup of tea to ease the stress I have needlessly brought upon you?"

"Do whatever you wish," he muttered without even sparing her a glance. "Your flights of fancy during the daylight hours are of no concern to me."

The Queen of Torrelin held her head high. Biting back a retort that would surely see her thrown in the dungeons beneath the castle for a night or two. Bowing low once more instead, before exiting the office. She headed straight to her own wing, in the heart of the castle. Climbing the stairs to her private kitchen a level below her tearoom, she brewed up a steaming pot of the king's favourite tea. A special recipe passed down from her mother. She found he always was more agreeable after a soul warming cup of the specialised blend.

CHAPTER TEN

Same Old Tricks

Solveig woke in a plush bed with fur-lined sheets, dressed in a simple white cotton slip. The air was different. Instead of the scent of damp, there was salt. A warm breeze, not chilled, drifted through a solitary window. She winced against the bright light of a cloudless sky that illuminated the small room.

She was in Farrenhold; it hadn't been a dream. They'd made it.

"You've been out for five days." A gravelly voice came from her left. "How you didn't die from the blood loss, the gods only know. Still, the healers drew the infection from that wound you allowed to fester, but there was nothing to be done for the scarring." Solveig met the impassive silver eyes of Jasper Etana, who leaned against the closed door to the room. "You know yourself there's only so much hydromancy can do and creating fresh skin to prevent the need for stitches is not one of them."

She tried to sit up, but couldn't move even an inch, as heavy air pushed back against her. "Jasper. If I wanted to hurt you or your family, I could've killed Malik and sent his body back in pieces." She tried in vain to push against the unnaturally dense air.

"Why did you do it?"

"Does it matter at this point?"

"You know it does." The message was clear, it mattered to Adira.

"I owed a debt. Setting Malik free was my penance."

Suddenly there was a commotion of scuffles and shouts beyond the closed door, before a lone authoritative voice called, "Commander, tell your guards to stand down or so help me. The second I officially relieve our father of his sovereignty. I'll have you demoted to stable boy."

Jasper chuckled softly to himself. "I'm merely trying to prevent you murdering the woman before we get some answers out of her."

"You can do that with me in there."

Jasper stood silent for a moment, studying Solveig, whilst she remained silent. This was his call.

"Guards. Stand down. Let the future sovereign pass." Jasper moved from his position as the door flew open and Adira strode in. They carried all the ferocious grace of a future ruler, dressed much as they had been the night she and Malik had arrived.

"Did I not warn you the night you stole our brother, that if you set foot on Farrenhold soil again, I would have you incapacitated on sight?" Adira placed a hand against the wall, leaning down into Solveig's face. "The only reason I didn't hold true to my word was thanks to the spectacular job you did of fulfilling my promise yourself."

"Believe me." Solveig whispered, "it was not a decision I made lightly. I ordered Malik to leave, but he wouldn't."

"How noble," Adira hissed. "Do you want a thank you for not killing him? After you left him to rot in that prison? Whilst you killed countless others?"

"Fifty."

"What?"

"I counted every single one, Adira," Solveig muttered, her face impassive. "All fifty of them. I won't apologise, nor am I asking for forgiveness. I did what I judged to be right, and I hold to that."

"Did you ever stop to think that some of those people you executed could be innocent?" Adira countered, rubbing circles into their temples to chase away the phantom pain of a headache. "If Malik's name had never come up on the docket, you'd still be murdering on the whim of your family," they scoffed. "Your family, who hold themselves to such grandeur. Casting judgement on the rest of us from that towering, rotten keep." Adira's eyes raked over Solveig's stark appearance, pallid white skin, and raven black hair. "The golden family indeed until you came along. The shadow to their light."

"No."

"No?" Adira asked, their voice echoing round the room. "If you wanted me to believe that the killings would have stopped long ago."

"I won't insult you by claiming I always intended to save Malik because I didn't." Solveig bit out, "When I lost Aldrik, I was in free fall. Then, to find out *Malik* had attempted to steal from Leader Ezekiel that same night." Solveig shook her head, eyes low. "I followed the law. I obeyed my family. They were all I had left. What would you have done in my place?"

"The girl I knew at Erynmar Academy," Adira began, "the girl Aldrik loved, the same girl who spent holidays with my family in Farrowvale." They shook their head, mouth in a thin line. "I cannot reconcile her with the version of you that lies before me now."

"I don't expect you to,"—Solveig shrugged—"because I'm not her. I have no fight with your country or your people. I had orders, I obeyed them, until—"

"Until Malik." Adira finished, and Solveig nodded.

"I know what his death would initiate. I refuse to wear the responsibility for that. If it's war they want, they can trigger it themselves."

Adira nodded, glancing at Jasper, who remained silent at the foot of the bed. "Free her."

"You sure?"

Adira beheld Solveig once more. "She poses no immediate threat to Farrenhold."

Solveig exhaled as the heavy air around her lifted. She made to stand, to walk toward Adira, but they took an immediate step back.

"We are grateful to you for returning Malik, and you can stay here in North Watch as long as you need, but make no mistake. This is not me forgiving you. We are a long way from that, but for the sake of our two countries, and what I hope they may one day become." Adira paused, glancing back at Jasper once more, their jaw clenched, "I want to work toward trusting you again."

"Understood."

"Malik has asked that you join us for dinner this evening. Eleric has travelled up from Evrosei to see him."

"I would be honoured."

"Very well." They nodded. "The day is yours to do with as you please. I'll have healers come up to check on those wounds," Adira muttered as they exited the room without glancing back.

With her wounds cleaned and bandages changed, Solveig dressed in a flowing white shirt and brown cotton pants. Wincing slightly as she bent to lace up a pair of leather boots; her stitches pulling with the movement.

Tentatively, she left the chambers to explore the grounds of North Watch, desperate for fresh air and a walk. She passed the growing fields and cattle stalls, walked across to the armoury and barracks. Everywhere she went, she sensed eyes on her, curious, angry, and suspicious.

Still, Solveig felt as though she could breathe properly for the first time in years. Dust kicked up around her feet as she walked back across the main courtyard. To her right, a group of guards practiced their sword skills. Clashing steel echoed through the air like a sweet song, but a mouth-watering collection of fragrances drifting from the keep soon distracted her.

The scent of toasted bread, topped with ripe tomatoes, cheese and garlic oil dressing, danced toward her. Stomach groaning, she headed in search of the food, hunger suddenly at the forefront of her mind. She would need to keep up her strength now more than ever. Food first, then maybe she could convince those guards to go toe to toe with her for a time, to reshape any lost muscle from her brush with death.

Sweat ran in rivulets down Solveig's flushed skin, soaking the edge of her shirt collar. She heaved another deep breath. Eyes focused on her opponent. The blunt sword she held growing steadily heavier as she tried to ignore the churning in her stomach. Everything about being back in the salt-soaked air of Farrenhold made her feel lighter, even as a dull ache still snagged at her wounds.

"You're turning rather green, ready to give up?" her partner asked, quirking a brow.

"Not likely." Solveig smirked, adjusting her stance to parry another blow. She ducked and twisted at high speed. Expertly dodging his next two strikes as they spun to face each other again, swords locked in a stalemate.

"We agreed best of three. I won't be forfeiting now, but please, don't let me stop you," she teased.

Her partner was a member of Adira's guard. A visitor to North Watch, same as she, and it did not escape her notice that he had been the first to step up to her challenge. A silent show of respect to his future sovereign, that anyone, no matter their gender, could hold their own in a fight.

With her thoughts distracted, the guard moved to land another stinging blow against the leather vambraces covering her arms. But another sword entered the fray, blocking the move. This one gleaming under the light of the sun.

"And here I thought you knew better than to get lost in your head during a fight," Adira muttered with a cunning smile.

Solveig grimaced, pivoting on one foot, but Adira read the movement as though they'd already seen it happen. Stepping into Solveig's path, they swept her standing leg out from under her, leaving sprawled on her back in the dirt.

Adira held the sharp point of their sword at Solveig's heart, the tip dangerously close with every rise of her chest. "Same moves as four years ago. Someone ought to teach you some new tricks."

Solveig laughed, slipping her hands beneath her lower back to where she had stowed twin daggers. In swift movements, she used one to brush Adira's sword aside, and the other stabbed into the dirt, giving her leverage to push to her feet.

"Not all my tricks are old," she stated, pulling her dagger free of the ground, facing Adira head on.

"Not all, but enough that I could have you on your back again easily." Adira shrugged. "You should be more careful. That you managed to not vomit your lunch all over the courtyard is one thing. But your wounds are still healing. You should be resting."

"And you,"—Adira spun to face the guard—"shouldn't have agreed to the match."

A smirk broke across his face. "I wanted to see if the Dark Princess would live up to her fearsome myth."

Solveig's gaze hardened on the guard as she slipped her daggers back into the waistband of her trousers. "And?" she bit out. "What's the verdict?"

The guard only chuckled. "Does it matter what I think? I merely wanted to sate my curiosity."

"Your name?"

"Unnecessary information, I would think, Your Highness?"

"Call it sating my curiosity," she parroted back on a smirk.

"His name is Elias." Adira sighed, rolling their eyes. "And he should be running drills with his unit right now." Their eyes flicked to the barracks in the distance, dismissing him.

Elias's whole demeanour changed at the order. He bowed stiffly to his commander before collecting the training swords and stalking off toward the barracks.

"When I said the day was yours to do with as you pleased, that was not me giving you the freedom to sharpen your skills." Adira said. "You want to earn my trust? Then you ask my permission to train with my guards."

"Understood." Solveig nodded, reluctant to push the subject further.

"Now, if you're quite finished with your little game, follow me this way," Adira ordered again, spinning on their heal toward the Elysian Bridge.

CHAPTER ELEVEN

Moves and Countermoves

"A messenger arrived," Adira whispered. "Jasper has been dealing with it, but he is refusing to speak to anyone except you." They cast her a side-long glance. "As long as you remain on this side of the bridge, you are under our protection."

As they came to a stop beside Malik and Jasper, Solveig finally got a good look at the messenger. From the cropped hair and pinched facial features. To the copper emblem pinned to his chest, and the three silver stars atop four alternating stripes of his turquoise and gold epaulets. She recognised him instantly as her brother's right-hand man.

"General Anik," Solveig hissed, reaching for her dagger.

"Ms Maleen." The general smiled, staring down at her as though she were a soldier in his command. "The king has given orders for you to return to Torrelin at the earliest opportunity. Refuse and you'll be stripped of your titles and placed under warrant to be delivered to Luxenal for correction."

"As Commander of North Watch." Jasper stepped forward. "I shall respect whatever decision the *Princess* of Torrelin makes." None of them had missed the general's omission of her title. "I will judge any attempts to remove her from Farrenhold against her will, as acts of aggression and *will* respond in kind."

General Anik glared at Jasper, "who are you to treat with me boy, a second-born son too weak to usurp his bastard sibling to take the crown?"

"You will refer to the future sovereign of this nation with the respect their position requires," Malik seethed; the general's gaze crossed to him at last.

"The criminal prince." He sighed, gaze flicking to Solveig. "What a fine collection of companions you have collected for yourself, *Princess*. I'm sure your parents would love to hear this. I would add the slight to your already extensive list of charges if I were them."

Adira had heard enough, drawing their bow. "Did I miss something, General? Do you carry a missive stating that the Kingdoms of Torrelin and Farrenhold are no longer allied?"

"I was merely giving my opinion, Your Highness."

"You'd be wise to keep your *opinions* to yourself, lest they be interpreted as that of the king's. Unless you want to bring the might of an entire nation down on their heads with a few poorly chosen remarks."

The ground shook beneath their feet as a chasm formed between them and General Anik. Breaking away to leave the man nary a small spit of rock to balance upon. His face paled as he stared down the newly formed gouge in the earth, so deep he could not see the bottom.

"You've spoken to Princess Solveig. Now go scurry back to whatever hovel you crawled out of." More dirt and rock fell away from the edge. General Anik cursed as they forced him to hop around on one foot like a fool as he turned to tightrope walk his way back to the bridge. Once there, Adira allowed the ground to return to its original state, barely a speck of dust out of place.

Solveig stared at the dimming glow of the emerald gems in Adira's cuffs as they walked away, with Malik in tow.

"Exactly how powerful has Adira become?" she whispered to Jasper in awe.

"We aren't sure. They've never been properly tested." He shrugged.

"You're concerned." Solveig guessed.

"Should I not be?"

"I wouldn't worry about Adira," Solveig said, touching his arm lightly, bringing his stormy gaze to hers. "I'd worry about those who challenge them."

"You should rest," Jasper said, his gaze shuttering. "Your body is still healing, and if you plan to return to Torrelin—as I think you will—then you're going to need all your strength."

They walked to the keep in silence. Jasper left her to climb the stairs to her room alone. Where she sank into the cloudlike softness of the bed. Sleep claiming her mind instantly.

Chapter Twelve

A Family Reunion

Through the eyes of a Torrelinian, the banquet hall at North Watch was underwhelming. The stone walls were bare except for a few bronze-coloured sconces holding flickering candles and a large crackling fireplace at the far end of the room. The smoky scent of burning wood permeated the air.

Solveig and Malik exchanged few words as they waited for the rest of his siblings to arrive. Jasper came first, taking a seat to the left of the head of the table.

When the doors opened again, it was as though the air was sucked from the room. Eleric Etana strode in and locked eyes on his younger brother for the first time in years.

"Four years in a prison camp and somehow you still look ten years old, Mal," he quipped as he crossed the room, gathering Malik in a tight embrace.

Malik pulled free from the hug first. Arms circling around himself, as he smiled. A gesture that didn't quite reach his eyes. "What happened to your hair?" He laughed hesitantly. "Too many jewels to count—got you stressed?"

Eleric ran his hand over his shorn head with a scowl. "Someone's gotta make sure everyone gets their fair share. Even if it means I must sacrifice my own good looks to the cause."

Malik choked on a laugh, but still with all the joy of it, his eyes remained dull. "They shall have to build a statue in your honour. I'm sure Adira could enquire about it once they've locked me up in a treatment facility in Trivellian and can focus on something other than fussing over me."

All humour died in Eleric's eyes, Jasper's too, who had been watching their exchange silently from his seat.

"Adira won't do that, Mal." Jasper insisted.

"Won't they?"

"I won't let them." Eleric countered.

"Careful, El, it was naivety and cocksureness that got me locked up for four years. Adira will do whatever they believe is necessary."

"We'll discuss it later, the four of us," Jasper ordered, ending the discussion.

"Right." Eleric nodded before he turned to face Solveig. Taking her by surprise as he pulled her into a hug, too. "You saved my brother's life, but you'll forgive me if I'm not quick to trust you implicitly." His silver eyes darkened.

"I would feel the same if our places were reversed." Solveig whispered.

"Good, then we understand each other." He peered around the room. "Adira's delayed. If we can't eat, we should at least start on drinks."

"Nice to see some things never change." Malik rolled his eyes. Taking a seat beside Jasper, shifting his chair slightly to allow himself more space, leaving Eleric and Solveig to sit beside each other. A kitchen aide hurried in, carrying a tray of glasses, and a crystal decanter of whiskey, serving each before exiting once again in silence.

"To family reunions," Eleric said, lifting his glass.

"To surviving," Malik countered, his haunted gaze flicking to Solveig, who lifted her glass with him.

"To Farrenhold," Jasper declared.

"Long may she soar!" Adira finished from the open doorway. Before crossing the room to pick up the glass set before their place at the table, drinking it down in a single swallow. The rest of the group swiftly followed, for it risked infinite bad fortune if one failed to drink following a toast.

Adira took their seat, and not a second later, the side door opened once more, and the workers hurried in to lay trays of sizzling foods before them. As with most things, the food in Farrenhold was simple, but that did not mean it lacked flavour. That night they dined on warmed bread. A tray of hard cheeses accompanied it. There was salt roasted pork with leaf greens and mixed nuts tossed with balsamic apples. Alongside roasted root vegetables and shredded braised red cabbage with carrots. Dessert followed, a syrupy blood orange sponge cake with autumnal berries and spiced cream.

Only once the sounds of polished silverware on plates had faded and they sat back, stomachs full. Each nursing a second glass of whiskey, did Solveig finally address the room. "I have decided to return to Torrelin," she said, her voice echoing across the now quiet banquet hall.

"Are you crazy?" Malik spat.

"Tomorrow." Solveig finished, eyeing him pointedly.

"No." he shook his head, eyes blinking ferociously as he tried to process her words. "You'll be in the gallows before the weeks out."

"I'm going, Malik," Solveig said firmly, a hand fisted beneath the table. "I cannot hide in Farrenhold forever."

"He's right," Adira said, placing their glass back on the table as they wiped their mouth with a napkin, "or rather he's partially right."

Solveig's jaw clenched. "How so?"

Adira rolled their eyes. "All I meant was that you're in no fit state to up and leave on horseback tomorrow. We'll go by sea instead, in a day or two."

Solveig mulled the offer over for a moment, thought of how her wounds still ached and skin itched around the stitches. "Fine."

Malik stared at them. "You can't be serious."

"Solveig is a grown woman, Malik, a princess of the realm. We cannot stop her from leaving," Jasper tried to reason.

"They'll kill her."

"I can take care of myself," Solveig snapped.

"You were knocking on death's door days ago," he fired back.

"My return to Torrelin will not cause a physical fight Malik, you spent four years in that mine, but didn't learn how the higher ups operated?" She raised a brow. "Or perhaps you did." Her eyes narrowed. "As you said, there was more than physical torture going there."

The colour drained from Malik's face at the implication of her words as she nonchalantly sipped her drink.

Malik laughed bitterly. Head shaking in defeat. "I should have known," he muttered, desperately trying to pull his features into a cold, indifferent mask. "You didn't earn the name Princess Pain, for nothing did you, Reaper?"

"It was earned fairly," Solveig agreed.

"Enough of this," Adira hissed, their head falling back against the chair with a sigh. "Solveig and I will sail for Torrelin the day after next. Malik, you will go with Eleric to Evrosei. I'll meet you there in a few days and we'll travel home to Trivellian together."

Malik didn't spare Solveig another glance as he stormed from the table. It was better this way. Better that he believed Solveig had played some part in all the horrors he may have endured at Luxenal.

The following day, Malik was nowhere to be found. He had his meals brought to his room, and only left to use a bathing chamber. The others continued as normal. Eleric went with Jasper as he oversaw the daily pressures of command over North Watch. Adira helped wherever they were needed, with Solveig joining them. They harvested grain and milked cows. Mucked out stalls and helped sharpen the swords and daggers in the armoury. As they spoke, both tried to put their differences aside, and the past behind them. It would not be easy. There would always be that edge of mistrust between them that had not existed before, but Solveig knew deep down it was already more than she could hope for.

That evening, only Solveig, Adira, and Jasper dined together. Eleric claimed he wanted to eat in his rooms and sleep early ahead of his return to Evrosei, and Malik was still avoiding Solveig.

"I sent word to Torrelin that we would arrive by sea tomorrow evening. What welcome should we expect?" Adira asked Solveig.

"It's me they want. There will be guards waiting, but you'll have nothing to worry about on your end."

"It isn't me I'm worried about," Adira hedged.

"As I told Malik." Solveig muttered, sipping on a mug of ale, "I can take care of myself."

Adira only nodded, finishing the rest of their meal in silence.

The sun barely kissed the eastern horizon when Solveig and Adira headed for the dock the next morning. It lay within the chasm far below the Elysian Bridge and serviced only the small craft sufficient for their quick journey. Adira sent out guards the night before, who had the ship ready for departure when they arrived. The journey to the port outside Marrelin City would be short, with favourable winds they would arrive before sundown.

No one spoke as the sails rose and Elias took the helm of the ship. He steered them safely out of the tight chasm with the aid of an Aire Wender soothing their passage. The Elysian Bridge loomed above them, casting an enormous shadow as the last dregs of night faded.

Hours later, Adira sat beside Solveig on the deck, snapping her from her reverie. Solveig eyed them warily; having not spoken a word to each other since dinner. "Did you mean what you implied to Malik the other night?"

"No," Solveig whispered, "I may have held the title of High Inquisitor, but I wasn't involved in anything other than their last trial. Any other experiments were in the guards' remit."

"Experiments?"

"Luxenal is more than a mine, Adira. I don't know when it happened, or who ordered it, but it has happened. Testing poisons, training guards and healers? It all comes at the prisoner's expense. The crematorium has been working overtime to keep up. It's rarely out of use."

"But why let Malik think—"

"You know why," Solveig interrupted.

Adira looked at their friend solemnly. "Cruel way to go about it."

"I saved his life to repay a debt I owed; it's best he doesn't romanticise it."

"Why go back." Adira implored. "Surely you know by now who you're dealing with. They don't care about you beyond staining your soul and making you a villain in their stead."

"I don't trust them."

"Does anyone?"

"It's more than that." Solveig sighed. "Whether it makes sense or not, I know I can do something on the inside."

"Do what?" Adira questioned.

"Warn you if they plan to make a move. Save any I can."

Adira scoffed at the last part, eyes raising toward the sky.

"What?" Solveig asked.

"It's a bit much to claim you want to save people when you've spent two years killing them."

"And people can't change?"

"Not this quickly." They eyed Solveig knowingly. "You're telling me things you think I want to hear out of fear of losing me?"

Solveig only stared at them, head nodding slowly.

"Then stop, because you already did." Adira bit out. "Lying to me, pretending to be anything other than what you are, is a sure-fire way to keep us apart."

"Then what do I do? How do I fix it?"

"You can't fix something this broken Solveig." Adira sighed, reaching out a hand to hold hers. "We can only start over. Build something based on the people we've become rather than who we were."

"What if who I am is someone you don't like?"

"You are Solveig. My friend. The Reaper of Luxenal? She is someone else, a shell you inhabit to protect the real you from the pain of all you've done."

"How do I get back to Solveig?"

"You don't."

"But I—"

"You merge the two," Adira interrupted. "Aldrik made you soft. He protected you from the harsh realities of the world. You needed to break. Now you must find the balance between Solveig and the Reaper."

Solveig had no words. How could it be possible to merge two vastly different people, especially when she had been one continuously for the last two years?

"Your family is going to try to bend you back to their will, Solveig," Adira said, eyeing the coast of Torrelin on the horizon. "You mustn't let them. Fight enough to keep yourself safe, but please." They squeezed her hand tightly. "Don't abandon your heart in the process. There is a life for you beyond the creeping shadows of that castle. There is more before you if you only have the courage to stand and take it."

"How can there be more?" Solveig asked, a chill running down her spine as the shore grew closer. "Torrelin is ice. The longer I'm there, the more frozen I become."

Adira watched her. Saw the fear in her eyes, fear that she would never be free once she stepped back on Torrelinian soil. "It isn't too late, you know."

"If I don't face this now, I never will."

Adira nodded. "Then if you ever need help, get word to Jasper. He's under orders to assist, should you need it. We'll get you out before you're frozen here."

Solveig's eyes narrowed. "You'd risk an already tenuous alliance to help me?"

"I have my reasons, Solveig," Adira stated with a finality that said they would not elaborate.

Both stood as they approached the dock and within minutes of them tying the ship up, heavily armed Torrelinian soldiers surrounded them.

"Your Highnesses," General Anik said, moving to the front of the pack, "will both of you be joining us?"

Solveig and Adira shared one last glance before the former shouldered her pack and made her way down the gangplank. "Just me, as requested."

"Pity." He smirked, pulling a pair of shackles from behind his back. They glittered with gems of red, green, and white to stifle her hydromancy. "Necessary precautions, Princess. I'm sure you understand." He took her pack before snapping the shackles around her wrists.

"Solveig," Adira called, walking to the edge of the gangplank to meet her. "Can't have you going into the lion's den completely at their mercy now, can we?" they whispered, hiding a dagger beneath the waistband of her trousers. "Fight Solveig. That is all I ask of you. Don't let them win."

"She's all yours," Adira smiled, stepping away, "send my regards to your king and queen. We are truly grateful for the safe return of our brother."

The general said nothing as Adira re-boarded their ship and their men readied to leave. General Anik tightened the shackles around her wrists, eyeing her for a moment before he reached behind her with a smirk to pull the sheathed dagger free.

"I'll be taking this. Don't want you getting any ideas," he said, handing it off to the nearest soldier.

"You'll ride upfront with me. I hope you enjoyed your little boat ride. We'll be on horseback until we reach the city."

Solveig mounted the horse wordlessly, taking one last look behind her as the ship pulled away from the dock, leaving her to face the fate that now lay before her. She could only hope that her years in the mine had prepared her for whatever the golden trio could throw at her.

CHAPTER THIRTEEN

The Princess of Many Names

With every step the mare took, Solveig felt a sickening pull on her stitches. By the time they had cleared the road between the mountains and the city had come into view, a sheen of sweat coated her greyed skin.

With the snow-capped mountains to the north, and the towering defensive wall that surrounded it, Marrelin City was a fortress. Her ancestors had carved the keep, High Tower Castle, into the mountains hundreds of years ago. It was a terrible beast, looming over the meagre dwellings below. Rivers bordered the city, lifelines that supplied the otherwise remote locality with fresh water and easy fishing grounds. Pipes funnelled much of it into the castle, but for now, at least there remained enough in the channels to feed the ever-growing population.

The company came to a halt on the bridge to the western portcullis. General Anik dismounted, making his way over to where Solveig sat slumped atop the mare.

"We're to remove the shackles before entering the city."

Solveig stared at him in perplexed silence.

"Orders are orders." He shrugged. "Try anything and I'll take you down."

"Now that would cause a spectacle," Solveig muttered.

"What?"

She rolled her eyes, shifting on her saddle to face him. "I don't pretend to understand my parents' reasons for having you remove the chains. However, I can guess that they are trying to avoid a spectacle before they've decided what to do with me." She eyed him expectantly, but he remained silent. "I don't know about you, General. But I think the murder of a princess in broad daylight would cause exactly the show they are trying to avoid."

General Anik smirked. "You've been away a long time, sweetheart, long enough for opinions to form in your absence. I'd be willing to bet everything I own on the citizens of this city throwing a party at seeing your pretty head severed from its body."

She ignored him. "If the king wanted a show, he'd have you take me straight to the gallows. But he hasn't, has he?"

"How many people did you kill in the last two years, Princess?"

"Fifty."

"Did you know they announced every single one of them in the city square? They had us guard the wall for days to ensure their names didn't appear."

"I followed my king's orders. They can think what they want. But they won't get to celebrate until the king pops the wine himself." She smiled, and General Anik returned to his own horse in silence.

Wrought-iron gates screeched open, and a myriad of sensations hit Solveig all at once. A deafening cacophony of market stalls, and the stench of sweat and sewage. The sickening taste of rotting fruits and vegetables stuck to the back of her throat as the ramshackle buildings of the lower city surrounded them.

They cantered through the uneven, broken cobbled streets. Citizens stared as they passed. Whispers grew as gaunt faces followed their path until every set of eyes in the city were casting judgement down upon her. As the whispers grew to shouts; Solveig couldn't make out most of the words, but a few choice ones hit their mark.

"Twisted bitch."

"Murderer."

"Wraith witch."

"Reaper."

"Rot in the pit, Princess Pain." On and on the insults came, only quieting when they passed up into the higher city and cantered by the Holy Site of the Temple of The Oracle. No one would dare utter such heinous words within its shadow. Mercifully, the upper city was calmer, quieter. Here lay the elemental guilds and the homes of the king's members of court. People who were far more likely to scheme behind your back than insult you to your face.

Soon they approached the winding tree lined road that led up to the fortified gates of High Tower Castle. Solveig's back straightened. She would not cower in the castle's shadow. Not under the strain of the journey, nor the stress of wondering what waited. Certainly not under the weight of hateful stares and whispered malice. She would ride through the gates of High Tower Castle for the first time in two years, with her head held high.

Once they were away from the prying eyes of the city's inhabitants, the general placed the shackles around her wrists again. The chains rattled, a light echo of the orchestra she had once listened to through the daylight hours at the mine. Though it was much quieter, with only one set.

They stood before an ornate set of carved wooden doors. General Anik knocked once, waited, and then knocked a second time. Solveig could hear the hushed whispers beyond before the deep commanding voice of her father, King Emerson Gunnar of House Maleen, called,

"Enter."

CHAPTER FOURTEEN

Guilty as Charged

Heavy doors swung open, their hinges groaning as they twisted in the woodgrain to reveal the throne room. Blinding light from the arched windows lining both walls lit the room. A strong floral scent assaulted Solveig's nose. Drifting from copious, overflowing bowls of flower petals, desperately trying to mask the stench of centuries-old damp.

General Anik dropped Solveig's arm as he sneered, "Good luck little witch, you're going to need it." He backed out of the room slowly, leaving Solveig to walk down the long, blue carpeted aisle alone.

Guards lined the way, barely a foot of space between them, up to the dais where three gilded thrones sat. Each member of the trio had dressed in all their lush velvet finery and best sparkling jewels. They sat unmoving, emotionless as statues as she walked toward them in day's old clothes, a harried mess from her journey.

Each throne sat before a large window, from where the sun poured in, casting their faces in shadow, gilding their crowns. Their hair shimmered equal to freshly spun gold as she halted before them.

It was Solveig who spoke first,

"Brother."

"Mother."

"Father," she said, watching each of them.

Queen Asta rose from her throne, her deep red velvet gown rustling around her. "You stand accused!" she screeched, eyes sharp as daggers before her husband and king raised his hand.

"SILENCE! Guards. Leave us, this is a family matter."

One by one, the guards slowly filed out of the room, their armour clattering as they walked. The king rose from his throne, and Solveig had to arch her neck to peer up at his ageing face.

"Solveig Aila Maleen, Princess of Torrelin, Master of Hydromancy." The prince to the king's left sputtered a poorly concealed laugh at the last part and Solveig cut him a threatening glance, one that he met with equal fervour.

"High Inquisitor of Luxenal Copper Mine," the king continued, unfazed. "You are called before us today to answer the charges levelled against you by your superior, Commander Dissin Sellen."

"What charges?" Solveig asked, her tone bored to mask the irritation that coiled in her stomach at the idea of Commander Sellen ever being superior to her.

The queen's jaw clenched tight at the disrespect in her tone. "You may be a princess, but when you stand in chains before us, accused of serious crimes, you will address us in the proper manner."

Solveig's eyes slid from her father to her mother and back, "fine. What charges, Your Majesty?" Solveig repeated. Dipping into a bow so low, she had to bite back the grimace and curse that fought to escape her mouth as white-hot pain lanced through her stomach. Killian's eyes danced with amusement.

"Feeling okay there?" He drew a long, pale finger across his lower lip. The corner tipped up in a sly smile, eyes glittering.

"Never better," Solveig gritted.

"Enough of this!" the king commanded. "You stand accused of dereliction of duty, aiding the escape of a prisoner marked for execution and the murder of no less than three guards. How do you plead?"

Solveig made a grand show of thinking it over for a few moments before shrugging her shoulders with a resigned smile. "Guilty as charged. Your Majesty."

"Insolent little brat, who do you think you are?" Asta seethed.

Solveig folded her arms across her chest as best she could, with her wrists still chained. "Let's see, there was Witch Bitch, Princess Pain, Reaper, Wraith, but plain old Solveig works too, Mother."

"Watch your mouth," the queen bit out.

"Or what? What exactly will you do? Put me through an actual trial?" She took a step closer. "Why haven't you made what I did public? You bet I'm guilty. Worse, I must confess because I didn't aid his escape, I planned it." Solveig stared at her mother, a woman who had never been warm and yet somehow in the two years since she'd last seen her, Asta had become colder than ever. As though their separation had severed any remaining kindness the queen had harboured for her daughter.

Asta Maleen rose from her throne, body shaking as though she were trying to hold back her rage.

"You're to present yourself at the Temple of The Oracle at dawn tomorrow for further questioning. You will also put yourself forward for your long-delayed offering. If you don't, I will ensure that every soul in the shadow of this castle knows precisely what you did."

Solveig cocked her head to the side as she regarded her father. "I wasn't aware that the queen was now in charge of decision-making. How progressive of you, father."

The king shook his head. "Your mother is merely parroting a decision I made days ago."

Solveig yawned. "Am I free to go then? I could do with a bath and a change of clothes. How would it look for a member of the king's court to show up to temple so..." She glanced down at herself. "Unkempt?"

"Oh, you may laugh now, little lamb, but a lot has changed since you last went to the temple." Killian smirked from where he slouched on his own throne. "Let's hope you keep that spirit up. Gabriel will be there after all. Your betrothed, remember him?" His gaze shot down to her naked ring finger. "You should wear gloves. He won't be too happy if he spots a certain diamond missing." He rose from his chair and Solveig followed his every step warily as he came close. As a teenager, Killian had often accidentally used his magic on her. With Aldrik beside her, the accidents had stopped, but she had no way of knowing which version of her brother faced her now. Lifting her hand in his, he kissed the finger where the ring should have been.

"It truly is good to have you home." He smiled up at her, and Solveig gasped as his hand became intensely hot in hers. She tried to pull away, but he only gripped her tighter. His skin beneath hers burned as he pulled her closer. Her palm blistered beneath the sheen of flame he conjured between them. "Better get that seen to, amongst your other injuries." His gaze flicked up and down her. "We need you in top condition tomorrow." Solveig bit her lip through the searing agony in her palm as he burned through the skin there before releasing her, shouldering past to exit the throne room. Killian, it seemed, had reverted to his old ways, though he wasn't hiding anymore, rather revelling in the pain he wrought.

"You're dismissed, Solveig," the king muttered, pretending not to notice, as Solveig stared down at her blistered skin.

"A guard will escort you to your quarters and a healer sent to check you over. You remain under charges and may not leave your room unless escorted by one of us or a member of the royal staff. Do I make myself clear?"

"Crystal," Solveig sneered, "and the shackles?" She shook her arms, the sound echoing along the walls.

"They'll remove them when you are safely in your room. We wouldn't want you getting any ideas about using that strange magic on any more innocents now, would we?"

Chapter Fifteen

Desperate to Forget

Through the open windows of the princess's bedchamber, the faint orchestra of the city travelled along the wind. From the stall holders shouting their deals at the market, to the ethereal singing of The Oracle's acolytes. Almost drowned out by the banging and sawing of trades men; desperately trying to fortify the houses of the common folk before the winter months crashed down upon them.

Solveig lay on the chaise at the foot of her bed. A woman dressed in the grey tunic and pants of the healers knelt before her. Face creased with deep concentration lines as she studied the princess' many injuries.

"You mend these wounds y'self, Highness?"

"I was too busy lying unconscious from the blood loss."

"Couldn't channel some of that hydromancy?"

"What need does an executioner have of healing ability?" Solveig snapped, watching with satisfaction as the healer's mouth fell into a grim line.

"Nothin' I can do for the scarrin' I'm afraid. You can thank whoever did the rush job of stitching you back up for that," she muttered, changing tack. "How's your pain?"

"Fine. As long as you don't ask me to stand." Solveig grimaced, recalling the sickening ache merely standing in the throne room had wrought.

"It's common to have lingerin' aches from injuries such as these. Try to stay off your feet for a while." She rummaged through her bag of supplies on the floor beside her.

"Terin root and Gabos leaf potion for the pain, two sips morn, noon and evenin' for the next three days should fix ya up."

When Solveig didn't move to take the potion, the healer instead placed it on the mahogany table beside her head. Sweeping her eyes down the princess' body when she spotted the burn on her hand. "How d'ya get that, then?" she asked with a raised brow.

"I got burned trying to build a fire."

"You build a fire ridin' horseback from the port all night?"

"No. Why?"

"Too fresh a wound to be any later than a day old."

Solveig merely shrugged.

"I checked your records before I came up here, difficult bein' a new healer and all. It's quite thick for someone of your age and social standin'. Lots of burn injuries over the years."

"Drop it." Solveig's voice dripped ice; her gaze promised swift silence. She had no desire to discuss her brother's sadistic tendencies.

The healer held her hands up in response. "Healer's job to ask ya, understand?"

"There's nothing nefarious going on here."

The healer rummaged through her bag once more, pulling two more glass bottles out. "Aloe leaf gel, for the burn, as needed, and peppermint oil for when all that tension ya holdin' onto brings an inevitable headache. My legs aren't what they used to be, could do without havin' to make the trip to your tower twice in one day."

Solveig starred at the healer with a furrowed brow. "You know who I am, right?"

"Yes, ma'am," the healer said, shouldering her bag.

"Why do you care this much about my pain levels?"

"Healer's code. We don't deny care to anyone. Good day, Your Highness."

Solveig drank the potions as the healer left, waiting for the pain to dampen before standing and heading toward the bathing chamber. She twisted the taps at the sink. The old pipes rattled loudly as they pulled water from the reservoir deep within the castle. Once full, she dipped one hand into the frigid water, closing her eyes. Searching down into her consciousness where the still dangerously low well of power lay, she connected with it and instantly sensed the water becoming an extension of her. She thought of the burn on her other hand, willing her power to use the source of water to cool the ache and inflammation.

Sweat beaded at her hairline, brows furrowed in concentration. Still, nothing happened. Solveig ripped her hand from the sink, sending droplets flying across the room in frustration as she stormed from the chamber to grab the aloe leaf gel from the table. Control water, yes, drain water, easy as breathing. Heal with it? No, that wasn't something she had ever been capable of.

With her physical aches masked, there was only one thing left to deal with. Solveig stalked over to the windows, closing the heavy velvet drapes to block out the daylight before heading for her bed. At the side of it, she drifted a hand down the cool stone wall, until she came across a small crack in the stone. Pushing lightly to dislodge it, revealing a small glass vial of calming draught she saved from four years ago. A time when she had been incapable of making it through a single night without screaming the castle down with her nightmares. One small drop on her tongue and she would be dead to the world around her within thirty minutes.

She pulled back the heavy blue sheets and crawled beneath them, staring at the ceiling. Her mind resolutely going through sword play moves. Unilaterally focused to ensure that she wouldn't drift to the darker thoughts that fought to resurface with being back in the castle; in this room that held too many memories.

CHAPTER SIXTEEN

Layers of Armour

The sound of a key turning in the lock yanked Solveig from her sleep. Her hand dived beneath the pillow for a dagger that was nowhere to be found. In all that had happened the previous day, she had let it slip her mind that her weapons were yet to be returned to her. She couldn't be in this castle, let alone in this city, without them. Years ago, she'd had the protection of Aldrik, and even when she lost him, people steered clear. But now? She didn't know who or what could be lurking beyond the next corner and needed to be ready for anything. Especially if she had fifty disgruntled families on her tail from her exploits at Luxenal.

"Ma'am?" a voice called from the doorway. The surrounding room lit suddenly with the blue light of elemental flame. Solveig eyed the woman at the door, someone she had never seen before. She was young, with deep red hair that appeared almost purple in the flames light.

"And you are?"

"Teris, ma'am, your ladies' maid."

"Whose servant were you before mine?"

"I was with the prince; I have worked in the castle for six months now."

"You have a strange accent. Where do you call home?" Suspicion roiled in her gut. No one had mentioned a maid to her.

"Apologies, ma'am, but now is not the time for chatter. You're expected at the temple within the hour. I'm to help you dress and escort you downstairs." Solveig eyed Teris as she flitted about the room. Her words were too proper, her appearance too healthy, to be a pauper desperate enough to go into service at the castle.

"Shall I have them prepare breakfast in your sitting room, ma'am?" Teris asked after she finished preparing the bath.

"No, the table by the chaise will do," Solveig said, too quickly to be natural, causing Teris to shoot her a quizzical look.

"Very well. Do you require help in the bathing chamber, or shall I set out some clothes for you?"

"The clothes please," Solveig stated as she walked toward the other room, locking the door behind her.

After a quick bath in warm lotus flower scented water, Solveig reopened the door to find a screen covering the entrance. A dress hung over it, under things placed on the ottoman to the side. Quickly, she slipped the items on, grateful that Teris had opted for practicality and comfort.

They rolled in breakfast as Teris tied Solveig's hair in a simple knot at the base of her neck, a few wisps left out to frame her face. Solveig stared at her appearance in the mirror. She may not have been a prisoner at Luxenal, but it had taken its toll on her, regardless. Looking good to Solveig was akin to donning another layer of armour, but she had left all her cosmetics behind at the mine. They would need to be replaced quickly, along with a much-needed haircut.

She sipped on sweetened lavender and honey milk coffee as she chewed a few scant pieces of fruit, having no interest in the overly sugared pastries. Two years of basic rations at the mine and she'd lost much of her appetite for the fancier delicacies favoured by the rest of her family. The lavender and honey milk coffee, however, was an imported delicacy from Farrenhold that she had sorely missed.

"Ma'am, the carriage is waiting."

Solveig turned in her chair to see Teris holding a large box. Her eyes narrowed.

"Your mother has requested you wear this." Teris lifted the lid to reveal a thin golden circlet lying atop plush green velvet. Solveig rolled her eyes. She should have known; gold was the family signature. They couldn't have her walking round completely devoid of it. Teris placed the circlet atop Solveig's head, before offering her hand to lead her from the room and down to the entrance hall. Once there, she draped a long black cloak around Solveig's shoulders, pulling up the hood to cast her face in shadow as they led her out to the carriage.

CHAPTER SEVENTEEN

Ceremonies and Offerings

A weak yellow dawn broke across the snow-capped peaks to the back of High Tower Castle as the princess's carriage wended its way down to the higher city. Solveig caressed the jewelled cuffs at her wrists as she watched the common folk through the sheer drapes covering the windows. As a child, they'd been cumbersome to the point of pain. Yet with every pair she'd grown out of, she had also grown older, stronger; they became easier to bear. She almost forgot they were there. Until she witnessed citizens, like the stall owners setting up at the market and the bakers pulling fresh loaves from the ovens, walking through life without them. Content in their simple, powerless lives. Joined in their obscurity by the countless others who failed to manifest with every passing year.

They passed The Wall where a few citizens lingered, freshly picked flowers held in tight grips as tears tracked down their cheeks. Some placed a hand upon it, caressing the name etched beneath their palm, remembering their dead in the only way they could afford. As the years had passed, many had fallen to the strange sickness that was taking hold within Osvolta. From the snow-capped peaks of Torrelin to the salt kissed shore of Farrenhold, hundreds of elementals had succumbed to gruesome deaths. Fine one day and drowning in their own blood the next. The lords and ladies of her father's court who had suffered losses were remembered in The Hallows, a burial site beyond the eastern gates of Marrelin City. The common folk had The Wall and their families' names etched within. Solveig had to force her gaze away, as she fought to swallow the emotion clogging her throat. She had lost someone as they had. Held him as he choked. Sobbed as his body went cold in her arms, but she would never be one of them. Would never share in their pain whilst she caused them more, cursing them to a life of unending grief.

Finally, the carriage pulled up alongside the Temple of The Oracle. The golden dome atop the stark, white walled façade was a beacon glowing in the early morning sun. Solveig repositioned her hood, bowing her head to wait for the carriage door to open as protocol dictated. Once it did, she took the gloved hand that reached within and stepped out into the chill air. Temple acolytes lined the pathway on either side, silent in their pale blue and white garb. Solveig climbed the polished steps, coming to a stop in front of two men.

"Praise be The Oracle, and the balance hard fought. May we always be worthy of their court." She bowed low as she spoke.

"Rise, dear child," came a kind voice. Solveig raised her head and met dark eyes set in an unearthly pale face, crowned by long white hair. The voice of The Oracle in Torrelin, their prophet. Chosen from a sea of acolytes following his predecessor's death ten years prior.

"Leader Ezekiel," she murmured.

"Blessed child of Oracle protected Osvolta. Welcome home." He drifted the back of one icy hand down her cheek. Shivers ran over her body from his touch. "To what do we owe this auspicious visit?"

"I come to pay my delayed respects to our benevolent protector, so their light may continue to shine upon me."

"You are most welcome, dear child. Please follow me this way." Leader Ezekiel's white robes kissed the floor as he spun.

Solveig made to follow when the other man stepped in her path. Her eyes shot up to meet the familiar blue belonging to Gabriel, Leader Ezekiel's son, and her betrothed. He said nothing as he offered her his hand to lead her inside, where an acolyte waited before a basin of Caldera Lake water. Gabriel helped her shed her cloak, revealing a dark blue dress as he handed it off to the acolyte before taking her place.

"Bless those who come to this temple to make their annual offerings." Gabriel dipped two fingers into the sacred waters and drew two overlapping circles at the centre of her forehead over the golden circlet she wore. Binding her to her family and The Oracle.

"This way Princess Solveig, your ceremony shall begin momentarily." Gabriel offered his hand to her once more, this time realising that she had not worn the gloves as Killian recommended. Her gaze flicked up to Gabriel's, where she almost missed the sharp glint in his eyes and the tightness in his jaw before he wrenched back his control.

Their footsteps echoed along the polished white stone floor. Ordinarily, when a member of the royal house came to pay their dues at the temple, they lay a turquoise blue carpet edged in gold out for them. Not for Solveig. She was more reaper than princess these days.

Sweet smelling smoke wafted out from the private worship rooms. Choral singing drifted from the main hall that Gabriel led her toward and then passed. Solveig twisted in his grip, staring at the doors to the hall as they went. "Where are we going?" she asked as Gabriel marched her further down a long, dark hallway. He remained quiet until a locked door blocked their way.

"We have a few questions for you before the ceremony." Gabriel said at last, squeezing her hand tightly as though in support, but it only sent shivers down her spine.

"We who?" she countered, jaw set, and eyes narrowed.

"They shall reveal all once you enter."

"You won't be joining me?"

"I wish I could, dearest Solveig. It has been too long since I last gazed upon you. Alas, I am needed in the main worship hall whilst we finish setting up for the ceremony." He patted the top of her hand warmly, but a stark coldness lurked beneath his eyes. With a wave of his hand, the white gems on his own cuffs glowed as the door clicked unlocked, swinging open slightly.

"Please, let us not delay any further."

Solveig entered the room alone, its dark walls were cast in an eerie blue and green glow. The blue Solveig quickly realised came from elemental flame. The green, however, came from some other monster. A copper cube sat atop a pedestal, framed in blue light from the smouldering wood lying on a tray behind it. Thin copper wires, similar to those used for chain mail, extended from it. At the end of each wire were circular disks edged with sharp teeth. A green substance lay in the centre, travelling up the underside of the wire to the cube.

"Ready to reveal all your secrets, little lamb?" Solveig's eyes shot to where Killian stood behind an empty chair.

"I'd rather give you a matching scar for the other side of your face," she muttered, taking a step backward.

"Good luck doing that without your daggers," he retorted. "You want them back? All you must do is take a seat right here. I'll connect these wires to a few areas around your scalp. Nothing to worry about."

His smile was too sweet, words dripping with false comfort. There was a trap here, but she knew she had no choice but to go through with it. She'd made that decision the moment she boarded Adira's ship.

Reluctantly, Solveig sat in the chair next to the pedestal as Killian placed two of the wires beneath the hair at her temples. Two more at the crown of her head and the last two behind her ears. He took a step back, checked the positioning, smiling as he spoke.

"Shall we?"

Solveig nodded as best she could. Her movements restricted as Killian snapped his fingers and the smouldering logs became an inferno as he slid the tray into the cube. The green substance along the wires glowed like the gems of their cuffs when their magic ran through them.

"Now then, Solveig, why did you free Malik Etana?"

Images flew through Solveig's mind, completely out of her control. Her eyes watered as she tried to fight it, but as she fought, pain lanced through her head between the points of contact where the disks met her skin. Some other presence took up residence in her mind, ripping apart her consciousness piece by piece.

"Hello, Princess," a ghostly voice spoke in her head, as it wrenched control of her memories away.

And Solveig screamed.

CHAPTER EIGHTEEN
Where Loyalties Lie

H er body felt achingly out of reach. She couldn't speak, think, or move. For someone else, *something* else was at the helm, forcing Solveig into a tight cage in the recesses of her mind.

"*Shhh* little lamb." Killian's whispered words echoed through her. "Don't fight. It will only make this worse."

She ached where the sharp disks dug into her flesh. The green substance burned her scalp as a ghostly presence ripped her apart, tearing through her memories at will. And though it burned, she was grateful for the pain. For that miniscule shred of proof that she was still connected to her physical self.

"*My turn,*" a dark voice echoed through the void in her mind, "*why did you free Malik Etana?*"

Solveig fought against them, but it was no use. They cut through her mind, peeling back the days to the moment she had decided to save Malik, leaving her raw. Exposed.

"*You're playing a dangerous game, Princess. Shall I show these treasonous thoughts to your brother, or keep your little secret between us?*"

Solveig's blood ran cold as the words seared her mind, revealing who had seized control over her.

The Oracle.

Across the vast distance from Marrelin City to the Elysian Caldera, somehow, they had built a device capable of communicating with The Oracle directly. It relinquished just enough control to allow Solveig to respond mentally.

"What do you want from me?"

"It makes no difference to me, child, whether you remain loyal to your family, as long as the balance of power does not shift. Remain devoted to me and you may do as you please."

"Have I ever given you a reason to doubt me?"

"Your missed offerings over the last two years were enough."

"They sent me to live at Luxenal Mine, prevented me from returning until now."

Solveig sensed The Oracle digging through her mind again. Bile rising in her throat as they gouged into her memories of being sent away.

"It's time for you to make yourself useful to us," Queen Asta spoke from where she sat framed in light behind her desk.

"What will you have me do?" A younger Solveig whispered, staring down at the hands on her black leather clad thighs. She had known this moment would come, eventually.

"Luxenal needs a High Inquisitor. It's rumoured to be a breeding ground for anti-magicist sympathisers. You are to be our eyes and ears. Judge, jury and executioner." Queen Asta looked at Solveig's hands then too, hands that now wielded terror. "Using all means at your disposal."

"You want me to torture people," Solveig said, meeting her mother's gaze.

"If you must put it so bluntly, yes."

"For how long?"

"As long as we deem necessary. You will remain there year-round, and your father shall give you special dispensation to skip your annual offerings. Your obligations to crown and country take precedence now."

"Father doesn't have the power to grant such an exemption, only The Oracle may do that."

"Family first, Solveig. You will do as we ask, and we shall deal with the temple," Asta commanded.

"I see you have been truthful." The Oracle agreed.

"I believed they obtained your approval," Solveig stated, though she had no way of knowing if The Oracle would spare her.

Silence reigned for a moment. The images in her mind remained still, frozen in time as Solveig sat suspended between the physical and mental plains.

"What comes first, Princess?" The Oracle whispered.

"Balance."

"And who safeguards that balance?"

"The Oracle."

Pain seared her consciousness once more, as though a hot poker was thrust straight through her grey matter.

"Your family had no right to deny me your offering, and I will deal with them. Yet I cannot ignore that not one person here trusts you. I see things, my dear, small pieces of a puzzle that are slowly coming together. Be careful."

Solveig's eyes flew open, their colour milky as she met Killian's. Her mouth opened and a voice that was not her own spoke through her.

"The princess remains loyal. I have searched her memories and found nothing incriminating. The rescue was a moment of weakness, easily corrected."

Killian bowed his head slowly. "Blessed Oracle, we thank you for your help in this matter."

Solveig's eyes fell closed once more, her limbs tingling as they slowly came back under her control. Piece by piece, The Oracle relinquished their grip, leaving a parting gift, a warning, etched in flame in her mind.

"You've crossed a dangerous line,
daggers sharp, power in decline.
You intend to hide,
but your hands are tied.
Your choices put us all on the line."

Solveig woke with a start, gasping for air as tears spilled from her eyes. Her skull throbbed; scalp burned.

"WHAT WAS THAT?" she screeched.

"A gift from The Oracle to help root out the liars."

Shall I keep your secret, Princess?

"The Oracle is at the Caldera. How is it possible that I could hear them?" She paused, staring blankly ahead. "Feel them, in my mind."

Killian shrugged. "It's not necessary for you to know."

"It's barbaric."

"And that is why you will never be queen; you aren't willing to do what's necessary, Solveig."

"Fifty dead prisoners aren't enough for you?"

"Should've been fifty-one," he muttered, folding his arms across his chest as he leaned against the pedestal.

Frustrated, Solveig reached for one of the disks attached to her scalp, intending to pull it free.

"I wouldn't do that if I were you," Killian smirked. "They need to cool off. Your skin will be delicate, rip them off now and you'll give yourself some fresh scars to add to your collection."

Solveig's hands fell back to her sides. "Can you see the memories The Oracle rifles through?"

"Not yet," Killian smirked, his eyes sparkling at the idea of being able to see into someone's head. "They merely tell us what they have seen, in your mind and in the stars. A person can lie, but their memories, their destiny, cannot."

"Who else have you used it on?"

"A few prisoners at the mine, ones scheduled for execution."

"Why them?"

He regarded her as though she were missing the obvious. "Couldn't risk them telling their allies about our new device."

A chill skittered across her skin at his words. "You had me murder your test subjects?" she shouted, nostrils flaring, hands fisting. All this time, she believed she had been executing traitors and murderers when, in truth, they had been using her to cover their tracks. She was a fool. How had she not seen it? All this time they had preached about her being useful and what better way than hiding their crimes?

Killian's eyes narrowed at the shift in her demeanour. "Perhaps The Oracle was mistaken. You don't sound loyal to me."

"No one ever said I had to be loyal without question."

"Then allow me." Killian surged forward. "You will do as you're told; eat, sleep, walk and talk at our sole discretion. Mother wants you reminded of exactly who you belong to." He ripped the wires from her scalp, one by one, as she resisted the urge to wipe at the blood trickling down her scalp. She wasn't safe here, that much was clear. She needed information. Proof that she could use against them, and that lay within the castle walls. In her father's office. She had no doubt they had a plan for her, and she had to be ready, but the only way to do that was to stay. To remain part of the fold.

Discover their end and do what she could to stop it. No matter the cost to her, her soul was damned, regardless.

"Get up," Killian spat. "It's time to welcome you back into Torrelinian society."

Killian took Solveig's arm in a vice like grip, pulling her from the room and back down the dim hallway to stand before the doors of the main worship hall.

CHAPTER NINETEEN

The Benevolent Oracle

Choral music rang out as two female acolytes escorted Solveig down the aisle, their high-pitched melody twisting her already addled mind. The scent of powdered rose invaded her nose as sweat beaded at her nape from the heat in the room. The many white pews sat empty, save for one. At the front of the chamber, her parents sat beside Gabriel, watching as she made her way down the long aisle, to where Leader Ezekiel stood atop the dais.

Solveig glanced behind him to where the sun shone through an arched wall of stained glass. The art depicted an image of the Elysian Caldera on the day of The Oracles ascension. It had taken over fifty of Torrelin's most talented pyromancers, more than a year to complete. Even now, years later, there was a sect solely responsible for its upkeep. It had been thousands of hours of work that had all gone unpaid in the name of honouring the beloved Oracle.

Leader Ezekiel's voice interrupted her thoughts, as Gabriel channelled his Aire magic to carry his voice across the vast room.

"Welcome all on this auspicious day! We thank you for taking precious time out of your days to bear witness to the long-awaited return of our princess, Solveig Aila Maleen. As she prepares once more to give her thanks in offering to The Oracle."

Silence permeated the air, and Solveig remained rooted to the spot.

"Come forth, child." Leader Ezekiel beckoned with an outstretched hand. Solveig held her head high despite the pounding ache between her temples. Shaking her arms free of the acolytes, she walked toward the grand copper pedestal.

"Is there anything you wish to say before we begin?" he asked with a soft, warm gleam in his eyes. The words came to her as easy as breathing.

"I, Solveig Aila of house Maleen, wish to give my thanks to The Oracle for their unwavering love and protection. They who have kept us on the righteous path, safe and sound, these many centuries. It is not duty, but an honour to present myself to The Oracle."

"The Oracle receives your gift with gratitude." Leader Ezekiel smiled. "Place your hands within the pedestal." She stared at the gleaming copper, decorated with gems for every known power, so similar to the cube hidden in the back rooms.

At twenty-five, she'd been through enough ceremonies to know what they expected of her. She knelt before the pedestal, a sign that no one, not even royalty, was above the will of The Oracle. A window of light shone on her to symbolise their ever-watchful gaze.

Every blue gem on the pedestal glowed, as did those within the cuffs at her wrists. Excess energy collected by the cuffs would be drained into the pedestal, where Leader Ezekiel used his power to channel it down deep into the earth. The temple was situated atop a powerful ley line; the pedestal lay at the cross point of that power. Leader Ezekiel's magic allowed the offerings to flow through the earth across the many miles to the Elysian Caldera, where The Oracle ruled at the heart of Osvolta.

Solveig's knees ached the longer she knelt. The ceremony seemed more drawn out than she remembered. Sure, she had two years' worth of excess power that needed to be drained. Yet she felt off centre, as though something was drawing her closer, pulling harder. There was a twinge in her chest as if the pedestal were pulling power directly from her and not from her cuffs.

Then a voice laughed in her head once more.

Payment for keeping your secret, Princess.

Had her wrists not been trapped, Solveig was sure she would have fallen to the ground in shock. She'd heard The Oracle in her head again, long after the connection with the cube was severed.

She stared up at Leader Ezekiel, who watched her with rapt attention. And in that moment, she knew. It was the same magic that allowed theirs to travel the ley lines that gave The Oracle access to her mind. The ancient pedestal and the cube were practically the same, and now The Oracle knew how to manoeuvre her mind. All they required was the power of an Earth Breaker to connect them across the many miles, straight through the ley lines.

Her power felt as though it was gushing out of her as she fought to keep her eyes open, shadows creeping around the edges of her vision. Solveig thought she heard someone cough. Her eyes flew wide as a splash of dark red appeared on the floor before her. Her chest rattled, the muscles of her neck clenched as more coughs ripped from her, wet and choking and aching. Blood dripped from her mouth and nose, body shaking, skin as white as the walls of the temple. She slumped forward.

"Release her," commanded a voice that Solveig couldn't place. She drifted in and out of consciousness, becoming lost in a spiral of terror. More coughs racked her body as she slid to the floor, arms stretched up to where her wrists were still trapped in the pedestal. Her breaths came thick and fast. Lungs heavy as she fought for air around the blood that clogged her throat. A strange tingling sensation began in her stomach, before traversing her body, like tiny shockwaves. She stared helplessly at the stream of red running down the pedestal, the splatters decorating the white stone floor as though a violent murder had occurred.

Blood.

Her blood.

Solveig's mind was not her own. She fell deep into her memories. A patchwork of moments stitched crudely together by The Oracle.

Violins sang. Icy wind bit her skin as the iron rich scent of blood infiltrated her nose. All at once, her vision spun, tilting beyond sense and reason. The violins refrain became jumbled. Screams, shouts, and rattling coughs echoed through her mind. She was feverish and bitterly cold at the same time. There was happiness, though her heart speared with aching loss. No image, nor feeling held for more than a few seconds. Suspended in a maze of faces, sensations, and scents.

Round in circles, The Oracle spun her consciousness. Over and over. Her senses assaulted with the overload of memories being forced through her mind.

And then it stopped.

There was only silence.

And an image of herself. Lying in a pool of blood on the cold stone floor as she stared unseeing into the shadows that crowded the edges of her vision before they consumed her entirely.

CHAPTER TWENTY

All for Show

The scent of alcohol burned her nose. Washing away the stench of blood as Solveig fought through the fog clogging her mind.

"Easy there," a gentle voice commanded. "You're in the temple infirmary. You're safe." Gabriel ran a hand down her arm in what she imagined he thought was a calming caress, but to her was akin to being scrubbed with pumice stone.

She opened her eyes to stark white walls, cabinets filled with little glass vials and gleaming instruments. They'd changed her out of her lush velvet gown into the pale blue and white smock of the acolytes, her own dress having been spoiled with blood. She paused as fragments of images returned.

Blood.

Coughing.

The Oracle invading her mind, ripping away her power, in payment for keeping her secrets. It all came back in a rush, her heart rate ticking up slightly.

"Take it easy Solveig. I don't want to put you under again." Gabriel murmured; his voice was cold as steel. His grip tightened around her wrist.

"Don't you dare steal my air again, Gabriel Orson."

"You're angry at me for that? I was helping you come down from that ridiculous panic," he spat, all pretence at warmth abandoned now.

"You could have killed me."

"I guess I won't be getting a thank you then?"

"It should be thanks enough that you don't have my death on your hands." Solveig tried to sit, only to find she couldn't move. Her eyes narrowed on Gabriel.

"LET. ME. UP."

"I'm not sure that's the wisest course of action."

"Gabriel Orson, I am a Princess of Torrelin, and I command you to release me at once."

"Your orders mean nothing here, Solveig, you know that."

"And if The Oracle commanded you to release me, would you?" she challenged.

Gabriel smirked. "Father is the voice of The Oracle, and you are here under his orders."

They stared each other down. Solveig picturing all the ways she could slowly flay him with her daggers. Gabriel mentally listing all the reasons he was going through with this sham engagement.

"Where's your ring?"

"Lying in the mud at Luxenal."

"That ring cost…" Gabriel gritted his teeth, one hand fisting. "Forget it." He blew out a breath. "I'll get you a new one by tomorrow."

"Thank you, dearest."

"You could at least pretend you're happy to see me, Solveig. We were friends once."

"You'll forgive me if I'm not exactly thrilled to be held against my will."

Gabriel softened slightly at her words, releasing his grip on her wrist.

"You saw it again, didn't you?" He sighed. "Aldrik's d…"

"If you value your tongue, you won't dare finish that sentence."

"It's been four years; don't you think it's time to let it go?"

She knew he was right, but old memories died hard, and the death of loved ones were some of the hardest to set free. Gabriel stood when she did not respond, heading for the door.

"Your family returned to the castle as scheduled, an acolyte posing as you travelled with them. We're under orders to keep you here until mid-eve, so you may as well enjoy the rest whilst you can."

The day passed slowly, though the pressure of Gabriel's Aire lifted, another's soon replaced it. They kept her tied to the bed, under the watch of at least one temple acolyte, often more.

Gabriel returned at sundown, relieving the acolyte to allow them to attend evening worship.

"I was thinking you'd forgotten about me," Solveig gritted.

"Never thought I'd see the day you'd be happy to see me again."

"You've had me trapped in this bed all day with only silent acolytes for company. I'm about to lose my mind."

"Sorry, love, but you know your family. How'd you think they'd react if I let you wander around the temple all day for anyone to see? Appearance is everything to them, isn't it?"

"I thought you said it was Leader Ezekiel who ordered me to remain here," Solveig stated with narrowed eyes.

"He did. Your parents requested it, and Father agreed it was best."

"What's best would be you allowing me the ability to visit a bathing room in private," she seethed, changing tack. It was clear she wouldn't be able to get Gabriel to talk.

He had the decency to appear sheepish.

"Right, of course." He coughed and almost immediately, the weight lifted from her chest. She stretched out her arms and leaped from the bed, swaying slightly on her feet.

"To your left, second door on the right," Gabriel called after her. Solveig merely waved a hand in his direction as she made a beeline for the door, heading in the opposite direction. Back toward the shadowed room that hid the crude device behind its locked door.

She wasn't sure what her plan was. Destroy it, inspect it, steal it. But she knew she had to do something useful whilst they had her trapped here. As she approached the door, chills skittered down her spine, as though The Oracle was watching her every move. The door was locked, not surprising, but thankfully a locked door had never stopped her before. Sure, Solveig didn't have her lock picking tools with her, but she could make do with what she had, a few pins and some patience. The only thing she didn't have was time.

She pulled two pins from the hair style Teris had constructed that morning, kneeling beside the door. Listening for every twist, clang, and snick of the locking barrel as she manoeuvred its inner workings. Anxiety peaked as the lock fought against her. It felt as though hours had passed by the time she heard the final click, allowing the door to swing open, revealing a pitch-dark room beyond it. There was no glow, no blue, no green, nothing.

The cube was gone, the pedestal with it.

"Looking for something?"

Solveig spun, brandishing the pins as though they were daggers.

"I got lost." She shrugged, eyeing the shadowy figure of Gabriel Orson as he stood in the doorway, arms crossed, his face concealed by the darkness.

"And you thought you'd have to break into the bathing room?" He stalked to her, leaning in as he grasped her arm.

"What exactly did you plan on doing when you found it?" he asked, his grip tightening to the point of pain as Solveig tried to pull her arm free.

"I was looking for the bathing room," she insisted.

"Right," Gabriel scoffed. "And I'm the Prince of Elithiend."

The thought was so absurd that Solveig had to stifle her laugh in case it angered him further. The prince had a reputation almost as long and twisted as hers. His entire kingdom did. Here in the north, it was merely a distant memory. A myth whispered over campfires. But from Rialtus Keep to the south, the whirlpools and rocky seas that surrounded them were all too real.

Gabriel dragged Solveig unceremoniously back into the infirmary. Ripping all the remaining pins he could find from her hair.

"I can't stand and watch you constantly, and I won't punish an acolyte by forcing them to miss their duties to babysit you either," he said before locking the door and shielding it with a thick layer of weighted Aire, blocking out all sound and rendering any hope of escape futile. She could break the door down if she wanted, but she would never make it past his shield without Aire magic of her own.

CHAPTER TWENTY-ONE

The Shadow of Him

After returning to High Tower Castle under the cover of complete darkness, Solveig woke the next morning to a harsh rap on the door to her bedchamber. A second later, Teris waltzed inside. Two servants scurried in behind her with eyes downcast, each carrying a large velvet bag.

"Good morning, Your Highness." She beamed. "Feeling better after a night's rest, I hope?" She walked toward the windows, throwing the drapes wide, allowing the sun to cascade into the room, shining off her slicked back red hair.

The two servants left the bags lying on the chaise at the foot of the bed, racing to leave as quickly as they had arrived. Teris stared at them, a playful gleam in her eyes. Solveig reached warily for one bag, grimacing at the unexpected heaviness as she tipped it upside down on the bed.

Daggers, throwing stars and knives of all shapes and sizes, scattered across the bed. Some Solveig recognised, others she didn't. Those were shinier, newer, likely never even used. Her gaze caressed each gleaming blade from largest to smallest. Her fingers itched to test each of them for balance and sharpness, longed to hear them sing through the air.

She reached out a shaking hand to pick up the two smallest and most expensive daggers. They were a matching pair and had been the last gift that Aldrik had given her.

"For when your outfit doesn't afford a hiding spot." Aldrik had laughed, as she slid closer to him on the couch. Fire flickering in the background, somehow cooler than the heat that bloomed across her skin from being close to him.

"Why don't you show me what you pictured?" she whispered over her shoulder. She'd heard his shaky exhale. Revelled as his fingers drifted along the length of her neck, across one shoulder, and down her arm. His touch left gooseflesh in its wake and tremors in her blood. He plucked the daggers from her hand and carefully slid them, crisscrossed over each other through the knot of her hair. Only the obsidian jewelled hilts and shining steel points were visible.

"If I'd known sharpened steel was the easiest way to your heart," he whispered, placing a kiss to her nape. "I would've bought you an entire armoury years ago." Solveig twisted on the spot, sealing her mouth over his,

"You never needed to work for it," she whispered between breathless kisses. "My heart was always yours."

Solveig forced the memory back into the confines of her mind, where it belonged. In a locked chest covered in dust, never to be reopened. She gripped the twin blades fervently. Watching as they caught the light shining through the windows, her reflection distorted within the steel.

"Your Highness?" Teris asked from where she stood beside the bed. Concern clear in her creased brow, Solveig glanced up at her expectantly. "Their Majesties, King Emerson, and Queen Asta, wanted to welcome you back to High Tower Castle. They had your belongings retrieved from the vaults last night, and they will reinstate your funds by this evening."

Solveig eyed her, frowning as suspicion coiled. Whatever the test had been at the temple, they had clearly decided she had passed, despite the blood spill.

"The queen," Teris continued, "has also requested that you join her in the tearoom this afternoon. Master Gabriel and Leader Ezekiel will join you as well."

The delight at having her daggers returned to her, guttered immediately. The last thing she wanted to do was sit around one of her mother's delicate tables. Sipping her special blends of herbal tea from floral cups. She wished for the dirt and screams of Luxenal once more. But at least it gave her the morning to go searching for answers within the castle.

"Where are my parents this morning?" she asked Teris, trying to appear disinterested as she toyed with the weapons before her.

"The queen is with her ladies, preparing for the upcoming manifestation ceremony."

"And the king?"

"With his advisors," Teris swallowed, and Solveig's gaze rose to see Teris's lower. "They've gone to The Hallows. There's talk that the grounds may need expanding soon." Teris's voice was gloomy as Solveig's blood ran cold in her veins. That The Hallows needed expanding was a frightful thought. The mere idea that the dead may soon outnumber the living as the blood curse ran rampant through the realm.

Solveig rose from her bed, careful of the daggers still scattered across the sheets. She slipped into her robe, heading for the bathing chamber without a word, for there was nothing more to say. No words existed that could comfort either woman when faced with the harrowing truth that either of them could be next.

When she exited, hair still damp, Teris handed her a fur blanket, to keep her warm against the morning chill. "Sit," she ordered. Teris removed her hair from the towel wrap, letting it fall down her back. Solveig was instantly grateful for the blanket, shivering slightly as Teris set to work, brushing it free of tangles.

Soon a gentle warmth caressed her scalp, her eyes drifting closed as Teris worked her magic. When she opened them again moments later, her hair was completely dry. Teris made quick work of pulling the princess's hair into a bun, but when she moved away to grab her clothes, Solveig reached for her.

"I want to wear these in my hair from now on," she said. Staring up at Teris, whose gaze fell to the small twin daggers. To most, they would be nothing more than a daring accessory. But Solveig knew, as Aldrik had, that she had the skill to make them every bit as deadly as full-size daggers.

With an almost imperceptible nod, Teris took the weapons from her. Placing each one carefully through her bun until they crossed each other like swords beneath a coat of arms. Once upon a time, Solveig hadn't been able to even look at them without falling apart completely. Now, she would wear them with pride. She would carry a piece of him with her everywhere, including to tea with her betrothed.

CHAPTER TWENTY-TWO

Secrets...

A floor-length gown wasn't ideal attire to go skulking around the castle in, but it was midmorning and there were too many people around. She would have been out of place in all black, more obviously up to something. At least in the gown, if she were caught, she could claim herself an innocent, ditzy princess.

Solveig's footsteps echoed through the cold stone hallways, travelling the stairways, and sneaking beneath doors. The bleak day beyond the windows gave little light, and she watched as servants hurried by, checking that each blue flamed sconce remained to light the passageways. High Tower Castle was built as a fortress, the mountain stronghold, resulting in too few windows. This had been fixed on the lower levels where hundreds of years prior there had been none, to ensure no easy access for would be invaders. Earth Breakers had shattered rocks to allow light into the entry of the castle, but they left the higher levels, where the public did not venture, as they were. Easier to hide secrets and misdeeds in the shadows than the blinding light of day.

Up and up, Solveig climbed, her thighs burning with every step as she fisted the skirt of her gown to avoid tripping on it in the low light. The higher she climbed, the closer the air became. Every breath felt like she was inhaling water as the rising heat mingled with the damp. Finally, six stories above her own chambers, she pushed through the burning ache in her thighs to reach the door to her father's chambers. Where she came face-to-face with not one, but two heavily armed guards.

She'd been prepared for this. As soon as their gazes locked on her, before they could even reach for their swords, Solveig's hand flew to her chest, eyes growing wide as she gasped.

"Oh, thank The Oracle!"

The guards' eyes flicked to each other before focusing back on the princess.

"The king needs you!" she cried through sharp, shallow breaths. "Anti-magicists have descended on The Hallows. You must go assist them!"

Neither guard tried to move.

"For Oracle's sake, I will guard the door. Go help your king!" She gestured frantically toward the staircase she had ascended moments ago.

"Perhaps one of us should stay," the guard to the right said, his words trailing off as he took in the princess's reddening face, fists shaking at her sides.

"You refuse to assist your king in his hour of need?" she spat. "I should have you in the gallows for dereliction of duty." She watched as the guards' faces paled. "Or better yet—" A wicked smile spread across her face as she lifted a hand, blue gems in her cuffs glowing. "Why don't I sentence you now? What use is a guard that's reluctant to do what's necessary?"

A solitary step forward was enough to send both guards running. Their armour clattered as they raced down the spiral staircase. All to aid a king who didn't require it and would have their jobs for abandoning their posts. But sacrifices had to be made in times like these, and Solveig needed the information behind that door to keep herself safe.

Her footsteps echoed throughout the landing as she walked, checking that no one lingered before returning to the once guarded door to pick the lock she'd sworn to keep safe. She bent low, ear pressed close, listening for each catch and snick as she worked. Her movements were steady, sure that she would have more than enough time to get in and out before the guards returned. If they did at all.

The Hallows lay beyond the city's eastern gates. Giving her a minimum of an hour or two before anyone came looking.

Beyond the door lay the king's grand office, walls lined with leather-bound books, their titles etched in priceless gold. The sturdy desk sat before a large arched window. The glass in the centre was clear, allowing a vast view across the city below. But the edges were a border of stained glass, a mosaic of blues and reds, the powers of the royal house. Intricate metal work of lead and copper held the pieces together, but also drew shapes. Vines and flowers that appeared to shift into snakes that weren't seen in these lands, creatures that called the Jewelled jungle of Farrenhold home. Their depiction caused Solveig to pause, stepping closer to study them. Why were they here? For what purpose? The glass was said to change with every ruler. The reds and blues made sense, the vines, and flowers too, for the king's mother had been an Earth Breaker. But the snakes they didn't belong. Wolves, horses, birds of prey and cattle called Torrelin home, their climate was much too cold for snakes.

It was a mystery that would have to be saved for another day. She turned to face her father's sprawling desk, noting scorched patches across the surface that had yet to be sanded out. A pot of ink and a quill sat to the side next to blank sheets of pulped paper. Beside that lay a jar of wax pellets, envelopes, and finally king's royal seal stamp lay atop a pedestal. The king, though quick to temper, was still meticulous. Unlike Commander Sellen, no documents had been left out on the desk, leaving Solveig no option but to tangle with the locked drawers, one by one. All six of them. She only hoped whatever she was searching for was hidden within the first.

But luck, as was often the case, wasn't on her side. As she flicked through files and stacks of paper. Missives between him and Guild Leaders. Decrees he had passed and some that still required further scrutiny. Yet through each drawer and every sheet, not one made any mention of Luxenal Mine, nor the ordered executions.

Solveig cursed, slamming the last drawer shut as she lowered to the floor. She leaned back to rest her head against the desk as she stared up at the stone ceiling held up by rotting wooden beams.

The information had to be here somewhere. There was no way the king didn't track who he put to death and why. He was far too prideful to let any piece of his legacy be forgotten.

Slowly she rose to her feet, spinning on the spot, scanning for any hidden nooks or holes. None were to be seen, and she hadn't the time to go through every book in the room to search for hidden files. But she would come back. Every day if she had to.

She headed for the door. Steps cushioned by the rug in the centre of the room until a squeak and groan echoed around her.

She froze. Gaze falling to her feet. Hesitantly, she pressed down again with her leading foot and watched as the floor depressed beneath her weight. A creaking groan sounded once again before she lifted her foot and ran to the edge of the rug. Shoving heavy chairs out of the way to roll it up, revealing a wooden door in the centre of the stone floor.

Solveig's hand shook as reached for the handle set flush within it, twisting to find it unlocked. The hinges screeched as she wrenched it open. The scent of dust and damp greeted her as she stared into a small hole barely a meter wide, crammed full of files. She reached in as far as possible, grabbing the top three. She settled on the cold stone floor, not wanting to waste time re-laying the rug in case footsteps sounded on the staircase beyond the door.

Solveig stared down at the top file, emblazoned with *'Project Luxenal: Subject 51'*, and knew in her gut these were the files she needed. The answers she craved from the moment Killian had confessed their deeds to her. She flipped the cover and scanned the contents. Malik's name and description listed at the top, followed by a history of his arrest and sentencing. There were detailed accounts of his time in the mine, every guard interaction, every infraction. Every test and punishment, and finally records from his well-being assessments.

Leader Ezekiel had been present at them all. How had she never known he had been at Luxenal? The notes on the assessment were in his hand. Each time, the question had been the same. Why did he steal the book? And his response never changed. Not once over countless sessions, as though perfectly rehearsed.

'Subject continues to insist he worked alone and not at the behest of his sibling, Adira Etana, nor their father, Sovereign Warwick Etana.'

Each file was more of the same, lists of transgressions, notes on well-being sessions overseen by Leader Ezekiel. The second file belonging to Connall Kano. On and on it went. Every project number was a prisoner she had executed. Yet not one file contained an execution order nor death certificate. A missing piece of evidence that could only be within the confines of Luxenal. The last piece that tied the experiments and the executions together. The proof of what her family had been doing for the last two years, and what they would have continued doing if she hadn't refused to kill Malik. How many Luxenal projects would there have been? Would they have ever stopped? Questions only her father could answer, and she was in no position to ask without the proof in her hands to stop him evading her.

As she was reaching to replace the files from where she found them, her ears picked up the sound of footsteps beyond the door. She rushed, haphazardly replacing the files. Reaching for the door, closing it is as quietly as possible to avoid the screeching hinges before hurriedly straightening the rug and chairs to hide her discovery. She raced for the door, closing it behind her, as the shining blonde head of her brother cleared the landing. His eyes zeroed in on where she leaned against the wall, ankles crossed in a nonchalant stance.

"Should I be insulted that you believed anti-magicists would pose a threat?" he paused. "Or impressed by how easily you manipulated those guards to abandon their posts?" He stopped before her.

"I'm sure I don't know what you mean," she simpered, staring up at him with false innocence.

"You didn't tell two of the king's most trusted guards he needed their assistance?" He quirked a brow.

"I saw two guards running down the staircase and found the door to Father's office unguarded. No more, no less."

"So you decided to stand here and wait for them to come back?"

"I assumed someone would be along to check, eventually."

"Lucky then that I arrived before you could get yourself into more trouble," he stated, taking a step forward.

"Again, brother," she said, taking a step back until she was flush with the icy wall at her back. She fought the shiver from the chill stone against her warm skin that she knew Killian would attribute to fear of him instead. "I was simply guarding an unlocked door. I had no nefarious intentions."

"Then you'll be happy to hear you're relieved of your post. Mother is looking for you. You're late for tea." Solveig scowled at his sarcastic tone, and the laugh he barely held back. "Do enjoy your leisurely lunch, Solveig." He smiled. "It is, after all, a woman's place in court to be seen rather than heard."

CHAPTER TWENTY-THREE

And Unexpected Guests

Queen Asta's tearoom sat in the heart of the highest tower. Spanning an entire floor, surrounded by windows draped in lacy curtains that led out to sun washed stone balconies. Intricate mosaic tiles made up the floor. The walls were lacquered white and decorated with delicate, hand-painted flowers and vines. Candles and incense lay sporadically around the space, giving a heady smoke to the air as it worked to mask the ever-present stench of damp. Except the result was an overpowering sickly-sweet smoke, as though they were in the workshop of an expert herbalist.

Solveig was the last to enter, late as her brother had said. Still wearing the deep green gown that matched her eyes, a black choker gracing her neck to hide the imperfection beneath that she knew her mother would hate. Asta eyed her sharply as she drifted toward the table, not missing the twin daggers adorning her hair. But there were more that she couldn't see. They'd strapped an ornate iron dagger to her thigh beneath the dress too. The same one she had used to give Killian the scar that marred the right side of his face during a sparring match as teenagers. He would claim a prisoner had attacked him, but they both knew it was her. His little sister had bested him, and the shame had eaten at him until he'd grown to hate her.

She walked around the table to sit between Gabriel and the queen. Servants poured their tea, and a myriad of plates adorned in small sandwiches and delicate iced cakes appeared on a golden cart.

"Thank you for inviting us, Your Majesty," Leader Ezekiel spoke first, as he sipped his tea. "I must confess, I look forward to your mysterious concoctions whenever we visit."

"Old family recipes," Asta said with a wink as she delicately stirred her tea with a small golden spoon.

Leader Ezekiel laughed. "Perhaps we shall be fortunate enough to share them once we unite our houses."

Solveig remained silent, her gaze on the artwork behind the leader's head. Ezekiel, Gabriel, and the queen ate and sipped their tea in silence for a few moments. Solveig touched none of it. Not only wary of her mother's *family* recipes, but her stomach twisted with sickness from what she had learned in her father's office as she stared at Leader Ezekiel. The voice of The Oracle in Torrelin, who had taken that power and subjected countless prisoners to torture by the device in The Oracle's name. Gabriel placed his cup down with a clatter, hand trembling slightly. Solveig's gaze snapped to him as he stood and then knelt before her.

"My love," he whispered, his eyes conveying none of the false warmth his mouth vomited. "I must rectify the loss of your ring at once, if you would be so gracious as to accept once more."

Deftly, he pulled a small velvet box from his pocket to reveal a stark white diamond, overly large and completely obnoxious.

"Solveig Aila Maleen," Gabriel swallowed, "will you marry me?" She stared down at him, feeling as though the weight of the entire world crushed her. They were trying to force the chains back around her, and she could see no way out, not without the files at Luxenal Mine. Gabriel knelt there, waiting silently, ashy brown hair gleaming in the sun, hazel eyes with a vicious glint stared back.

"Yes," she whispered reluctantly, and Gabriel slid the new, larger ring onto her finger. Solveig fought back the memory of when Aldrik had done the same, with a smaller ring that the king and queen had forced her to bury with him. Memories she had locked tightly away that The Oracle's invasion had set free.

"Fantastic." Asta exclaimed, clapping her hands loud enough that Solveig jumped slightly in her chair. "Now that Solveig is back," the queen continued. "I see no further reason to delay the wedding. We should set a date as soon as possible." Ezekiel nodded as he chewed on a strawberry tartlet, the red jam smudged like congealed blood on his cheek. "Spring perhaps? Once the snow thaws enough to allow visitors to reach the city. Let's see... " A knock at the door interrupted her before she could suggest an exact date, much to Solveig's relief.

"Yes," the queen called in a clipped tone as one of her many ladies-in-waiting entered with a white knuckled grip on the copper handle, her eyes downcast.

"Apologies, Your Majesty," she whispered, bowing low, "but the princess has a visitor, and I am afraid they are demanding to see her at once."

"And who, pray tell, would turn up unannounced demanding an audience with my daughter?"

"The Duchess Xanthe Whitlock, Your Majesty," the girl whispered, as Asta sat back in her chair.

"That woman," she hissed. "Fine, you're excused, Solveig. We will hammer down an exact date later." Solveig wasted no time leaping to her feet as she hurried from the room, leaving her tea untouched.

"I shall receive the duchess in my quarters, have her escorted up." Solveig said to her mother's servant as she raced for the stairs.

Solveig threw the door open before the duchess had even finished knocking. The two women stared at each other when the duchess pulled her into a tight embrace, and Solveig burrowed her face in Xanthe's neck as tears brimmed in her eyes.

"Solveig, my dear, I came as soon as I heard." The princess lifted her face from the soft warm skin at the duchess's throat, blinking back her tears to meet the icy blue gaze that was identical to Aldrik's. Xanthe's eyes were full of concern as Solveig gripped her hands tight. "Something's wrong," she whispered.

Xanthe led her into the room, shutting the door behind them as they walked over to the chaise. "Come sit, tell me what's happened. I'm sure it can't be all that bad."

"I should be dead. Or locked away in Luxenal."

"Come now, you're a princess."

"For two years, Xanthe, they had me kill their test subjects. I followed every command without fail. Never once questioning whether any of them were truly guilty of anything more than going against the trio's orders. I broke a prisoner out, killed three guards, and they swept it all into the shadows. They used to relish any opportunity to focus public discourse in my direction. I laid a golden opportunity at their feet, and they aren't using it."

Xanthe wrapped an arm around Solveig's shoulders, pulling her close.

"You know I've always thought of you as a daughter, no matter what you've done or will do. My son loved you, and you loved him." Xanthe turned, facing her.

"I must ask you though, if you are thinking of taking them to task, how far are you willing to go?"

Solveig blinked. "I don't understand." Her head tilted to the side slightly.

Xanthe caressed Solveig's cold cheek. "My dear, they've beaten you down for over a decade, but you must know they're afraid of you now more than ever. Why else would they be doing this, shoving you into the spotlight to disguise all their misdeeds, tarnishing you so they could shine?"

"I've tarnished myself plenty without their help," Solveig scoffed dismissively.

"Perhaps, but they've done everything in their power to make it known."

Solveig frowned, eyes downcast. "What is it, dear?" Xanthe asked.

"At my offering ceremony, something strange happened." She blew out a deep, shaking breath. "I ... I coughed blood. I was choking..." Her eyes searched unseeing as she tried to make sense of all that had happened. "Like what Aldrik went through that night."

Xanthe went stiff at her side. "What are you saying?"

"They told me Aldrik died of poisoning, but what if he didn't? What if he was simply a victim of the curse that's killed countless others?" she implored, eyes unfocused, lost in her thoughts. "Or maybe he was poisoned, and I executed the wrong man?"

Xanthe remained rigid. Voice tentative. "From what I've heard, you suffered severe physical and spiritual damage during your escape." She gripped one of Solveig's hands. "Is it not possible that all of this could be but a culmination of that experience?"

"Perhaps," Solveig hedged, "but what if it isn't?"

"Then you won't stop until you discover the truth."

The princess and the duchess talked for hours, each filling the other in on all they had missed in the last two years. They talked until the sun hung low in the sky, and the scents of dinner wafted up through the cracks in the old stone walls.

"It's getting late," Xanthe said. "I should make my way."

"Stay," Solveig whispered. "You'll never make it to the keep before dark now." She pointed toward the orange hued sky. "Stay, eat some food, rest a while and you can leave at first light instead."

"Sounds perfect." Xanthe smiled.

Solveig had Teris bring their meals to her room that night. Queen Asta had never approved of their close bond and Solveig refused to subject the kind-hearted duchess to her mother's scrutiny. She slept on the chaise, allowing the duchess her bed. It was the best sleep Solveig had had in four long years, without the aid of medication.

At dawn, they shared a tearful goodbye, hugging each other tight with a promise to visit as soon as they could. The queen stood watching from her balcony as Xanthe took Solveig's hands in hers one final time.

"My dearest child." She smiled, ice-like eyes overflowing with warmth, "how I wish things could have been different for you and my son." She cupped the princess's face with a gloved hand, stroking her cheek gently. "Don't let them snuff you out, you're stronger than they could ever hope to be. Whenever you are ready to take that step, you'll have a supporter in me."

"Xanthe…" Solveig murmured, but the duchess squeezed her hand once more, a silent gesture to let the princess know it was okay, that she understood. Her carriage pulled up, and Xanthe headed down the steps to meet it. Solveig pulled her cloak tighter. As she turned away, the chill morning air seeped into her bones, when a sound beyond the chorus of birds and the howling wind drummed in her ears. A sound that sent an arrow of ice straight through her heart that had nothing to do with the wintery mountain air.

Xanthe had coughed.

Once.

Twice.

Three times.

An awful, wet, gurgling sound echoing as she clutched her throat.

CHAPTER TWENTY-FOUR

Remember, You Were Warned

S olveig turned; time slowing as she watched a thick, dark red liquid drip from Xanthe's chin. The frosted ground thawed where the droplets landed. She thought she saw fear in Xanthe's eyes for a second before she collapsed. Her body wracked with shakes, coughing around the blood clogging her throat as she fought for every hopeless breath.

High above, Queen Asta surveyed the ruckus from the safety of her balcony, calling for immediate aid from the castle healers as her gaze fell on the bloody scene below.

Solveig lurched, running for the duchess, knees screaming as she slammed to the ground in time to catch her before her head collided with the stone. Blood dripped from the duchess's blue lips.

"I was s... supposed to have m... more time." Xanthe struggled, bringing a shaking hand to the princess's face. Solveig fought to keep her mind in the here and now as she watched her dead lover's mother meet the same grizzly end.

"Run," Xanthe gasped, eyes full of terror, hand gripping Solveig's arm, "You have to run, you must see."

"What, Xanthe?" Solveig implored, shaking the duchess's still form. It was too late. Duchess Xanthe Whitlock's chest rattled, a death knell of finality. Choking on her last breaths as the healers finally arrived but were of no more use than they had been the night Aldrik had died. From poisoning, they'd said. And yet, here was his mother. Dead in the same way. No poison in sight.

"Your Highness?" a guard said from beside Solveig, where she sat, clutching the duchess's blood-stained form to her chest. "You must release the duchess now." She stared up at the guard, enraged, as she whipped a dagger from her back.

"Who are you to give me orders?" she hissed, climbing to her feet, holding the gleaming point toward his throat.

"Please, drop the weapon, Your Highness," another guard said, his palms raised, facing out.

Solveig laughed at the sight, a dark sound devoid of life. "What is happening here?"

"We just have some questions. Drop your weapon."

"I'll drop mine when you drop yours." She starred pointedly at the swords hanging from their hips and the arrows now pointing toward her from the guard towers.

"Lower your weapons," the guard commanded to his men. Solveig waited until every single one clattered to the ground before lowering her own.

They seized her arms immediately, placing her hands behind her back in shackles.

"You think I killed her?"

"No one is accusing you of anything right now."

"Sure feels that way with these shackles you've got me in," she spat, as they led her back inside the castle. Down steep, slippery staircases entombed in darkness toward the dungeons.

"Not guilty, huh? Not being accused of anything, yet you're throwing me behind bars, anyway."

"We're following orders, ma'am," said one as they closed the gate behind her, the lock screeching as it twisted shut.

"Whose orders?"

"The queens,"

"And how long does my mother plan to keep me here?"

"She's awaiting Leader Ezekiel to perform the interrogation."

"And why, pray tell, do they need Leader Ezekiel for that?"

"New protocols."

Solveig's blood ran as cold as the ice on the ground as she took an unsteady step away from the bars. High Tower Castle sat atop a ley line that ran straight to the Caldera. They needed Ezekiel for the connection. They were going to force her into that unnatural experiment again, have The Oracle tear through her mind when she hadn't even repaired it from the last time. She could still remember how their sharp claws ripped her open, searching for her darkest thoughts. What price would The Oracle demand this time to keep her secrets?

Alone with her thoughts, Solveig had no recollection of time beyond the monotonous dripping water along the moss-covered stone walls. There were no gaps for sunlight to seep through, no scents wafted down from the kitchens to mark mealtimes. It was like existing in a void. One in which she had all the time in the world to think over all she had learned. The sinister truth about what her family had her do. Her suspicion that Aldrik may not have been poisoned made only stronger, as she replayed the memory of holding his mother through her dying moments. Events that had been identical to his in every way. Had there ever been a poison? And if there had, who was the real culprit? They'd had her execute Aldrik's killer, and yet his mother died in the same way. Was it a group? Or was the answer something far simpler and infinitely more sinister? Was it her family?

Seeking to isolate her from every source of warmth and kindness. Abusing their power, twisting The Oracles teachings to their own advantage, using a deadly curse to cover their tracks. Round and round her mind spun, desperately trying to make sense of what happened and yet still coming up short. Because she still had no proof.

Hours. Days. Weeks later, she wasn't sure, but they eventually came back. Dragging her up to the throne room in chains, still dressed in her nightwear that had become stained with dirt and blood, her skin chilled to the bone. The king and queen sat atop their shining thrones as the guards placed Solveig in the chair. Prince Killian, Gabriel, and Leader Ezekiel watching close by. She felt the bite as they attached the disks to her skin. Tensing as she waited for the glow of her brother's cuffs to power the device. Gritting her teeth as the burning began, and the claws tore through her consciousness once more.

"Back so soon, Princess?" The voice of The Oracle echoed through her skull as she writhed in her chair.

"You told the duchess you had become suspicious of the circumstances of her son's death. Care to share your reasoning with me, Princess?"

Solveig did not respond.

"I can see that you played no conscious hand in either death, but your lack of cooperation saddens me. Perhaps you need a lesson in what it means to defy me."

The Oracle ripped through her mind again, memories of their violent deaths playing on repeat until they were burned into her mind. Impossible to forget.

"Stop!" she screamed. "No more!"

The Oracle merely laughed as they took full control of Solveig's body once more to speak through her to the waiting crowd.

"The princess is innocent—she is free to go."

This time, The Oracle did not linger.

This time, Solveig did not wait for the machine to cool down before ripping the disks from her inflamed scalp. Knowing now what countless prisoners had suffered before being forced before her to keep this secret, her rage took over.

"Destroy it," she demanded through angry tears as she leaped to her feet. No one moved. "Fuck this." She lunged for the nearest guard, taking him by the throat, the gems on her own cuffs glowing as the guard screamed.

"Let him go, Solveig!" King Emerson ordered.

"Destroy that *thing* and I'll consider it."

"Child, be reasonable. It is a gift from The Oracle," Leader Ezekiel argued.

"Destroy it. Or he dies!" she cried as the man continued to scream beside her, his skin and muscles pulling tight around his bones.

"I cannot sanction that."

"I warned you." She shrugged, as an eerie calm came over her. Her face twisting into a vicious sneer. If they wanted to hate her, fear her, then fine, she would give them a reason to. Agonised screams echoed as she drained every drop of fluid from the guard's body. She dropped his desiccated corpse to the ground at her feet as though it were a doll.

"Destroy it," she said once more, staring at her family. "Or I will burn this place to the ground."

Fire flew at her head in fast bursts that Solveig quickly deflected with her own magic, using the liquid pooled on the floor. The ground around her feet began to shake and fall away, upsetting her balance as Killian threw fire ball after fire ball at her.

"Now, son," Leader Ezekiel ordered on a deep inhale, as Gabriel stole all the oxygen from the room. Blood trickled from Solveig's nose, eyes widening, when she realised what was happening a moment too late as she fell to the ground unconscious.

CHAPTER TWENTY-FIVE

The Captain

The fading autumn sun beat down clear and bright. Only the salt drenched mist of Letalis Falls provided the city of Vhallakyr with respite from its scorch. A woman stood on the salt baked planks of the dock that had once been a bustling trading port, now reduced to housing pleasure craft for the rich.

The light breeze ruffled her copper waves, though she had tied the front pieces back to stop them from catching along her face. She wore a pale sea foam green tunic and pants, made of a light cotton to help combat the midday heat. Her arms crossed beneath her chest; one dirt covered boot tapping on the wood as she watched her brother's ship slowly sail into the port.

"Prepare to make port," called the deep, travel worn voice of the captain. He jumped on to the starboard side rail, scaling the shrouds to take in the view of his home. A wry smile appeared on his face as he spotted his sister.

"Drop the winds."

The breeze scattered his brown, sun warmed curls across his forehead, momentarily hiding the long-healed scar that lay there. He adored being out on the open water. At the mercy of nature, as they explored the shores of the scattered Isles off the coast of Osvolta. Still, nothing could compare to the joy of returning home after weeks at sea. To sail down the shrouded darkness of the Malum Channel and wait as the inner isle of Elithiend revealed itself.

Deep terracotta, sunny yellow, and pale orange buildings with white-washed windows littered the coast. They sat along tangled, cobbled pathways. Rivers ran down toward the falls, glittering like diamonds in the sun. The breeze brought the sweet tang of orange and lemon peel from the groves to the west. And there, in the centre of it all, the crown jewel sat slightly back from the water's edge. Valentia Palace, all shimmering white stone walls, burned red roof and sea foam green tiles around the windows and edges.

He was home.

"Tie her up nice and tight," the captain called as he scaled back down the shrouds, jumping to the sun bleached decked below. "There's a limitless tab at the tavern in the square for one night only: drink up, soak up, welcome home!" His sailors cheered as they busied about readying the ship for its stay in port.

"You'll have them all in early graves if you keep this up," Valentina called as she helped tie the lines to the dock.

"Happy sailors bring an easier life, Val." The captain said as he wandered down onto the dock with her. "They put their lives on hold at will whenever they're called out to join me. The least I can do is ease them back into life at home."

"They wouldn't need easing in if you didn't spirit them away so often."

"Something to say Val?"

"No. I'm merely curious whether you plan on staying put for longer than a month this time."

"As long as Father is fit and healthy, and I continue to maintain the barriers, I am free to do as I please. What's got into you?"

Valentina bit her lip. "We've received word from the mainland."

The captain stumbled, his easy, carefree smile dropped instantly. "What news?" he demanded, picking up pace toward the palace. "From whom?"

"We should wait until we're inside," Valentina hedged. "Mother and Father are waiting, as is a cold bath and dinner. Honestly, you spend weeks on the water and yet you don't bother using it to bathe?" she raised a brow, trying to lighten the mood.

"The stinks a sure-fire way to make sure you don't get any grand ideas of stowing away."

"Who said I planned to stowaway on one of your ships? I've grander ideas than that."

"I'm sure you do," he said, slinging his bag over one shoulder and his other arm around his sister, pulling her close. "Missed you Val."

"I missed you too, Rich, arrogant peacocking and all." She pulled free of his embrace, and he laughed with a deep smile, though the lines scattered upon his forehead betrayed the heaviness that loomed from the news awaiting him.

They'd deployed spies across Osvolta for centuries, but it was notoriously difficult to keep up communications. They hadn't received more than single sentence, hasty scribbles in over two years. Something had changed, and he wasn't sure he was altogether ready to know what it was.

"Tell me you're joking." The captain's voice echoed across the white walls of the throne room as he stared at his parents sat atop their limestone thrones.

"This is some sick joke, right? Punishment for being away for this long. You thought it would be funny to make me see the type of news I could return to."

"It's not a joke," Valentina whispered, from where she stood beside her mother, eyes downcast, arms wrapped around herself. The two women were complete opposites. Where Valentina was fire, Queen Audra was ice. They shared the same pale, almost translucent complexion. The same ice-blue eyes, but Valentina's hair was that of writhing flame beside her mother's snow white.

"Son, your father and sister speak truly, the duchess." His mother paused, swallowing her own grief down to remain controlled. "Her grace, Xanthe Whitlock, died three mornings prior."

"How," he seethed, hands fisting. It had become commonplace for elementals to die on the mainland, especially over the last few decades, but it wasn't common for a noble to succumb to that fate.

"There are rumours that the princess may be responsible. Word is she returned to the city. It's the story that is widely accepted on the streets of Marrelin City."

"Is the story without substance?"

"They say she spent the night alone with the duchess before she died. For all anyone knows, the princess could have slipped her poison."

"That's not her style," he retorted, rubbing at the steadily forming ache between his temples as his mind raced through everything he knew about the Princess of Torrelin.

"We shouldn't put it beyond her. People like her change tactics all the time."

Prince Emmerich swallowed down bile. She was a killer, that wasn't a secret. Some said she revelled in it, enjoyed the torture she'd grown to master. Bathed in the blood of her victims. Rumours said she was as stunning as the old gods, a siren in human form luring her victims to their death. Others said she was horrifically scarred in a murder attempt as a child and had been seeking revenge ever since. Few claimed she was the living embodiment of The Oracle, a vessel for them to wear and do their bidding in disguise. Regardless of who or what the princess was, she had become a nightmarish legend across Elithiend and now it seemed she may pose them a genuine threat.

"How many elementals have died this year in Torrelin?"

"It's hard to know for sure, but estimates suggest at least seventy, possibly more."

"How many of noble blood?"

"Three, including the duchess."

"And by the princess's hand?"

"Latest reports out of Luxenal Mine suggest twenty-two this year."

"Gods," Emmerich muttered, staggering back a step. She was truly evil, perhaps from birth, for there was little he could think of that would warp a person to do what she did willingly.

"So, elementals are dying, and their princess has an unquenchable blood lust. If it is her, she can't be working alone. She must be taking up another's mantel."

"What makes you say that?"

"These deaths were happening before. There's no way she's in this alone."

"And the other option," the king demanded.

"It's a disease, one that's gaining strength."

The silence that permeated the throne room was deafening, save for the cawing gulls beyond the windows and the rolling waves on the coast.

"I have to go," Emmerich sighed, hands delving into his hair as he worried his bottom lip with his teeth.

"WHAT?"

"NO!" the queen and the princess exclaimed simultaneously.

"They'll kill you on sight," Valentina continued, her knuckles white where she gripped her mother's throne.

"We would have to make a formal request." The king eyed his son, his mirror image, golden brown skin, deepened by the sun, and dark brown curls interspersed with red and gold in the sunlight. "They'll attack first, ask questions later if they discover you on their shores without permission." A solemn look crossed the king's face as he recalled how he had landed himself on the throne. He'd been young when his father was caught sailing in their waters, but still he remembered every detail of the moment they'd told him he was gone. Passed on to the Netherworld.

"How soon can you draft it?"

"By end of day."

"You can't be considering this!" Valentina hissed.

"Silence Valentina, control your emotions." The princess looked desperately toward her mother, whose hand came to rest upon her daughters. The two women agreed, but Audra knew there was no debate to be had; the king and his heir and made a choice, and that was that.

"My emotions are in check. It's Emmerich's sanity that isn't. Even if they don't kill him, what if it is a disease? You'd risk sending your heir—the future of Elithiend—into the vipers' nest?"

"We've little option Val," Emmerich reasoned. "Surely you can see that."

Valentina's shoulders straightened as she ripped her hand from her mothers. "I'll go." She swallowed, to hide the tremor in her voice. "It's less risky and this way you don't lose your heir." She glanced at her father, her king, for approval. He did not meet her gaze, instead appearing to be having a silent conversation with his son.

"That's not possible, Val." Emmerich sighed, shoulders slumping.

"We've had the same training. I'm every bit as powerful as you. I can do this!"

"They don't even know you exist! We've fought long and hard to keep your existence a secret."

"You'll miss the Harvest Festival at least, maybe even the solstice," she tried desperately.

"So would you."

"I'm not the future ruler of Elithiend. You are!"

"My duty is to protect Elithiend, whatever the cost," he fired back.

Valentina looked at her parents and brother. "One day, Emmerich," she said, eyes burning, "you're going to need my help. I only hope your ego doesn't get in the way then, too."

"This isn't about ego, Val. It's about your safety, our safety. I need you safe. The kingdom needs you safe."

"I'm more than this, Emmerich!" she exclaimed, arms flinging wide, the gold plates on her palms glinting in the sunlight. "I'm more than the last piece of your puzzle."

"You're staying in Elithiend, Valentina, and that's final," the king declared.

"Have my ship readied for immediate departure," the prince ordered a guard.

"Son, that ship has just returned from a month's long voyage. It needs tending to. Not to mention its size and crew requirements would send entirely the wrong message," Queen Audra warned.

"Then have the Valdrych readied, and Commander Bleeker and her soldiers called up."

"Right away, Your Highness." The guard bowed as he hurried from the room.

"If you'll excuse me." Valentina huffed, shouldering past her brother. "I have training to oversee." Emmerich watched his sister go with a heavy heart. She could hate him, if that's what she needed, but as long as she was safe in Vhallakyr, he could focus. He could do what needed to be done to keep the rest of his people safe.

The king stood from his limestone throne, gripping his son's shoulder as he left. "Set sail now and I'll make sure you're granted safe passage."

"Yes, Father."

"One of these days you're going to push her too far," Queen Audra said as she stood, moving with a timeless ethereal grace, her voice a soft, lilting song.

"At the end of it all, she is still your sister. She is more than the power in her blood. Never forget that."

The dawn broke in warm orange and yellow hues over Vhallakyr whilst the prince finished repairing the barriers that protected Elithiend from unfriendly eyes. He could only hope that they would hold long enough to protect his people for however long this mission endured.

Soon the prince, Commander Bleeker, and her men boarded the Valdrych. A small crowd gathered to wish them well. He could see his parents from the balcony at the palace, but there was no copper in sight. Valentina had not come.

Commander Bleeker took the helm, as the prince filled the ship's sails with wind to spur them on their journey. Slowly, they drifted down the dark passage of the Malum Channel toward an unknown fate.

CHAPTER TWENTY-SIX

A Mother's Love

In the central turret of High Tower Castle, the Queen of Torrelin rifled through her stocked cabinet of dried herbs and spices. Behind her, a pot simmered on the stove. Steam wafted around the room, sweet and warm. She was searching for one last ingredient, an ancient herb that was no longer found in these lands. Her supply was running low, and her last connection to access it had passed beyond the veil a year prior. She would need to make other arrangements, or she'd run out completely.

Still, she considered these to be desperate times; it had been three days since Duchess Whitlock had met her ghastly end on the frozen steps of the castle. Her husband, Duke Whitlock, now a widower and heirless, had arrived at the castle the day before to help prepare for the funeral.

Every member of the royal house walked not only the halls of the castle, but the streets of the city below, in mourning black. An appropriate sombre mask schooled into place across their faces. All except for one. No one had seen the princess in days. Whispers spread across the kingdom, words exchanged in hushed tones between market stalls, over warm ale in the dimly lit taverns. That the princess may have had a hand in not only the duchess's death, but a guard's too.

Asta sprinkled the last ingredient, Nexun Weed, into the pot just as the princess stirred across the room. "Right on time," she muttered, glancing toward her daughter. "It is frightfully difficult to pour hot tea down the neck of someone unconscious."

Extinguishing the wood-burning stove with a burst of water, she strained the tea into another pot before pouring a cup and walking it over to her. Solveig sat up in the bed, as much as her bonds of rope would allow.

"Are you going to release my arms or pour it down my throat for me?" Solveig sniped as her mother sat on the edge of the bed beside her.

"You know I prefer to keep your father's henchmen away from my quarters. The bonds will stay." She tipped her head to the side, slowly eyeing her daughter with a shrug. "For now, at least."

"Are you going to tell me what's in it, or will you poison me in secret as you have before?"

"Before? You've become paranoid, my dear. When have I ever poisoned you, or anyone else for that matter?" The queen laughed as she tucked a fallen strand of hair behind Solveig's ear, causing the princess to flinch away from her touch.

"You think I don't see how some people become more agreeable after a cup of your *special* tea? Or how some misremember facts, or forget them entirely? Who am I to say how far you'd go, or whether you have already?"

Asta's eyes darkened, her mouth in a tense, thin line at odds with the bright cheer of her voice as she spoke. "You're traumatised by all that's happened, my dear. It's nothing more than a basic calming blend. It's a mother's job to care for her daughter, is it not?"

"You've never cared before. What makes you think I'd believe you do now?"

Asta sighed. "As much as I'd enjoy you becoming a dribbling mess, bending to my every command, we've too much to do for the time being to allow for that."

"I'm not thirsty,"

"Nonsense. You've been asleep for two days. You need fluids now more than ever."

"Then I'll take water, not whatever concoction you've brewed up from your secret stores."

"You are not leaving this room until you have swallowed every drop."

"I have no intention of drinking that."

"Shame." Asta shrugged as the door across the room opened. The queen stood, placing the cup on the crystal table as she glanced over her shoulder to where Gabriel Orson entered the room.

"I gave you the option of drinking willingly, child." Asta sighed. The air around Solveig grew thin, her breaths laboured. "You chose wrong."

Gabriel's eyes flicked to the still bubbling pot on the stove, and the cupboard to the left, its door still ajar. Crammed full of a variety of pots, jars, and vials.

"What's in that tea, Your Majesty?"

"Orange peel, honey, clove, cinnamon, apple, and a dash of Nexun Weed." Asta mused, stroking her sleeping daughter's hair.

"Nexun Weed?" Gabriel questioned, gaze skirting back to the cupboard.

"Yes." The queen said, following his gaze. "Some things are better forgotten. Now leave, whilst I tend to my daughter." She stood, teacup in hand, moving to close the cupboard.

When Solveig was next allowed to wake, she was safely back in her own chambers.

"It sure is good to see you awake, ma'am," a voice called as they pulled the velvet drapes wide.

Solveig had to shield her eyes from the blinding light as she muttered, "How long was I out?"

Teris looked over at her, sympathy in her warm gaze.

"Two days. The healer had you sedated"—her gaze fell to the floor—"after witnessing the duchesses' death, you were inconsolable."

Memories came flooding back then, some clear as day, others hazy. She remembered the night she and Xanthe had spent talking. Remembered the duchess falling, coughing, choking on her own blood. But after that, there was nothing but a black void in her memory, as though they had stolen something from her.

"I'm told it's normal to forget things, ma'am," Teris said gently as she sat beside the princess. "After my father passed, I could barely function." A sad smile played on her lips as the ghost of a painful memory flooded her unseeing eyes. "Try not to fret too much. Whatever's missing, it will come back."

"Thank you, Teris," the princess said, her voice thick with unshed emotion, as she squeezed the woman's hand.

"Now, now, we mustn't wallow. We've appointments to get to today at Queen Asta's request. She has given me quite the list of beauty treatments and baubles to purchase in preparation." Teris busied herself as Solveig remained in her bed, confused.

"Preparation for what?"

Teris stopped suddenly as she reached for a gown from the princess's closet, turning to face her once more. "Of course," she laughed. "How silly of me. You've been asleep. How could you know? A visitor is coming to Torrelin, ma'am." She almost danced with her excitement. "He'll be here in a matter of days; the entire kingdom is talking about it!"

"Teris." Solveig warned, "For the love of The Oracle. Would you stop talking in riddles? Who is coming?"

A dark, mischievous gleam entered her eyes, "The Prince of Elithiend, Your Highness."

The blood drained from Solveig's face, her jaw slack as she whispered, "That's not possible."

"Of course, it's possible," Teris laughed. "Now, up you get. We don't have a moment to lose."

Still, Solveig didn't move, "Emmerich." She paused. "Emmerich Ryker Anders is coming to Torrelin?"

"Do you know of any other Elithiend Prince?"

No, she didn't. There wasn't another, just him. The future ruler of the enemy kingdom lurking beyond the Dead Strait.

CHAPTER TWENTY-SEVEN

The Vipers Nest

Marrelin City was silent. Every citizen, young and old, stopped to watch as the foreign prince and his entourage wended their way through the grim, stinking streets.

"He should be in chains!" came a voice from the gathered crowd. Sparking a cacophony of hushed whispers from too many voices to keep track.

"Cuff him! Any elemental on our soil should follow our laws!"

"Send him home and take the witch with you!"

As the company came upon the Temple of The Oracle, a small group of people had gathered. They dressed in similar garb to the acolytes—theirs black and grey instead of blue and white. Each held a sign aloft in silence.

Royal Villains.

Seek the truth.

Three of them stood in the middle holding a larger sign that read, *may The Oracle bring true balance through the death of the users.*

It had never occurred to Prince Emmerich to consider that scenario. That those families whose magic had abandoned them may seek to rid the mainland of it altogether. The temple faded into the distance and the company continued toward the looming darkness of High Tower Castle.

"Bit dramatic, don't you think?" Commander Bleeker quipped, staring up at the grey monstrosity.

Emmerich couldn't help the laugh that bubbled at her bluntness. "It's the perfect fortress. Give them that."

"Still." She shrugged. "They could do to ask their Hydromancers to give it a dousing. I'm sure it'd be more welcoming once they wash the stench away."

"Something tells me the stench is coming from within." The prince muttered.

"Into the vipers' nest then?" she quirked a brow.

"Into the vipers' nest," he confirmed as they made their way up the incline, iron-tipped arrows pointed directly at their hearts with every step.

They had not decorated the halls as they would for any other visiting nobles. King Emerson and Queen Asta sat on their matching thrones, dressed in their finest threads, dripping with their best jewels. To the king's right stood the Crown Prince. His golden hair draped about his shoulders like liquid gold. Clad in a dark blue suit with a red fur-lined cloak draped over his shoulders. The spot to the left of the queen was noticeably empty, for Princess Solveig had yet to be seen exiting her chambers that morning.

Only the most trusted guards surrounded the golden trio. Servants lined up at the entry as they prepared for the imminent arrival of their unwelcome guests.

"Do you realise the danger you have put us in?" Asta hissed. "You can't keep your own daughter in check what makes you think you can control a wayward prince of an enemy kingdom."

"It isn't necessary for you to understand my decisions."

Asta simmered with her rage but had no opportunity to act on it as the arched castle doors swung open and the squire announced.

"Presenting His Royal Highness. Emmerich Ryker of House Anders, Prince of Elithiend, and Lady Wrenn Bleeker, Commander of the Royal Guard."

It felt as though all the air had fled the room. No one moved as the two newcomers strolled in, beaming smiles on their faces. Neither one had bothered to change into something more formal for the occasion.

"Chilly in here," Wrenn said with a mock shiver as she looked around the empty room before her eyes landed on Prince Killian. "Aren't you a pyromancer? Do us a favour and light that fire. Your kingdom's a fair bit colder than ours."

Killian aimed a fireball at the commander's head that she snuffed quickly. Creating a vacuum of air around it before it could set the drapes behind her alight.

"Well, that is a new way of giving a warm welcome," she mused.

Prince Killian glared at her. "You did say you were cold."

"I asked you to light the fire, not my hair, bit out of practice, are we?" She smirked back, purposely trying to rile him.

"Commander Wrenn, is it?" The queen simpered with a tight smile as she looked her up and down, distaste bitter on her tongue, Wrenn only nodded. "I'm not sure how things work in your kingdom, but we demand a certain level of respect here. We would appreciate it if in the future you used our titles when addressing us."

"My apologies, *Your Majesty*. Years of serving this one here has me forgetting my manners. Emmerich isn't one for formalities," she joked, slapping a hand on his shoulder.

"You can imagine my surprise to receive your father's letter, Prince Emmerich, though he was quite scant on the details of why you wanted to visit us," King Emerson declared.

"Your Majesty." Emmerich lowered his head almost imperceptibly. "Lady Wrenn and I came to help uncover the mystery behind the deaths of your rapidly declining elemental population. We're offering a truce of sorts, and once we solve the issue, we can go back to happily hating one another from a far."

"Insolent boy! You think we need help from your runt of a kingdom? We can protect our own."

"Your Majesties please, show me the same courtesy that you demand." He smirked. "Insolent prince will do. Besides, it seems you've more than dying elementals to contend with. Those anti-magicists we saw on our way up here could be quite troublesome if left unchecked."

"That rabble is of little concern to those of us with magic. They can spout their words of war against us, but what chance would they stand against the might of nature?"

"Poison could do the trick." The prince mused, flicking a speck of dust from his jacket, "I'm sure there's one out there capable of causing the deaths you've seen."

"And how would you be privy to that information?"

"I have my sources, Your Majesty. Are you going to pretend that you don't also?"

The king surged forward in sudden anger. "I should have you, lo..." but his words died on his tongue as the echo of footsteps sounded from an upper floor. Steady, sure, and pointed.

Everyone but the prince turned to watch the new arrival who stood atop the grand stone staircase. Wrenn elbowed him in the ribs, hissing under her breath, "Eyes up, Em. This meeting just got a lot more interesting."

The prince's eyes lifted at his friends' words and collided with the distant gaze of the witch princess herself. Stood with a delicate hand atop the balustrade. Her gaze fierce to the point that even he thanked their precious Oracle that she didn't have the gift of pyromancy. Or else he would've surely become ash and bone on sight.

CHAPTER TWENTY-EIGHT

A Warm Welcome

Solveig stared at the prince taking up valuable space in the castle entry. Hatred roiled in her gut at the sight of him, this descendant of the man responsible for her own grandfather's death. She'd often wondered what would have become of her father had his own lived to old age. Would King Emerson have become the paranoid, unpredictable ruler he was, or would things have been different? Would her life have been different if they hadn't caught the prince's grandfather sailing too close to the border without permission? Then her own grandfather's ship wouldn't have given chase. The maze of whirlpools along the southeast coast of Osvolta wouldn't have trapped them in its thrall. Taking minutes only for the ship to succumb. They had named Emerson king that same evening. Their kingdoms' separate histories set them on opposite sides of a cold war. Their personal history sealed their fates as bitter enemies. She cared little for the whims of her parents now, after all she had learned. But here stood a living descendant of the man who set her life on the catastrophic course it had become, and she hated him for it. Hated everything he stood for, everything he had that she didn't. Freedom. Power. Hope. She couldn't stand the sight of him.

Sensing his blue eyes track her up and down as though she were his prey, and not the opposite, she moved slowly, purposefully, to descend the staircase. Dressed in her usual black leather fighting suit, she'd layered it with a turquoise-coloured tabard, its material embroidered with swirling patterns in gleaming copper coloured thread. She'd cinched a jewelled belt around the waist to give it shape. Her black hair twisted into a knot, adorned only by the small daggers that Lord Aldrik had gifted her those years ago.

Even as she came to a stop at her mother's side, the two young royals continued to stare at each other. Her eyes burned with an unnatural fire. His were cold as ice as the tension grew thick around them.

The prince moved first. A small smirk lifting the right corner of his mouth as he raked his eyes up and down her form. "Princess Pain," he began. "Reaper, witch, wraith." He took a step closer, one brow crooked in silent challenge. "Your legend precedes you, and yet still, I expected something a little darker."

Solveig growled through gritted teeth, eyes narrowing as she slowly lifted one arm as though to reach behind her head to scratch an itch. Her hand curled around the black jewel encrusted hilt of one dagger, letting it fly quickly, before the prince could even blink. So fast he hadn't the time to move before he found himself pinned to the mahogany door at his back.

Prince Emmerich stared down at where the dagger cut clean through the shoulder of his jacket. Lodging itself in the wood grain before his eyes drew back to the princess. "Your poor aim ruined my jacket."

"Watch yourself, Prince," Solveig sneered, stalking toward him with a full-sized dagger now in hand as she crowded into his space. Close enough that the warmth from his body radiated through her clothes as she held the point of the blade against his throat. "If I wanted to hurt you, I would have done it. My aim is unmatched, and I find a threat is useless if its intended recipient dies before I can deliver it."

Emmerich swallowed. The action causing the dagger to shave away at the days' old stubble growing on his throat as he brought his eyes to hers. Their breaths mingling, as heat, hatred and respect radiated through him.

"Where did you hide that thing?"

"You'll have to earn my secrets." She smirked, raising a brow to match his earlier challenge as she leaned close to pull the dagger from his jacket. The heady amber scent of his skin lingered around her as she placed it back in her bun.

"Enough, Solveig." The king ordered. She turned to her father before reluctantly withdrawing to her place beside her mother. Leaning a shoulder against the throne, she spun the dagger between her fingers. Her gaze never leaving the prince.

"Well." Commander Bleeker cleared her throat. "Who knew there were so many ways to deliver a warm welcome?" Her eyes flicked over to the princess. "If that's how you greet your enemies, sign me up."

"A fan of daggers, are you, Commander?"

"Oh yes, big fan, he is too." She gestured to the prince. "Though he would say otherwise right now."

Solveig's gaze slid back over to the prince. "You can call me Solveig."

"I prefer Dark Princess."

"You wouldn't be the first." She rolled her eyes, pressing the point of her dagger into the fleshy pad of her right pointer finger until a bead of blood welled on her skin. Without taking her eyes off the prince, she raised it toward her painted red lips, cleaning the blood away with a flick of her tongue. She didn't miss the flutter of the prince's throat as he swallowed, his gaze tightening on her mouth.

"When you're finished," the king declared, "I have a proposition." Solveig snapped her eyes back to her father, lowering her hand.

"Since our visiting prince here is determined to uncover the truth behind the deaths, and you are on leave from Luxenal. Who better than you to work with him on this?"

Solveig stiffened. "I'd rather rot in the darkest tunnel of Luxenal."

"Be careful what you wish for, sister," Killian muttered.

"I would be honoured," Emmerich replied with fake sweetness.

"Stay out of my way, Prince, and maybe you'll return home with all your limbs still attached."

"Promises, promises, Princess," Emmerich smirked, earning him a glare.

"Then it's settled," the king ordered. "Servants, take the prince and his companion to their rooms." His head turned to his daughter. "Solveig, a word." But she did not remove her gaze from the prince until he was far enough down the hall that she could no longer see him.

"Solveig," her father snapped.

"Yes, Your Majesty?"

"You're to watch them. Learn what you can. You'll be his escort around the city. Whatever it takes to uncover their secrets, do it. We cannot pass up this golden opportunity."

"You remember I am engaged, right?" she said, absentmindedly twisting her brand-new engagement ring.

"Whatever it takes. Solveig. You can escort him to The Gathering this afternoon."

Killian and the king left, leaving Solveig alone with her mother.

"This is your last chance. Do this and you'll be free to live your life as you choose."

"Free from the mines? Of the engagement? Free of this place?"

"Baby steps, dear. First gather the information, then we'll talk." And with that, the queen left as well.

Solveig, overwhelmed by her rising frustration, threw the dagger she held straight at the wooden doors. Narrowly missing a servant's head, not stopping to apologise before she stalked back to her own chambers. Wondering how she was supposed to get close enough to her enemy that he would eat out of her palm. Her magic couldn't help her here. This was all down to her and her winning charm... they had screwed her before she even started.

Chapter Twenty-Nine

Lord Wautin

T he Gathering had always been one of Solveig's least favourite rituals. Once a month, her family would open the gates and allow entry to all for a *short* audience with the king. No topic was off limits, but you wouldn't necessarily get an answer either. As Teris pulled the laces of her dress tight, Solveig nursed a glass of whiskey. She watched from her window as the common folk wandered their way up to the castle gates, dodging the carriages that splashed them with dirt as they raced by.

"Will Gabriel be attending with you, ma'am?" Teris asked as she tied the laces together and concealed them within the folds of the skirt.

"No." Solveig said tightly, taking another, larger sip. "I'm to escort our visiting prince today." She felt rather than saw Teris's hands pause, turning slightly to study her.

"Everything okay?"

"Yes, of course, my lady." Teris stammered, "Just ensuring everything is tied correctly." She smiled at the princess, but it was a tight smile. The kind that spoke of unease. Teris was nervous.

"Have you spoken with the prince yet, ma'am?" she asked, trying now to appear cheerful.

Solveig smirked into her glass as she turned back around. "We spoke briefly this morning. I will say he is not as fearsome as his myth would suggest."

"Oh?" Teris questioned.

"Oh, indeed." Solveig smiled, remembering how the prince had stared as she licked her blood from the self-inflicted wound. How his mouth had tightened, and throat bobbed as he swallowed, his gaze never leaving her lips. She had affected him, that much was clear. Now she needed to get him on her side, but he was an unknown entity, and she sort to uncover those secrets whilst keeping her own hidden. There would be no safe landing place for her when this was over, yet she wasn't sure she would even need one. Not if the recurrent nosebleeds and the new instance of coughing blood meant what she suspected it did. The only question was, how long did she have?

"Time for the tiara, Your Highness." Teris declared, yanking Solveig from her reverie. She downed the last dregs of whiskey, placing the glass on the table beside her as Teris came forward carrying a polished wooden box with a copper clasp.

"Your mother selected it from the vaults," she said as she opened the box to reveal the tiara lying atop plush pine green velvet. It was a stunning piece, one that had belonged to her grandmother at her age. A woven golden vine wrapped around the band, twisting up and around gems of sapphire and diamond in various sizes. It was a tiered shape comprising three spikes on either side ascending to meet the larger and significantly more detailed central one. She bent, allowing Teris to place the tiara upon her head, holding back the wince as the edges pressed against the still healing wounds on her scalp. As soon as it was secured, she righted herself, brushing her hands down the pale cream gown that her mother had also chosen. Made of a tight corseted bodice, capped sleeves, and flowing skirt with two front pleats giving the appearance of a second skirt beneath them with an intricate silvery pattern.

"Last touch," Teris stated as she crossed the room to gather the long flowing cape that had been laying across the princess's bed. The outer fabric was that of turquoise velvet, the underside lined with coppery satin. The top hem had been decorated with hand sewn golden beading to give the appearance of rays of sunlight bursting from within. They were the colours of the royal house. Marking her as one of them. In appearance, at least.

Cacophonous chatter echoed off the arched stone passageways as Solveig approached the throne room. Her unwelcome companion walked two steps behind her, still dressed in the same outfit he had arrived in hours earlier, complete with the dagger torn jacket.

"You could have changed." Solveig hissed over her shoulder as they approached the entrance.

"If I'd known my appearance mattered to you, I may have even brushed my hair." He smirked as he came to stand beside her. "Mixed signals, Princess, where I come from, we don't hold daggers to the throats of people we care about." Solveig laughed for a split second before reigning back her control, glancing down at him with an irritated gleam in her eyes. In her heels, she was barely an inch taller than him, but he enjoyed the view too much to care. In the long flowing cream gown, she could have been a different person, but the attitude was all her. That was something he had learned even in their brief time together.

Solveig reached out a hand, tapping lightly on the closed door. "You're here to observe, nothing more. Do you understand?"

"Aye, aye, Captain," he joked with a wry smile.

"This isn't a game, Prince," she bit out, "you came to our kingdom, respect our customs or I'll have you removed."

"And go against your king's orders?" he jested. "Seemed to me as though you weren't keen on defying him." Their eyes held each other's in a silent war. Solveig instinctively reached beneath her cape to a small, concealed pouch at her back where Teris had helped secure a pair of daggers. But the doors swung open, halting her movements.

Emmerich watched as her face changed in an instant, from irritated but relaxed, to cold, hard stone. A mask of indifference.

"Presenting Her Royal Highness, Solveig Aila of House Maleen, Princess of Torrelin." Solveig stepped into the room first to little fanfare as the announcers called her companion. "And His Royal Highness Emmerich Ryker of House Anders, Prince of Elithiend." Every face in the room stared at him. This phantom that had hung over their heads, made real in flesh and bone before their eyes. As he and Solveig made their way down the carpeted aisle, every pair of eyes in the room tracked their movements. Right up to the dais where the thrones stood. Solveig took her seat beside her mothers, and Emmerich stood beside her, one step back, appearing as more bodyguard than visiting prince.

The ballroom had been decorated for the citizens and nobles of Marrelin City. No expense had been spared. Copper pedestals topped with blue flame braziers lined either side of the turquoise carpeted walkway. The windows had been covered with heavy velvet drapes, except for the ones behind the thrones giving the appearance of light shining down upon the royals, hiding the shadows within. Glittering chandeliers had been polished, fresh candles replaced old ones, all individually lit. Bowls of fresh picked rose petals surrounded the room, hiding the stench. It was clear to any familiar with the space that a considerable amount had been spent to make the usual cold and dreary castle appear warm and welcoming.

Soon after Solveig, Prince Killian, Queen Asta and King Emerson entered, each taking their seats. And one by one, citizens were led to stand before the dais. The requests were typical for the time of year, more wood for fires, more stone to shore up properties, more food, more, more, more. Offerings were made in any way the citizens could afford. Crops from meagre gardens, spare coin that could have been spent on the items they needed and would never see from royal hands.

It was rare that the crown helped the citizens, except in times of great need when it was unavoidable. In fires or floods, they would be the first to be seen donating supplies. Image was everything, so long as they got something out of the exchange.

"Lord Wautin, for His Majesty." A guard bowed as he led an aged man before them. Solveig watched as her father stood, a move he had not made for any previous attendees.

"My friend," the king began, with a hand over his heart, palm outstretched.

"Friend?" Lord Wautin snapped, spearing the king with a hateful gaze. "You have the gall to stand up there and call me *friend* when you did nothing to save my only son's life?"

Solveig tensed, arm reaching back again, but Emmerich placed a light hand on her shoulder, pausing her movement. "Easy," he said, bending low to whisper in her ear, "How would it look to harm a broken man who's made no threats?"

"Remove your hand," she hissed, shrugging him free, but her hand returned to her lap, heeding his warning as they both turned their attentions back to the Lord.

"You sit there on your gilded thrones. Dripping in jewels and the finest fabrics, pretending to care, and yet when I asked for your healers to attend my son, I was met with silence. I had to watch as he drowned in his own blood. I'll never get the stain out of the floor. It will be with me always, that final reminder of how *you* allowed him to die."

"My friend—" the king tried again, taking a step closer to the Lord, who now stood with shaking shoulders and a tear-drenched face.

"Don't call me friend when I am little more than an ant to you. *You* who have known for years that people have been dying and have done nothing to stop it. You claimed you had *her*—" Lord Wautin pointed to Solveig. Staring at her with equal hatred he had given the king "—kill the culprits and yet they never stopped dying. One after the next." The lord turned to face the gathered crowd, voice breaking as he shouted, "Do you know what he was doing a few days ago? He was overseeing plans to expand The Hallows. He sits there and tells you that all is well, all is under control. Princess Solveig is executing them one by one, and yet all the while he's preparing for more of our loved ones to die. No more," he cried. "NO MORE." He turned back to face the Torrelin royals then. "You have had years to fix it, years to save us, and you have failed. I think it's time you learn how it feels. Perhaps then you'll finally do something to save those who are left."

Time seemed to slow as Lord Wautin raised his hands. The red gems in his cuffs glowing as the fire in the braziers grew hotter, larger, spreading across the room under his control.

"I doubt she'll be missed." He shrugged. "Not by the families she's torn apart, anyway." His arms spread wide as the flames came racing toward Solveig, who launched to her feet, cape billowing as she whipped out both her daggers, sending them flying. The first hit his shoulder, distracting him, the second sliced clean through his neck, and the flames died instantly. Leaving the carpet scorched, her cape torched and the skin of her hands and forearms singed. Solveig walked forward as Lord Wautin fell to his knees, blood dripping from the wound in his throat, running from his mouth as he bled out.

"May The Oracle bless your passage to the netherworld," she said in a monotone voice before leaning down and pulling the blade from his throat. Blood spurted, staining the front of her gown as he slumped to the ground, lifeless. Solveig stared ahead at the shocked crowd.

"Clear the room!" King Emerson ordered, and the guards rushed to herd the citizens away. Solveig remained still.

"Will you punish me for this, too?" she asked once the doors slammed shut.

"Your life was threatened, and you acted. There will be no case to answer." The king surmised. Solveig turned to look at her father, nodding her head, before moving her gaze to the stunned prince still stood beside her throne.

"Didn't I tell you my aim was unmatched, Prince?" she seethed, stowing her still dripping blade before turning to stalk from the room, the tattered remains of her cape dragging solemnly behind her.

CHAPTER THIRTY

Strengths and Weaknesses

I t was unseasonably hot. Arid winds, drawn up from the Scorch, mingled with the intense humidity of Torrelin, caused sweat to drip down Solveig's back. She weaved, bobbed, and parried strikes from her two opponents as the sun baked them. They'd been sparring since dawn, hoping to beat the heat, but it had come on thick and fast that morning.

The down time brought on from her injuries had left her horribly out of shape. Her skills weren't as sharp as she needed them to be. More than once, she had unintentionally left herself open to a killing blow that neither opponent had spotted. She was distracted. It had been two days since the prince's arrival in Torrelin and the catastrophic events at The Gathering. She'd spent minimal time at the castle since then, beyond eating and sleeping. Instead, choosing to spend most of her time at the Hydromancer's guild honing her skills and avoiding *him*.

Solveig's breaths grew laboured, but so were her opponents. She focused back on the surrounding fight, trying to read their manoeuvres before they made them. She feinted left. Distracting one before knocking his feet out from under him, grabbing hold of his sword as it flung from his grip.

Brandishing it at his throat as she met the remaining opponent strike for strike one handed. In a split-second decision, Solveig flipped the sword in the air. Manoeuvring to knock out the opponent on the ground with the pommel, before facing the remaining attacker with both swords. She trapped his blade between her twin ones, pulling it from his grasp before crossing her blades at his neck.

Slow clapping rang out behind her from the edge of the training field. Solveig spun. Wooden swords falling to the ground in favour of her real daggers. She found the blue flame eyes of Prince Emmerich slowly dragging up and down her sweat drenched frame. Dressed as she was in a blue vest and skin-tight leather pants, his gaze bordered on inappropriate.

The princess stowed her daggers in the holster at her hips. Shaking her head as she helped her opponent back to his feet. "How'd you find me?"

"I made friends with your lady's maid this morning when she delivered my breakfast. It was all too easy to charm her into divulging your whereabouts."

"I'll be having words with Teris about my privacy tonight," Solveig said, shouldering past the prince without a glance to grab her skin of water.

"Don't blame her," he chuckled, crossing his arms over his chest as he continued to watch her. "If you hadn't been avoiding me for the last two days, she would have been too busy tending to you. As it is, she was merely doing her king's bidding; he did order us to work together."

"I wasn't aware that this was a matter of urgency," she said, feigning indifference as she sipped her water.

"As lovely as your kingdom is, Princess, I'd prefer to make it home before the snow traps me here until spring."

"You can leave now for all I care." She turned to stride across the fields back toward the guild, but the prince reached for her arm, bringing her to a stop. Solveig's gaze landed on where their bare skin touched. Lightning spread through her blood.

"Let. Go." He immediately dropped her arm as though she had burned him, though his eyes remained fixed on where he'd touched her.

"I get it, alright. You're the big, bad, Dark Princess. You don't trust anyone." He took a step closer, crowding her space. "Well, I don't trust you either, but like it or not, we have a common enemy here. Surely, we can put our differences aside for the sake of that."

"Not likely," she scoffed, stepping back to give herself some much-needed space.

Emmerich sighed, head tipping back as he rubbed his eyes. "What's it going to take to get you to work with me?"

"I would rather eat dirt, six feet under, gasping for every drop of air than spend another minute alone with you."

"Now, now," he berated, cocking his head to one side as he appraised her. "We both know that was a lie. In fact, I'd be willing to bet there's something we could learn from each other."

Solveig's muscles stiffened as she turned from him. "There is nothing I need or want from you," she called over her shoulder as she walked away.

"I heard your magic is weak. I could help train you, and you could teach me some of those fancy fighting moves."

Solveig stopped on the spot, head falling back, to stare at the cloudless sky. "You're welcome to spend as much time at all the guilds as you want, but as I said, there is nothing I need nor want from you." Her head spun, gaze piercing his. "Now leave before I use your throat for target practice."

Emmerich held up his hands in defeat. Humour danced in his eyes as he walked toward her. "No need for that, Princess. How about we use those actual targets and practice together?" He gestured to the sheets pinned to the perimeter wall of the guild.

"Do what you like, but don't blame me if you end today with steel lodged in you."

"Aren't you vicious?" He said with a laugh. "I think you might be protesting a little too much." He took another step, so close now their booted feet touched. "Do I get under your skin?" he whispered. The soft exhale sending shivers racing up her arms despite the heat. Emmerich didn't miss the gooseflesh they left in their wake. "Grab those daggers, Princess. What do you say? Best of five?" He threw his own dagger at a target, hitting the bullseye dead on. Solveig had never been one to back down from a challenge. She wasn't about to now. Without turning to face the target, she whipped a blade from her holster, letting it arc through the air to the centre of the bullseye.

"And here I thought you learned your lesson at The Gathering." She smirked as Emmerich blinked at the direct hit she'd managed whilst staring at him. Using fish for moving targets had finally paid off.

The prince was good, though she loathed to admit it. She watched him narrowly miss the bullseye on his last attempt. Smiling to herself, she stepped up, taking mere seconds to aim. Her dagger arched through the air, striking straight through the bullseye, one last time as she turned to face him.

"Thank you for the practice." She grinned, a cunning gleam in her eyes. "It was truly *helpful*."

"How so?"

"We're even now. You know my weakness and I know yours." Arms folding across her chest, she looked him up and down.

"What weakness would that be?" he laughed.

Solveig was standing in the same position he had when he challenged her, toe to toe, until she could feel his breaths skitter across her cheek as she whispered. "When did you injure your left arm, Prince?"

She noticed his body stiffen beside her, giving him away as he tried to deny it. "I don't know what you're talking about."

Solveig slowly tilted her head, watching him intently. "Now, now," she parroted his own words back at him. "We both know that was a lie." Their eyes met, as the prince did not confirm or deny her suspicions because he knew she didn't need him to. She was a hunter, a killer, practised in spotting and exploiting weaknesses.

"No skilled prince fights one handed by choice, and you made every single throw with your right hand. All signs point to an old injury that didn't heal right."

"Or perhaps I'm merely that good," he whispered, leaning in closer. "Perhaps I don't need both arms to win."

"Then you're in dire need of more practice, Prince. If you ever hope to beat me, that is." She smirked, stepping away finally so they could both breathe. "My magic may be weak, Prince, but at least I can win a fight without it. Can you honestly say the same?"

CHAPTER THIRTY-ONE

At the Queen's Behest

The next morning brought colder weather and with it an invitation to breakfast from the queen. Solveig didn't dare ignore it, not when she held a tight grip on her future. She dressed quickly, before heading to her mother's central wing, stopping dead in her tracks when she entered the circular tearoom.

Prince Emmerich sat at the table, sipping a steaming cup of tea. Solveig's lips curled around her words as she spoke, "You again?" she yanked out a chair, the legs scraping across the tiled floor.

"Desperate times, Princess," he said, taking another sip before placing his teacup back on the saucer delicately. "Hated to go over your head, but this is bigger than you or me."

Solveig eyed the prince, taking in his dark curls where the sun had revealed hidden strands of gold and red within as they lay in a disarray across his forehead. His white shirt wrinkled to the point that she thought he must have slept in it. She shoved the image away. Reluctant to think of the prince in bed, somewhere within the castle. His smooth tan skin covered by velvet sheets, curls tangled, face relaxed, safe within the realm of dreams. No, she absolutely could not think of him that way. As something entirely human. He was a means to an end to her, and she had to keep it that way.

Asta cleared her throat as servants placed a pot of tea and a tray of breakfast food before the princess. "There's a Manifesting Ceremony at the temple today," the queen said with a pointed stare. There appeared to be bruises beneath her eyes, discolouring her otherwise pale skin, her hair pulled back hurriedly. The queen did not appear at all herself today.

"As a representative of the Hydromancer's Guild, mother, I was already aware."

"Good. Take him with you." Asta flicked her gaze to the prince as though there was any mistaking who she was referring to.

"You think it's wise to give him intel on the inner workings of our society?"

"Solveig," the queen warned, "you are working to discover why our kind are dying. What better place to start than the moment their powers first manifest? Now eat quickly, the ceremony begins in a few hours, you must not be late."

Solveig remained silent, knowing any argument was utterly pointless. Instead, turning her attention to the prince, who still sat happily drinking his tea, her eyes narrowed on the cup in his hand. She inched closer to him, all the while keeping her eyes on her mother, who sat barely a few feet away, reading her morning correspondence.

"I'd stop drinking that if I were you," she whispered in his ear, pointing to the cup he still held.

Emmerich paused, his eyes searching hers as he swallowed another mouthful. "Why?"

She shrugged, before rearing back suddenly, watching to see if her mother had noticed, but Asta stayed focused on the papers in her hand, oblivious to the warning. Her eyes met the princes once more before flicking to her mother and then back again. Emmerich followed her gaze. Placing his cup down as though he understood her silent warning. Turning to ask a nearby servant to fetch him a glass of water instead.

Solveig stood in the castle entry way, picking at the fragmented edges of wood in the door where her dagger had landed days ago. Now here she was, about to escort her target out in public, to the Temple of The Oracle, no less. Teris had dressed her in a demure blue, long-sleeved gown that kissed the floor as she moved. Her cuffs remained visible at her wrists.

They had clipped a veil to her hair, ready to be draped over her face once they arrived at the temple. As a leader of the Hydromancers Guild, Solveig was required to dress similar to the acolytes of the temple, for the Manifesting Ceremony at least. It was symbolic. A prominent position within your elements' guild was akin to being as close to The Oracle as the Temple Leader. Specifically chosen for the balance you would help bring.

"What's so interesting about that wood grain?" Emmerich drawled as his perpetually booted feet stomped unceremoniously down the wide stone staircase.

"I was imagining how much better it would look if I'd stained it with your blood."

A smirk spread across the prince's face, eyes shining bright. "Aren't we about to embark on a holy excursion? Surely, it's blasphemous to talk of bloodshed."

Solveig spun to meet him head on, taken aback slightly to find him standing closer than she had first thought.

"You," she scoffed, incredulous. "An outsider, presume to tell me how to best serve..." Her words trailed off as her eyes finally took in what he was wearing. "You've got to be kidding me," she groaned, head falling backward slightly.

"What?"

"You lecture me about the appropriateness of my thoughts when you intend to visit a temple, dressed in that."

Emmerich's gaze swung down to his scuffed and dirt encrusted boots. Scanning up the leather pants, sword holster, black v neck ruffled shirt, and leather jacket that still sported the hole she had decorated it with.

"TERIS!" Solveig shouted, her voice echoing along the bare stone walls. "You'll have to change immediately. I cannot escort you into the temple dressed like some rogue who wandered in from the battlefield, half drunk."

"I'm not drunk," he laughed, though he did not deny the rest of her assessment, as Teris appeared atop the staircase.

"Thank The Oracle," Solveig muttered.

"You needed me, ma'am?"

"Yes Teris, please take the prince upstairs to change," her gaze flicked back over to him, "you'll find him something more suitable to wear in my chambers. Quickly, if you please, I fear he is purposely attempting to delay us." She eyed him with suspicion and the sly grin he responded with told her she was right.

Teris hurried the prince up the stairs and out of sight without a word. Ten minutes later, he returned, dressed in a pale blue tunic atop black trousers and polished shoes. His skin glowed against the colour. She'd also taken a few minutes to slick the prince's curls away from his face.

"Happy now?" he asked, flinging his arms wide as he spun slowly for her approval.

"Much better. Now come along."

They sat in silence on the brief carriage ride over, neither catching the other's gaze, content to be silent in each other's company. Soon they came to a stop and Solveig hit him with a sudden glare, "You do not speak unless spoken to. Keep your head down and we might make it through this."

"Careful, Princess, I wouldn't want anyone to think you cared what happened to me."

"I'm more concerned about having to spill your blood on the white temple floors if you do or say anything against The Oracle inside their holy house." Solveig could feel his ardent gaze rake over her.

"Are you carrying, Princess?" he whispered conspiratorially.

"Wouldn't you like to know?"

The prince groaned in response. "You're just tempting me to find out where you're stowing those daggers in that conservative get up."

"I didn't think I would have to say this to you, of all people, Prince. But I am engaged."

"Oh, I know," he laughed, leaning in closer to get a waft of her lotus flower scent. "I'm simply enjoying that blush creeping over your cheeks. It makes you look more alive." He flung the carriage door open, ignoring her orders completely as he held out a hand to help her down. A job that was supposed to be reserved for her betrothed.

Yet Solveig gripped hold of Emmerich's hand regardless, a small gasp escaping her throat as she felt a strange warmth bring life back to her icy fingers. She thought she saw a fleeting glimpse of a knowing stare within the prince's eyes, but had no time to ponder when she heard someone clear their throat. Her gaze snapped up, colliding with Gabriel Orson's, his jaw clenched tight as anger simmered beneath the surface.

Solveig tore her hand away from the prince's. "We should head inside," she said without meeting his eyes, as Gabriel helped her pull the veil over her head to conceal her face. He placed her arm through the crook of his. Leaving Emmerich to be escorted in by one of the many waiting acolytes. All the while, Solveig couldn't ignore his burning gaze on her retreating form.

CHAPTER THIRTY-TWO

Blessed Children of The Oracle

In Elithiend, Prince Emmerich was all too aware of his societal position and the subsequent attention it brought. Yet a slither of unease still coiled in his gut as every pair of eyes in the temple fell on him. He stared down at the attire his escort had forced him in to, wondering why she had men's clothes in her chambers at all. Clothes that from the looks of him certainly wouldn't have fit the man that she currently claimed to be engaged to. Gabriel was at least a head shorter than Emmerich.

Princess Solveig was turning out to be as vicious and secretive as she was beautiful and utterly enthralling. Technically, she was his enemy, a descendant of murderers and usurpers, worshippers of a false god. Not to mention the long line of bodies she had piled up on her own. He couldn't trust her. He knew that. She was a means to an end, but that didn't mean he couldn't glean some enjoyment out of the situation.

"Bless you, child of The Oracle," an acolyte intoned, stopping Emmerich in his tracks. Their head bowed in silent prayer as they dipped a finger into the water and drew two overlapping circles upon his brow.

Emmerich coughed, shifting on his feet as he watched her. "Erm yeah, same to you," he muttered before stalking away to find his murderous princess, leaving the acolyte to gawk after him. But he refused to be held responsible if the princess was going to withhold essential information on social customs.

He paused as he entered the worship hall, taking in the pristine white walls, row after row of pews, carved with a myriad of images depicting Torrelin's history. But it was the stained-glass mural at the far end of the room that saw his fists clenching as his mood soured. The intricate image showed the Elysian Caldera mid-eruption. They celebrated this. He recalled learning of it through his youth, how the mainland cheered for the deaths of thousands, as though their *sacrifice* forged a path to a better world. It made his blood boil. Sick to his stomach, he forced his eyes away lest he attempt to launch one of the empty pews straight through its heart to shatter the illusion.

Slowly, he regained control of his anger, inhaling deeply as he took in the crowd milling about the space before finally spotting *her*. She sat at the front of the room, hair dark as night, covered in a lacy, pale blue veil. A quick glance around the stark space informed him that her betrothed was standing atop the dais. Emmerich approached her, hoping that the empty seat beside her was for him.

"I think I scandalised that poor acolyte practicing finger painting in the doorway," he whispered as he slid into the pew beside her. "You could have warned me about protocols."

"And why would I do that?" Solveig's shoulders shook slightly with her laughter. "It's much more entertaining to watch you squirm."

"You've had your fun. Now tell me, what am I supposed to say when someone blesses me as a child of The Oracle?"

Solveig studied him and even through the gauzy lace material, he could see the amused smirk on her face. "Praise be The Oracle, and the balance hard fought. May we always be worthy of their court. Think you can remember that?"

"Hopefully there won't be a next time," he muttered, slouching in his seat like a petulant child.

As the doors to the worship hall slammed shut behind the last visitor, Emmerich snapped to attention. He watched as the Temple Leader strode up onto the dais, dressed in pristine white and gold robes.

"Welcome, blessed children of The Oracle," Leader Ezekiel declared, voice bright and clear as his son projected it around the room. Solveig elbowed Emmerich in the ribs, harder than was necessary, as the congregation recited the words in unison.

"Praise be The Oracle, and the balance hard fought. May we always be worthy of their court." The words rang loud and clear as a grimace fell across Emmerich's face.

"How many times are you lot going to say that today?" He shifted closer to her, all the while keeping his eyes on her betrothed, enjoying the irritation on his face as he glared in their direction. To where they sat so close, their thighs brushed.

"You'll be a natural long before the ceremony is over, Prince. Better settle in. We're going to be here for a while."

"Fan-fucking-tastic," Emmerich muttered. Trying to ignore the zing of lightning firing from where the princess had only briefly touched his leg. He stared at her from the corner of his eyes, but she seemed oblivious to the sensation.

Leader Ezekiel stood before his ever-obedient congregation, a sea of pale blue. "Today we gather, to share in the joy of this month's new elemental gifts. We give thanks to our Oracle, our saviour and protector of the balance." Solveig winced as a phantom pain sliced through her skull at the mere memory of what they had forced her through in this building. A place where the power in the earth grew more focused and potent.

"You, okay?" Emmerich whispered, leaning closer to her, fathomless, ocean eyes drenched with concern.

"I'm fine," Solveig shrugged, "pay attention."

Emmerich's narrow gaze hesitated on her for a second before sliding back to the leader atop the dais, but he made no attempt to move away from her.

"But first we remember those we lost this past month. Our blessed elementals stolen by the cruelty of the anti-magicist rabble." Leader Ezekiel raised both hands to the ceiling as the congregation stood with heads bowed, right palms resting on their hearts. "Almighty Oracle. Wondrous and true. Bless those who lived in service of you as they walk the path beyond the veil. May they find the peace that was stolen from them within your loving embrace. We ask you to welcome into your realm, Her Grace Duchess Xanthe Enya Whitlock." A candle lit on the altar behind Leader Ezekiel. "Carinex Wautin." A second candle ignited. On and on until five candles danced behind the leader in memory of their fallen elementals. "We ask that you watch over them in the Netherworld as you blessed in them this one. Until we may greet them again, our stories at last united under the gaze of your unending glory."

Silence reigned through the hall for a moment as Prince Emmerich remained seated in his pew surrounded by stoic worshipers. Holding his breath as tension seemed to grow thick in the air, not daring to move lest he draw attention to himself. Finally, Leader Ezekiel's arms lowered, and the congregation sat in synch with him.

"In their memory, we march on. Never balking before those who would wish terror upon us. As such, one by one, our blessed children who came of age this month shall stand before the four pedestals of power. To reveal their affinities as either Hydromancer." The cloth covering the first pedestal flew away with dramatic flair, to reveal a vessel of water. "Pyromancer." Again, the cloth flew away to reveal a solitary lit candle. This time Emmerich had to stifle a laugh, as he spotted the slight wave of hand from the Temple Leader's son. He was the one flinging the cloths around. On the other two pedestals stood, an empty glass teetering on the edge for the Aire Wenders, and a vine plant for the Earth Breakers.

"What? No Aether or Electromancer pedestals?" Emmerich hissed. Solveig's head snapped toward him, as did many others.

"Hold your tongue, Prince, to even mention such magic within these walls is akin to blasphemy. Those, those..." She struggled for the right words as her hands fisted in her lap, knuckles turning white.

"People?" Emmerich supplied with a raised brow. Solveig glared at him through her veil.

"Those power-hungry manipulators are dead. All of them and we're better off for it. There is no balance in one person holding all the powers, and only one other person being able to defeat them." She turned back to the front, staring resolutely at Leader Ezekiel.

"Some would argue that it is balanced. Do you even know how their magic works?" Emmerich pressed, reaching for her still clenched hand.

"Balance, according to The Oracle's teachings, is us all being of equal standing. One power, one life, in perfect harmony," she snapped, pulling her hand away before he could touch her. "I don't know how their power works, nor do I care to know. There hasn't been an Aether nor Electromancer on these shores for centuries."

"You're judging something without holding all the facts."

"I know The Oracle's teachings, and that is enough. That is what matters."

"Is that what you told yourself every time you slaughtered someone in that mine?" Solveig's gaze slowly slid back to Emmerich's. Body rigid as she seethed, "Watch your tongue. I won't tell you again."

"Anara Nexa of house Bonida," Leader Ezekiel called, snapping them back to attention. A small girl made her way up the steps, hands shaking.

"Miss Bonida, please reveal your gift," he pressed, taking the girl by the hand toward the first pedestal. Solveig's eyes flicked to the right, where a woman, an older image of little Anara, watched intently. Her palms were together as she muttered a prayer.

Anara moved down the line, focusing on each pedestal. The water did not churn; the flame stayed trapped to the candle's wick; and the glass didn't move. Finally, she stood before the last pedestal, the vine plant. Anara closed her eyes. Focusing as she thrust out her hand once more.

One breath.

In and out.

Two breaths.

In and out.

Three brea... A vine shook, then slowly, one by one, they wrapped themselves around the pedestal, under the complete control of the girl standing before it. A gasp echoed through the hall before the congregation broke out into cheers. Anara's mother cried as Leader Ezekiel led her daughter over to where the alchemist stood. They fit her with copper cuffs adorned with the sparkling green gems of the Earth Breakers. Blue elemental flame glowed as they sealed them. Every few years on the anniversary of their manifestation, they would be invited to have them adjusted as their bodies grew, but they would never be completely removed, even upon death.

Anara moved to the next station, where she signed her name upon the scroll that would enlist her with the Royal Guard. A second sob, this one infinitely more broken than the last, came from the right. Solveig's gaze swung to the child's mother once more, and she realised that the woman hadn't been praying for her daughter to manifest. She had been praying that her daughter would be powerless. That she would be safe.

"It is my blessed honour to present, Anara Nexa of House Bonida," Leader Ezekiel called. "Earth Breaker."

"Praise be The Oracle, and the balance hard fought. May we always be worthy of their court." The congregation sang again, only this time Solveig couldn't bring herself to join in. Watching as little Anara scurried down the steps straight into her mother's waiting arms. The woman held her daughter close, placing kisses atop her head as tears ran down her sunken cheeks. For Anara was no longer Mrs Bonida's to care for. She was a ward of the royal family, a soldier in their army. She would commence training at the Guild of Earth Breakers that same evening.

Beside them sat a young boy, with the same rich black skin and tight curls as his mother and sister. He couldn't be more than a year or two younger than Anara. What would happen when his time came? Would he manifest as she had, or would he be safe by his mother's side? Powerless and forgotten, but safe.

The next child took the stage, a boy named Tern Ackman of House Genard. He stood before the pedestal of water and within seconds; he had it bending to his whim. Creating swirls and whorls and tiny creatures with it. A family of five cheered off to the left. Solveig recognised them all, the Genard's were a family of Hydromancers. They hadn't had another power manifest in decades.

Tern followed Leader Ezekiel to be fitted for a set of cuffs that would match the one's adorning the princess's wrists. He signed his name upon the scroll with a grin, standing tall and proud before the gathered congregation as Leader Ezekiel called,

"Tern Ackman of House Genard, Hydromancer," a chorus of cheers sounded as the ever-faithful crowd echoed. "Praise be The Oracle and the balance hard fought. May we always be worthy of their court."

"That's it?" Emmerich hissed, eyes fixed on where the boy had strolled back to his family.

"What's wrong now?" Solveig snapped, meeting his gaze, only to find horror lurking in the blue depths. His shoulders shaking with what she assumed was repressed anger.

"He controlled water, so he's a Hydromancer for life?"

Solveig couldn't stop the laugh that bubbled up. "That can't be what you're upset about. Everyone knows that the first power to manifest is the strongest. Of course he's a Hydromancer for life." Her gaze shot to where Tern and his family celebrated. "And by the looks of it, he's proud to be one, too."

"And what of Anara?" Emmerich fired back, gesturing to where her family still sat huddled together in silence with ashen faces and downcast eyes. "She and her family don't appear to be proud."

"We draft all elementals in Torrelin into the Royal Guard upon manifesting. Many find the prospect to be scary, though we've been living in peace for centuries and there is no need for them to be concerned. Unless your presence here is more sinister than you're letting on?" Emmerich only levelled her with a glare in response.

"With magic becoming scarcer, my family wanted to ensure that their guard stayed strong should they ever need to be called upon." Solveig whispered, trying to avoid any attention from those around them, hoping she sounded convincing. Yet the words were ash on her tongue. Lies.

"It's no wonder you've a problem with anti-magicists." He muttered.

"Meaning?"

"Who would want to be blessed with powers when all it ensures on these shores is conscription? Forced to live your life according to your element, with no say in the matter?"

"Why would anyone desire to abandon their gift?" Solveig asked, shocked at the mere idea. The prince eyed her solemnly, his mouth a grim line as he spoke. "Some people want a simple life Solveig, who are you to deny them that?"

"You would never understand. You haven't lived here; haven't seen the tough choices my family has had to make for the greater good."

"The greater good, or *their* greater good?" Emmerich needled, his words picked efficiently at the wounds set deep within her. She refused to look at him as she fought to hide her hurt. She couldn't allow him to see her as separate from her family, even though that was exactly what she was becoming.

When Emmerich finally realised that she wouldn't respond, he turned in his seat, where they sat in stoic silence as the ceremony continued around them. Solveig only spoke when needed. Emmerich no longer even tried to appear as though he was joining in, sitting resolute as the minutes ticked by. One by one, each child took to the dais. Three failed to manifest, and Emmerich thought he saw relief in the eyes of their families.

Hours later, they had presented and anointed four new Hydromancers, five Earth Breakers and nine Aire Wenders. Only one showed an affinity for pyromancy. Though that wasn't uncommon, most pyromancers had come from Estrellyn. They rarely saw their power these days, and most resided within the royal house.

"Renit Dawn of House Teria," Leader Ezekiel called, but no one moved. No child appeared, and the longer time went on, an uneasy murmur rumbled through the congregation.

"Renit Dawn of House Teria!" he called again. Still, no one approached the dais, and Ezekiel shot a pointed glance at a guard by the door, who stood to attention and exited immediately.

"What's going on?" Emmerich whispered.

"It would seem the Teria family has chosen to not bring their child forward."

"And?"

"If they're not dead or dying, the parents will go to Luxenal for a minimal sentence."

"You can't be serious."

"As the grave," she hissed, eyes still facing forward.

"And the children?"

"If they manifest, they will live with their guild until they release their parents."

"And what if they don't?"

Solveig hesitated. "The orphanage," she said in an emotionless voice. She knew now how cruel it was, but it was the law. The same law she had spent the last two years upholding at Luxenal through spilling blood. If she spoke against it now, her game would be over, her secret revealed far too soon.

"You'd see a family ripped apart over this?"

"It's the law." Solveig bit out as quietly as she could, hands fisting tight in her lap as her fingernails cut into her palms.

"Whose law," Emmerich hedged. "Yours or The Oracles?"

"Leader Ezekiel's. As the voice of The Oracle in Torrelin, it's his duty to ensure that we worship The Oracle as they deserve to be. It isn't new, everyone knows it and still they defied it. They've only themselves to blame."

"You can't honestly believe that horseshit," he declared a little too loudly.

"I spent two years upholding the law at Luxenal. What do you think I believe?"

The doors swung open again, and the guard returned, dragging a girl behind him. Sweat drenched her skin, face pale, eyes full of unspeakable terror.

"Renit Dawn of House Teria?" Leader Ezekiel questioned.

"Y... yes," the girl stammered.

"By The Oracles records, you came of age last week. It is required that you attend today's ceremony. Follow me to the dais and we shall begin."

The girl didn't move, but with a small flick of the leader's head, the guard hauled her up, planting her directly before the first pedestal. Except now when she cried, the vessel of water did too. It dripped first. Then ran down the edges, before overflowing and rushing so suddenly that the entire room was ankle-deep in water before the guards could wrestle the girl away.

The congregation sat stunned. Renit Teria wasn't only a Hydromancer, she was a creator, she'd manifested early, and her parents had tried to hide it. Creators, those who could manifest their power from nothing, to create more of a finite substance, were becoming fewer. Most never developed beyond simple manipulation of an existing substance. Solveig knew this was more than a standard six-month sentence in the mine. Knowingly concealing a manifested child, one of creator level at that, carried a minimum of life imprisonment. It was likely that Renit Dawn of House Teria would never see her family again.

They dragged the girl from the dais to have her cuffs welded shut, but the tears never ceased. "Please no, what about my brothers? Where are my brothers?" she cried.

Solveig gasped. Her hand clutched Emmerich's tightly. Even as the tingling spread through her skin and up her arm, she didn't let go. Neither did he. He squeezed her hand back in silent comfort. Throat bobbing as he stared at their joined hands.

CHAPTER THIRTY-THREE

Swift and Terrible Justice

That night, what lingered of the blistering heat from the south shattered as rain pounded Marrelin City. The streets flooded and the rivers beyond the stone walls overflowed, yet two figures sat on a raised surface in the castle grounds, hidden from public view. A hooded figure stood beside them, daggers at their hips, sword at their back. The rain soaked the black leather ensemble they wore.

The two figures cowered in fear as they looked up, "P... p... please." One of them stuttered. "We were trying to protect her, protect all of them."

"There is little use in begging. Your fate has already been decided. For the crime of harbouring a manifested child. We have sentenced you to death. Do you have any last words?" The icy, unfeeling voice of the princess declared. Her hands shook, but she hid it well. Fighting to block from her mind the thoughts of how many more citizens she would kill before she could bring her family down. "We loved them. Everything we did was to protect them."

"Your children will never hear that message. They will grow up in the care of those who will teach them that your actions were criminal. You tried to deny that child the right to her magic."

The princess grabbed each of them by the throat as their screams filled the night, moving through the otherwise silent grounds like smoke. It wasn't long before the eerie quiet took hold as they slumped to the ground and the wraith towered over them, placing gloves over her hands.

The execution had taken place under the shadows of night, away from the city, to hide the identities of the victims. The king was wary of the up-roar a full public display would cause amongst those who already dissented. Publicly, the conviction would be life imprisonment at Luxenal, a secret to protect the peace within the kingdom.

Yet a figure stood in the shadows, watching the scene unfold. They'd listened to their screams and cries. Watched as they slumped to the ground lifeless, before walking away, leaving the Reaper to deal with the mess of her own making.

Solveig's clothes dripped rainwater on the stones of the entryway as she pulled off her gloves and cloak. She made to climb the stairs and disappear to her chambers unseen and unheard when a voice called out to her from the shadows.

"The laws of my country would have me strike you down for what you have done." Solveig paused on the steps, one hand gripping the cold railing.

"Then it's good we aren't in your country, we're in mine. And our laws state I carried out justice."

"I thought the rumours were exaggerated. Now I see every one of them rings true."

"Who are you to pass judgement upon me, Dark Prince?"

"Take one step inside, Elithiend, Princess, and you won't hear those words uttered against me. I don't even have to leave the castle to hear nightmarish stories of the things you've done."

"Why are you still here, desperate to work with me, if I repulse you?" Solveig questioned with an irritated sigh.

The prince stepped out of the darkness, and she gazed upon his handsome face, turned hard as stone, devoid of all warmth. "I don't have to like you to get what I need from you."

"Good, the feeling is mutual."

"Training tomorrow?"

"I'm busy with the new recruits at the guild tomorrow."

"Then I'll tag along."

"You're here to figure out why elementals are dying. You do not need to see our training methods."

"I disagree," he took another step closer. "I need a complete picture if I'm to root out the cause."

Solveig shook her head at a loss. "Then you'll need permission that I don't have the authority to grant."

"And who does?"

"My father, of course," she said saccharinely. "Good night, Prince."

Solveig could feel his gaze burning her like hellfire as she ascended the stairs. "You know, for someone who proclaims to hate every piece of me, you spend an awful lot of time watching me," she fired over her shoulder.

"It's possible to abhor someone and still find them pleasant to look at. Sweet dreams, Princess."

CHAPTER THIRTY-FOUR

Practice Makes Perfect

Solveig stood before the group of newly anointed Hydromancers. Tern Genard was front and centre, with a hungry gleam in his eyes. Behind him were Tasy Roy, Sigra Rozen and Charla Laxie. The three girls huddled with their heads pressed together as they whispered. Renit Teria stood alone on the far side of the room; her eyes remained red as tears continued to flow.

"Welcome Hydromancers, for those of you who aren't aware, my name is Solveig."

"You're the princess." Sigra said, her eyes wide and shining, voice dripping with wonder. The other girls in her group giggled mercilessly at her outburst.

Solveig's answering smile was tight. "I am indeed. However, within the guild, titles and social standings are of no concern. Your position here will depend solely on how little or how much you choose to train your powers. You'll have daily training sessions here with guild leaders after your regular schooling."

"First, who here can tell me some benefits of the Hydromancer gift?"

Sigra's hand flew to the air as she wriggled on the spot, desperate to be chosen. Solveig's answering smile was kind. She saw a lot of her younger self in the girl. Eyes full of wonder at what the future may hold, not yet tarnished by the reality, nor the hatred of the anti-magicists. To her, her power was still new, exciting, and Solveig hoped it would stay that way for as long as possible.

"Sigra?"

"Manipulators can wield water that already exists. They can heal the injured, stop waves and rain," she rushed, barely able to contain her excitement.

"That's good Sigra, thank you." Solveig smiled at the girl. "Anyone else?"

"Charla? How about you?" The girl swallowed as she met Solveig's gaze. "Can you tell me what a creator can do with hydromancy?"

Charla nodded. "They erm—" She paused, taking a deep breath. "Creators can manifest water from nothing. They can make rain in a cloudless sky, waves in a dessert, drinking water in the middle of the ocean."

"That's right, well done." Solveig smiled encouragingly once more. "Last, can anyone tell me about the dangers for both manipulators and creators?"

"They can die," Tasy Roy stated flatly.

"Yes," Solveig agreed, "but how?"

"Use too much and you risk burning out all your energy. Creators are most at risk, because of the power it takes to create from nothing, but even manipulators should beware. Some may be tempted to use ley lines to boost them, but they can drain as fast as they give." There was no feeling in Tasy's voice as she spoke, staring straight ahead, and Solveig realised now why the girl knew so much. Her parents had burned out attempting to drain flood waters from the city three years ago. She'd been in her grandmother's care since.

"That's correct, Tasy, thank you." Solveig smiled again, but this time it was solemn, in recognition of all the girl had lost.

"You'll go over all of this and more in greater detail over the next few years, but before we begin your first session, are there any questions for me?" She surveyed the room. There was silence for a moment, and then Tern raised his hand.

"Yes, Mr Genard?"

"Are we going to learn how to harness our power the way you did?"

"You will have the time and opportunity to develop your powers as you see fit. For now, we'll be starting with the basics. Some of you may already have some experience, but others." Her gaze landed on Renit. "Require more help. Momentarily, I will have a water vessel brought in and one at a time you will practise creating a stable ball of water. You'll let it hover in the air before returning it to the vessel without losing a single drop. We will do this over and over until you are all able to complete the task. Remember, you're a team and all of you must succeed to progress to the next step. Is that understood?" The group nodded. "Fantastic. Then let us begin," Solveig said, spinning on the spot.

She made to open the door, but it swung out before she could even reach for the handle, and in sauntered the Prince of Elithiend. With a water vessel moving along ahead of him, of its own accord. So, this was the prince's power, Aire Wender.

"Afternoon," he said with flippant ease. As though he wasn't an enemy prince and hadn't revealed himself as an Aire Wender, who had no business being inside the walls of the Guild of Hydromancers.

"Emmerich, Aire Wender." He gestured to himself. "Don't mind me. In fact, pretend I'm not here." His eyes alighted on Solveig, and he chuckled, as though he could see the anger rolling off her skin in waves.

Solveig grabbed his hand, pulling him to one side. "What are you doing here?"

"Easy, Princess. I came to observe." He smiled nonchalantly, eyes glistening with humour, his gaze falling to her mouth for a beat before meeting her glare once more.

"And I told you, you needed permission to be here."

"Relax, would you? They granted it this morning, the king's seal of approval and all." He pulled a scroll from the back pocket of his trousers to show Solveig the written confirmation. "Now carry on with your class, pretend I'm not here." he smiled as if it was the easiest thing in the world to pretend that the Prince of Elithiend wasn't there.

She stalked back to the centre of the room, muscles tense as she stood before the vessel, taking a deep breath as she reached down to her well of power. Even now, it still felt significantly depleted, as barren as the Scorch.

The manipulation side of elemental magic was one of the easiest parts to learn. It was why they used it as a test in the manifestation ceremony. Anyone with an elemental affinity could manipulate with little training. What they taught in the guild was how to adapt and grow. How to pace your power to avoid burnout. That was the single most important lesson an elemental could learn. It was the difference between life or death. However, manipulation magic was also the only form that Solveig had ever mastered. Much to her family's dismay. It was also the only class that she was qualified to teach.

Solveig held out one hand. Feeling her magic connect to the water within the vessel. Sensing every part as though it were an extension of herself. And then, silently, she commanded a section to separate from the rest. Raising the other hand to form it into a ball of water, perfectly round without a single ripple.

Manipulation may be the only magic she was capable of. But Solveig had honed her skills to the best of her abilities. Which she proved by dropping her hands and moving to walk around the room. The ball of water stayed exactly where she'd manifested it. Not one drop fled, as she controlled it with her mind alone. This was the first class that Solveig had taught at the guild after returning from the mine. She was pleased to see that it felt as though she had spent no time away.

She approached Tern first. Who had more interest in the world outside the window — where a group of teenagers engaged in weapons training — than he did in the class.

"Mr Genard, since you showed such incredible manipulation skill at your ceremony yesterday, you'll go first," she said. Her back to her own sphere of water as she directed it to return to the vessel from where it had originated, without once disturbing the rest of the water.

"Easy." The boy said. With a little too much self-assurance for a ten-year-old. He sauntered over to the pedestal and thrust out a hand. The rest of the group waited with bated breath.

Tern's brow dropped low in concentration. He managed to gather some water from the bowl, but no matter how hard or how long he tried. He could not get it to form into a ball, as she had asked.

"Thank you, Tern, that's enough." Solveig said, ordering him to stand back with his classmates. Whilst, she returned to the front, staring directly at the disgruntled boy.

"Lesson number one. The only reason some of you could perform the tricks you did in the ceremony was because of the temple itself. Had the ceremony taken place here, none of you would have succeeded. That is because they built the Temple of The Oracle on the cross point of two ley lines. Just by being in the temple, you could connect with the energy radiating from within the earth. It helped to manifest your power. Now you must learn to do it entirely from within. That, Master Genard, is why you could create none of those fancy shapes you were capable of yesterday. Next time, pay attention. And I won't have to embarrass you in front of your classmates again." Tern glared at Solveig; his face reddened slightly.

"Yeah, right," he muttered. "You thrive off people's pain, that's what my mum says. What they all say, isn't it?"

Emmerich pushed off from the wall he had been leaning against, as though he was ready to fight a ten-year-old over a bunch of harmless words.

Solveig shook her head, spearing him with her eyes, a warning to back down.

"Some people say that yes." She shrugged, turning back toward the boy. "All I care about within these walls is that you show me the respect I have earned as a Guild Leader. The same respect your other instructors will also require. If you decide to not pay attention, you must be prepared to back it up with impressive skill, which you have not done."

The boy continued to glare, and Solveig ignored him. "Would anyone else like to give it a shot?" she asked, looking at each of the students. Until her eyes fell upon Renit. "How about you, Miss Teria?"

The girl met her gaze and wordlessly stood. Shoulders shaking as she made her way toward the pedestal. She held out a hand, closing her eyes for a moment before a cruel smirk took over her face and the water began rapidly flowing over the pedestal at her command.

Solveig blanched. "Miss Teria! stop this instant."

She didn't. Merely staring at the princess, her gaze devoid of any life.

"Out, everyone out," Solveig commanded. Emmerich took charge, herding the rest of the children down the stairs, leaving Solveig to deal with Renit alone.

"Well, that didn't go as planned, did it?" Emmerich walked up to where Solveig was attempting to dry off her sodden trousers in the weak sunlight.

"Something always goes awry on the first day. This is all new to them," she said, trying to shrug him off, but he came to sit beside her instead.

"There's something I don't understand though,"

"And what might that be?"

Emmerich eyed her thoughtfully. "Of all people you could have chosen to go next, you picked the one child in the room who showed creator abilities from the off."

"Was there a question there?"

"Why?" he pressed.

Solveig smirked. "I was curious what power she would have away from the ley line."

"That would be fair, or..."

"Or what?" She sliced him with a sharp stare.

"Or maybe what you truthfully wanted was to cause a diversion."

"And why would I do that?" Solveig laughed, though her eyes narrowed on him.

"I'm not sure," he leaned back on his elbows, eyes falling shut, "but I will figure it out, Princess, that you can count on."

"Can't wait," Solveig said as she stared down at the citizens milling around the market, one level below them. Grateful that the chill air dulled the ever-present stench of rot billowing up to assault their senses.

"Since your class finished early, how about that training session?"

"Just because we're supposed to be working together, Prince, doesn't mean we have to spend every waking moment bothering each other."

"Oh, I know," he smiled, leaning toward her. "But I showed you my affinity today. If you were so curious about what little Renit Teria could do, aren't you even curious about what I can do?"

Solveig turned, meeting the prince's gaze with a wry smile. "Oh, you want to play, Prince?" she jumped to her feet, holding a hand out to him. "Fine then, let's play."

CHAPTER THIRTY-FIVE

Perfect Sync

They stood on the training field, away from the curious eyes of the market below. Their stances mirror images of each other.

"Swords, elements, or both?" Solveig called over her shoulder as she withdrew the wooden training swords from their stowage.

"Both. Let's make this interesting." He smirked. Solveig threw him a sword, and he manipulated the air around it so that it landed gracefully in his waiting hand.

"Ready, Princess?" Emmerich raised a brow.

"Are you?" she bit back, before launching her first attack.

They moved as though they were part of a dance that only they knew the steps too. Left, right, right, left, forward, back. She struck, he parried and on it went. Wooden swords clashed, sticking together from the force for a moment. Emmerich drew close, breaths hard, skin flushed.

"You're toying with me," he accused, as her scent engulfed his senses.

Solveig blinked, eyes shining as her hands clenched tighter around the hilt. "I was merely trying to spare your ego."

"Did I ask you to go easy on me?"

"No."

He pushed down on their swords, leaning into her space, "then let go," he whispered, never once breaking eye contact. He saw the darkness descend, the wicked gleam that edged her gaze now.

"There's no need to beg." She inhaled the scent of his skin like a hunter would their prey. Wrenching her sword free, she spun out to land a blow on his back. "We'll pretend that was a flesh wound." She smirked as Emmerich turned to follow, striking out with his sword, a move she deflected with ease.

The vibrations reverberated through their bones. Sweat graced both their brows despite the chill. They drew an audience. Small at first but rapidly growing as word spread around the guild of the two royals engaged in battle; meeting each other blow for blow, in perfect sync.

Solveig reached out with her power to draw the lingering damp from her pants. She manipulated it to spread on the ground around the prince, creating a slick mud patch beneath his feet. Emmerich lost his balance momentarily, and that was all the opening she needed.

She moved to strike his unguarded left flank, but he threw up a shield with his Aire to protect himself. With his concentration distracted, Solveig drew more water into the ground, this time causing him to lose his balance entirely. He landed in a heap with the point of Solveig's sword pressed against the hollow of his neck.

"You should be less ambitious with your choice of opponent, Prince. You rely too much on your right side, leaving your left unguarded."

Emmerich gritted his teeth as he realised how easily she had read him. "Help me up, would ya," he snapped, and Solveig held out a hand to him, a smug grin on her face at the sight of him riled up. The tension creeping into his usually calm stance. Yet she didn't release his hand right away, pulling him closer to her instead, until she could smell the warm amber of his skin mingled with the fresh air.

Her voice trembling slightly as she spoke. "You don't have to tell me why you don't use your left side to fight. That's your business, but you must learn how to use it in some capacity." Her voice hardened. "If you ever want to stand a chance against comparable opponents, or even those who aren't under your command." She dropped his hand, taking a step back so she could look him in the eye.

"That was always the benefit of growing up magically weak, Prince, an advantage you have failed to realise. When my magic failed me, I had to learn other ways to protect myself. You rely too much on something that another elemental could easily stifle. Strength of arms, however, is something no one can ever take away from you."

"Who did you need to protect yourself from?" he whispered, eyes narrowing.

"Everyone who ever underestimated me,"

Emmerich made as if to say something, but Solveig beat him to it. "I'm done here Prince. Meet me tomorrow at the Grand Library. Perhaps some mental investigations will give your wounded pride time to heal."

The tavern stank. Cheap watered-down ale, stale piss, and rotted wood. It was the perfect place to go unseen. Dark enough for the dregs of society to come and play without being disturbed.

This was where the prince found himself that night, sat in the back in a shadowed alcove, nursing a warm ale, as he stared at the cloaked woman before him.

"It was you who got the message to Elithiend, wasn't it?"

"Your Highness," the woman started, her accent strange, as though born of many places.

"You got close to them. You're on the inside. Tell me how she died?"

"I did not see the princess that night, beyond bringing them supper. It's possible someone slipped something into the duchess's food either before or after that, but I cannot be certain."

"And her death?"

"Exactly the same as her son's, it appears."

The prince mulled that over silently as the woman continued, "I know you think little of the princess, but I believe you can trust her. She isn't as enthralled with her family as she may appear."

"She's murdered for them before and has continued too since I arrived," he fired back.

"Perhaps, but things are changing. I can feel it. Don't give up on her. She needs someone to believe she can be better than what she has become."

"It cannot be me," the prince said resolutely. "I have a duty to my people. I can't risk exposing them to her."

"You underestimate your people, and her."

"If she has changed, as you claim, why would she murder that girl's parents?"

"I have no answers for the decisions the princess makes, Your Highness. I'm not in her head. All I know is that not everything is as it appears."

The prince dropped a heavy velvet pouch on the wooden table between them, the coins within rattled against each other. "For your continued discretion and service."

The woman nodded in silent acceptance. She grabbed the bag and made her way out to the alley. The blue glow of a sconce revealed deep red hair in a low bun, against freckled pale skin before she winked it out with a flick of her wrist. The action hid her from the view of the figure above, lurking between the chimney stacks. They watched them both come and go before disappearing into the night.

CHAPTER THIRTY-SIX

Something to Look At

Torrelin's Grand Library sat in the shadow of High Tower Castle. Its exterior, an ancient style of design, was the only remaining relic that pointed to the old dynasty of Seers that once called it home. The iron-grey stonework had become stained by years of neglect, now shrouded in creeping ivy. Its spires bedecked with gargoyles who wore an untold number of expressions. The grey slate tiles were so dark they could almost pass for black, especially on rain-soaked and cloud ridden days. Much like the one that saw the Prince of Elithiend shivering outside the library's heavy wooden doors.

Summer was a distant memory, and autumn too would soon yield to the icy grip of Torrelinian winter. Even now, snow capped the mountain peaks, and it wouldn't be long until those flurries drifted down to the city below. He had not packed for the cold. Hadn't been expecting to stay through the winter, underestimating how quickly temperatures would drop in the north. He wondered if he was better off sending Wrenn straight back to Elithiend to retrieve them some warmer clothing. But he knew it was pointless. Anything he owned to survive winter at home wouldn't suffice here. In the north, winters were devilishly bleak. Snow and frost plagued the citizens for months on end. Even once the worst of the frost thawed spring met them with bitter, icy rain.

Emmerich had seen snow a few times in his twenty-seven years. Solveig had seen it in every one of her twenty-five. As was clear when she walked up to the library in far more suitable attire. Her pants appeared to be of a thick woollen material tucked into heavy fur-lined boots. She wore a knit sweater beneath a wool cloak, its hood trimmed with the same fur as her boots. The princess had pulled her dark fall of night black hair away from her face into a high ponytail, the black choker ever-present around her neck.

"It's been dawn for at least thirty minutes," he sniped, shoulders shaking as he shivered against the bitter wind.

"I was delayed."

"Clearly."

"You want an apology?"

"It wouldn't go amiss." Solveig eyed the pissed off prince and his silent friend who appeared to be napping against the door.

"I could spout words of apology, or I could unlock the doors and let you inside to defrost your wounded ego. Your choice, Prince, I'm plenty warm." She smiled, burrowing down into her cloak, as a tell-tale blush dusted the tip of her nose.

"Open the damn door, Princess."

"That's what I thought."

Solveig turned, unhooking a key from the waist belt of her pants. "Wake your friend up whilst you're at it," she muttered, flicking her chin in Commander Bleeker's direction. Emmerich hastily pulled her away from the door, causing her to jump in shock as Solveig shoved the gargantuan library doors wide. The cast iron hinges screeched as they moved.

"You're welcome," Solveig called after them as they stormed inside.

Light cascaded down from windows cut into the sides of each tower, unlit sconces encased in glass lined the edge of every bookcase.

"You touch nothing without my say so," Solveig ordered. "The Grand Library is open to the public, but only in certain sections. Even I am not allowed in all of them. You touch one book out of line, you even breathe in their direction, and we're finished here. Is that clear?"

"That what happened to that prince from Farrenhold," Commander Bleeker yawned.

Solveig paused mid-step. "Excuse me?"

"He touched a book out of turn, right?" Wrenn continued, enjoying that she had struck a nerve with the princess. "That's what landed him in Luxenal. Pretty steep price to pay over a book." She whistled, dragging a finger down the closest gold dusted spine. "Though word has it, he's safely home in Farrowvale Palace now, after four long years. You know anything about that?"

"I don't see how that's any of your concern, commander," Solveig gritted.

"Just making conversation."

"It's polite to be quiet in libraries, Commander. Didn't you know that?"

"No one else is here."

"For now, but not all day. Best we start practising." Solveig walked off toward the central tower, slinging her cloak over the back of a chair by a long row of mahogany tables. She lit the fireplace beside them to chase away the morning chill that had followed them inside.

"They permit the northern and western towers for public use," she said without turning to them. "Pull anything you deem useful."

"And where are you going?" the prince questioned.

"To the section permitted only for the royal family's use," she said simply, eyes narrowing. "Remember what I said, Prince."

"Yeah, yeah, no touching a single book outside the lines you've drawn."

"Good. after all, you wouldn't be the first prince we've locked away over it." She shrugged, heading off to the eastern tower, making swift work of the rolling ladders.

"You're right," Wrenn said, moving to stand beside the prince.

"About?"

"She's a real piece of work, but gods know she's something to look at, at least,"

"Less gossiping, more reading," Solveig shouted from a landing area two stories above them.

"I guess I'll take the western tower; you take the northern one."

"Quicker that way, less opportunity for gossiping, as she so eloquently put it."

CHAPTER THIRTY-SEVEN

Needs and Wants

Solveig spent most of the morning traipsing up and down ladders with every few books she found, holding titles that seemed promising. Prince Emmerich, however, utilised his magic to help himself and Wrenn float their picks down to the tables on a gentle breeze.

An hour of searching passed, and they each had four stacks of books. Solveig summoned lunch to the library as they tirelessly combed through each tome by the flickering firelight. Hoping they would find anything that might explain what was happening to the magic. A reason why some people were dying when others were simply losing their powers, and if there was anything they could do to stop or reverse it.

Lunch arrived, bringing with it a welcome reprieve from their fruitless search. The library hands brought them tender salted pork on soft white rolls with butter and applesauce from the city markets. And a flagon each, filled to the brim with steaming winter punch. Their bellies full and souls warmed a touch, Solveig moved to grab another book from her stack, when Emmerich released an annoyed sigh.

"Out with it, Prince," she muttered, flicking the page, "I'm no mind reader and if I wanted to see amateur dramatics, I'd head to the theatre."

"Cute," he quipped, placing his book down on the table.

"If you're giving up, say the word there are far better things I could do with my time than sit in a dusty library with the two of you all day."

"Desperate to get back to Luxenal, Princess?" Emmerich snapped. "I'm sure there is a long line of prisoners waiting to feel the bite of your blades by now."

Solveig's gaze darkened, her grip turning white around the book as she closed it, moving to stand as Wrenn Bleeker did the same, sensing the threat.

"Can you stop sniping at each other for more than a couple of hours?" Wrenn sighed.

"Tell your prince to watch his mouth, or he'll be sailing home in a coffin leaving his kingdom heirless."

Wrenn and Emmerich shared a look, neither of them speaking.

"What?" Solveig hissed; eyes narrowed as they flicked between the pair.

"Nothing," they said in unison. Suspicion roiled in Solveig's gut. They were hiding something, that much was obvious. Solveig knew she should dig for the information, to keep her parents from getting suspicious, but right then, she'd rather a stack of books fell on her head.

"I'm going for more books. When you two idiots decide you want to get back to work, let me know."

Emmerich watched as she walked away, her hips and ponytail swaying in unison. He watched as she gripped a railing and made light work of pulling herself up to the second level with smooth feline grace. He kept watching until he felt someone smack something across the back of his head, a little too forcefully.

"Focus," Wrenn hissed. "You can watch, but you can't touch. That girl is bad news."

The prince blinked, steeling his face. "As if I could forget," he said nonchalantly, "she's still under suspicion for murder after all."

"Yeah," Wrenn said, with wide eyes, mouth twisted in a knowing smile, "better send the message to your eyes then. They were far too preoccupied with her arse."

"Fuck off." Emmerich swung a book at Wrenn. Downing the last of his winter punch, he muttered, "next time let's have them bring that stuff spiked. I could do with the kick right now."

"Spiked punch is the last thing you need to be drinking around her."

Emmerich threw Wrenn a glare, shoving a book across the table at her. "Read that and make any notes on mentions of The Oracle and their power."

Her eyes narrowed. "You think they have something to do with this?"

"That thing has invaded every part of their lives. They worship it for the power it's given them, and the power it's taken away. It cannot be both things, so read."

"You got it, Captain."

Another hour passed before either of them resurfaced from their chosen books, and Solveig still hadn't returned.

"Look..." Wrenn hedged, "maybe you should go make peace with her."

"You can't be serious."

"Before you consider whacking me again or shipping me back off to Elithiend with orders to do grunt work as punishment, hear me out, okay?"

Emmerich placed his heavy leather-bound tome back on the table next to him, crossed his arms over his chest, one brow raised expectantly. "I'm listening."

"You said yourself whatever is going on here has something to do with The Oracle, right?"

"Right."

"And she said that certain sections of the library aren't open to the public, which means there are books in this library that they don't want common folk seeing. Books that are important enough to send an allied prince to a prison camp for."

"You think the book they caught Malik Etana with is the same one we need?"

"Possibly. And if it isn't, I'd be willing to bet we'd find it in the same area. Areas that only she has access to..." They both turned to look in the princess's general direction.

"You don't have to trust her, but you do need to get her to trust you. Do you honestly think she's going to share everything she's reading in those books? No, you need to read them with her. And the only way to do that, my dear Prince, is to go make peace."

"If I die, it's on you."

"Give her something. Make it appear as though you're being open with her and maybe she'll return the favour."

"If I have to go play buddies with a murderer, you can clean this mess up." The prince said, gesturing to the book strewn table before them.

"Sure thing. Just maybe don't call her a murderer to her face."

"Whatever."

Emmerich found the princess sat cross-legged, leaning against a dusty shelf rammed tight with old books and sheets of parchment.

"You shouldn't be here, Prince. Thought I made that obvious," she said, without looking up from what she was reading.

"Find anything interesting?"

"Maybe, maybe not."

"We're supposed to be working together on this."

"These books aren't for your eyes. If I find anything I think you need to see, I'll let you know. You can go back to your friend now, so she knows I didn't add you to my kill list."

"Actually," he hedged. Solveig looked up at him, her green eyes shadowed by the dark surroundings. "I thought we could take a break." Still, she didn't respond. "I wanted to apologise for what I said earlier. You're taking time out of your day to help me, and all I've done is insult you and remind you of the mistakes you've made."

Solveig's gaze shuttered immediately, clueing him in that he had said the wrong thing already. Her eyes swung back to the book in her lap as she spoke.

"Who said I've made mistakes, Prince? They made a choice for me. And I have lived with it the only way I knew how. No more, no less. I won't apologise to you or anyone else for what I had to do to survive. False platitudes help no one."

"For fuck's sake, woman, would you put the bloody book down and look at me?"

"Excuse me?" She jerked her head back, blinking up at him.

"Before you go reaching for one of those pointy daggers you're fond of, will you hear me out?"

"By all means," she said with narrowed eyes as he sat across from her, the tight space between the shelves forcing their knees to touch.

"Your family graciously allowed me access to your kingdom to do research, and at every turn, I have belittled, laughed, or argued about everything. I've judged you for making the *choices* you had to make to survive. And for that, I'm sorry."

"Remember what I said about false platitudes, Prince," she said, gaze probing his.

"I'm not trying to placate you. It's true. Whatever you did before. I've no reason to judge you for it now. Multiple times you tried to get me to accept help with my arm. Help me strengthen my weakness that you pointed out within seconds of watching me, when everyone else I've surrounded myself with kept quiet."

"What happened?" she pressed.

"There was a shipwreck. My powers had barely manifested when a typhoon hit. I wasn't strong enough to control it. Many died. I suffered severe nerve damage and walked away with a pretty scar on my head, to boot. But I lived." Tears brimmed around the edge of the prince's eyes.

"Healers couldn't do anything to repair the damage?"

"They didn't find me for days. By then, the work they did was the best I could hope for."

"That's why you kept shutting down, isn't it? You know you'll never regain full strength in that arm."

"Partially. But also, because I'm a prince of the realm, I'm supposed to be formidable. The Dark Prince, that's what your people call me, right?" Solveig nodded. "A prince capable of wielding a sword with only one hand suddenly doesn't sound formidable. He sounds entirely beatable."

"You are beatable. I've done it twice now." She smirked. Emmerich's head dropped, shaking slightly.

"Why do you do that?"

"Do what?"

"Pick at people's deepest hurts to ward them off when they're getting too close."

"You're the one laying all your weaknesses at the feet of your enemy." The book slid from Solveig's lap as she knelt, leaning into the prince's space. So close that the scent of him masked the scent of aged books and ink.

She watched him with the keen eye of a hunter, the bob of his throat, his shallow breaths and slow blinking eyes. And he watched her, as she raised a dagger to lift his curls away from his forehead, revealing the scar there.

"It would be so easy," she murmured. "To take you out. You wouldn't even have the chance to scream."

Emmerich's hand shot out, grasping the wrist where she held the dagger perilously close to his skin, he felt her pulse flutter beneath his fingers. As their gazes held each other.

"Then teach me how to be better. Stronger."

Solveig only laughed. "What kind of predator would I be if I taught you how to defeat me?" She pulled her arm from his grip, trailing the flat side of her dagger across his neck, then lower down the front of his shirt. Before leaning in closer, lips at his ear.

"You'll have to try harder than that to make me bend and break. I spent two years in a prison camp. I learned how to play games with the best of them."

"Who said I'm playing games?" Emmerich swallowed, blinking furiously to clear the haze from his mind at her proximity.

"You told me your sad story and what you thought I'd spill my guts to you in return? Like some babbling fool, desperate for attention until she breaks at the smallest touch of it?"

"I think you're starved of kindness. Of warmth. Not attention, the Reaper stirs enough of that for you already."

She laughed. "You think you'll be the one to show me kindness?"

"I could be. If you let me. If you let go of those walls, you're so desperately clinging to."

"I don't want your kindness."

"Who said anything about want? Needs and wants are two different things."

"And what do you want, Prince?"

"To earn your trust."

Solveig sat staring at him for a moment, puzzling over how to respond. Their gazes holding, when Emmerich moved into a kneeling position too, so close now that they almost touched.

"I want you to be honest with yourself," he whispered. "Even for a moment."

"I—" Solveig began, but the spell he held her under shattered with the heavy echo of Wrenn Bleeker's approaching footsteps.

Solveig and Emmerich jumped away from each other as though burned. Sat as they were, they both smacked hard into the bookcases at their backs, desperately trying to hold back the wince of pain as Wrenn rounded the corner.

"You could do with getting someone to blow some clean air through the dust up here." Wrenn joked. Her sharp eyes landed on the pair.

"There are hundreds of years of history on these shelves. You cause even a speck of damage, and I won't allow you within a mile of this place again," Solveig seethed.

"Interesting,"

"What is?"

"Damaging a thousand-year-old piece of parchment carries a much lighter sentence than merely stealing it." Solveig froze. "Guess I should return this book I slipped into my jacket. Wouldn't want to be shipped off to the mines now, would I?"

Emmerich stared at his friend. Not even half an hour ago, she lectured him about playing nice with the princess. And yet here she was, riling her up again.

"Out of curiosity, what type of book would it take to get me sent to the mines?"

A look of death crossed Solveig's gaze as she made to retrieve her dagger, but Emmerich was faster this time, catching her arm with his hand.

"Wrenn's an idiot. Ignore her."

Solveig's gaze pierced his as she shook her head. "Or maybe she's more honest than you," she spat through gritted teeth, wrenching her arm free before turning on the commander. "Not that the content of the book matters, commander, but it was a history of all known powers and their connection to the earth and The Oracle itself. They sentenced Malik to Luxenal because he took the book from Leader Ezekiel's private library."

"And?"

She took a step closer. "Even my father can't enter Leader Ezekiel's private library. If the King of Torrelin can't. How would you deal with a foreign prince with an unknown agenda breaking not just into the library itself, but into a restricted area? Then attempting to walk out of there with a book on the same night his sibling attended a royal ball? Because if you ask me, the Etana family is lucky they only locked one of their children up that night. Adira's saving grace was that they found no proof of them working together. And with Malik swearing that he acted alone, he faced the consequences alone, too."

Solveig squared up to the commander, dagger twisting in her grip. "You got what you wanted," she sneered, glancing between her and the prince. "I think it's time we left."

"Wait, please!" Emmerich called after her.

"No, I won't wait. You've shown your true conniving colours today. I should applaud you for it, but you'll forgive me if I don't feel like it right now. Stay out of my sight for a few days if you know what's good for you."

Solveig pushed past the commander, storming down the stairs and straight out of the library, leaving them both behind. Emmerich looked at Wrenn.

"What was that?" he raged.

"I said play nice, not play lovers."

"I was getting her to trust me, and you had to walk in and take us back to ground zero. She's never gonna help us now."

Wrenn shrugged. "She left that book behind and those notes."

"No."

"Oh, come on. No one's gonna find out. Aren't you interested in knowing what the Dark Princess found important enough to make notes about?"

Emmerich warred with himself for a moment before sighing heavily, rubbing his temples. "Fine, but hurry before someone else sees."

The commander slipped the stolen tome and notes beneath her jacket as they exited the library into the bitter evening air.

CHAPTER THIRTY-EIGHT

Under Storm Covered Darkness

Winds ripped at ancient stonework. Icy rain battered against shutters as a ferocious tempest blew in from the Eastern Ocean. Only the flames of the strongest pyromancers kept Marrelin City from plunging into unearthly darkness, whilst the storm roiled, an insatiable, mythical beast.

Citizens took refuge in their ramshackle homes, many still not shored up for the coming winter. Desperately trying to prevent their dwellings from flooding. Those who lived close to the riverbanks wouldn't sleep that night.

Yet through the howling wind and sheeting rain, a lone figure raced across the rooftops. The storm afforded them more cover than they would normally have from darkness alone. When they reached their target, they tore a pair of shutters open, and two smaller figures crawled out of the compact frame, escaping into the night with the taller one. They raced through barren city streets, their footsteps sloshing through the already ankle-deep water. The wind at their backs pushing them along. None spoke, not even as they reached the city wall, and a fourth figure emerged from the shadows. They took a swift route up the wall, pulling the smaller ones with them, cresting over the top and disappearing into the long black night.

It would be morning before anyone realised anything was amiss.

Prince Emmerich stood by the rattling shutters. The hinges groaning as they tried to hold on to the wall that the wind was determined to rip them from. A blue fire crackled in the hearth behind him as he listened to the storm ravage the unsuspecting city below. Nursing a crystal glass filled with whiskey that burned his throat, chasing away the chill in his heart and bones.

They were waiting for dinner to be brought up before they would settle in for a long night. Studying the book Solveig had been reading and the notes she had hurriedly made. Wrenn sat across the room as close to the fire as she could get. In a plush armchair nursing an ice-cold glass of ale, the glass weeping with condensation.

They were used to storms like this. As the clouds had darkened over the city, they had seen many elementals racing out into the streets. Watching as they aimed their magic toward the sky, trying to halt it in its tracks. Though their efforts only angered the storm further. In Elithiend, they left storms to build and pass as nature saw fit. Their homes and palaces built to withstand them; ships moored tight in the harbour to prevent extensive damage. They saw storms as nature's way of resetting.

A knock rapped against the door. Wrenn jumped to her feet when a familiar face entered the room, a trolley laden with food in tow.

Teris.

"What are you doing here?" Wrenn exclaimed, tears shining in her eyes as she ran across the room. Wrapping Teris in a tight embrace, she buried her face in the warm crook of her neck as the prince watched on from the window.

"I'm a servant in the castle," Teris whispered, holding Wrenn, stroking her hair softly, inhaling her scent that she had missed more than anything. "My mistress is not in residence for the evening. As such, I've been deployed elsewhere." She placed a kiss atop the commander's deep brown hair, eyes squeezing tight, as the weight of their time apart crashed down around them.

But the prince came alive at her words as he demanded, "where is she?"

Teris's head shot up as she rested her chin on Wrenn's hair. "She's a princess, Your Highness. She doesn't need to tell anyone of her comings and goings, especially not her servant."

Emmerich slammed a hand against the cold stone wall. He was a fool, a damned fool. Whilst he had been trying to woo her to see his side; she had been plotting a way to escape. Wrenn, the stupid, impulsive fucker, had given the princess exactly the opening she had needed to keep them away.

"This is on you!" Emmerich shouted, as he drained the rest of his whiskey, making to exit the room.

"Your Highness, if I may," Teris called, trying to go after him, but Wrenn kept a tight grip on her.

"No! Teris," the prince fired back, "you chose to come here, and my family pays you handsomely to watch them and report back whenever you can. And yet here you stand, telling me that the princess is somewhere out there in that beastly storm doing gods know what."

"Is it concern for her, or for what she may do that has you worried?" Wrenn said flatly, finally raising her face from Teris's neck.

"Excuse me?"

"I saw you two today, in the library, gazing into each other's eyes. I never would have told you to get closer to her had I known how close you already were."

"Watch your tone, Commander. You allowed your assumptions to cloud your judgment when we're still no closer to figuring out what's going on here," Emmerich shouted, taking a step closer. Wrenn moved to stand in front of Teris, blocking her from the prince's view.

"Sit your arse in that chair Anders, you're gonna eat some food, and together." She gestured between the three of them. "We're going to go over these notes and see what Princess Pain unwittingly left behind for us."

"I can't stay," Teris said, leaning around Wrenn, gripping her hand tight with a sad smile. Wrenn twisted, taking her face in their hands. "I haven't laid eyes on you in two years, and by chance I get to accompany this self-righteous idiot into enemy lands and even then, all I get is crumbs."

"I volunteered for this Wrenn," Teris whispered, leaning her forehead against the commanders, "I knew what I was getting myself into."

"I want you home."

"And I will return when the work is done."

"Lady Teris," the prince whispered, "your sacrifice does not go unnoticed, believe me, but you must understand the importance of your work. We cannot afford to slacken now. Is there anything else you haven't told us?"

Teris's eyes flew to the ground as she turned to face the prince, guilt warring in her heart and mind as she worried her bottom lip. Wrenn's hand, never leaving hers, squeezed in silent comfort.

"What is it?"

"It's not my place, nor my story to tell," she whispered.

"You're keeping secrets for her now?" Emmerich exclaimed in disbelief.

"It's not like that," Teris fired back. "I know she's done terrible things, but this is different. Please understand, my prince."

"Don't force me to question where your loyalties lie."

"Her loyalties are with us, as they have always been," Wrenn declared, pulling Teris closer to her.

"I should go," Teris whispered, but Wrenn's arms banded around her as she buried her face in her neck once more.

"I miss you," she whispered, pressing a kiss to the fluttering beat of her heart in her neck, her words whispered across her skin.

"My love." Teris exhaled, pulling her face to the commanders, "no matter where I am, or where you go, I tied my heart to yours. It will stay that way until the end of my days."

"I need you safe." Wrenn pressed a kiss to Teris's mouth, feather light at first, before she groaned, the commander's hands spreading across her back. Teris's twisting in her hair as they deepened the kiss, tongues tangling and teeth clashing.

When they pulled apart, they didn't go far. Foreheads touching. Breaths mingling. Gazes wrapped tight as Wrenn whispered, "my place or yours, I don't care which. The moment you step foot back in Vhallakyr, we aren't spending another second apart."

"Deal." Teris whispered, tears threatening, as a hopeful smile spread on her face. She pressed one last kiss to her swollen lips as she detangled herself from Wrenn's grip and hurried to exit the room. Her cheeks flushed as she passed the prince, who was making a grand show of looking anywhere but at the two lovers.

Teris paused as she reached for the doorknob, her head hitting the etched wood. "She was to head out to Luxenal Mine in the morning, likely guess is she left early. If you leave at daybreak, you might catch her."

"Thank you, Teris," the prince implored.

"You didn't hear it from me," she said firmly. "If the princess finds out we talked, you'll jeopardise my position here."

"You have my word."

"And, Prince?"

"Yes?"

"The clothes you wore at the manifestation ceremony?" She swallowed, debating whether to continue, "they've been gathering dust in the princess's closet for four years and that is all I will say on the matter." She exited the room swiftly, the door slamming shut behind her.

CHAPTER THIRTY-NINE

Patterns in History

The prince and the commander ate in silence, working their way through a goat's cheese salad with beetroot and honey-soaked red onions. A main course of roasted lamb with a rosemary mint crust. Alongside roasted garlic and clementine carrots, zesty greens, and a red wine gravy with crusty ale risen bread to the side. Dessert was a liquor drenched orange tart topped with light as air chocolate cream. All washed down with fruity wine for the prince and more ale for the commander.

Wrenn was the first to break the silence that had surrounded them. "If I was out of line earlier, I apologise." she wiped her mouth with one of the silk napkins. "But you asked me to come here, to keep you in check, and honestly, I'm concerned."

"About?" Emmerich said without looking up.

"The way she looks at you."

"Like she wants to watch my blood swim at her feet?"

"No." Wrenn laughed, "far from it, like she wants to devour you whole. And you the same."

"There is nothing going on between me and the princess."

"Not yet perhaps," Wrenn shrugged, "but I worry that the more time you spend together, the more likely you are to lose focus on the real reason we're here."

"And you haven't?" Emmerich fired back, "I'll stay away from the princess as soon as you stop risking Teris's cover!"

"Teris is my wife," Wrenn seethed. "My wife. Emmerich. That princess is your enemy, our enemy. Stay away from her."

"You forget your place," Emmerich launched to his feet, "you don't give me orders, commander, you follow mine. When I need your advice, I will ask for it."

Wrenn swallowed, biting back a knee jerk retort, "whatever you say, Your Highness."

They sat on opposite ends of the room, tension thick in the air as they poured over the book and the princess's notes, late into the evening. So late that the winds battering the castle had finally died down.

The princess's handwriting was barely legible, her notes vague. From what the prince could decipher, she had spent more time researching the origins of her own power than anything else. She'd created a list of all previously recorded uses of hydromancy, healing, wave bending, drinking water supply, rainmaker. The list went on and on with no mention of hers. She was searching for evidence of someone else having used hydromancy in the way she had, and either they'd stopped her mid-search, or she had failed to find it.

"You find anything?" he asked as he flicked through the notes, freezing when he reached the last page. Wrenn was talking, but he wasn't listening, too busy trying to understand what he was reading.

"Emmerich? Hey, snap out of it!" Wrenn clapped her hands, trying to catch his attention.

"Sorry what?"

"I said this book is a history of illustrious magic users across the years, nothing of much importance."

"Say that again," Emmerich said slowly, his eyes drifting from the list toward Wrenn.

"It's just a history of powerful elementals, Emmerich."

"I think our favourite princess was working on a theory."

Wrenn's eyes narrowed. "What did the notes say?" Emmerich crossed the room, gripping the pertinent sheet tightly.

"Most of it was notes on hydromancy, but on the last page, it's a list of names."

"Okay?" Wrenn hedged.

"A list of families who have had members die, and a list of magically weakened families."

"And?"

"There's no crossover."

"Say that again," Wrenn parroted Emmerich's earlier words.

"The weakened families. Their names don't appear on the list of the dead and vice versa."

"Read me some."

"Sellen,"

"Not here,"

"Teria,"

"Yep, they're here," Wrenn muttered, flipping through the book.

"What does it say?"

"Powerful in hydromancy and Aire Wending, the ancestors could manipulate both."

"Vieret."

"Grand masters of pyromancy, ancestors hailed from Estrellyn."

"Whitlock,"

"Em..." Wrenn's eyes flew up.

"Just check," he insisted.

Wrenn sighed, shaking her head as she flipped through the book again. "Powerful across all elements, ancestors once thought to have mouldable magic." She closed the book in her lap. "So, what's the connection?"

"They're dying."

"What?"

"All the powerful families on this list and in the book are dying."

"And the weakening ones?"

"Just loss of power, no gruesome deaths,"

"So, either we're looking at the same culprit with two different side effects, or two different ones."

"What's more likely?"

"Just one," Wrenn muttered.

Emmerich nodded, rubbing his face, legs bouncing nervously. "We need to find a way into old Ezekiel's hidden library."

"You're fucking with me," Wrenn sputtered. Emmerich merely stared at her. "Shit."

"Prince Malik was on to something," Emmerich insisted, "what we hold here is a history of known powerful families. Malik was after the connection to The Oracle. He was searching for something and we're going to find out what."

"Or die trying," Wrenn muttered.

"Something like that."

CHAPTER FORTY

Missing Children

A yellow dawn broke over the eastern horizon, bringing with it clear skies. The prince and his commander mounted a pair of tan mares, carrying meagre supplies with them and a single map with directions to Luxenal Mine. Instructed to keep a steaming pace if they wanted to reach it by nightfall. Still, they had packed enough supplies for at least one night in the woods should the worst happen. Teris had got them each some warmer clothes to protect them from the bitter chill that rolled down from the northern mountains.

"I hate horses," Wrenn grumbled. "I'm a woman of the ocean, built with sea legs not made for riding atop four of them, five feet from the ground."

"It's the quickest way to travel," Emmerich muttered. "If we went on foot, we risk arriving at the mine long after she's already gone. I don't fancy my chances of turning up at a prison camp, a prince, and an army commander from an enemy kingdom without an escort."

"Yeah, I got it," Wrenn huffed. "Doesn't mean I have to enjoy it though."

"Gods above, you're a commander of the Royal Guard. Do you whine this much when you're leading them in training drills? Gods only know how you've kept your position this long."

"Isn't it obvious?" Wrenn laughed, "If we weren't friends I would have been out on my arse within a week."

They trotted toward the western portcullis through the city streets. Commotion built as more citizens ventured out of their homes to inspect the storm damage. A woman spoke with two guards, her hands gesturing frantically as others swept away storm debris from their stoops, pretending not to listen.

"You've gotta do somethin'! Boys don't just up'n vanish into the night!" she screeched.

"Listen lady, two little boys couldn't have survived that storm alone. They're likely dead already. Best you move on."

"And what of their sister, eh?" she fired back.

Emmerich's ears pricked at that. Two young boys missing, and a sister? It was too much of a coincidence. He directed his horse toward the woman and the guards.

"Word has it she hasn't shown her face at school, never mind the Hydromancy Guild! She's kidnapped 'em I reckon!"

The guard yawned. "Whether she has or hasn't is no concern of yours now."

"That girl is a danger to us all. They should've locked her up with her parents."

"What's going on here?" Emmerich enquired, puffing out his chest to which Wrenn had to stifle a laugh, causing Emmerich to shoot daggers at her with his eyes.

"Nothing that concerns a foreigner," one guard sneered.

"I would have thought even here that missing children were a priority."

"Wards of the state go missin' all the time, ain't nothin' to be done. With no one left t'care for 'em, they either come back to the only warm bed they have left or die out there alone."

"They're children!" Emmerich cried.

"And not your concern. Now run along," the other guard ordered.

The woman stalked back toward the building she had emerged from, muttering curses at the guards. Emmerich paused momentarily, before deciding to chase after her, "Hey wait!" he called. The woman turned on her heel, staring dumbfounded at him.

"The two boys and the girl. Are you talking about the Teria children?"

"Why do you ask?" she said carefully, eyes narrowed.

"I want to help."

"You're about as useful to me as those guards. You should go home, Prince. No one in this city will work with you."

"Just answer the question."

"Yes, it's the Teria boys, and I have it on good authority that the girl hasn't been seen since her first day at the guild. The two boys, Nex and Milas, vanished into the night. That girl has taken them. I know it. She's going to get them all killed, mark my words."

"Thanks," Emmerich rushed as he ran back to Wrenn and his horse.

"Don't know what ya thankin' me for. I didn't do nothin'," the woman shouted after him as she headed back into the orphanage and the two companions set off back on their journey as the cogs in the prince's head turned.

CHAPTER FORTY-ONE

Return to Luxenal

Her soaked leathers clung to her skin, leaving her wondering if she would ever be able to peel them off again. Had she been at home. Closeted in the cold damp of High Tower Castle, she would've taken a knife to them without a thought and crawled into her bed to sleep for a week. But she wasn't. She was crossing the winding river, racing through the trees of the forest back toward the mine. With every step closer, the weight that had lifted over the last few weeks slowly slid back into place. What would she find when she stepped back into the cacophony of the mud drenched shithole that was Luxenal Copper Mine?

Solveig had known that she would have to return at some point. Either to reclaim her post, or to search for those missing execution summons. Fortunately for her, Commander Sellen had grown impatient, snapping up the opportunity of her absence with rampant glee. He'd declared her position had been filled internally. Leaving her no choice but to remove her belongings; or risk him turning them to ash in the crematorium with the next load of Luxenal's victims. He'd unwittingly given her the perfect excuse to return without arousing suspicion.

As the sun dragged itself higher in the cloud drenched sky; she soon heard the crashing, clanging and squelching orchestra of the mine's open pit in the distance. Solveig tried her best to block it out, but with every step closer, it grew louder. Coming to a head as she walked up to the arched wrought-iron gates and came face-to-face with her old commander.

"Finally decided to show your wretched face, Reaper?" he sneered, eyes cold.

"Commander Sellen."

"They have your things in the operations building. We wouldn't want you roaming in any areas you're no longer allowed."

"As if I have any interest in spending a second longer than necessary in this cesspit," she said with an air of boredom as she moved to walk around him, but he snatched her arm tightly.

"You'll have an escort at all times, and you'll leave your weapons here. Only my guards may walk the grounds armed."

Solveig's eyes narrowed as she wrenched her arm free from his punishing grasp. "You think I'm going to wander around here with no protection?"

"Hence the escort, Princess. My guards are more than capable of protecting you."

Solveig stepped closer, leaning into his space, whispering with dead eyes and emotionless words. "I killed three of your guards the night I left. You'll forgive me if I'm not confident in their ability or their willingness to watch my back."

The commander only shrugged. "Leave the daggers here or go home," he insisted. Solveig unsnapped her holster, shoving it toward the nearest guard. "If there's even a speck of dirt on those when I return, I'll be cleaning your blood off them on your own uniform," she hissed.

Heads turned as they escorted Solveig through the gates, expressions ranging from fear to disgust, anger to sorrow. Some prisoners, those who weren't chained in the open cast, spat at her feet as she walked by. It seemed the news of her stepping down had travelled swiftly. She refused to react.

After everything she had done, Solveig knew she had no cause to be upset over some spit. Not when she refused to apologise.

Whispers travelled the muddy walkways like the wind. Silence had once been their greeting of choice for her. Still, the names and gossip were hardly new. Solveig merely allowed them to fuel her myth, feed the legend of her name.

A good myth was hard to kill. They could spit at her feet all they wanted, but they'd never dare touch her. Each of them was still too scared to lose what insignificant life they had left, especially those who had survived more than a year in the pit. Those who had something to hold on to, something to hope for. Hope was the greatest killer. Without it, you stood no chance, but when the hope died, it took you with it.

Her escort led her straight to the operations building, and Solveig froze. Sat at the desk was a familiar face, but not the one she had been expecting. Solveig had thought salt and pepper jewelled braids, and haunting silver eyes would greet her.

"Where is she?"

"Who?"

"Viana, the woman who worked the desk before I... left."

The guard stared at her as though she were being purposely stupid. "No one by that name has worked here," he muttered. "Only Miss Everly there."

Solveig knew that wasn't true. The young woman sat before them had indeed worked at the mine. She knew her face had dealt with her before, but she wasn't there the day leading up to her departure.

"You've never seen a woman walking around here with grey eyes and braided hair?"

"No," the guard scowled, eyes flicking back toward the door they'd come through.

A chill danced its way down Solveig's spine. Who was that woman if she wasn't an employee at the mine? How did she know so much about the operation?

"Ah, Miss Maleen, right on time." Miss Everly smiled. "Your belongings are over here." This was the same girl who had cowered from her before she'd executed Mr Kano. Yet here she stood, smiling, and chattering away as if they were simply old friends.

"With respect." Solveig tensed. "I am still a princess of the realm, whether I remain employed here or not."

Miss Everly laughed with a wave of her hand. "My apologies, Your Highness. I got so used to seeing you here that I forgot who you were on the outside."

These people weren't afraid of her anymore. Solveig had killed and tortured. She'd broken a prisoner out, and yet they acted as though none of that had happened.

"I don't need all of it," she said. "Only a few items of personal value."

"Well, the boxes are over there. Go through them and anything you don't want, leave it here and I'll have it sent to the crematorium this evening." She shrugged, moving to sit back behind her desk.

Solveig stared after the woman for a moment. She'd been away from the mine for a month, and it was as though everyone had had their memory wiped.

She paused as realisation struck. Her breaths grew short, eyes wide, pulse rapid.

Malik had said that physical torture wasn't the only type going on within the mine. And Killian, he had mentioned them testing the machine that had allowed The Oracle to rip through her memories on prisoners.

What if the testing was over?

What if this was another side to what the machine could do?

Implant false memories, change a person's perception of reality, their personality. Bend someone's will to another's. And Solveig had allowed them to hook that thing up to her. How many times did it take to become pliant?

She needed sleep, and a drink, not necessarily in that order. Her eyes alighted on a lone bottle of whiskey lying in one box. "Thank The Oracle," she muttered, pulling the cork free, savouring the burn as it helped quiet her frantic mind.

"Your Highness!" Miss Everly sputtered indignantly, "it's not even mid-day yet!"

"Your point?" Solveig muttered, taking another swig, "I travelled through the night. To me, it may as well be nighttime."

The woman looked unsure as she worried her lip between her teeth. "Perhaps we should find you somewhere to rest for a few hours, and you can continue your journey when you're more... coherent?" Solveig looked down at the bottle in her hand and back up at the peppy woman before her.

"Fine," she muttered, "but I'm taking the bottle with me."

"I wouldn't dream of parting you from it," Miss Everly murmured, lips pursed as she walked away, leading Solveig out of the operations base. They headed for the guards' bunk house, past the reception desk and down the left-hand corridor, stopping at the first door.

"This is my room." Miss Everly said as she fished a key from her pocket. "Clean yourself up, have a nap." She eyed the bottle again. "And maybe eat something before you drink any more of that." Solveig gave the woman her best attempt at a grateful smile, though it wasn't convincing as she headed inside and closed the door without another word.

Solveig snatched the desk chair and wedged it beneath the door handle. It wouldn't stop anyone who was truly determined to get in, but it would at least give her a small window of preparation. She listened as Miss Everly's footsteps faded away and then began tearing through the room. She didn't know what she was searching for, and it was highly likely that Miss Everly wouldn't have any sensitive documents hidden in here. Still, it was worth a shot.

In a drawer of the desk, her hand drifted over a rumpled sheet of paper. It was a measly scrap, completely unassuming, yet it pointed to things not being as they seemed within the mine. An appointment slip, to see the healers, dated not two days prior, for a 'mental well-being assessment.'

She needed to get to the infirmary. If they kept records on the usage of that device, they had to be there, but first she had to get around the mine, unseen.

Chapter Forty-Two

Mental Well-being

It was a categorically stupid idea.

And yet she had no other choice.

She needed to get into the infirmary without arousing suspicion, and the only way was to dress as though she were a prisoner. She would be too recognisable in anything else. Even then, once inside, she would have to find her way into the back rooms, through who knew how many locked doors, and numerous watching eyes to find the files. But she had to know for sure.

She pulled a grey scarf from Miss Everly's closet, rubbed it along her mud splattered boots, ripping the edges slightly before she tied it over her hair. Step one complete. Now she needed to reach the laundry room. As she poked her head out of the door, she saw the coast was miraculously clear. She hurried, not wanting to chance her luck.

Inside the laundry room, Solveig took a pair of standard issue women's garments and raced back to Miss Everly's room to change. Back outside, she found a window down the hall and hid her boots in a wastebasket. They would have given her away all too easily, before clambering up and out of the window, falling in the mud on the other side. She sighed, grimacing against the sting, but at least the dirt and dust would help to disguise her.

She slumped at the shoulders as she walked. Careful to avoid the stones tearing into her bare feet. She hadn't been able to find any shoes in the laundry room. Thankfully, it wasn't uncommon for women to walk around without, especially if they worked in the sorting fields instead of the pit. Still, she prayed no one would notice her unchained hands and feet as she made her way to the infirmary.

Once inside, she almost fled straight back out. It was busier than she had expected. Rows and rows of prisoners sat waiting to be seen, and she wondered when the guards had started to allow so many the time to visit the infirmary. They usually reserved it for employees, not prisoners. She kept close to the wall, slinking off to one corner, and listened.

"What number is this for you?" one mud slicked prisoner asked.

"Third, you?" replied a man who appeared older than he was.

"First time."

"Ah," the older prisoner muttered, "nothing t'worry 'bout. Hurts the first two times, but smooth sailing after that. It'll be over before you know it."

"Prisoner 5967, this way." Solveig watched a man stand, pulling off his scarf to reveal a shorn head littered with red welts. She peered around the room then. Sure enough, every prisoner who had already removed their scarves sat with shorn hair and matching red welts. Just like the ones beneath Solveig's hair.

The cube was here, and they were using it on everyone, under the guise of a mental well-being check. There was no way of knowing what they were being fed, without being hooked up to the machine too, something that Solveig wasn't willing to do. Yet still, she needed to get closer.

"No, no, I've changed my mind, please." Solveig cried suddenly, collapsing to the floor, arms wrapped around her legs as she rocked back and forth, face buried in her arms as she muttered over and over. "Please, I can't do this."

She sensed the shadow of a person standing over her and then kneeling beside her. A gentle hand stroked the back of her neck. A healer. It had to be. Guards would have dragged her to her feet, with a blow to the stomach to silence her cries.

"Come now, child, there is nothing to be afraid of." A kind voice whispered.

"Please, I can't," Solveig continued.

"It can be overwhelming the first time, but this is normal." The voice said, "You're taking a big step toward your rehabilitation, and that is to be commended. Don't give up now."

"Do I have a choice?" Solveig felt the hand on her neck pause.

"There is always a choice," they said. "But if you wish to one day leave this place, then this is the only way."

No choice then. Solveig surmised. Who would choose not to do this if the alternative was dying in this cesspit? "Can." Solveig swallowed, trying her best to sound afraid, weak. "Can I go somewhere private and collect myself?" she asked, lifting her head slightly to meet the gaze of a woman. Hair greyed, matching the colour of the standard issue healer's tunic.

The woman hesitated for a moment, glancing around for her nearest colleague, when she realised everyone around them had grown silent and was now staring at the two of them.

"Okay." The woman muttered, "I can give you ten minutes in an exam room, but then you must come back out and be brave, okay?" she insisted, taking Solveig's hand to help her stand, leading her through to the back on shaking legs. She sat her down on the chair beside the examination bed, before kneeling before her.

"What's your name?"

Solveig panicked. Names would be on a register, and she did not know who would be on the list. "I'd rather not," she replied, not meeting the woman's gaze.

"And why might that be? You're safe here."

"If my commanding officers hear of this, they'll double my quota," Solveig rushed, trying to sound terrified.

"Medical matters are not discussed with guards, my dear." The healer smiled.

"Please, I've already had my quota doubled twice this week, and my rations cut. Solveig forced herself to shake, desperate to drive the message home. If this gets out, who knows what they'll do to me!" she cried.

"Okay, okay. Tell you what." The healer smiled, patting her knee. "I'll give you ten minutes to take some deep breaths, then I'll have the next available healer fetch you, okay?"

Solveig nodded, sniffling lightly as she wiped at her dry eyes.

"Okay." The healer repeated, "ten minutes, try to relax. It will be over before you know it."

Solveig shuddered for real this time. That damn phrase, the pure lie of it. Because she knew it wasn't true, The Oracle decided when it was over, and she would not risk being attached to it again. Not here. She stayed where she was, waited to hear the healer's footsteps fade away beyond the door before springing to her feet.

Ten minutes, that was all she had, and she had to make it count.

She rifled through cupboards and drawers, but there were no records to be found. It was nothing more than a standard exam room; the files had to be somewhere else. She crept toward the door with gentle steps, pressing her ear against it, listening for voices, or movements. When nothing came, she pulled it open slightly to check outside; the halls were empty as she snuck out and began checking doors.

She'd been in exam room one, passed two and three before coming upon the kitchen. The next room was labelled Guards Quarter. Solveig tried the door but found it locked, so she moved on instead of wasting time. She'd come back if the rest of her search came up empty. Rounding the corner, she came to a stop. One room remained ahead of her, emblazoned with Records Room. This was it.

If the information she needed existed, it would be behind that door. She walked forward, testing the handle, locked.

"Dammit," she hissed, slamming a hand against the wood. She had no pins in her hair to help her this time. She needed to think and fast. She had to get inside that room. Ordinarily she preferred to not leave a trace of her activities, but she had no time left and little options. She had to break the door down. Squaring up, she leaned back on her strongest leg, placing her foot as close to the handle as possible.

It was going to hurt; she knew that breaking down doors in boots was bad enough, but barefoot was madness. If she misfired and hit the handle, she'd break something. She took a deep breath and then surged forward with a large crack. Thankfully, there was no immediate pain. She tried again, and again, and finally, on the fourth try, the door cracked open. Wood splinters flew in every direction as she raced inside, careful not to put too much weight on her smarting foot.

Time wasn't on her side as she flung open door after door, searching by year until she found this past one. *498 OA*. She flicked through the names, searching for any she recognised, stilling when she spotted the first. Celerin Firachen, then another, Connall Kano, Malik Etana, Flotare Grepino. She had no time to rifle through them, instead stuffing them down the front of her pants to hide them on her way back to the officer's residence.

She backed out of the room, closing the shattered door behind her as best she could before turning to walk back down the hall. Voices sounded as she passed the kitchen and, with nowhere to go, she backed inside to find it mercifully empty. She waited by the door for the voices to pass before heading back out the way she had come with the healer. Making a beeline for the entrance, not sparing a glance at the gathered prisoners as she pushed through the doors, keeping her head down to avoid attention. She slipped outside and straight into the path of a guard.

"What have we here?" he muttered, leering down at her, eyes sparkling. "Where are you running off to?"

"Back to work," Solveig said as meekly as she could manage. The papers she hid beneath her clothes felt heavy as rocks as he beheld her.

The guard's eyes narrowed. "You aren't skipping your check-up, are you?" His gaze slithered over her body. "You know it's important for your rehabilitation into society." Solveig had to force back the scoff at his words. Few ever rehabilitated back into Torrelinian society. If the mine didn't kill them, the guards found a way.

"Of course not."

His gaze halted on her wrists then. "Who removed your chains?" he demanded, reaching for his baton. Missing the lack of scars or welts that should have been present from perpetual use.

"They forgot to put them back on."

"That right?" the guard muttered, taking a step closer, his eyes boring into hers. "Why'd they take 'em off in the first place?"

"I panicked, sir. They said it would help me submit to the assessment better, that I could get new ones when I returned to work." It was at least partially true. If he asked anyone inside, they could vouch that a female prisoner had panicked in the waiting area. She only hoped that none of the healers would confess that they had let her slip away out of fear of facing their own repercussions from the guards.

"What's your number?"

"5967," she blurted without thinking.

"I'll be checking on you later, 5967, and you'd better be back in your chains."

"Yes, sir," Solveig muttered, bowing her head. It was overkill, but still it couldn't hurt.

"Hurry back now, you wouldn't want your hours extended for missing quota." Solveig knew then that the poor prisoner who worked under that number was about to have his daily quota doubled. There would be no sleep for him tonight.

Solveig hurried back toward the open cast, glancing over her shoulder a few times. Once she was sure the guard had stopped watching her, she ran for the window she had originally jumped from, as someone else shouted.

"Stop right there!"

She kept running, lungs labouring from a night of no sleep and no food, her arm wrapped around her stomach to hold the papers in place. She risked a glance over her shoulder. The guard wasn't chasing her but running for the main entrance of the sleeping quarters to head her off on the other side. Solveig pushed herself harder. Faster. Lungs burning as she launched herself at the window. Stomach smarting as it collided with the metal edge, scraping the soft skin, despite the added padding of the files she hid. She dragged herself inside and pulled on the boots she had stashed to hide her muddy footprints. Making it back to Miss Everly's room as the thundering clatter of standard issue guards' boots ran past.

Smiling to herself around deep breaths, she ripped the scarf from her head, shirked her boots and clothing and headed straight for the adjoined bathing chamber. Washing away the grime and dirt of the mine and a long night of travelling through the storm. Before slipping into the bed for a few hours of shuteye, just as the alert for a prisoner on the run sounded.

Perhaps after she had slept, she would feel truly guilty for duping that innocent healer and throwing Prisoner 5967 to the wolves. But at that moment, she was far too preoccupied with diving headfirst into sleep.

CHAPTER FORTY-THREE

Someone Has to Care

The sun was drifting low in the frost-coloured sky by the time someone started pounding incessantly on the door. Solveig dragged her sleep heavy body from the bed to wrench it open.

"What is so important!" she demanded; eyes fierce despite the lingering haze of sleep that called her back to the still warm sheets.

"Miss Everly had us bring you dinner," answered a prisoner. They were dressed in the beige garb of those assigned to kitchen duty, and the fear in the woman's eyes told Solveig that this one remembered her. The lack of red welts peeking out from her hair line said she had yet to be sent for *rehabilitation*.

"You remember me?"

"Who could forget the Reaper of Luxenal?" the woman hissed.

"Some have,"

"Because they chose to. I don't want to forget. I never can."

"Forget what?"

"The hopelessness on my husband's face as you used that wicked magic to drag every drop of life from him." Solveig swallowed tightly, the only sign that she felt anything.

"It's probably best if you leave," she insisted, refusing to apologise. The words would offer the woman little comfort now.

"Probably," the prisoner parroted, as she walked away with one last hate filled glare over her shoulder, her chains ringing a solemn tune.

Solveig ate the standard prison fare of watery cabbage and onion soup and a square of dense bread, the echo of pickaxes her only company. It was as tasteless as she remembered, but it was hot, and it filled the gaping hole gnawing at her insides. She sat back down, eyes alighting on the boxes lying on the empty bed opposite her.

After she'd forced down the last drop of soup, she went through the boxes again. Most of it, such as old bedsheets and clothes she could replace in the city. There were random books worn with dirt, ripped and water damaged from the damp surroundings that wouldn't survive the journey back. In another, her hand drifted over the shining steel of her remaining daggers. She smirked to herself at the commander's oversight. He'd taken her weapons at the gate only to hand her old ones to her like a gift. They had folded her spare leather training outfits beneath the weapons. Those were irreplaceable, custom made solely for her.

Solveig sorted through each box, packing her bag with her belongs atop the files she had stolen, praying no one would go rifling too deep before she left. Soon, all that remained was a small jewellery box containing two items. Her ostentatious engagement ring and a chain holding a dainty sapphire encrusted locket. She left the diamond in the box. It wouldn't burn in the fires of the crematorium, but it could stay there in the smoke and ash forever for all she cared. The chain, however, she slipped over her neck, the locket pendant hanging beneath her shirt lying close to her heart.

She couldn't bear to open it; wasn't sure she could ever witness his handsome face again, but still she wanted to keep the memory of him close.

It was all she had left of the boy who made her believe she could have any life she wanted. Until he took it all with him when he departed for the Netherworld.

With her belongings packed and energy somewhat restored, Solveig readied herself to leave the mine for the last time, when a commotion picked up, echoing toward her. She stepped out into the hallway as Miss Everly rounded the corner, racing toward her.

"Thank The Oracle you're already dressed. This way please!" she rushed as Solveig turned to grab her bag.

"What's going on?" she replied. Hands ringing impatiently before her.

"You have a visitor." Miss Everly said, a grimace twisting at her mouth. "And the commander isn't too happy about it."

"Who?"

"Now I can't say I've seen an image of him. But I'd be willing to bet my Oracle blessed powers it's that mysterious prince from Elithiend everyone has been chattering on about."

Anger simmered in her veins, head falling back on an exasperated sigh. "That stupid, arrogant son of a bitch. I'll kill him myself," she swore, slamming the door shut, as Miss Everly spun on her heel to lead her to him.

"That won't be necessary if we don't hurry," she said over her shoulder. "Commander Sellen may beat you to it."

The two women raced for the gate, where the commander stood with a team of heavily armed guards at his back against two travel weary companions on horseback.

"You must possess a death wish to even consider coming here, Prince," she called as they grew closer. Emmerich couldn't hide the relief in his eyes when he heard the rasping anger of her voice.

"You left without a word. What else was I to do?"

"You were supposed to stay out of my sight for a few days," she seethed, brandishing a dagger in each hand. Wariness creeped into the prince's demeanour at the sight of them.

"I didn't want to lay eyes on you in my home. What makes you think here is any better?"

"Why did you come back?"

"That is none of your concern."

"Depends."

"On nothing, Prince, it wasn't a question. My parents granted you access to Marrelin City. They did not give you permission to wander throughout Torrelin unaccompanied."

"I wouldn't be unaccompanied if my guard dog hadn't vanished into the night like a wraith," he shot back.

Solveig glared at him, and the silent commander trying desperately to smother her laugh beside him. "I should kill you now," she muttered. "Put you out of your misery, for your own stupidity is bound to catch up to you eventually."

"I'd enjoy seeing you try." Solveig could see the smirk lifting one side of his handsome face as her hand tightened around the hilt of a dagger.

"I've held a weapon to your throat twice now, Prince. Wasn't that proof enough that I'm more than capable?"

"Physically sure," he shrugged, gaze pinning her to the spot, "mentally though, I'm not convinced." His smile only widened as she moved to launch for him, only halted by Commander Sellen's exasperated bellow.

"MISS MALEEN!"

"WHAT?" she snapped.

"A word, if you'd be so kind." He tipped his head. Anger plain in the reddening of his cheeks. Reluctantly, she followed the commander a few steps away when he turned on her.

"I know you went skulking around today, Princess," he muttered. "A prisoner without chains seen running for the guards' quarters. Vanishing without a trace after scaling the window." His eyes drifted with an oily slowness down her body, settling on her stomach. "Shall we see that bruise you're hiding?" The commander reached out to grab the hem of her shirt. But Solveig read his move, wrenching his arm back suddenly as her other hand hit dead centre with a sickening crack. Commander Sellen's forearm bent at an unnatural angle as she brought his back to her front, pressing the point of her dagger into his neck until blood welled.

"I can't tell you how long I've waited to have you under the bite of my blades, Commander." She hissed in his ear, "Touch me again and I'll give them something to investigate me for." She dug her dagger further into his neck, slicing deeper as blood poured from the wound. "Or maybe I should kill you now. Put a stop to whatever evil you're taking part in behind those gates."

Distracted by the bliss of finally having Commander Sellen at her mercy, she didn't see the guard creeping up behind her. A sword poised to lacerate her back until he landed with a thud at her feet, a throwing knife protruded from his neck.

Solveig spun, releasing the commander. She found Emmerich staring at her, panic clear in his eyes. "Did I ask for your help?" she sneered, wiping the commander's blood from her dagger on her pants.

"No." Emmerich scoffed, shaking his head as he walked closer, bending to pull his knife from the guard's neck. "But that doesn't mean you have to do it alone all the time."

Solveig studied him for a moment, ignoring the commander groaning at her feet as he desperately tried to staunch the blood from his neck with his uninjured arm.

"I thought the laws of your country had you strike down cold-blooded murderers."

"It's not cold-blooded if your life was in danger."

"Why do you care about my life?"

"Someone has to," he muttered, stowing his knife as Solveig turned back to the commander without a word.

"Run back to your castle and take your moronic lover with you before I have you all in chains," the commander cried.

"I'd like to see you try." She laughed, pressing on his snapped arm with the toe of her boot before snatching up her bag. "It's a good job you love this place so much." She muttered, turning to face him for the last time. "Because if I see your face in Marrelin City, I'll have you rotting with the sewage in a day."

Facing the prince and his commander, she ordered, "You two follow me and try not to fall off your damn horses with exhaustion. We've got a long ride before it's safe to make camp."

"Why did you come back?" Emmerich asked, mounting his horse and trotting after her.

"I was settling old affairs."

"What sort of affairs?"

"No offence, Prince." She sighed, staring up at him. "But that is none of your concern."

Emmerich stopped pressing, and they travelled on in silence until they reached the tree line of the Cuprum Forest, the sun setting behind them. They walked for another hour, until the chill rattled their bones, clear skies stealing any warmth the day had provided.

"We'll make camp here tonight," Solveig said, coming to a halt. The prince and the commander jumped from their horses, grabbing their own packs.

"I don't suppose either of you have a hidden talent for pyromancy up your sleeves," she asked, but neither spoke. "Old fashioned way it is then, surely you two are capable of that. I'll take care of dinner."

She turned, heading toward the river, a straight path through the dense trees. Their shadows formed spectres in her peripheral vision. Images that would terrify anyone unfamiliar with the territory.

The storm had created a rush of water, but it would not deter Solveig. If she had to face the prince on an empty stomach, she was liable to gut him before the moon even rose. She made a bed of thick leaves, taking a seat at the riverbank, pulling out her dagger, taking aim as she had done countless times over the last two years. Before long, she had caught them each three fish. That would hopefully keep them going until they could reach the city.

She returned to their camp where a roaring fire was already glowing, casting the trees and dirt around them with its warm orange haze. The prince and the commander sat before it as she dropped the fish beside them.

"Think you two can cook these?" she muttered. The prince only stared at the catch and then back up at her, and back down at the gaping wounds in each of the fish's heads.

"Did you... did you throw your daggers at these?" Emmerich asked in bewilderment, taking one in his hand.

"Not much in the way of target practice out here, Prince. You've got to learn to be resourceful."

"You caught fish. Using daggers. Live, swimming fish?" he whispered in cautious awe.

"If I wanted you dead, Prince," Solveig sighed, "there are far easier and faster ways than feeding you festering fish."

"Not what I was implying," he said with a shake of his head. "But fair enough."

"What?"

Emmerich laughed, looking up at the canopy of trees above them. "I never stood a chance when I challenged you to that target match, did I?" He smiled. A real, genuine smile that was higher on one side than the other. His eyes sparkled with it, and to her surprise, Solveig couldn't help but smile back as she quipped.

"No, you didn't."

CHAPTER FORTY-FOUR

Ifs and Maybes

Solveig sat against the rough bark of a tree. Her arms curled around her knees as she twirled a dagger between her hands, keeping her mind occupied as she fought through the sleep deprivation. Only the roaring fire kept her company in the dark. She was staring through the rustling canopy of the trees to the starless sky above, when soft footsteps sounded behind her, breaking her reverie.

"Mind if I join you?" the prince whispered from the shadows.

"What's this? Another misplaced act of kindness."

"No." Emmerich said, as he took a seat before her. "Wrenn is snoring in my ear. I can't sleep for shit." Solveig said nothing as she continued to stare up at the sky. "You're not going to sleep, are you?" he asked.

Solveig shook her head as she lowered her eyes to meet his thoughtful gaze.

"Will you tell me why?"

Solveig warred with herself for a moment, tilting her head back against the tree as a soft breeze caught her hair. "I never trusted Commander Sellen. And now that you and I showed him and his guards up at the gates. I trust him even less." She sighed, a deep cleansing breath. "He let us go for now, but I have no desire to sleep when his men could creep up on us at any moment."

"Here, I thought nothing scared you."

"Luxenal was never a paradise, but it's not the place I knew. Something has changed." She stared over the prince's shoulder into the shadowed enigma of the trees as her mind whirled.

"Are you going to tell me or leave me guessing?"

Solveig eyed the prince. "If it becomes pertinent to your investigation."

"And if I was your friend?"

"You and I can't stop lying to each other long enough to even try." She said, shaking her head in defeat.

"We could start now, clean slate." He moved to sit on his knees as he extended a hand toward her.

"What's the price?" She didn't move an inch, eyes narrowed on his outstretched hand.

"Renit Teria. Is she..."

"She's safe. The boys too." Her shoulders slumped in defeat as the prince's mouth fell wide open. "I took everything from them. The least I could do was give them back their freedom."

"The parents are dead, then?"

Solveig's head shot up; jaw clenched. "You mean to tell me you threatened my life when you weren't even sure if I'd killed them?"

"I hoped more than anything that perhaps you aren't as lost as you appear."

"Hope is a fool's errand; you should have left it in Elithiend. It abandoned these shores long ago."

"Why do you say that?"

"I have my reasons, and they aren't for you to know."

"And yet you let the children go free," Emmerich whispered, at a loss.

"The children were innocent." Solveig shrugged, "misled by their parents' poor choices."

"She was an elemental, a powerful one, and you still let her go."

"Don't paint me for a saint."

He was fighting a losing battle against a princess, with a moral code blurred beyond recognition. Had tried to shove her into the box of the heartless killer, her parents' puppet, but it wasn't as simple as that.

He watched in silence as she leaned her head back against the tree once more, at a loss for what to say, when a silver chain glinted at her neck. The unfamiliar jewellery pulling his focus. Then he stilled. Ice in his veins as his eyes zeroed in on her choker free neck, and the faint scar that it revealed on one side.

"How did you get that scar?" His muscles were tight as tension invaded his system, hands fisted, jaw set. His eyes appeared almost black, churning like charred firewood as he continued to stare.

"It's a long story," she muttered, meeting his gaze as her hand moved to cover it. Surprise colouring her words at the intense anger that simmered beneath his. "And nothing more than I deserved."

"Friends. Remember?" he gritted through clenched teeth. "We've got all night."

Solveig stared into the prince's eyes. Trying and failing to understand where his sudden concern had appeared from, before taking a deep, steadying breath as she began.

"I hadn't been at Luxenal long when the first execution summons arrived. It was for a man charged with treason and attempted murder. They wanted flare and drama. They had trained me for it for years."

"It had rained all night long, but that didn't stop them. They set up a stage right on the edge of the open cast, where they chained the man to the floorboards from the waist down."

"He should have been the one screaming. Every test of my new power told me that, but as I bent and gripped his neck, closing my eyes to delve down into my power, it wasn't him, but me."

"They hadn't chained his arms, and I, in all my cocksureness, had failed to notice. He had grabbed a fistful of my hair that I had naively left down and yanked me toward him. Stealing one of my daggers to hold it tight at my throat. Hard enough to break skin."

"I can still remember the stench of his breath as he whispered, *'what a show it would be to slit your pretty throat and watch you bleed out instead.'* He'd pressed deeper as he drew the blade across my neck. I felt the bite and tug. The warm sticky fall of my blood and then it was over. Blood splattered across my face as the blade fell from his hand, and his body slipped to the floor with it, a bolt protruding from his neck."

"If you check the records, the kill is mine. Even though if it hadn't been for that guard, I would have been dead. The healers patched me up, and I was back on my feet the next day. Where a shiny new execution summons waited on my desk. For Dorian Illsen, Guard of Luxenal Mine. His crime? The unwarranted murder of a prisoner."

"I had to go back on that stage and face the chained down man who had saved my life and take his in return. I had to watch as every glimmer of life drained from his eyes until all that remained of this man — whose only crime was saving a stupid girl's life — was a dried-out husk."

With her eyes trained on the floor, she heard rather than saw the prince move. Felt him in the sparks across her skin as he drew close. And with slow, excruciating tenderness, he drew a fingertip across the scar. Her pulse flickered beneath his touch as her eyes met his.

"How old were you when they trained you to become... this," he whispered. His voice was low, fingers resting on the crook of her neck, feather light but infinitely distracting. She swallowed, trying to regain her composure, as her pulse raced, blood heated, and skin tingled beneath his attention.

"Twenty-one." She let out a shaky breath. "I lost someone close to me. It was the same night they arrested Malik. After that, I didn't particularly care what happened to me."

"They manipulated you," he hissed. Pulling away from her as his hands fisted, leaving her cold without him.

She shook her head, coming back to her senses.

"Yes, Solveig," Emmerich insisted, taking both of her icy hands in his. "You were finding your feet in a new world where a friend had betrayed you and you lost someone you loved. They took that weakness and spun you into a mythical monster fit to do their dirty work under the guise of giving you purpose."

Solveig's head continued to shake with every hope filled kindness that drifted from the prince's mouth.

"Be honest with yourself," he pleaded, "if your friend hadn't died, would you have become the person you are today?"

"I can't answer that," she bit out, nostrils flaring, as she tried to push the pain in her heart back into the box that she kept padlocked shut.

"Why?"

"BECAUSE THEY DID DIE! AND I DID BECOME THIS PERSON!" She wrenched her hands from his, slamming her dagger to the hilt in the dirt beside her as she stared up at the sky, fighting to calm her erratic breathing. "What use are ifs and maybes when they won't change my reality?"

Emmerich reached out again. Gripping the hand that had gone white at the knuckles. Pulling it away, he massaged the hurt in her muscles as he whispered, "they let you know who you are. Who you truly are deep down if this world wasn't so broken." His voice was soft, as though he spoke to a wounded animal.

But as Solveig's heart rate slowed, her breathing followed, and her eyes shuttered. She pulled her hand back from his grasp, removing the dagger from the earth as she spoke. "It's a beautiful sentiment, Prince. I can only imagine what life in Elithiend is like for you to have grown up which such whimsical notions in your head."

"We are not without cares. My people had to adapt the same as everyone. Our ancestors' reluctance to join with yours in their worship of that, that, thing..." he sputtered.

"The Oracle," Solveig bit.

Emmerich ignored her. "They cut us off from everything. We had to learn to provide for ourselves and we have become stronger for it. Elithiend is a nation reliant on itself and we have earned our place through the blood, sweat and tears of our ancestors."

"Perhaps one day I'll get to see this magical place." Solveig scoffed.

"Now who's thinking whimsical notions?"

The crackling fire was the only sound between them for a while, aside from the faint snoring of Commander Bleeker. Solveig resumed gazing at the starless sky, and the prince stared at her. The real her. Her mask and armour dropped slightly in the relative anonymity of the woods; she appeared younger, softer, more human. He hated to ruin the almost carefree look on her face, hated that he was about to cause any amount of tension to creep back into her muscles.

"There's something I need to tell you," he said at last, and Solveig's gaze shot back to him, instantly wary.

"We took your notes," he whispered, crushing dry leaves between his fingers nervously, "and the book you were studying."

Solveig's face clouded. A storm brewed in her eyes, her voice cold as death as she hissed, "Are you insane?"

"We were desperate!"

"How am I supposed to trust anything you say when you're going behind my back?" she spat. "You'll return that book the minute we get back to the city. And you'd better pray to anyone out there that still listens to you that the library hands haven't noticed it's missing."

"You were on to something," he interrupted.

"What?"

"Your list of names, the dead, the weakened. Why were you writing them down?"

"Why would I tell you that now?"

"I think we solved it. The people who are dying come from families who historically had a significant amount of power." He paused. "And the families whose magic is failing all together don't. There's no crossover, not in the names you found."

"Since you solved it, why don't you tell me what it all means then, tell me how we stop it."

The prince hesitated, fumbling with the leaves once more. "That we haven't figured out yet."

"Of course you haven't."

"Because we need your help."

Solveig's eyes narrowed. "For what?"

"I need you to get us into Leader Ezekiel's library."

Solveig laughed, but when he didn't join in, she froze, staring. "You're insane."

"Can you do it?"

"It's not a question of *can I*. It's: will I?"

"Will you?" he pressed, voice shaking.

"No." She scoffed, as though the mere idea was completely nonsensical. "Not now, not ever."

"This could be the key," he tried. "What if there's a way to save your people from this horror?"

Solveig hesitated, remembering the sight of her own blood splattered on the stones in the temple. Memories of chest rattling coughs that echoed from the duchess and her son flooded her mind. "I'm guessing at some point you considered me a suspect, but that idea must be at the back of your mind now. So, tell me, what is it you're after?"

"Whatever it was, Malik Etana took. We think The Oracle has something to do with what's happening here, and to prove it, I need to know how elemental magic reacts to its presence. Information that only your temple leader has."

"We're finished here." Solveig's eyes shuttered, locking him out completely. As she made to stand, Emmerich grabbed her hand. The Oracle was their saviour, not their destroyer. She believed that. He was chasing a false lead.

"Wait," he implored, staring up at her, "Please, what happened?"

The princess stared down at their joined hands wistfully before pulling herself free of his grip.

"The Oracle is Osvolta's saviour. They brought blessed balance to our country." She said simply, "You're on the wrong track, Prince, investigate elsewhere."

"I think it warrants looking into," he insisted.

"Then you'll be doing it alone. I cannot go up against The Oracle. Don't ask me too again. This is the only warning I'll give you. I won't report you for what you have already done, though Oracle knows I should." Solveig walked away, lying down on the opposite side of the fire, her eyes never closing as she watched and waited for the dawn to crest. Giving birth to a new day without answers, another day closer to making friends with death.

CHAPTER FORTY-FIVE

Beneath the Monster

T he morning after returning from Luxenal, Solveig woke to a letter resting atop her desk from her mother, demanding an audience with her that same afternoon. She would expect an update, something Solveig could not give her. Her parents had no interest in the dying citizens. All they wanted was information on Elithiend, and she had garnered little to none in her time with the prince.

She stared at the files on her desk. The entire journey home from Luxenal, she'd felt as though they were burning a hole through her bag trying to reveal themselves. Taking a steadying, damp ridden breath, she reached out to flip one open.

Project Luxenal: Subject 48: Celerin Firachen – DECEASED.

She skimmed the data, his arrest and sentencing, the length of time at Luxenal. He'd been subjected to the cube five times, all under the supervision of Leader Ezekiel. They weren't the execution summons, as she'd hoped, but what they did contain was still useful.

The results and decisions made afterward.

Initial Testing: FAILED

Secondary Testing: FAILED

Reconditioning: FAILED

Discovery: FAILED

Final Testing: FAILED

She didn't know their purpose, but each test ending in failure suggested that some were less susceptible than others to the cube's effects. The next paragraph summarised Leader Ezekiel's findings.

Subject 48: Candidate Unsuitable – Recommendation: Terminate experiment via S.A.M.

Solveig's blood ran cold. The papers fell from her hands.

S.A.M.

That was her. Her initials. She grabbed the next file; heart racing as she scanned the pages.

Project Luxenal: Subject 49: Flotare Grepino - DECEASED.

Initial Testing: FAILED

Secondary Testing: SUCCESS

Reconditioning: FAILED

Discovery: FAILED

Final Testing: FAILED

'Subject 49: Candidate Unsuitable – Though minimal success in secondary testing, the candidate is resistant to further rounds. Recommendation: Terminate experiment via S.A.M.'

Each file was more of the same. Failed tests all ending with termination via S.A.M. Solveig Aila Maleen. Killian had been telling the truth. They'd had her murder their test subjects, and she held the proof in her hands. Only Malik's file was different.

Project Luxenal: Subject 51: Malik Etana – ALIVE

'Candidate success rate is inconclusive. S.A.M interference before cessation of testing. Recommendation: Reconditioning of S.A.M to prevent future issues.'

This had been their plan all along. From the moment she had set Malik free, their aim had been to get her back to Torrelin. Back under their watchful, controlling gazes. Reconditioning her to their way of thinking. And she had walked straight into their trap.

A knock sounded at the door, causing Solveig to jump as she gathered the files and stuffed them into her desk drawer, calling, "come in." As bright as she could manage.

Teris waltzed in, some of the princess's garments in hand, "your mother's asking for you, Your Highness." She stated simply, entering the room to put away the freshly cleaned dresses. "She's on edge this morning. Best to hurry on up, I think."

Solveig had dressed in a simple gown, her hair swept up into a bun, face devoid of cosmetics. Taking a seat at the table in her mother's tearoom, she sipped lightly on the warming cinnamon and apple blend that she had Teris bring up for her.

Soon the door swung open, and the queen waltzed in wearing a dress made of a heavy cream material with golden velvet accents. Her equally gold hair curled to perfection. Pinned expertly around a crown that shimmered in the midday sunlight streaking through the large arched windows.

"You know it is customary to stand when a queen or king enters the room," she said airily, taking a seat in front of her daughter.

"I figured since we're alone, you wouldn't mind forgoing some of the usual formalities, mother."

The two women sat in silence for a moment. A servant hurriedly brought in a tea tray for the queen, and a small étagère of cakes and sandwiches that neither woman touched. Asta brought her teacup to her artfully painted red lips. Blowing across the surface of the liquid before taking a small sip, her gaze never once leaving her daughter's face.

"I have news," she said finally, setting the cup down gently with a soft clink. "We have apprehended the citizen responsible for Duchess Xanthe's death."

Solveig stiffened. "I wasn't aware you had even ordered someone else to investigate."

"You believed we would leave it to a couple of incompetent children? A murder this prominent needed to be resolved quickly."

"Where is this perpetrator now?" A messenger scurried into the room, placing a brown folder on the table between the two of them. Solveig's blood turned to ice in her veins.

"He's languishing in the dungeons below our feet." She gestured to the folder, "all the information is there."

"Why are you telling me this?"

"I think you know why, dear." The queen smirked, sipping her tea. "Open the folder."

Solveig swallowed noisily, hand shaking as she lifted the cover. Immediately, her eyes zeroed in on the heading.

EXECUTION SUMMONS:

Erick Connall of House Kano

Charged on this day, the twenty-fifth of the Harvest Season,

with the murder of Her Grace Duchess Xanthe Enya Whitlock, via poisoning.

His Majesty King Emerson Gunnar of House Maleen decrees for Mr Kano to be executed the following afternoon. The twenty-sixth day of the Harvest Season by Her Royal Highness Princess Solveig Aila of House Maleen.

Dread roused a sickness in the princess' stomach. All Marrelin City was about to see her monstrous magic for themselves for the first time.

"You have a team of executioners on hand, why me?" Solveig seethed, hands fisting beneath the table.

"Who else?" the queen shrugged. "You were a daughter to her. You who held the duchess through her dying moments. Who better than you to exact justice?"

"Don't make me do this."

"Your king has commanded this of you. You may refuse, but if you do." Asta paused. "We'll have you in Luxenal at the earliest opportunity, under charges of dereliction of duty." This was it, Solveig realised, the choice that lay before her, toe the line, or be sent to Luxenal. What did they need her around for staining their reputation if she was no longer useful as their chief executioner?

Solveig stared in resigned silence as the queen continued. "Believe me, Solveig, he will drag out the investigation into your crimes for as long as possible."

"Why are you doing this?"

"You once prayed to The Oracle for the opportunity to be of use to the family." The queen said simply, "and The Oracle blessed you with a power never seen. You would throw that back in their face now?"

"This is no blessing but a curse," she seethed, her hand fisting atop the discarded folder.

Asta's face darkened as she spoke in a low tone. "If you were anyone else," she punctuated her words, "I'd have you in the dungeons for blasphemy." She slammed a delicate ringed hand on the table, china plates and cups rattled in her wake. "You will present yourself at dawn for The Oracles' blessing. After which we will all go to the city square where you will carry out the sentence as commanded by your king, using your Oracle blessed gifts. Then we shall host a ball in celebration of the duchess's life. Prince Emmerich will announce his return to his kingdom, never to darken our doors again."

"What happened to getting information from him?"

"Do you think me blind, child? I have eyes everywhere. The more distance between you and that boy, the better. You are to be married, Solveig, and that marriage will go ahead whether you like it or not. You made the choice to throw away your freedom at Luxenal. Now you will pay the price. You'll marry Gabriel and join the temple as an honorary acolyte heading up the department of investigations."

"You call being a glorified executioner freedom?" Solveig scoffed, leaning back in her chair. "No, Your Majesty, I merely swapped one cage for a significantly more gilded one."

"You played the game and lost, Solveig. Now you must live with the consequences."

Neither woman uttered another word as the queen finished her tea, waving a hand in Solveig's direction. A silent dismissal. With the folder a heavy weight in her hands, Solveig left the tearoom, wandering through the dark, dank, echoing hallways of High Tower Castle. Her thoughts were a million miles away.

Lost in the dark recesses of her mind, she hadn't thought of the direction she was heading. Yet somehow, she found herself outside the door to the prince's quarters. She should leave, walk away now. They weren't even friends. Who was she to turn to him now?

Still, her hand hovered in front of the door, hesitating. Before she could gather the courage to knock, or the good sense to run, it swung open before her. Leaving her staring into the fathomless blue warmth of the prince's eyes that swiftly grew alight with concern.

"What is it? What are you doing here?" he rushed.

"I... I didn't know where else to go." She shrugged, clutching the locket with one hand and the folder with the other.

"What's going on?" He took a step toward her, but Solveig stepped back, shock crossing her face as she swallowed.

"I'm sorry," she whispered, eyes staring blankly through him.

He'd seen enough. Reaching for her hand this time, Emmerich pulled her into the room, away from prying eyes and once the door was closed, he wrapped her tightly against him.

His arms leached the cold from her skin as she buried her face in his chest, one hand running up and down her back in soothing strokes. The prince was warm and strong and safe, and she clutched his shirt as though desperate to get closer to him. Vaguely, she heard the voice of Commander

Bleeker whispering, "I'll give you some space." Before she left the room, closing the door softly behind herself.

Solveig didn't move from her place in the prince's arms. Savouring the warm honeyed amber of his skin. She felt his hand lift from her back as he utilised his Aire Wending powers to shield the doors and windows from intrusions. Leaving them utterly alone.

Taking her hand in his, Emmerich led her to the sofa next to the fire. Never once relinquishing his hold on her, as though she may vanish. Afraid he would lose the intoxicating feel of the sparks thrumming in his blood from her proximity alone.

"Now tell me what's wrong," he whispered, his voice strong, sure that he could fix whatever it was.

"I'll never be free." She whispered, "I'll always be a monster." A shudder wracked her body.

"You aren't a monster, Solveig," he insisted, drawing her tighter into his side.

"But I am, because I'm about to take a life to save my neck."

Emmerich stiffened beside her. "What are you talking about?"

Reluctantly, she pulled away from him, revealing the folder that had stayed crumpled between them. He took it from her, eyes widening as he read the contents.

"What is this?" he demanded; voice harsher than he intended.

"They say he killed her." She sighed. "If I don't execute him tomorrow, they'll send me to Luxenal, and you will go home, your task complete." Her eyes were cold, as he looked her over, completely devoid of emotion as though this was the only way she could protect herself, to feel nothing.

Emmerich threw the folder on the floor at his feet, the papers scattering. Papers she would have to read that night to familiarise herself with whatever historic charges he had.

"You believe this?" he implored. "That this, this, I don't even know what to call him. Low rung anti-magicist murdered a duchess?"

"They have witnesses stating he gave her food. What other explanation is there than poisoning?"

The prince's eyes darkened as he beheld her. "You know the other explanation."

"No," she said firmly, stiffening under his touch, "don't do that."

"Do what?"

"Don't make outlandish theories. I've been warned once already today about my blasphemous ways. I can't risk going there again, not when you have no proof beyond speculation."

"Then help me find it," he whispered.

"I need to show you something first," she said, taking his hand. "Do you trust me?"

"Beyond reason."

Dressed in matching cloaks to disguise their faces, Solveig led Emmerich out of the castle. They wandered down the hill to the higher city, past Lord Wautin's now boarded up home, and through the gates to the other side of The Wall. In the middle of the afternoon, there were few mourners allowing them a small degree of privacy.

"What is this?" Emmerich asked as they walked the length of the wall, taking in the endless list of names, from the freshly carved to the weather worn barely legible ones.

"This is The Wall." Solveig said. "It's the memorial for the dead amongst the common folk. They can't afford burial chambers and remembrance stones, so instead, the names of their loved ones are carved into this wall to allow them somewhere to mourn their dead."

They stopped in front of the most recently carved names. "They're organised by year," Solveig whispered. "Do you see anything missing?"

Emmerich studied the names, tracing them back. None of them stood out to him until he realised that at least two should have. Renit Teria's parents weren't on the list.

"Why aren't Renit's parents here?"

"Because I executed them. I condemned them, Torrelinian law states that no criminal is allowed a public memorial. Not one of my executions at Luxenal is on this wall. I ripped families apart in my parent's name, stole loved ones, and in doing so I stole their right to remember them too. One of those names should be Connall Kano. He was my last kill at Luxenal, before—" she hesitated.

"Before you freed Malik?" Emmerich finished, and Solveig nodded. "Why is he important to you now?"

"Because tomorrow I'll be killing his son." She gasped, fighting back the tears that fought to resurface at the reality of her situation. "I'll be taking away another member of that family, condemning them to be forgotten by history, and—"

"And?" Emmerich whispered. Stepping closer, he placed two fingers under Solveig's chin, raising her face to meet his gaze. She almost collapsed at the kindness in his eyes, the openness, how he refused to shy away from the horror of who she was. He stood there and listened, and he didn't hate her for it.

"And I'm not sure he's even guilty."

Emmerich launched forward, encasing her in his arms, protecting her from view. To the outside world, they appeared as two ordinary mourners; he hid the truth, the horror.

"Then help me." He whispered after a moment, "Help me, help you."

"There's no time."

"This isn't you," he implored, stepping back, holding her at an arm's length, forcing her to look at him. "Don't give up. We can still stop this."

"No, we can't." Dread filled Solveig's stomach. "If it's not him, there will be someone else, and another after that, there always is until they get what they want. I have to accept my fate at some point."

"Where is Ezekiel's library?"

"I can't," she pleaded. Her neck arching as she gazed at the cloud drenched sky where rain threatened to fall and soak them, like the blood that drenched her black soul.

"You can," Emmerich said, taking one of her hands in his again. "This is the only way." He entwined their fingers as gooseflesh ran up her arm in their wake.

"You know where it is. I know you do. You're engaged to his son." Her skin paled at that, and she tried to pull away again, but the prince refused to let her go. Taking her face in his hands, drawing her gaze back to him as he stroked the soft skin of her temples.

"Let me help you," he whispered. "You've taken care of yourself for so long. Let someone else shoulder the burden."

"You can't help me." She sighed; a sad smile lifted one corner of her mouth. She twisted her fingers against his, marvelling at their strength, his warm brown skin against her pallid white. "Just promise me…"

"Anything," he interjected, rubbing circles along her jaw with his thumb.

"You don't even know what I'll ask of you."

"Name it, Princess, and it's yours," he insisted. "You have me by the damn throat, regardless." Her eyes widened at the impossibility of his words.

"Promise me that when tomorrow is over, you won't hate me. Promise you'll remember the person beneath the monster."

"You aren't a monster," he repeated.

She smiled despite herself. "No false platitudes, remember? Surely, you've seen how the people view me," she whispered, glancing around at the few people milling nearby. "You've seen me kill with your own two eyes. How can you see me as anything but?"

"I'm not trying to placate you," he insisted, dropping her hand to frame her face entirely, forcing her to look him in the eye as he punctuated every word. "You. Are. Not. A. Monster. Your past does not define you. The things they have forced you to do are not your burden to carry. You have killed, there is no denying that. It's likely you will be forced to kill again before this is over, so long as you never lose yourself to this nightmare."

Solveig closed her eyes, leaning into his touch. When was the last time she'd been touched with such aching tenderness, handled as though she were precious? It made her long for things that couldn't be hers, but she wanted to fight for them. She opened her eyes and stared past him to the towering spires of the Grand Library.

"It's high above, beneath the central spire, glass floor, entirely open. You'll never get in and out without being seen. It's a suicide mission."

Emmerich turned. Following her gaze. "Don't underestimate my determination to save you from yourself, Princess," he joked. "After all, they don't call me the Dark Prince of Elithiend for nothing." He turned, pulling her into his chest once more, holding her tight, and she did not fight him.

"Thank you," she whispered, her breath skating across the skin at his neck as she felt the stubble of his chin graze her forehead with his reply.

"For what?"

"For seeing beneath the mask, even when I fought against you. For not turning me away when you had every right to." Her voice broke, and he held her tighter still. "For not hating me after all I have done."

"You aren't responsible for the things your family forced you into, and you don't have to thank me for anything. It's what friends do."

She lifted her face from his chest, his scent, his warmth, his very presence invading all her senses as she spoke. "Is that what we are, Prince?"

"We could be."

"Even when you're a world away by next week."

"I have a multitude of ships at my disposal, Princess. You want to see me again after this? Say the word and I'll be here." She allowed herself to revel in his hold for a moment, the calming sensation he wrought over her soul.

"Let me help chase away your demons," he whispered into her hair, "and then, when you're ready, I'll walk you back to your rooms."

Hours later, the prince kept to his word. Once she could breathe easier, he escorted her back to the castle and up the six flights of stairs to her rooms, but did not linger with her.

The Prince of Elithiend had a book to steal.

CHAPTER FORTY-SIX

Not Worthy of a Promise

Solveig may as well have slept on the hard, damp floors of the dungeons for all the sleep she managed in her bed that night. She'd tossed and turned for hours. Even the calming draught hidden in the wall didn't help. Once the inexplicable, soothing warmth of the prince's presence had faded, her mind refused to quiet. Plagued by thoughts of the boy she was to slaughter.

Could he be innocent?

Was his only crime his relation to a known—and now dead—anti-magicist?

The same man who was her last *official* execution at the mine.

No, there had to be more than that. Sending an innocent man to Luxenal was one thing but slaughtering them in front of the entire city. Would her family stoop so low to protect themselves?

How many of those she had committed to early graves had truly been guilty? Did she want to know? She had a mind to storm straight to the prince's room and confront him for the part he had played in the softening of her heart. Despite her best efforts, she'd allowed his kind eyes and warm smiles to penetrate her shadows. Deep enough, she was sure she'd never be free of him.

A knock sounded at the door, followed by Teris's swift entry. The usual breakfast tray wheeled in behind her, but in place of a pretty dress. Today she carried Solveig's black leathers, the costume of the Reaper.

"Good morning, ma'am," Teris said, as she laid the outfit across the chaise. "You're wanted in the great hall after breakfast." She brought a dressing robe for Solveig to slip into. Stomach churning, she walked over to the breakfast set up, knowing she would have to eat to keep up her waning strength.

The king and queen had chosen her because they wanted a show, and that meant the boy would have to die by Solveig's magic and not her blades. She would need all the strength she could get to sustain it.

She watched as Teris poured her a steaming cup of coffee. Mixing it with honey syrup and lavender milk, as she dug into a bowl of porridge dressed in autumnal berries and dusted with cinnamon sugar. It warmed the freezing, aching parts of her that surreptitiously longed for the prince's touch.

She dressed quickly, the black suit fitting like a glove before Teris braided her hair into a bun. With each button, clasp and scrape of steel she donned, the wraith stirred in her mind, falling into a stoic mask, gaze utterly blank and unfeeling.

Solveig stalked the castle passageways, every inch the reaper. Once she arrived before the doors to the great hall, she took one last steadying breath. Locking away the princess whose heart the prince had softened, before swinging the doors open with her head held high.

Ice-cold water splashed violently across his face, biting the tip of his nose and the edges of his mouth. Prince Emmerich shot up in his now sodden bed, cursing under his breath.

"What the fuck?" He grimaced, wiping the icy liquid from his sleep drawn eyes.

"Get up." Teris tossed a robe at him.

"Teris?"

"Where were you last night?"

"Out."

"Doing what?"

"That's none of your concern."

"I swear to the heavens if you have jeopardised your family."

"What Teris?" Emmerich snapped, standing from his bed. "What are you going to do? You forget that the only thing keeping me alive here is their belief that I am the sole heir to Elithiend. They won't risk open war by locking me up or worse."

"These are the same people who turned their daughter into the perfect weapon. They ordered her to kill innocents for years. They would care little about adding your name to her roster."

The prince hesitated, and Teris, sensing the weak spot, lunged for it. "Tell me, Prince, do you think Solveig would hesitate? If it were your life or hers, do you think she would hesitate to kill you?"

Emmerich stared at her in silence, because truthfully, he didn't know. He and the princess had formed an uneasy alliance. He cared for her despite knowing it was unwise, but he didn't know where her heart truly lay. Could only assume that she would act the same as him. If taking her out meant saving himself, saving his kingdom, if there were truly no other choice, then no, he wouldn't hesitate, he would do it. As would she.

"I'm going to take that as a no," Teris surmised, "and yet last night you were reckless. You think I don't know what you were up to, but I do. Wrenn talks in her sleep, Your Highness." She stabbed a finger in the centre of his chest. "I said to get to know her, not put everything on the line for her. She, who wouldn't only watch the lights leave your eyes. She'd be the one stealing them."

Emmerich went on the defensive at the harsh truth in her words. "Why are you in here at the break of fucking dawn telling me all of this?" he snapped.

"Because you've already risked everything to get that book, you're hiding under the pillow." Her eyes flashed over to his bed. "You should at least put it to some use."

Emmerich eyed Teris, his brow wrinkled beneath the mess of curls, heart thudding in his chest. "What do you know?"

Teris stood rigid, tension leaking through her voice, "that she's going to be in council with the king and queen all morning." She hesitated at the forlorn look on the prince's face before continuing. "You'll have one window of opportunity to get information to her."

Emmerich scrambled for the book so he could start reading.

"You have two hours," Teris muttered, and he stared at her dumbfounded, head shaking slowly. Two hours wasn't enough time to read and decipher a book large enough to be a doorstop.

"She'll go to the temple via carriage then. I can get you inside, and you'll have however long it takes to get down to the temple to tell her what you know." She eyed the thick tome in his hands. "You better start reading."

Solveig walked two steps behind King Emerson and Queen Asta as they headed out of the castle. Killian would meet them at the square shortly before the event. Whereas they were heading to the temple for The Oracle's blessing. The scent of snow, pine and stagnant water drifted across her nose, carried along by the northern wind.

Teris waited beside her carriage to assist her inside, but she was to travel alone. "Good luck, ma'am," Teris said, not meeting her gaze. It seemed even her closest attendant could not reconcile with her today. Solveig took her offered hand and stepped into the carriage.

No sooner had the door snicked shut, a hand clamped over her mouth. Solveig jerked, whipping a dagger from her holster, flipping it deftly to gut the fucker who dared come after her. Her pulse thundered in her ears. Was this why Teris couldn't meet her gaze? Had she known someone was in here, waiting for her? A firm hand grabbed her wrist before she could slice into their abdomen.

"You've a funny way of greeting your friends, Princess."

Solveig's heart practically stopped in her chest as the warm voice caressed her ear. If the spark travelling up her arm hadn't given it away, his smooth whisky voice did. She nipped lightly at the hand covering her mouth, and he slowly moved it away.

"You're the one lurking in the shadows of an empty carriage. What was I supposed to think?"

"I thought, perhaps, Teris had warned you."

"When would she have done that exactly, and more to the point, why would she? How long have you been conspiring with my attendant, Prince?"

"Long enough to get her to believe I'm on your side."

"That is impressive, since even I'm not sure that you are."

He stiffened slightly behind her. "We'll discuss that later. Right now, there isn't much time." The carriage shook beneath them as they travelled onward.

"Time for what?"

"I think I can prove the boy is innocent."

"You think, or you know?"

"I know."

"Go on."

"I think The Oracle is draining your powers."

Solveig laughed in his face. "No shit, Prince, tell me something I don't know."

"What?" he demanded, a little too loudly in his confusion.

Solveig sighed, leaning back against the plush velvet bench seat. "Every time we use our magic, our cuffs siphon off trace amounts of it that we then offer to The Oracle as a gift for the continued peace that we enjoy."

Emmerich only stared at her in stunned silence for a moment. "When were you going to share this detail?"

"It wasn't something you needed to know."

"Even you can't be that bloody dense."

"Excuse me," Solveig's eyes narrowed.

"You wear magic cuffs that steal your powers and still you wonder why some family lines are weakening or losing it all together?"

"Those losing powers have never been our concern, Prince, only the ones who are dying horrible, bloody deaths. But here's the thing," she whispered, encroaching on his space. "Lord Aldrik, Duchess Xanthe, and the rest. They have attributed all those deaths to poisoning. That has nothing to do with The Oracle."

"And what if that isn't it, Solveig? What if it is the cuffs?"

"Stop!" she cried. "The Oracle has been nothing but good to us. You're asking me to walk into their house and blaspheme them for all to see to save my own neck, when you still have no proof."

"But you will take a man's life to save yourself." He said solemnly, shaking his head. "Maybe you are a lost cause."

Emmerich heard her sharp intake of breath as his words hit her. He regretted hurting her. The thought alone was abhorrent, but he wouldn't take the words back. Harsh as they were, she needed to hear them.

Solveig stared at him and found the same hurt in his eyes that she was sure lay in her own. "You won't even try, will you," he continued, "you're going to go along with it, because that's the easy choice."

"Easy?" she sputtered. "No, it's the only choice." She could almost feel her heart cracking in her chest, as she fought to lock it up tight to prevent further damage.

"You know that isn't true," he pressed, crowding her space now. "Deep down I know you do."

The carriage came to a stop then. "We're done here."

"Looks that way," he muttered, and Solveig shook her head in resigned disappointment, tearing her gaze away from him.

"For what it's worth," she whispered, "I'm grateful that you tried, even if it was hopeless, and I'm sorry I wasn't worthy of your promise."

CHAPTER FORTY-SEVEN

Leader Ezekiel's Suspicions

Solveig was numb to the chill as she strode into the temple. She would have to be for what came next. Locking away her softened heart that the prince had wounded as she cursed herself for allowing him to affect her.

An acolyte anointed her with waters they claimed came from the lake at the Elysian Caldera. She repeated the prayer back to them in a daze before they led her through the echoing hallowed halls. Two steps behind her parents, as always, to Leader Ezekiel's private chambers.

The king did not knock—royalty was above the law in Torrelin in many respects, this being one of them. Face-to-face meetings with the Temple Leader were available to few people, but the ruler of Torrelin had an open-door arrangement with the temple and vice versa.

"Majesties." Leader Ezekiel beamed as he stood from behind his desk. "Your Highness," he echoed as his eyes caught on her. His arms stretched wide in welcome. White robes trimmed in gold, somehow still pristine despite the dirt hallways that spun off from the public areas of the temple.

"It is an honour to welcome you to the temple ahead of today's... festivities." His gaze grew hard on Solveig for a moment. "Please sit." He walked around his desk, motioning for King Emerson to take the seat he had vacated. "There is something I wish to discuss with you all before we proceed." Solveig and Asta each took seats to the side of the desk as Leader Ezekiel moved to stand before them in the centre of the space. "It pains me to trouble you with concerning news on a day such as this." Creases formed above his brow as he looked toward Solveig's parents. "But I must bring to your attention an alarming discovery from my private library this morning." His eyes flickered to Solveig for a beat.

"What discovery?" the king ordered.

"My Acolytes were taking morning inventory when they noticed a book appears to have vanished into the night."

"Which. Book?" the queen seethed, crushing the skirts of her deep red gown in her fists.

"The same one that Prince Malik attempted to abscond with." This time, when Leader Ezekiel's gaze fell upon Solveig, it lingered, piercing and cold.

"Your Highness, I know that you have been studying in the library of late. I sincerely hope you had nothing to do with this." Solveig met Leader Ezekiel's gaze head on.

"I ceased all my research on the topic the moment the queen informed me they had apprehended our culprit."

"And is there anyone who can vouch for your whereabouts last night?"

"I sleep alone, Leader Ezekiel. Only The Oracle could tell you if they saw me slipping out into the night."

Leader Ezekiel turned to face the king and queen once more. "I should endeavour to speak to our visiting prince to ensure he had nothing to do with this." Queen Asta looked between Solveig and the temple leader for a moment, her eyes narrowed, mouth pinched.

"The boy is to return home soon, but we shall ensure that he pays you a visit first," King Emerson agreed.

Solveig seethed in silent fury from her chair. The prince was a stupid, reckless fool. And now he may pay the ultimate price.

"If you would, Your Highness," she heard Leader Ezekiel say, pulling her from her thoughts.

"I'm sorry?"

"I said I should like to conduct a mental well-being check before your trial this afternoon. To ensure all is in order."

Solveig's blood ran cold, for she knew what that meant. Prisoners within Luxenal had referred to it as a mental well-being check, too. Was this how they would pass it off to the masses?

"She would be happy too," the queen spoke for her. Solveig's head swung to her mother. Unable to hide the hurt that sliced through her.

"Excellent." Leader Ezekiel clapped his hands and two acolytes entered, each taking one of the princess's arms to lead her from the room. Ezekiel, the king, and the queen followed them.

"Your father and I shall pray in the main worship hall, dear. Come find us when you're done, and we'll head to the trial together."

They led Solveig down a separate hallway. With the two acolytes at her front, and the temple leader at her back, escape was futile. Their footsteps echoed across the dirt floor and up the white walls. This deep within the temple, the hallways were narrow, dark, and cold.

"Is this necessary?" Solveig muttered, as she desperately fought to hide the growing fear from her voice.

"You've spent a concerning amount of time with that foreign prince. Gabriel and I worry about what effect he may have had on you."

"You think I'd be here today if I wasn't loyal to the cause?" Still, it did not stop the acolytes dragging her further and further down the dark passageway.

"It is merely a formality, Your Highness. And it shall be over before you know it." It was pointless arguing with him. His life began and ended with worshipping The Oracle. But Solveig knew it wouldn't be over before she knew it. Knew that it would last as long as The Oracle wanted it to. Knew that her scalp would burn with the remnants of their power as they shredded her mind to allow them entry.

They said The Oracle was omniscient. If that was true, then they shouldn't need that device. The realisation only numbed her further. She didn't fight as they strapped her into the chair, didn't flinch as the copper disks bit into her scalp. She did nothing. Not until the burning began and the pain, like a knife cleaving through her skull, was too much to take in silence, even for her.

CHAPTER FORTY-EIGHT

Kill or Be Killed

R aucous chattering filled the city square. Hordes of citizens surrounded the stage that had shot up overnight. Royal banners were strung across buildings alongside The Oracle's emblem, a united front of divinity.

The Prince of Elithiend stood in the crowd to the right of the stage. His friend, Commander Wrenn Bleeker, beside him. The stench of sweat and beer invaded their nostrils. This was an execution, and the citizens of Torrelin jostled, drank, and feasted as though it were a festival.

"When are we getting out of this rot?" Wrenn whispered, eyeing the jovial crowd with disdain.

"Soon. There's some grand ball planned for this evening to celebrate the execution."

"This isn't enough for them. They want to dance on the man's corpse too?"

Emmerich slid his gaze over to Wrenn, his agreement clear. Though his words disagreed. "Who are we to judge a country's traditions?"

"Something tells me this isn't a tradition, rather a message." Wrenn muttered.

A hush travelled over the crowd as a man took to the stage dressed in gleaming white robes trimmed with shimmering gold thread. Emmerich recognised him as the leader of the temple, Ezekiel Orson.

"Welcome, citizens of Marrelin City. We gather here to bear witness to justice. Our wonderful, blessed Duchess, Xanthe Enya Whitlock, was murdered, and The Oracle has commanded that the perpetrator must pay for his sins before all of you." He paused, eyes skating across the crowd as he turned. "Bring forth the accused." His voice echoed on the wind as he flung out his arms, robes dancing around him.

Clanging metal rattled through the square as two hooded guards dragged a young, scrawny man up the steps. His clothes were filthy and torn, all the exposed areas of his skin were streaked black from his stay in the rotting damp of the castle dungeons. Behind him, the royal family ascended one by one. First the king, followed by his son and the queen. But *she* didn't appear, not yet.

Leader Ezekiel faced the crowd again, never once turning to the prisoner at his feet. With arms outstretched, he addressed the crowd instead. "Erick Connall of House Kano, you stand accused of murder. How do you plead?"

Emmerich watched as the boy, who couldn't be any older than him, twisted in his chains, the rusting metal no doubt biting into his skin. Erick Kano did not speak, only stared out at the crowd in defiance, refusing to acknowledge the leader as he had him. Even from this distance, Emmerich saw the leader's eyebrow twitch at the boy's overt defiance.

"You understand, *boy*, that this is your last opportunity to save yourself. I hear your father refused to cooperate in his execution also and now he's little more than ash fertilising the earth. So, speak."

Emmerich had to bite back a laugh as Erick Kano only spat at the leader's gleaming robes. Teeth bared as he struggled against the bonds that held him at their mercy.

"Something tells me this isn't going the way they expected." Wrenn smirked.

"I doubt they care. The boy is doing little to prove their accusations false." Emmerich grimaced, because he knew the likelihood of this boy being responsible for the duchesses' death was small. There was a narrative being spun in this kingdom that both crown and religion were desperate to uphold.

"I accept your silence as an admittance of guilt. And to carry out that justice," Leader Ezekiel called, voice carrying louder now across the gathered crowd, arms wide as he stepped to the side. "Your Oracle has chosen Her Royal Highness Princess Solveig Aila of House Maleen."

Emmerich's heart caught in his throat as he watched her ascend the stage. Head low, a hood pulled forward to conceal her face in shadows. Dressed in all black, this woman was every inch the Reaper. When she finally lifted her head, he saw the bleak calm in her gaze. She had shut down. Shut everything out. To everyone else, she appeared cruel and uncaring, but to him. He saw it for what it was. A defence. To save whatever pieces of herself she could.

Heckles and jeers broke out across the crowd.

"Reaper."

"Witch."

"Rot in the pit, bitch."

"Defiler of magic."

One after another, as though the princess were the one on trial. Still, Solveig barely batted an eye as she stepped forward. Dropping her hood to look the boy in the eye.

"Erick Kano," she intoned. "The Oracle has found you guilty of the murder of Her Grace, Duchess Xanthe Enya Whitlock. May they show mercy on your cursed soul."

She pulled a glove free, hand trembling slightly, almost imperceptibly. But Emmerich saw it. And that was when she saw him. Their gazes locked, and she froze for a moment. Barely a breath, before closing her eyes, severing their connection, locking him out entirely as she wrapped her hand around the boy's throat. The cuffs at her wrists shone, blinding the crowd.

Every other voice in the square fell deathly silent as Erick Kano's screams of agony filled the square. His body went ridged, foaming at the mouth. Jaw clenched, eyes rolling back in his head. Solveig held him there, and Emmerich did not turn away. Not even as a colourless liquid poured from every orifice, splashing on the planks of the stage as the prisoner and princess moved.

When suddenly the boy fought back, "I wish I had killed her. All of you deserve it, wicked freaks of nature. You'll meet your end one day soon," he spat through ragged breaths; his skin and clothes drenched from the forced draining of all the fluid in his body.

Solveig paused, blinking slowly as she stared down at the boy.

"What's happening?" Wrenn murmured.

"I'm not sure. Maybe it's part of the act," Emmerich replied, his eyes never once leaving the frozen princess as she blinked down at the suffering boy before her. He watched as her hand pulled back, barely an inch, fisting slightly.

"The time for talking has passed." The king ordered, as he stood, staring his daughter down. "Proceed with the sentence." Solveig blinked, head moving between her father and her victim. "Now, Solveig," he commanded with a tone of finality before retaking his seat.

She nodded. It was imperceptible, but it was there. Not a nod of agreement, but acceptance, Emmerich thought. There was no way out of this for her. The boy would die by her hand, or she would pay for it in kind. Either way, Erick Kano would die.

Her hand returned to the boy's neck, gripping tighter as she poured more power into her grip. His screams became strained. Blinded as his eyes shrivelled in their sockets. Soon he crumpled to the floor, body becoming sickeningly thin and grey, cheeks hollowed, and jaw dislocated from his endless screams.

Until finally, Erick Kano inhaled his last. And the princess dropped his lifeless body with a sickening splash in the puddle of his own bodily fluids.

A deathly quiet descended on the square. Gone was the jovial atmosphere as some in the crowd wrapped their arms around themselves, others covered their eyes and ears as the stench of vomit permeated the air.

Yet somehow, as their gazes met across the corpse and gathered crowd, Emmerich couldn't find it in his heart to hate her. Even as she embodied everything, he had sworn to protect his people from. He watched as she yanked the hood back over her head, a hand flying to her face as she turned from the crowd. Her shoulders jerking slightly as she stalked back down the steps without being dismissed.

Silence turned to screams in her wake as the citizens of Marrelin City stared at the rigid, desiccated corpse of Erick Kano. It seemed they had finally found the one thing that would turn the people of Torrelin off their drink.

CHAPTER FORTY-NINE

All Is Not as It Seems

Healers rushed to cover the body as they carried it away for disposal. Usually, the dead went to the temple for their holy rites, but they cremated criminals. Spread their ashes to fertilise the ground so that, at least in death, they would finally do something good for the kingdom.

Solveig walked the way back to the castle alone. Eyes resolutely forward. Murmurs echoed as she passed, but she paid them no mind. Even as carriages rumbled by, carrying supplies for the ball being held that evening. All she could see was the look on the prince's handsome face. Sadness, anger, and pain. It haunted her. She wanted nothing more than to wash it away, to pretend she didn't care, knowing she'd been naïve to ask him to not hate her.

She walked the winding pathways to the gates. The guards' armour rattled as they opened the doors for her and she disappeared into the welcoming dark of the castle. Dragging her body up the stairs; face a mask of indifference, though every step was like a boulder weighed her down and every staircase took an age to climb. Until finally she was closing the door to her room, safe and alone within the confines of her quarters.

She hid the blood-stained cloth she'd been holding on to. The substance had dripped from her nose and erupted from her throat after the crowd witnessed her power in full display.

She was getting weaker.

Ever since she had returned home, her strength had waned. Power failing her over and over. Was it an omen for the fall of her house? Was she to be the first of many to be born weak until no power remained in the Maleen line at all?

She was too exhausted to consider it, collapsing atop the bed, fully clothed daggers still attached to their holsters. The sun beamed down on her through the window. None of it mattered. She could have been floating on a cloud in a starless sky. Within minutes, her subconscious pulled her from the mortal realm into a deep sleep. To anyone glancing in, she'd appear dead. But to those familiar with magic, they would recognise it as the deep healing sleep after too much exertion. Her mind's last line of defence preventing her from expending herself completely.

Teris passed by the princess's chambers twice during the afternoon. Both times, she found her in the same position as before. On the third, she entered the room and set about removing her dirt covered boots, discarding the daggers on the chaise, and removing her cloak. Before using all her strength to roll the slumbering princess onto her back to cover her with a blanket, allowing Solveig to rest properly for as long as she could.

"How is she?" Emmerich rushed.

"Alive. Resting."

"Still?"

"The healing sleep, I think. Three times I checked, and she hadn't moved even an inch."

"I should go to her."

"No!" Teris grabbed the prince's arm. "You can't."

"Watch me," he snapped, pulling his arm from her grasp.

"Be reasonable, Your Highness." Teris pleaded. "The castle is bustling with prying eyes with the ball tonight. You'll never make it to her room unseen."

"She can't protect herself in that state."

"Princess Solveig is fine. I locked the door to her chambers when I left her last. No one is getting to her." Teris eyed her prince with sadness in her gaze. "I thought for sure today would be enough," she muttered.

The prince glared at her. "What is that supposed to mean?"

"I was wrong. We both saw what she's capable of. What she's done repeatedly. Yet here you stand, as enraptured with her, as if she saved that man instead of damning him."

"You don't know what you're talking about. You don't know how it makes her feel, you don't know her."

"Neither do you." Teris shook her head. "I'm not even sure she knows who she is. She's playing you for a fool and you're too blinded by lust to see it."

Emmerich had no response, no proof that she was wrong. Teris shook her head again. As if she saw every thought that passed through his head. "Listen to me, Your Highness. I beg you. You are infatuated with a version of the princess that doesn't exist. You cannot expect her to change for you. Either accept her as she is or let her go."

"You'll see. I know it."

Teris stared at him, this man who looked like her friend, her Prince. He had the same dark brown curls cascading on his forehead, the same tall, lean body, skin a deep brown. His eyes were the same fiery blue. But his thoughts, those weren't him. The prince, she knew, would put his country first, not forsake it for a person who didn't exist.

A knock sounded at the prince's door. "Enter," he called, gaze not leaving Teris as another servant walked in, pushing a cart of tea and biscuits.

"Afternoon tea service, Your Highness." She bowed.

"Thank you." Emmerich nodded, and the servant left.

Teris's gaze burned through the steaming cup atop the tray. "What is *that*?"

"It's tea and cake." He chuckled. Teris's eyes lifted to him.

"How long have you been having it?"

"Every day for the last week. It's a daily service for all castle residents."

Teris's teeth ground together as she stared at him, and his elemental flame gaze that now appeared off to her. Clouded slightly.

"No one receives a daily tea service. Not even the queen."

"It's only tea." The prince laughed, sipping on the fresh cup.

"Put it down."

"You can go now Teris," He declared with a bored tone, flinging the door open behind her with his magic.

"Emmerich, please."

"I said you can go."

There was no reasoning with him. She couldn't run to Solveig — even if she was awake — not without risking her cover. As the door slammed shut behind her, she paced back and forth before it. She didn't know how much time had passed when someone grabbed her by the arms, startling her for a moment before her gaze met familiar, safe, brown eyes.

"What is it, Teris?" Wrenn rushed, a hand brushing the hair from her face.

"He's taken something."

"Who has? What?"

"Emmerich and I don't know what, but he's been acting strange. Making decisions he wouldn't normally make. Surely, you've noticed."

Wrenn only nodded in the affirmative.

"Someone's been delivering tea to his room daily."

Wrenn quirked a brow at her.

"Don't give me that look," Teris seethed.

"Hey, slow down. He's overworked, bound to make some odd decisions."

"You don't understand. He said he was told it's a tea service that everyone in the castle receives. But no one does, not even the queen."

"What else aren't you telling me, Teris?"

She rubbed at her brow; eyes dazed as she pieced it all together. "The princess, I was there one morning when she took tea with her mother."

"And," Wrenn implored.

"She wouldn't drink it. Outright refused, had me bring her another drink, prepared outside of her mother's wing."

"You think the queen is poisoning him? To what end?"

"I don't know. But something is wrong. I've seen it more than once when she and the king have disagreed." Teris whispered, "The queen will run off and when she returns, a steaming cup of tea in hand, the king is suddenly much more agreeable. Ready to do anything she asks." Teris gripped Wrenn's hands. "Talk to the princess tonight if you get a chance. She'll know something's wrong. This has the queen's doing written all over it."

"I'll talk to her, but I'm sure it's nothing." Wrenn hushed, bringing her hands to Teris's face, caressing slow, calming circles into her wife's temples, holding her tight as their inevitable goodbye loomed over them.

CHAPTER FIFTY

The Princess and The Blessed

Solveig woke as the sun set beyond her window. She was stiff and aching and in desperate need of a bath. As the thought crossed her mind, the door to the bathing chamber swung open and Teris walked out in a cloud of jasmine and lotus flower scented steam.

"Good, you're awake." Teris smiled. "I was worried that you would miss the ball. I've been keeping a bath warm, and I'll send down for some food. You must be starving."

As she lay in the copper tub, staring out at the blue, purple, and orange tones cascading across the sky, her mind wandered. She hadn't attended a ball in four years. Tonight, the air would sparkle with false merriment as music filtered through the castle walls. Lords and ladies would dance the night away with copious amounts of sparkling wine, ale, and a table full of food that could feed a family for a month.

Solveig was about to play the part of the princess when the blood of the man she killed hours earlier was barely cold. To the nobles in attendance, she would be a hero. Someone to be wary of, yes, but still a hero. To the citizens lying in the castle's shadow, she was a monster. A witch, a killer. Certainly, no hero.

She climbed from the tub, wrapping herself in a plush robe as she exited back into her bedchamber, where Teris waited. This time with a tray of food on the desk and a collection of fine dresses in various designs and colours draped across her freshly made bed.

"Food first, I think," she muttered, eyeing the glass of water beside the tray, gulping it down immediately. "I don't suppose you have access to something stronger before we try on all those gowns?" she asked, a pleading look in her eyes.

Teris smirked. "I think I saw a few bottles of unattended sparkles in the entrance hall on my way up?"

"Perfect. Bring two and we can drink together." Solveig replied as she wolfed down a goat's cheese salad, followed by a bowl of fresh berries with sweet cream.

Solveig brought the fluted crystal glass to her lips, sipping lightly at her second helping of sparkling wine. A faint buzz clouded her mind as she surveyed the dresses laid out before her. With Teris's help, she had narrowed it down to two options. The first was a black, high-necked sheath style dress with a matching lace cape. The second was a cap sleeved ivory silk empire line that faded into black at the tulip shaped hem. Each dress came with its own matching headpiece. The ivory silk, an intricately woven leaf and vine design encrusted with brilliant diamonds. The black dress, with a twisted iron headpiece adorned with shining obsidian gems. It was dramatic, but a safe choice for a woman who had spent four years courting the night. The ivory gown would send a message that nothing was pure, that in the end, they all had a tendency for darkness.

"That's the one," she said, pointing at the ivory gown. "But I want the lace cape too."

"Let no one say that you don't have a flair for dramatics, Your Highness."

Teris helped her into the gown, slowly fastening each pearl button along her back. The silk was akin to cool liquid as it whispered across her skin. She took Teris's offered hand as she slipped into a pair of shining silver heels, the points so sharp they were weapons on their own. A slight tremor of a hand saw Teris topping up the princess's glass and Solveig received it with a grateful smile. She sipped away, standing at her window. Listening to the sounds of merriment drifting from below, where the ball had already begun, when a knock sounded signalling her date's arrival.

She placed the glass down on the tray, standing in the centre of the room as Teris opened the door, revealing Gabriel Orson on the other side. His blonde hair slicked back, dressed in a white suit and blue shirt, the colours of the temple. She saw his eyes travel the length of her body before meeting her gaze.

"There's *my* Dark Princess." He smiled, a hungry gleam in his eyes. "Shall we?" Gabriel held out a hand toward her. Solveig hesitated momentarily; she didn't miss the clench of his jaw as he noticed it. With a deep breath, she walked over to wrap her arm around his. The Dark Princess and the child of The Oracle blessed.

CHAPTER FIFTY-ONE

No One's Property

"If I have to go, you do too," Emmerich declared, dragging a reluctant Wrenn behind him.

The prince wore a black velvet tailcoat; the edges decorated with glittering gold filigree. Beneath it was more gold sewn into a patterned waistcoat over a ruffle collared shirt. On his lower half were black tailored pants with velvet panelling and shining black leather boots polished to perfection. A simple golden circlet sat atop his slicked back and parted curls.

"I feel ridiculous," Wrenn muttered as she fidgeted beneath the tight corset of her dress. "You better not be expecting me to dance." The gown was similar in fashion to Emmerich's waist coat. Only instead of black and gold, hers was in varying shades of green. The pattern was dense around the bodice. Its tone was not too dissimilar from the sage of the main fabric, but as the intricate pattern cascaded down through the box pleated skirts, it changed. Darkening through shades of juniper, seaweed and finally, the colour of pine on a starless night.

"Believe me," Emmerich muttered, adjusting the collar of his shirt. "I wouldn't dream of inflicting your sullen brashness upon them." The doors to the ballroom swung open for them then, and a squire announced.

"Presenting, His Royal Highness, Emmerich Ryker Anders, Prince of Elithiend and Lady Wrenn Bleeker, Commander of the Royal Guard."

Curious eyes swung their way. Mutterings skittered through the crowd, inaudible thanks to the swaying melody that drifted from the far side of the oval room.

They had decorated every available surface in shimmering gold, glistening gems, and warm copper. Along the northern edge of the room sat a long banquet table, covered in an array of food and drinks, being constantly refreshed by the castle servants. Along the western edge, between two gilded pillars, lay the dais. Atop it, three golden thrones lay empty.

"I need a drink," Wrenn muttered as a gentleman with expertly coiffed blonde hair, dressed in shimmering blue, dragged his gaze up and down her. "I will never forgive Teris for forcing me into this thing."

"Regardless, I'm sure the sight of you will be fodder for her dreams in the months to come." Emmerich smirked.

Wrenn glared at him. "You're lucky you're my prince, or I'd maim you for that."

Emmerich surveyed the room before him and the mass of bodies twirling across the sparkling dance floor. The steps called for the members to switch partners intermittently. As they spun, the women's dresses flared outward, revealing the array of colourful, gem encrusted shoes they had donned.

When Wrenn didn't return, Emmerich couldn't help but hope that some courtly lady or lord had whisked her away. He was laughing to himself at the mere thought of it, when the doors swung open behind him once more and he heard the squire proclaim.

"Presenting; Her Royal Highness, Solveig Aila of House Maleen, Princess of Torrelin. Escorted by Temple Guardian, Gabriel Xavier Orson." Emmerich spun, watching as the princess entered the room, on the arm of her betrothed. His gaze zeroed in on where her hand gripped Gabriel's arm, her diamond engagement ring shooting rainbows under the firelight.

Emmerich lifted his gaze slowly, inhaling and exhaling rapidly, as though the air had left the room in a rush as their eyes collided across the ballroom.

He allowed his own to sweep down once more, taking in her ivory gown that faded into black, and the sheer lace cape atop her shoulders. His gaze burned her skin as it journeyed up to a headpiece as white as fresh snow. Decorated with leaves, vines, and gems that glistened like morning frost against her hair. She was a siren song, calling to him, lulling him forward before he even realised that he had taken not one but two steps. Her eyes tracked him as though he were her prey.

"Your Highness," he whispered fervently, taking her hand in his, bringing it to his lips. Eyes never leaving hers. Her chest was heavy as she sucked in a breath. Their gazes burned and Solveig all too easily forgot about Gabriel.

"Prince," Solveig whispered, questions sparking in her jewel like gaze. Questions that they both knew she could not ask in such a public setting. Someone cleared their throat loudly, shattering the heady haze they'd drawn around themselves. Solveig ripped her hand from the prince's, pivoting toward the man responsible for the jarring noise.

"Gabriel," the prince said, his tongue clicking against the back of his teeth.

"Prince Anders," Gabriel replied with an almost imperceptible nod.

Emmerich brought his eyes slowly back to Solveig, tracing his burning blue gaze over her. "Save me a dance." He smirked before spinning on his heel in search of Wrenn, not allowing her an opportunity to refuse him.

Emmerich's scent invaded her senses, the warm decadent amber unfurling around her, but it was sharper than normal. As though mixed with something bitter. But she had no time to worry over it as a firm hand gripped her wrist, verging on painful as they dragged her out onto the dance floor. The sweet refrains of a new melody filled the room.

Gabriel's eyes met hers, their usual warm brown roiling with annoyance as he lowered his mouth to her ear, whispering, "Remember who you belong to." He twisted the engagement ring on her finger, placing her hand on his waist. Before joining their other hands as he spun them around the dance floor with dizzying speed. Faces in the crowd blurred. Her night black hair flicked around her. Breaths coming thick and fast as the music rose and fell, building toward its crescendo where Gabriel brought them to a sudden stop. Dipping her low, he pressed a harsh kiss atop her lips.

Solveig gripped Gabriel's arm to keep her balance from tipping over the edge as she tried to push him off, but it was no use. He had her at his mercy and there was nothing she could do except let the chill of his touch seep into her bloodstream and wait for it to end. When he finally placed her back on her feet, Solveig sidled closer to him. Her eyes conveying the warmth of lust when she struck, sending a dagger sharp heel stabbing into his foot.

Gabriel cursed, hobbling, as he tried to take the weight off his injured foot. Solveig watched with icy disdain before stalking off to the drinks table, leaving him limping in the middle of the dance floor.

She grabbed the nearest glass and whiskey decanter. Swiftly pouring two fingers worth before tipping it down her throat to chase away the chill in her bones that lingered from Gabriel's kiss. Out of the corner of her eye, she saw someone else slide up next to her.

"It's never boring with you around, is it princess?"

"Commander Bleeker," Solveig gritted as she poured herself another drink. "Can I help you?"

"You and your priest fighting?" Solveig's gaze slid over to her then, darkening to where the commander held up her hands, taking a small step back. "No need to get defensive."

"I've no need of your jokes nor small talk, Commander," Solveig declared, facing the woman. "Say whatever it is you have to say and kindly leave."

"I'm concerned for Emmerich."

"Why is that my problem?" She sighed, feigning indifference.

Wrenn pursed her lips, eyes narrowing as she considered her next words. "He's been receiving a mysterious tea service," she whispered, eyes darting left and right, relieved to find no one was paying them any mind. "The servant who delivers it claims everyone in the castle receives it."

Solveig shrugged as her heart spiked. "So what? Does he need a training partner to work off the extra cakes? Surely you can handle that yourself."

"He hasn't been himself."

"I'm still trying to figure out what this has to do with me."

"I see the way you watch him." Wrenn's eyes narrowed. "When you think no one is watching you. I see how your eyes follow his every move, how you lean toward him when he speaks."

"I'm engaged, Commander," Solveig drawled, raising a brow in challenge.

"And that's stopped people before?"

"Questioning my honour now? You're on a roll tonight, aren't you?"

"Well." Wrenn paused, wetting her lips as she looked the princess up and down. "I'm not sure a woman with a kill list as long as yours can refer to herself as honourable."

Solveig's eyes narrowed as she leaned closer. "Remember that you came to me for help before you insult me further." The two women engaged in a silent battle of wills as the ball went on around them. Wrenn was the first to yield, rubbing at her eyes as she spoke with a sigh.

"Think about what I'm saying. Maybe it's misplaced concern, but I heard a rumour that you won't drink tea from your own mother's kitchen." She took a step closer, voice lower. "That the king becomes more *agreeable* when he does."

Wrenn moved to walk away, shaking her head as Solveig grabbed her arm. "Who told you that?" she seethed; pale skin glowing as though energy rippled beneath her skin. The commander ripped her arm free of the princess's grasp as though she'd burned her.

"Let's just say a little birdy told me," Wrenn said once she recovered.

Solveig scoffed in annoyance. "Let's just say my mother's tea often makes the drinker more agreeable. The king isn't special in that regard."

Solveig could see in the commander's eyes that she was about to demand more, but stopped in her tracks as the ornate doors swung open. The golden trio swept into the ballroom; all eyes were now fixed upon them as the squire called.

"His Majesty King Emerson Gunnar of House Maleen and Her Majesty Queen Asta Cyrene of House Maleen." They walked arm in arm toward the centre of the room. The queen wore an exquisite cream gown trimmed entirely in gold, the hems and waist covered in jewels in a myriad of colours, shapes, and sizes. The king's suit styled to match. Atop their heads were magnificent crowns of dark blue velvet, glimmering gold and shining emeralds and rubies.

The squire cleared his throat once more, calling, "His Royal Highness Crown Prince Killian Gunnar of House Maleen." He strutted in like a peacock. With a suit in varying shades of blue and green and a cape adorned in feathers. A golden circlet inlaid with sapphires sat atop his brow. Killian scanned the room with a predatory grace before his eyes alighted on a woman with golden blonde hair, wearing a gown the same colour as his suit. He sauntered over, taking her hand in his, pulling her out onto the dance floor where the king and queen waited.

Once in position, the band struck up once more with a delicate waltz. Out of the corner of her eye, Solveig saw Gabriel rushing back toward her. A slight limp still present, fury marring his otherwise handsome features, when she heard a low, honey glazed voice whisper.

"May I have this dance, Princess?" His voice sent shivers through her. Heart thundering against her chest as she came face-to-face with the Prince of Elithiend. He watched her, waiting as she glanced back to see Gabriel was almost upon them. Without another thought, she took the prince's outstretched hand.

"I would be honoured," she said as he spun her into his arms and led her out onto the dance floor. Eyes followed them as the enemy prince stole the first official dance from the princess's betrothed.

The music swept the world away as they stepped, pivoted, and spun in perfect sync. Emmerich brought them closer together until their chests touched. Near enough that they could feel the other's heartbeat against the rise and fall of their breaths. Enraptured in a world of their own making.

"I've been dying to ask, Princess, where are you hiding your daggers tonight?" Emmerich bent his head to whisper against her ear. His brown curls tickled her skin, his voice captivated her senses.

"That's for me to know," she whispered back. "Though some would say a woman's shoes are weapons enough." The prince's blue eyes sparkled. He spun her, watching her feet as the bottom of her dress fanned, revealing the dagger sharp silver heels. Before he pulled her back against him, needing to feel closer, to know she was real. Her back to his chest as they swayed to the music in unison, his grip tight on her hips, mouth warm at her neck.

"Those shoes are wasted on him," Emmerich purred, his wine scented breath drifting along the column of her throat. The whisper of his lips on her feverish skin sending a tremor through her as his eyes glanced to where Gabriel seethed on the side-lines.

"Who said I wore them for him?" she shot back. Eyes falling closed as Emmerich spun her again. This time bringing them back face-to-face, and she looked into his eyes and saw nothing of what the commander described. She didn't even see the hatred she thought had lingered in the square that afternoon. No, his eyes sparkled with something else.

"Then why did you wear them?" He chuckled as he bent to lay his forehead against hers.

"To frighten away the weak of heart."

A sly grin lit up his handsome face. "Fortunate then that there's nothing weak about my heart." He spun her again in time with the music's dizzying crescendo. Swept her up into his arms, holding her steady above his head, spinning in a slow circle as the music faded out. In a daze, she sensed every eye in the room fixed on her as Emmerich lowered her, decadent and slow. Purposely gliding her body down his, every soft piece of her yielded against every hard piece of him. She stared wide eyed into his clear blue gaze, his thumb grazed lightly across her cheek.

He bent suddenly, and she froze. Time slowed as he appeared to take that last forbidden step, right there in the middle of the ballroom. A spectacle for all to see. But he brought his lips to her ear instead. His mouth turned up in a grin.

"To answer the question, you were too afraid to ask, Princess. No, I don't hate you. Even when I should have, I didn't. Even now, when you throw every dark and jagged piece of yourself in my face, I don't. I'm not sure I ever could."

He pulled away then, and she stared as he brought his lips down against her forehead. Her eyes closed, savouring the warmth of his mouth on her skin. She gripped his arms tight, desperate to hold on to this one perfect moment in a sea of dark. Praying she wouldn't have to open her eyes, that it never had to end. But all dreams end and their memory fades to be replaced by cold, harsh reality.

Solveig blinked away the warm, shimmering haze of the prince's attention, her surroundings coming into focus again. She saw the queen glaring; the king held her back with a tight grip. Prince Killian loomed with dark humour in his gaze, and the gathered crowd displayed a myriad of confused, shocked, and repulsed expressions. As for Gabriel, he was a simmering pot of anger, seconds from boiling over as he grabbed her arm and pulled her from the dance floor toward a balcony. As if it would afford them some privacy from the stares that followed their every move, stares that included the prince's flame hot sapphires.

Gabriel released her so suddenly that she stumbled into the balustrade. The force almost sending her over the edge were it not for the tight grip she found.

"What the fuck was that?" he shouted, thrusting a pointed finger toward the ballroom.

"A dance, Gabriel."

"Do not treat me as a fool."

"Then why don't you tell me? Since you know everything."

"It sure as shit looked like foreplay."

Solveig reared back, her eyes as cold as death. "You're disgusting," she hissed.

"And you're engaged to me." His nostrils flared. "I won't have you showing me up in front of these people, not with some two-bit princeling from an enemy kingdom after a good time." He took a step closer, crowding Solveig against the cold stone of the balustrade. His face burning like the red of fresh blood. "You belong to me."

"I belong to myself, Gabriel Orson. You'd do well to remember that, or do I need to bruise your other foot for the message to sink in?" she shouldered past him, but his hand swung out to grab her only this time, she expected it. Grasping his wrist before he could hers, she wrenched it painfully backward.

"Touch me in anger again and you'll find yourself with one less hand."

They stared at each other in heated silence. "You think I'm afraid of you?" He snapped through the pain, "A girl so scared of disappointing her family that she allowed them to turn her into a monster. But you aren't one, truthfully. Are you? Every life you take eats away at your resolve a little more. One day you're going to break apart. And when that happens, it will be me picking up the pieces. Not that prince you're mooning over. He'll be long gone."

Solveig leaned into Gabriel's space. Her chest heaving. Mouth twisted into a cruel smirk. "Is that a threat, Gabriel?"

Before he could even think to respond, an almighty crash of shattering glass and shocked shouts filled the air.

Solveig froze.

Memories fought to takeover, and she tried to force them back. It was an accident. It had to be. She ran, shoving her way through the jostling crowd toward the noise. Slowly, they parted for her, and she heard footsteps crunching over broken glass, followed by an aching cry ripped from Commander Bleeker's throat.

"EMMERICH."

Solveig pushed faster through the last of the attendees and came face-to-face with her nightmares made real. Though it wasn't her beloved Lord Aldrik lying on the ground, but the Prince of Elithiend.

His eyes closed, chest still.

CHAPTER FIFTY-TWO

To Save a Life

G lass shards shredded the skirt of Solveig's dress, biting into the exposed skin of her legs as she crawled to him.

"We need a healer." Wrenn shouted.

No one came to save the enemy.

They were alone.

Wrenn's gaze flew to the princess. "Please. Don't let him die."

"I. I can't," Solveig stuttered. "I never learned that type of magic." Her chest tightened with despair. This couldn't be happening, she thought, not again.

Emmerich convulsed, foaming at the mouth. His usually warm brown skin turned ashen. The acrid, bitter scent that Solveig had caught earlier invaded her senses. Potent now. When still no one came forward, Wrenn looked at her again.

"Try."

Solveig stared helplessly at the woman who, not thirty minutes ago, had reminded her of the pile of bodies she'd stacked up behind her over the years. She couldn't save the prince. They'd curated her magic to destroy, not rescue. But she knew she couldn't sit there and watch him take his last breaths and know she had done nothing to stop it.

Slowly, achingly slow, Solveig reached out a hand. Laying it on the prince's exposed neck. Feeling for his pulse. It was weak, but it was there. He was still there, his skin cold and clammy beneath her shaking fingers.

Closing her eyes, she searched down deep within her. Stretching her magic, unsure whether it would be enough. The darkness reared its head, answering her call. Waiting to devour, but she held it back, searching for something else. Anything else.

She could sense it. The bitterness that surrounded the prince was in his blood. Swimming through his body, aiming straight for his heart. This was something she could stop, or at least she could try. Either way, he was dead.

The Reaper held the prince's life in her hands as he lay dying on the floor. With every shallow inhale and even weaker exhale, his chest did not move. As the death knell approached, everything that made him, him, was slowly slipping away.

She opened her eyes, hand shaking as it reached for the split of her dress, to the hidden thigh holster releasing her dagger. She grasped the jewelled hilt, bringing the shining tip to his throat, when Wrenn grabbed her arm, eyes wide.

"What are you doing?"

"I am no healer, Commander. I'm going to save him the only way I know how."

"You'll kill him."

"He's dead, anyway."

They stared at each other for a beat before Wrenn finally released her arm. Solveig wasted no time slicing into the side of the prince's neck. The dagger clattered to the floor beside her as she placed her hand over the wound. Reaching out to her magic once more. Just his blood, she told herself. Nothing else. Drain the poisoned blood and he may live, lose control and...

Her head snapped to the Commander's. "Take his wrist." Her lips trembled as she thrust her dagger towards her. "If his pulse strengthens, his colour returns, his chest rises, anything, and I don't stop, you take me down."

Wrenn didn't respond as she grasped the weapon.

"I need your word, Commander," Solveig pleaded, her voice shaking.

"I promise. Now save him," Wrenn cried, her grip tightened on the dagger.

Solveig nodded, closing her eyes once more. Reaching out to her waiting power, this time she let the darkness rip free. The prince's blood flowed from his neck, pooling on the ground between them, staining all in its path.

Her plan was dangerous. There was always the risk that the poison had spread too far. That she could drain too much. She was a murderer playing a healer the only way she knew how.

As more of the prince's blood drained, she tasted the acrid bitterness begin to fade. Her arm shook. Breaths becoming laboured as pain ripped through her skull. She felt something dripping from her nose, mixing with the prince's blood on the floor.

"Solveig?" she heard Wrenn stammer through the haze of her power.

The commander's eyes fixed on the blood trickling from her nose, stark against her pallid skin and the white of her dress. But Solveig didn't stop. Would not stop until every drop of that bitterness left his body, no matter the cost.

As her vision faded, and her mind blacked out. That bitter taste vanished, and she could feel the prince's strong pulse against her hand. She used everything inside her. Screaming mentally and outwardly as she ripped her hand away and caged the darkness. Falling backward on the glass, the tiny shards biting into her skin.

Emmerich coughed.

Once.

Twice.

He was alive.

He was breathing.

And the Reaper of Luxenal had just used her darkest power to save a life in front of a crowd of her parents' most trusted advisors. A few minutes passed before a group of servants rushed over with a bed sheet instructed by Teris. They placed the prince atop it and made their way toward his chambers. Solveig and Wrenn followed behind them. As the doors to the ballroom closed, she heard Prince Killian shout.

"Grab a drink, restart the music, and someone clean this mess up." The ball resumed on Killian's command as if a prince of the realm hadn't almost died before their very eyes.

CHAPTER FIFTY-THREE

Give and Take

Bells chimed the early hour as partygoers filtered through the castle gates back down the winding hill to their homes. Solveig remained in vigil at the prince's side.

Watching.

Waiting.

For any sign that her dark magic had harmed him.

"We should get you cleaned up, ma'am," Teris said.

"I'm fine."

"Commander Bleeker will send for us if the prince's condition changes. I need to check your wounds lest they become infected."

"I said I'm fine."

"Your Highness, if I may..." Wrenn tried.

"No, Lady Bleeker, you may not. I have to know I didn't cause any lasting damage."

"You saved his life."

"With dark magic."

A hand landed on her shoulder, but Solveig flinched away.

"Your Highness, whatever means you used, you saved my prince's life tonight. My country owes you a debt of gratitude."

Solveig didn't look at her. "You should have your ship readied, Commander. Torrelin is no longer safe for you."

"I'll have a message delivered to the port at first light." Solveig only nodded as she watched the rise and fall of the prince's chest.

Dawn teased its way across the horizon, and still the princess sat in the cold. Her head resting on the prince's lap, breaths slow and even. She was dozing when she felt the hand in hers twitch. Her head flew up as she blinked away the haze of sleep, glancing toward the head of the bed, where the warm gaze of the Prince of Elithiend stared back at her. Healthy and whole.

"What are you doing here?" His brow creased as he raised a hand to brush a wayward lock of her raven hair behind her ear. His gaze falling to her ruined gown.

"What happened?" He tried to move, to rise from the bed, but grimaced with pain, falling back against the mountain of pillows Solveig had laid behind him in the night.

"What do you remember?"

His lips quirked with a ghost of a smile. "If you're wondering whether I recall spinning you around the dance floor. Declaring how little I hate you? Those memories are intact. It's afterward that's hazy."

Solveig's eyes dropped, a light blush creeping across her cheeks at the impossible memory of his words. "Please, I'm lying here feeling as though someone dropped a pile of boulders on me and there you are, dress torn, stained and bloody. What happened?"

"Honestly?" she worried her bottom lip between her teeth as she stroked the back of his hand with her thumb. Emmerich tracked her movements. "I'm not sure. I wasn't there when it happened."

"Yet, you're here now? And I'm guessing you were there for part of it, too?" Solveig nodded solemnly.

"I was with Gabriel on the balcony when I heard a crash back in the ballroom. I ran to see what had caused it and found you lying on the floor, unmoving, not breathing, and then you shook, and your mouth frothed." Her words were like vomit now. "No one came to help, though there were plenty of Hydromancers in the room."

Her eyes fell to the bandaged wound on his neck then, as a tear tracked down her cheek. Emmerich removed his hands from hers to wipe it away gently with his thumb. All the warmth that had been missing in his touch last night now returned, sending shivers through her body.

"Whatever it is, Princess. Just tell me."

Solveig took a deep shuddering breath before taking his hand again, laying it atop the bandage on his neck. "I sensed the poison, and I had to help you the only way I knew how. I had to drain it from you. From your blood. I'm not a healer. I don't know how to pull poison from the blood, I only know how to drain fluid itself. Even if it meant killing you faster. I—I had to try."

Her head fell in her hands, shoulders shaking. Emmerich sat up, despite the pain, pulling them away.

"Look at me," He demanded. When her gaze remained on her hands in her lap, he placed two fingers beneath her chin, and brought her face up to his slowly. She found his eyes full of nothing but wonder.

"However, you did it. I'm alive, because of you."

"But I—"

"No." He placed a finger against her plush mouth. "No buts." He lowered the finger slowly, directing it toward her heart between them instead. "You saved my life."

"What will it cost me?" she gasped, shoulders still shaking. Emmerich took both her hands in his, trying to warm the ice that had dug its teeth into her whilst he slept.

"Something that wasn't worth having."

A wry smile crossed her mouth at his statement.

"I guess I was wrong." He mused after a beat.

"About?"

"You had the guts to cut my neck after all." He laughed, and Solveig couldn't help but join in.

They were silent for a moment. Watching each other. Their movements mirror images as they pretended they couldn't sense the crackling energy that surrounded them. Couldn't feel the warmth spreading through their blood from where their hands touched and didn't let go.

"Did you clean those wounds yet?" Emmerich asked suddenly.

"What?"

He nodded toward her legs. "Those wounds you've got from crawling over broken glass to save me."

"No," she gulped.

"Bloody reckless fool. Grab the kit, I'll do it for you."

"Do what?" she exclaimed suddenly, pulling her hands from his.

He gave her a sardonic look. "Clean your wounds. You saved my life. It's the least I can do."

In a daze, Solveig stood from the chair, wobbling slightly on aching knees from being sat for hours. She grabbed the meagre kit from the adjoined bathing room and a small bowl of water before returning to the prince's bedside.

Emmerich had adjusted the pillows behind him in her absence, sitting fully upright now. His sun lightened curls sticking every which way from sleep, revealing the scar on his temple. The white shirt that Wrenn had dressed him in gaped open at the neck, revealing more of his warm brown skin. Her eyes lingered for a second too long when she heard a gruff chuckle from across the room.

"Eyes up, Princess," he jested, but she didn't meet his gaze. The blush on her cheeks deepened slightly as she approached him, slowly setting out the supplies on the bed before returning to her seat beside him.

She heard him chuckle before slowly patting his lap. She looked at him, mouth agape, as he raised a brow in return.

"I can't very well clean your wounds with your legs all the way down there now, can I?"

Solveig swallowed audibly, as she slowly lifted each leg onto his lap, the angle forcing her to lean back on her chair. The torn skirt of her dress falling to mid-thigh as she did so, needle sharp heels long since discarded.

"Shame," he tsked with a slight shake of his head.

"What is?"

"Those shoes would have been exquisite on these sheets. Another time, perhaps."

"If you're trying to charm me, Prince, I'm afraid to tell you it isn't working," she huffed, folding her arms across her chest to hide the rapid rise and fall.

"Liar," he replied with a smug smile. Reaching for a piece of cloth from the kit, dowsing it in cleansing alcohol before looking up at her again. "This is going to sting."

"Just do it."

Gently, Emmerich dabbed at the small cuts that littered her knees and shins. He wiped away the remnants of blood and glass, gaze resolutely focused on the task before him. Solveig tried desperately to calm her racing heart.

Next, he reached for the treatment solution, containing everything from Nyteberry seeds to honey. He placed a single drop over each cut before massaging it in. The wounds weren't deep enough to require bandages, and his caress felt like magic. His hands drifted from her shins to the back of her calves, where he kneaded the tight muscles there. Solveig's eyes fell shut as the pain relief properties in the solution took hold. Soon all she could feel were the shockwaves traversing her veins as the prince continued his self-imposed task.

A soft sigh escaped her lips as her body relaxed beneath his ministrations. She couldn't hide the blush that travelled from her cheeks down over her neck and chest. With the sound of her breaths hitching slightly, his hands suddenly fell away. She cracked an eye open to find him staring at her, the blush of her cheeks, the arch of her throat, where her head and fallen back against the chair.

"What?" she whispered.

"Nothing," he surmised, with a small shake of his head. Yet his eyes betrayed a blazing fire. Hot enough, she was sure he could set her aflame in both the best and worst way. He gripped the torn and bloodied edges of her dress, his eyes meeting hers as he reluctantly dragged it back down her legs. Covering her thigh holster that he'd wondered about as they'd danced. He swallowed; mouth suddenly dry as the desert as he dreamed of what it would be like to drift his fingers tips over her smooth skin. Would she tremble under his touch as he removed the weapon? In another life, perhaps. If things were different, if she cared for him as he did her. If they weren't on opposite sides.

"Will I live?" she quipped, breaking the silence, desperate to sound unaffected.

"I'd say your chances are high. Shame about that dress, though." He fingered the cool, blood-stained fabric. "I doubt even the most talented laundress could get all this blood and dirt out, never mind repair it."

His words should have elicited more shivers. It was yet another compliment, something he was becoming all too comfortable giving her. Instead, it jostled through her mind, dragging a memory from the depths of an ice-blue velvet gown that had been damaged similarly. On a night not too dissimilar to last.

Except for the blood staining that gown had been Aldrik's, this blood was hers and Emmerich's. And she had sensed the poison in Emmerich's long before it had ravaged him, without even knowing it. There had been no scent on Aldrik, nor Xanthe.

Just as Emmerich hadn't coughed. Hadn't choked on his own blood, chest rattling desperately for air, yet all three were supposedly poisoned. And she had killed the latest culprit, not even a day ago.

"What is it?" Emmerich asked, his voice on edge as he leaned forward, searching for an unseen threat.

"I... I have to go," she stammered, surging to her feet so fast she almost tripped.

"Is everything okay?"

"Yes. Why wouldn't it be?"

"Then tell me why you're running out of here, as though I asked you to marry me."

Solveig stilled at his words, turning to face him. "I have something I need to take care of."

"Are you going to tell me what?"

Her head dropped; shoulders bent inward.

"I'll take that as a no," he muttered.

"I'm sorry."

"It's fine. You don't owe me anything, Princess." But she could hear in the bite of his words that she'd wounded him again, this time without meaning to.

Solveig desperately wanted to confide in him, but something stopped her. She couldn't. Not until she was sure. Different poisons had different effects. There was no use concerning him without proof. There was a simple explanation for all of it.

There had to be.

CHAPTER FIFTY-FOUR

Seek the Truth

Solveig avoided Teris's gaze as she lit a sconce for her. Refusing to divulge why she needed it. Once the castle was sleeping, she crept out of the room, listening for passing servants. Determined not to be seen as she headed for the Infirmary.

The healer must've been called out, for the door was unlocked when she arrived. She slipped inside, heading straight for the Records Room. Knowing the healer could return at any moment. First, she retrieved the file on Xanthe, then she searched for the older one, fingers drifting across a slip of aged paper carrying Aldrik's name.

She walked over to the desk, placing her sconce down to study each of the death certificates. Both listed the cause of death as poisoning. Though the healer remarked, they could not find a trace of it after the fact. Whatever had killed the duchess, and her son, hadn't been in their systems when they filed the report.

Solveig felt as though she were drowning as she stared at the confirmation that she may have killed innocent people on her family's orders. Never once questioning it, until her friend's name came up on the docket. She was a monster. Despite Emmerich's protestations to the contrary. She had innocent blood on her hands.

Whatever saving Emmerich cost her, she deserved to lose it. She couldn't take back what she had done, but she could try to stop it from happening again. If Aldrik and Xanthe hadn't been poisoned, that meant whoever went after Emmerich was still alive and still had access to him.

She pocketed the death certificates and returned the files, before turning on her heel and heading, not for her quarters, but for her mothers. Whoever had done this was likely at the ball last night. They wouldn't have wanted to miss the culmination of their efforts. She needed the list of attendees and assigned workers. As Emmerich had suspected her of being Xanthe's killer, she now had to suspect everyone of being his.

Unlike the infirmary, the door to the queen's lady-in-waiting's room was locked. Solveig sank down on her knees, laying the glowing sconce against the stone wall. Casting, flickering, blue tinted shadows up and down the hall as she pulled pins from her hair and set to work wrestling with the lock.

As footsteps sounded down the hall, it clicked open, and she darted inside. She hid the sconce beneath the desk, praying its light wouldn't filter out beneath the door frame. Solveig held her breath as the steps came closer, louder. They paused for a second at the door, and she froze, as if even the slightest movement would give her away.

What seemed like an eternity later, the person finally moved along. Running to the desk, she pulled open drawers and boxes until she found what she needed. Then raced from the room in case whoever had lingered by the door decided to come back. The list felt like it was burning her skin as she moved. Someone on it had attacked the prince, and she was going to find out who, but it wasn't safe to investigate what she had learned in this castle. She needed to get away from watchful eyes and listening ears.

Commander Bleeker had sent word for the ship to be readied, as promised. Once Emmerich could finally walk more than a few steps from his bed, she declared it was time for them to go. They could do no more here, not when his life was on the line and Emmerich reluctantly agreed. Only requesting that they delay for one more day to allow him to say goodbye to the Princess, who had gripped his attention so thoroughly. They were talking in hushed tones over a light breakfast and steaming cups of coffee when Teris burst through the door.

"She's gone," she gasped.

"What are you talking about?" Emmerich demanded, shooting up from his chair, ignoring the ache still lingering in his body.

"Solveig. Some of her clothes and weapons are missing, as is she. I'm such a fool," she cried, covering her face with her hands.

"Start again." Emmerich exclaimed as he rounded the chair.

"Last night she asked me to light her a sconce, but wouldn't say why. I was wandering the castle half the night to see if I could spot her, but I never did except..." She paused.

"Except what?"

"I walked past one of the queen's offices. I thought I saw something, but no one was there. Now, I'm not sure."

"Why would she go there?"

"She was searching for something."

"Information she couldn't ask for," Wrenn supplied. Emmerich and Teris turned toward her.

"What information could she need?" Emmerich was almost shouting now, pinching his brow in frustration.

Wrenn turned toward Teris for help, whose only reply was a tight grimace. "Before the party, Teris was worried you may have been under undue influence from that tea you've been drinking. She asked me to talk to the princess about it. Something about not drinking tea from her mother's kitchen and warning you of the same."

"I remember."

"Well, the princess wasn't overly concerned, but now, maybe there's something." She shrugged.

"Something she's chosen to keep to herself." Emmerich groaned, his head falling back as he rubbed at his eyes.

"I warned you not to trust her."

"Something tells me that's not the problem here," he muttered.

"Then what?"

"It's just her. She doesn't trust anyone. Thinks someone in the castle poisoned me. I think she's found something that she thought wasn't safe to delve into here." He turned toward Teris. "Any ideas where she'd go?"

"Farrenhold."

"Why would she go there?" The prince and his commander glanced at each other, and Teris looked at them both as though they were stupid.

"Have you paid no attention to her at all? She's friends with the future sovereign, Adira Etana, and if that reason isn't good enough for you. Jasper Etana declared she would be under their protection whenever she was there until the end of her days. If she's found something she's not supposed to know. There's no place safer for her right now."

Emmerich eyed Wrenn next to him. "Change of plans, Commander. We're going to Farrenhold."

Wrenn rolled her eyes as she stood to write a message to be delivered to the port, as Emmerich prepared his belongings for departure.

"Wait." Teris shouted, throwing her hands wide. "You can't simply go to Farrenhold. You're a prince of the realm, remember? An enemy prince at that, you need permission to step foot on Farrenhold soil." Emmerich looked at Teris tersely.

His nostrils flared as he jerked his head toward Wrenn, flexing the muscles in his arms to loosen the tension there.

"Wrenn, you pack. I'll write the letter. And Teris, you make sure it gets sent out today. We're leaving before sundown."

CHAPTER FIFTY-FIVE

Race to Farrenhold

Solveig rode as if the wind carried hulking black monsters of the deep world. By day she rested, allowing the mare time to recuperate from the punishing pace they kept. Once night fell, they raced through the trees, a pair of wraiths in the blackness.

The journey lengthened as she circled far around the back of Luxenal Mine, right up to the base of the mountains to avoid being spotted by a patrol. Birds flitted and cawed over head as she picked at a piece of grilled fish she'd caught and cooked earlier that morning. Her supplies were running low, especially for the horse. She would need to reach North Watch by the next morning if she didn't want to risk damaging the poor thing.

It had been two days already since she had fled Marrelin City as though her life depended on it. She hoped and prayed that the prince and his commander had made the wise choice and were safely sailing back to Elithiend.

On the third day, she spotted flickering blue lights through the dense foliage, the lights of the Elysian Bridge. A few more steps and she would be back on Farrenhold soil. Safe. For a little while at least. Solveig jumped down from her mare to walk across the dense, echoing wooden panels. She didn't dare look down to where the chasm below was visible through the slats. A long drop and sudden stop. Two guards waited on the other side. One with his arrow already notched, the other with a hand resting on the pommel of his sword as she came to a stop before them.

"State your name and business," one ordered.

She held out a hand, a slight smirk decorating her lips as she said, "Solveig Aila of House Maleen, Princess of Torrelin."

Their faces blanched, and Solveig dropped her hand.

"I have to check with my commander," the guard with the arrow stammered. "They did not inform us to expect a visiting royal."

"By all means," she said, stroking the mare's mane softly.

As time wore on, Solveig took a seat on the ground beside her horse. Under the close watch of the remaining guard as she twirled, flipped, and aimed her dagger repeatedly. Every time she aimed it in his direction, he flinched slightly, almost imperceptibly, but Solveig noticed. Soon she saw dust rising in the distance as another horse raced toward them, with Jasper Etana riding atop.

"Solveig?" he shouted as he jumped down, racing over to her, "everything okay?" his eyes roamed her quickly, searching for injuries no doubt.

"I'm fine, physically at least."

"You look a fright." He took in the mess of her hair, dirt-stained clothes, and muddy skin. "What happened?"

Her eyes shifted to the guard stood a few feet away. "Not here."

"What I said before still stands," Jasper declared, rubbing at the stubble on his jaw, "as long as your boots stay in Farrenhold, you're under our protection."

"Good, I may need to ask you for that protection sooner rather than later."

Jasper quirked a brow at her, before turning toward her exhausted horse as he inclined his head toward the one he had ridden in on.

"Hop up, Princess. You need a bath, then we can talk."

Solveig found herself back in the room she had spent days healing in a month prior. They had already filled the tub with steaming lavender scented water. She wasted no time stripping out of her travel worn clothing, to wash away three days' worth of dirt and sweat from her pores. Warm water seeped into her bones, stinging as it lapped over some of the deeper cuts still marring her legs. Wounds that she hadn't taken the time to tend to since the prince had cared for them from his bed.

The memory of how his touch had burned and soothed simultaneously as they rubbed the ache from her muscles infiltrated her mind. She had allowed them to become closer than they should have. Her heart had pained slightly at the thought of leaving without saying goodbye, but she knew it was better this way.

They needed a clean break.

The winds weren't kind to the Valdrych and its crew as they sailed up and around the northern coastline of Osvolta. It was the second day of their sailing, and they were only now reaching the Elysian Bridge. Emmerich had been pushing hard, trying desperately to muster enough wind to fill their sails, but it battered against them instead. The seas were rough with an offshore tempest. They had sailed from Elithiend in the Valdrych because it was smaller and faster than the prince's other ships. In that moment, he would have given anything for one of his larger ones. They could better withstand the increasing swells that were already turning many of the deckhands green around the edges.

All they needed was to arrive in Trivellian soon after the princess. He couldn't allow her to have too much time to search and plot without him. She may have saved his life, but if she knew something, anything, about his poisoning, then she should have told him. He would not allow her to play the martyr. Not for him.

"You're headed for Trivellian?" Jasper inquired as he and Solveig walked the courtyard of North Watch after dinner. They had spent most of the day shored up in their rooms, trapped by a tempest making landfall.

"There are some things I need to investigate, and I'm concerned about the safety of doing so in Torrelin. There are eyes everywhere."

"What things?"

"Documents I may have stolen from the records in Luxenal Mine."

"About Malik?"

"About all of it. My family, our temple leader, what they've been doing these past few years."

"And you think Farrenhold is any different?" Jasper said, shaking his head. "Solveig, my father may not be as strict as yours, but he still answers to the Temple Leader. If it isn't safe there, it's not safe here either."

"I know, but I have to try." She tipped her head back to look at the cloud drenched sky.

"You've exhausted the mare. It can't go any further." Jasper said after a moment, "You'll take one of our stallions. They have better endurance on the drier terrain and can have you in the city in three days. You'll have to stop at Evrosei for supplies since you wish to travel light, but three days should still do it. Does Adira know you're coming?"

"No."

Jasper grimaced. "I'll try to get word out ahead of you tonight to give them some warning of your impending arrival."

"Think they'll be happy to see me?" Solveig jested, bumping his shoulder.

"Happy? No. Intrigued?" He chuckled. "Maybe."

CHAPTER FIFTY-SIX

What a Real Mine Looks Like

In the grasslands to the west of the Jewelled Jungle, halfway between North Watch and Evrosei Mine, Solveig made camp for the night. Not wanting to push the stallion too far. They wandered down to the river, giving the magnificent black and tan creature the opportunity to drink. Then she laid out some hay and carrots that the keepers at North Watch had packed with her. Before she headed back down to the river to fish for her dinner, something to add to the rice and pulses the chef had given her.

She rose with the sun the next morning, packing quickly to set off before the birds had even stopped their chorus. They raced across the drier terrain of Farrenhold. The towering trees of the Jewelled Jungle were still visible on the eastern horizon as they neared Evrosei.

If Luxenal were to be considered merely a mine, then Evrosei was a palace by comparison. There was no echoing orchestra of clashing chains, no torn clothing, or gaunt faces. Nor the terrible cry of a crashing whip. Armed guards were nowhere to be seen. Because the men, women and children who spent their days digging out the precious jewels and metals from the shafts below her feet were here by choice. And were paid handsomely for the hardship.

In Evrosei, there were no cramped and stinking quarters, only family homes and shared homes for those who didn't bring family with them. They weren't large by any means, but they were dry, and private.

"Can I help you?" a man with kind brown eyes asked. He wore what Solveig assumed was standard issue uniform, copper toed boots and heavy-duty overalls.

"I'm here to see Warden Etana. His brother Jasper sent me. The name is Solveig Maleen." The man's eyes lit up in recognition.

"If it isn't the Reaper of Luxenal at our gates." He smiled warily. "Got to be honest, love, not sure I should let you in. Word has it you're cursed." He leaned closer, whispering as though something evil lurked, "They say people drop dead wherever you go."

"And here I thought the people of Farrenhold no longer listened to myths and legends." The man chuckled at that, standing back with his arms crossed over his chest.

"Wait here, I'll go fetch the Warden. He can be the one to let you in."

As the guard wandered away, Solveig set about removing her supplies from the horse. Not stopping until everything, but the saddle and reins, remained. Her back was to the gate when a rough voice called out.

"If it isn't the hero of Farrenhold," she turned to see Eleric leaning against the gates. Even as the warden, he wore the same standard issue clothing as the previous man. A patch sewn to the front of his overalls, denoting his position, differentiated them. Sweat decorated his deep brown skin, gleaming under the afternoon sun. His silver-grey eyes shimmered as a broad smile grew on his face.

"What brings you to Evrosei? Come for some tips?" he jested, as he wiped his hands clean on the trousers of his uniform.

"I'm headed to Trivellian. Jasper ordered me to stop by and have the stallion tended to on the way." Eleric looked at the horse beside her then.

"Come on," he said, as he unlocked the gate and heaved it open. "I'll give you the tour, show you what a real mine looks like." His eyes glimmered as he spun on his heel.

Solveig fell into step beside Eleric as they walked toward one row of buildings. Workers waved to their Warden as they passed, smiles on their faces as Eleric led her inside.

"Afternoon, Davos," he called to the man sat behind a desk, "need to pick up some boots and overalls for my friend here." Davos only grunted in reply, as Prince Eleric dragged her off down the hall, fishing a stacked set of keys from one of his many pockets.

"Davos has been knocking around this place for as long as I can remember," he laughed. "I don't think I've ever heard him say more than ten words."

Eleric opened a door and led her inside. He rummaged through racks and bins before throwing clothes in her direction.

"Those are about your size. I'll give you a minute to change. Can't have you wandering around a working mine without protection now, can I? You'd ruin my streak of accident-free days, and I've got shares riding on it."

Solveig stared down at the clothing in her hands and the boots on the floor next to her. All of it was in stark contrast to the standard issue grey tunic and pants they doled out at Luxenal. The material was so thin it tore within the first day and stood no chance of keeping out the chill. The boots were a work of art, compared to the nonsensical fabric espadrilles they gave out in Luxenal. In truth, it was no surprise that many of the prisoners who survived often went home with at least one foot amputated. Sometimes both.

Once changed, she headed back outside to where Eleric appeared to be having an entirely one-sided conversation with Davos. The prince snatched her clothes, chucking them behind the man's desk.

"Hey!" she exclaimed.

"Don't worry," he laughed. "I'll have someone bring 'em to your room before dinner, and besides, Davos doesn't mind." They turned to the man. "Right, Davos?"

He only grunted in response.

"See," Eleric said, humour in his gaze as he turned back to her, "let's go, the tour won't wait and we're losing light fast."

They traversed the vast open dirt of Evrosei for hours. Talking about everything, except Malik and the rescue. Eleric explained how many of the people who lived at Evrosei didn't work in the deep dark earth digging for gems. There was a whole host whose jobs were to nurture the farmlands, harvesters, cooks, cleaners, laundry staff, all paid handsomely. Most everyone here worked in intervals, six months on, two months off. The mine closed for two weeks over solstice, allowing all operations to cease so everyone could see their families at their most sacred time of year. Even though the solstice was no longer a recognised celebration on the mainland.

For the Harvest Festival, which was little more than a week away now, the workers would all celebrate on site with a spread delivered from Trivellian.

Luxenal stopped for nothing, not the sick, injured, or dying. And here was Evrosei, shutting down for a fortnight long party. It was like they lived in a dream.

That night, the cool autumn air swept in through the window of the princess's guest room. She tangled in the sheets and pillows. Battling mental images and voices, from fanciful places with looming stone arches. Their centres swirling a sparkling black. To obsidian halls with red glass windows and some other place, with trees covered in twinkling lights. Silver walkways leading to small huts nestled in the branches of trees that towered so high they almost pierced the sky.

At first the images were wondrous, breathtaking, the promise of far-off worlds waiting to be explored. A place where life was untouched by the seedy black underbelly of corruption that had taken hold across mainland Osvolta.

She heard voices that were joyous, carefree laughter travelled along the wind until it twisted. The stench of sulphur and ash filled her nose and clogged her throat. Her skin felt as though it were set alight as she stared down at a bubbling, roiling magma chamber. A voice as cold and old as Osvolta itself echoed through her mind.

"Remember, I see all. I know all. You cannot run forever."

Solveig woke with a start. Sweat drenched her skin and hair, breaths coming in short, frantic pants. Try as she might, she couldn't banish the stench or taste of the nightmare as the eerie voice snaked around her mind. She was running out of time.

The room was dark as she fumbled for her clothes. Packing what little belongings she had brought with her, before quickly heading out. There was barely a soul in sight as she ran for the stables. Inside stood her stallion, her companion from North Watch already awake, as if it had sensed she was coming and needed to get away quickly. She loaded up their things, grabbing a small bale of hay strapping it to the back of the saddle as best she could before they rode off into the night.

The further away she travelled from Evrosei, the fainter the stench and taste of sulphur became. Until it was merely a memory that she could try to convince herself was truly nothing more than a bad dream.

CHAPTER FIFTY-SEVEN

Welcome to Farrenhold

The morning sun cast the deck of the Valdrych in buttery soft light. Prince Emmerich stood watching from the helm to where land drew closer with every beat of his heart. After days of battling unforgiving winds that threatened to capsize them. They had finally found favour sailing around the northernmost tip of Farrenhold and were at last sailing into the capital of Trivellian.

"Bring in the sails," Emmerich called to his crew, "we're getting close enough to drop some speed."

The Valdrych drew up alongside the dock and Emmerich and his crew were immediately engulfed in the heady salt air. Shouts from the fishermen filled the dock as they hauled in the morning's catch, ready to be sent off to market. Gulls cried above them, searching with beady eyes for scraps.

To the left, the city bloomed before them. Concentric around the port, spreading out wider and wider the farther back he could see, a mess of tangled alleys and dotted markets squares.

To the right loomed the sprawling sandstone palace, bedecked in gold and shades of green and blue tile artwork. Farrowvale Palace was heavily fortified, surrounded by high walls on all sides save one, where it sat on the edge of the ocean.

In the past, the royals of Farrenhold preferred their mountain stronghold. In their peaceful years since The Oracle's ascension, they had enjoyed more of the summer palace; until it slowly became their permanent residence. The keep in the mountain left to fall into disrepair.

Deckhands threw down ropes to the dock to help tie the ship up. Once Emmerich was sure that she was secure, he hopped down onto the dock below. Wrenn beside him, they headed toward the city, only to walk straight into a wall of steel.

Emmerich raised his head to meet a sea of anonymous helmets. They stood side by side, blocking their way. But through the centre of them moved a person, as graceful as they were predatory. Dressed in a cream gown cinched at the waist with a golden belt, a bejewelled hunting knife strapped to it. The colour of the dress glowed against their deep brown skin. Braided hair drifting around them in the salt kissed breeze, as the prince slowly met the storming silver gaze of the Etana heir.

"Never in my life did I think I would see an Elithiend march onto my dock as if he owned it," Adira retorted, circling him with a keen stare. "Search them," they ordered the guards with a flick of the head toward the visitors.

"Is that necessary, Your Highness?" Emmerich replied, arms raised as guards began pulling knives from his holsters.

Adira looked the prince up and down, arms crossed over their chest. "My father agreed to your visit. He did not agree to you arriving armed. You shall have your weapons returned upon leaving or when you prove yourself to be trustworthy, whichever comes first."

Once every weapon was uncovered and seized from them, Adira clasped their hands together, a crooked smile crossing their face. "Now, to the matter at hand, before I allow you to enter my city. Tell me, what can Farrenhold offer you, Prince Emmerich?"

Emmerich needed Adira Etana to trust him, and the only way to do that was to tell the truth. There was something about the way their eyes bore in to his, as if they could see deep into his soul. As though there was no use in lying because they would sense it instantly.

"Unfinished business with a certain princess. She left in rather a hurry, and I was hoping to speak with her."

"Why would Solveig Maleen be associating with you?"

"We were working together when I was poisoned, and she fled here. But only after she informed my second in command that we should leave their shores and never return. She's up to something, and since it affected me directly, I confess to say that I must demand to know what that is."

Adira regarded him. "And that's all you want with her?"

"Yes," he gritted. A lie. And he knew the minute the word had passed his lips, that it was outright and barefaced, and he could see on Adira's face that they knew it too.

"This will be an interesting way to pass the next few days." Adira muttered mostly to themself. "Princess Solveig arrived this morning. She's in her chambers freshening up, and the day is hers to do with as she pleases. Solveig has free rein across the country. She may sleep, eat, dance, and seduce her way through my city at her will. You, however, will be accompanied by a member of my guard or house. Is that understood?" Adira smirked, daring him to challenge them.

Emmerich tensed. But thought better of it. "Yes, Your Highness."

Adira smiled at that, turning toward their city with one arm outstretched.

"Then welcome to Farrenhold."

CHAPTER FIFTY-EIGHT

Interesting Dynamic

The sun was drifting below the western horizon when Solveig finally woke. Casting the city in shades of soft orange, blush pink and dusty violet. Boats swayed out by the northern harbour; their bells and rigs clanging softly against one another, as music and chatter from the port hub drifted along the wind. She pulled herself from the warm cosiness of the bed. Walking barefoot across the cool marble floor, the sensation odd against the still warm air.

When she arrived at the palace that morning, it had been like coming home. A servant led her to the chambers she inhabited as a child during term breaks from Erynmar Academy. Yet it still surprised her to find the wardrobe and cabinets stocked with everything she would need. As though Adira had prepared the rooms for this eventuality as soon as they returned from North Watch. It was Adira's own version of a peace offering, one that they had no need to extend but that Solveig would accept, regardless.

She wore a light blue gown; the material fluid as the ocean's rolling waves over her curves, cinching in at her waist with a golden belt. She stepped into a pair of jewelled leather sandals to walk over to the balcony as she haphazardly tied and twisted her hair back into a knot at her nape.

Running her hands across the rough sandstone, Solveig watched the last rays of sun fall away from the world, casting the garden in shadow.

Trivellian came alive with the blue glow of elemental flame. Voices sounded on the raised terracotta patio below, not loud enough to make out the words, but enough to catch her attention.

Two people sat across from each other beside the sparkling infinity pool. One was dressed similar to Solveig. Their golden accented braids draped over one shoulder as they reached out to grip the hand of the man before them. He had warm golden-brown curls falling haphazardly over his face, where his skin glowed even beneath the blue lights. Solveig's grip tightened on the edge of the balustrade as her eyes zeroed in on their joined hands. Wondering how and when the Prince of Elithiend had become a close friend of the future Sovereign of Farrenhold.

Under the flickering lights of the patio, Solveig's dress appeared darker, as though deepening with the souring of her mood. She stormed across to where the prince and the future sovereign sat. Mercifully, there was a good foot of distance between the two of them now. As she came to a stop, her fiery gaze alighted solely on the prince, who sat stoic. Refusing to meet her gaze, instead sipping slowly on the glass of water before him.

"I don't recall inviting you," she seethed, though Emmerich kept his eyes anywhere but on her. "A prince of the realm must be invited to visit another kingdom." Solveig continued as Adira swallowed down the amused chuckle that rose in their throat. Solveig's gaze swung to them.

"Since when are you friends with an enemy prince?"

"Who said I was?"

"You looked pretty friendly from the balcony," Solveig accused, throwing an arm toward her rooms. Adira's gaze followed it as another smirk crossed their lips.

"Spying again, Solveig? Perhaps I should reconsider the freedom I have afforded you."

"Why is he here?"

"I was bored." Adira shrugged.

"Bored? You were bored?"

"I'd heard rumours." They glanced between the two of them, "of the interesting dynamic between the two of you. I received your note first, whereas his arrived a day ago, and I must admit, I was more than a little curious to see this for myself."

Solveig only glared at her friend.

"Your jealousy is showing," Adira muttered. "Take a seat, order a drink, and cool off. Dinner won't be ready for another hour, which reminds me. I must check how things are progressing. Try not to kill each other in my absence. I hear it's terribly difficult to wash bloodstains out of the tiles."

Adira hurried back inside with a conspiratorial wink in Solveig's direction, as she took the seat Adira had vacated. She stared the prince down as he finally met her gaze, the blue swirling like a maelstrom, as a smile picked up one corner of his mouth,

"Hello, Princess. Did you think you could run from me that easily?" In one moment, the prince and the princess burned each other with their gazes. In the next, Emmerich was drenched head to toe as Solveig flung out a hand and sent a wave of water from the pool crashing over him. He stared down at his now water-stained suit, blinking in shock before an amused grin decorated his face once more.

"There's no need to ruin my clothes to get me to remove them," he chuckled, reaching for the lapels of his jacket. "You need only ask." He grinned as he slowly removed the jacket to hang it over the back of his chair.

The water had seeped through to his white shirt beneath, turning it transparent in places as it clung to every sun warmed ridge and valley of his chest and arms. Solveig realised a moment too late that she had been staring when she heard that smug chuckle escape his damned throat once more.

"My eyes are up here, Princess."

Solveig fought to keep the scowl on her face, but couldn't conceal the blush that travelled across her skin. Nor the drying of her mouth at the small glimpse of him.

Adira returned a moment later, coming to an abrupt halt beside them as their eyes went back and forth between the drenched prince and the blushing princess. They sipped at their refilled glass of wine, laughing lowly to themselves. "This is going to be rather entertaining indeed."

Solveig jumped to her feet then, ignoring her friend, "You were supposed to go home!"

"My investigation is far from over, which means, Princess, we are still partners." Emmerich stood, crowding her space until he engulfed her senses, and she didn't know where to look.

"Get used to it, Princess, you're stuck with me for a while longer." He leaned down, lips at her ear. Breathing in the soft scent of orange blossom that clung to her skin. "Besides, the sooner you get used to having me around, the easier this will get, and the drier we'll both be."

CHAPTER FIFTY-NINE

The Prince's Irresistible Charm

"You think whoever, or whatever, is killing the elementals is still out there?" Adira mused from behind their desk, gripping a steaming mug of black coffee. Early morning light filtered in through the balcony doors, casting soft shadows across their face.

"If it were just one person, the deaths would have stopped."

"And the reason you could no longer look into this from your own kingdom?"

"Whoever is doing this is close to my family. They got to the prince at the ball, mere hours after the new perpetrator was supposedly…"

"Executed." Adira supplied, mouth in a thin line.

Solveig nodded. "None of it adds up. There are eyes everywhere in Torrelin. I couldn't risk someone finding out my suspicions."

Adira studied their friend for a moment. "You realise this puts me in a difficult position? Farrenhold and Torrelin are still allies. If word gets out that I assisted an unauthorised investigation into the Torrelinian Royals, there will be the pit to pay."

"I understand,"

"Good." Adira placed their mug down, reaching out a hand to her. "Then make *me* understand. Give me a reason to allow this."

Solveig swallowed, her gaze falling to the floor as she whispered, "I have documents to support my theory, but in truth, the reason I'm here?" She sighed; head bowed. "I think I'm next."

"What?" Adira blinked, their mouth slightly agape.

"The signs are all there, nose bleeds, coughing blood. At first, I thought it was exhaustion, but when they went after the prince too, I realised they could be after me. That he may have been attacked by association?"

Adira stood, circling the desk to pull their friend into a hug, and Solveig held on tight, burying her face in Adira's warm neck. "I can give you access to the Royal Library. If there's information to be had, we'll find it there."

"Thank you," Solveig whispered.

Adira pushed back, holding Solveig at arm's length. "Now then." They smiled, popping a slice of honeyed melon into their mouth. "Onto more pressing matters."

"Such as?"

"What is going on with you and that oh so handsome prince?"

"Nothing."

"Careful now," Adira laughed, "you don't want to sound too defensive; it could make the wrong people suspicious."

"They forced us to work together, that's all. He was getting too close. I tried to put some distance between us, left without saying goodbye, hoping that he would get the message and return home."

"He doesn't seem the type to give up without a fight."

"There's nothing to fight for. I'm engaged, and he's the enemy."

"No one said it had to be a permanent deal," Adira winked. "He would be a damn good time, at least for a little while."

"I made a vow, and I intend to hold to it."

"You made that vow barely six months after Aldrik's death. They can't hold you to it. It'd be a healthy distraction."

"No," Solveig repeated, "I will not stoop to their level, not again."

Adira chose not to push the issue further. "I have some work I need to finish up this morning, but I can escort you to the library this afternoon, say one o'clock?"

"Sounds perfect." Solveig nodded before taking her leave.

In the more southern city of Trivellian, autumn still hung on. The sun blazed hot enough to allow the northern princess to sun herself out on the patio beside the pool. She lay in a one-piece bathing suit. Hair twisted on the top of her head; a glass of sparkling wine with a dash of orange juice on the table beside her. She drifted off to the sounds of the lapping waves against the moss-covered stone steps. She could get used to this life. Even in the summer, Marrelin City was rarely warm enough to allow this sort of activity. Those months brought rain, though they couldn't complain. The rain kept their lands fertile and the rivers full to bursting year-round. Unlike Farrenhold, they didn't have to rely on Hydromancers and Earth Breakers to survive.

Just as she was about to fall into the comforting embrace of sleep, Solveig sensed a shadow move over her, covering the upper half of her body. Praying it wasn't a building storm, she cracked one eye open to find the one person she had no desire to see standing over her.

"Nice to see you're keeping busy, Princess," Prince Emmerich quipped,

"Who said I came to Farrenhold for anything other than a holiday?"

"You're hasty disappearing act suggests otherwise."

Solveig shrugged, reaching for her perspiring glass of wine. "It was a spur-of-the-moment decision."

"Bullshit," the prince's retort echoed in her mind for a moment before she cracked both eyes open this time.

"Pardon me?"

"You heard me."

Solveig rolled her eyes. "I don't answer to you and I've no obligation to explain myself. Now if you don't mind, you're blocking my sun."

"I heard you're going to the library this afternoon."

"Your point?" She sighed, sitting up on her elbows.

"Whatever you're researching, I deserve to have input."

"If you want to come along and watch me select a few temperature raising, heart stopping romance novels, be my guest. But I doubt you'll find what you're looking for."

"Perhaps not," Emmerich whispered, "but you've provided me with an entirely new incentive to join in."

"And that would be?"

"Getting to watch that flush travel across your skin again when things get too... hot for you." His eyes blazed across her exposed skin. "I wonder if it travels beyond your cheeks and neck, lower perhaps. What I wouldn't give to uncover that little secret."

Solveig sat up hastily, grabbing her wrap to cover herself. "It isn't your secret to claim."

"Says who?"

"Says me and the engagement ring on my finger."

The prince only shrugged. "Nothing's official until you have the matching wedding band on. Until then, I won't stop until I've unravelled every piece of you. Little by little, chipping away at those walls you've so expertly built." He leaned closer, forcing Solveig to lean back as she stared at him. "I want it all, Princess."

"You can't have it all." Anger flashed through Solveig as she jumped to her feet, pushing the prince back a step, a hidden dagger pointed straight for his neck.

"You think you're so charming and irresistible, don't you?" she seethed. Stepping closer as he stepped back, gaze wary on the shining steel. "You're forgetting one thing."

"And that is?" He gulped, feeling the point of her blade graze his neck.

"That I'm not a prize to be won. I'm not a piece of furniture you can own. I belong to me and no one else. The answer was no yesterday, it is still no today, and it will be no tomorrow. There is nothing I want, nor desire to give you, and no reason for you to stay any longer." She ripped the blade away, hiding it once more. "Go home, Your Highness."

She turned to pick up her drink when the prince finally spoke on a shaking breath, "I'll go home, when you agree to go with me."

"Did you not listen to a word I said?"

"Oh, I heard you, Princess." It was his turn to step closer now, "But see, we aren't in Torrelin anymore. The only person who can command me to leave is rather entertained by having me here. So, you want me gone, fine, come with me." His eyes sparkled at the idea, "let me sail you around the coast of your beloved country, see it from another point of view."

"I can't stand to be in the same room as you, never mind aboard that miniscule boat forced to be close to each other for days on end."

"Liar," he quipped, not missing the slight tremor of her hand as she raised her glass to her lips.

Solveig did not respond this time; instead, resorting to the same tactics she had engaged in the previous night. Flinging out a hand to summon control over the water in the pool. Except today the prince was waiting. Anticipating her exact manoeuvre. He built a wall of solid air around them; watching as the water crashed above them, refracting the light from the sun in rainbows across her pale skin.

"That wasn't very nice, Princess."

"I never claimed to be."

"Come sailing with me."

"Fire will sooner reign down from the beastly maw of the Ignis Mountains than I will set foot on your ship."

"We'll see about that." He shrugged, dropping his hand. A few stray droplets of water splashed atop their heads. As he sauntered back toward the palace, he called over his shoulder, "What time are we going to the library?"

"Drown yourself and save me the trouble."

"That's your power, not mine, Princess, and I'd hate to damage one of those priceless books."

"The time," he repeated when she didn't respond.

"If I tell you, will you leave me alone?"

He pursed his lips. "For now, I suppose."

Solveig rolled her eyes, "two o'clock, here on the patio, don't be late or we'll go without you."

"I won't be. I'd hate to keep you away from all your heart stopping reads."

CHAPTER SIXTY

Secrets and Lies

The Royal Library of Farrenhold made its counterpart across the border appear more a hovel. A stark white building topped with a gleaming golden dome and spires at each corner. Beyond the great mahogany doors lay a bustling scene. People searching stacks and discussing books in hushed tones at tables lit by elemental flames. Torrelin's library was deserted. Though open to the public, the common folk of Torrelin had little time to indulge in the idea of reading for pleasure. There were many citizens who grew into old age, unable to read at all.

Adira rested their hands on their hips, surveying the room. "Did you bring the list?" Solveig nodded as she stared.

"Good. There's a private room in the back reserved for my family." Adira moved through the crowded stacks and Solveig followed, feeling every pair of eyes on them as they passed by.

Over the next few hours, they poured over the list and the little information Solveig had absconded with but could find nothing out of the ordinary. No names that stood out as not belonging. It was as Solveig had feared. Whoever had poisoned the prince was a wolf in sheep's clothing.

Everyone was a suspect, and she had no way to narrow them down, save one. Top of the list was none other than Queen Asta herself. She wasn't afraid nor foreign to slipping substances into drinks, but would she poison a foreign prince? Solveig couldn't be sure. Such a grandiose display of aggression wasn't her mother's style, she preferred more underhanded tactics.

Adira eyed Solveig hesitantly. "I don't think you're going to find the person responsible for the poisoning here. This is something you can only discover through observation."

"And the other issue?" Solveig pressed, sensing they weren't done.

Adira leaned back in their chair, running a finger across their bottom lip. "I'm not sure that our library will hold any books that differ vastly from yours. We can still try, but don't get your hopes up." They leaned forward, tapping their fingers atop the edge of the desk before meeting Solveig's gaze once more.

"You said the prince exhibited different symptoms?"

"Yes, Al…" Solveig paused, as the name caught in her throat, hands clenching as she spoke again with a deep sigh. "Aldrik and Xanthe both died, choking on their own blood. With Emmerich, there was this shaking, foaming at the mouth and…"

"And then?" Adira pressed.

"Nothing," Solveig whispered, her eyes downcast, "he was still."

"Anything else different?"

Solveig paused again, thinking hard about what little she remembered, her mind already hard at work boxing away the hurt as it had with Aldrik. There was Commander Bleeker, expressing concern about the prince's well-being, and the smell. That acrid scent and taste that had clung to the prince that night. Was it truly a hint of whatever had been lurking in his bloodstream?

"I think I sensed it."

"What?"

"Earlier in the evening, he smelled... bitter. Then when I was healing him," she spat with a shaking her head at the mere idea of what she had done being construed as healing. "I sensed it again. The more I drained him, the more it faded."

"Okay," Adira said, eyeing their friend beneath drawn brows as Solveig met their gaze once more.

"It wasn't there before, with Aldrik or Xanthe. I sensed nothing. Not as their blood pooled and clogged their throats, there was nothing except the tang of iron."

"What if it wasn't poison?"

"Sorry?" Solveig said, head shaking.

"Think about it. What's one of the first things we learn in the guilds?"

"How to use our powers?"

Adira sighed, rolling their eyes. "What else?"

"How to fight," Solveig said after a moment, "how to use weapons, make poisons and their antidotes..."

"Exactly, Solveig. Do you remember a single poison that was odourless *and* tasteless because I don't?" Adira jumped to their feet, pacing back and forth as they spoke. "They all left a marker. Either before or after death, and there you sit, telling me you sensed nothing as you held them through their dying breaths. We know their inspections showed no signs of lingering poison. You're a Hydromancer, Solveig, healer by trade or not. Part of your power is sensing the body's fluid."

"Okay?" Solveig hedged.

"What if it wasn't poison? What if it was simply the curse? And the two scenarios are linked only by their locations and the victim's proximity to you? Aldrik and Xanthe's symptoms in their last moments match those who died of the curse, but Emmerich's don't."

"It can't be," Solveig whispered, mind racing.

"Why?"

"I... I... How?" Solveig stared at her friend, slacked jawed, and misty eyed.

"First, we go for the books on known poisons and search for the markers."

"It could be something new. Something created by the anti-magicists."

"Perhaps," Adira allowed, before countering, "but then why not use the same method on the prince too?"

"I don't know," Solveig whispered, slumping in her chair.

Adira moved to sit on the desk beside her. "You have the perfect undetectable poison, and you decide not to use it despite its proven success? That doesn't make sense and you know it; these deaths aren't connected."

They poured over volumes of books on the known poisons and their recipes. From the sweet scent of oleander blooms to the stomach burning acidity of Nyteberry. The utterly paralysing Hemlock to the seemingly harmless glass of milk from cattle feasting on snakeroot. But as Adira had suspected, none were described as untraceable.

Solveig was fighting desperately to keep her tangled emotions in check. What if Adira was right? The idea was almost too much for her to stomach, because that meant she was living on borrowed time. That whatever had come for Aldrik and Xanthe was now breathing down her neck, too.

"You said the prince found you looking into records, right?" Adira asked, closing yet another book on poisons. All of them said variations of the same thing. If a poison were present at the time of death, it stayed, because the body would no longer be processing it.

"I was searching for correlations between the deaths and old powerful families, and then any connections to those who had seen their family line of power run dry."

"What did you find?"

"They were all there," Solveig stated.

"And the families whose power had run dry?"

"None of them were mentioned in any history of powerful families, nor were they on the list of deaths."

Adira sat back in their chair, rubbing at their eyes in frustration.

"It's a start, I guess."

"We have the correlation," Solveig agreed. "Perhaps we should look for the same pattern here in Farrenhold? See if we get the same result?"

"And if we do?"

"We cross that bridge when we come to it."

Adira only nodded their head and together they headed back out to the main room to pull even more books.

"You know I'm surprised the prince didn't demand to join this little excursion."

Solveig chuckled, avoiding her friend's gaze.

"What?" Adira leaned into Solveig's line of sight.

"I may have told him the wrong meeting time."

"Solveig Aila Maleen, you did not!"

"He's insufferable," she reasoned. "I don't need his help."

"Whether you think you need it or not, it's an extra pair of eyes to go over all these books."

"He'd only get in the way."

"How would he get in the way?" Adira smirked.

Solveig blinked, mouth in a thin line as she hoisted her heavy pile of books. "He was too close, too observant, too..." She paused, searching for the right word. "Much."

"He got under your skin?"

"Perhaps."

"No wonder you don't want to go there."

Solveig rolled her eyes and sighed. "I haven't much honour left. Who will I be if I break my promise to Gabriel now?"

Adira shrugged. "Well, you'd be a lot less tense for one." Solveig swatted their arm.

"I'm being serious."

"As was I!" Adira giggled. "What Gabriel doesn't know won't hurt him." They slid closer, although there was no one around to overhear them. "The walls of Farrowvale are thick. You could make a whole manner of noise, and no one would be any the wiser. Have some fun. He looks like he'd be a damn good ride."

"You've said as much before," Solveig muttered, "yet I don't see you offering yourself."

"He has more equipment going on than I would like."

"Thought that didn't bother you?"

"When I was sixteen, then I grew up and realised, women are much better at well, everything." They shrugged. "Maybe you should give it a shot."

Solveig choked on a laugh. "Believe me, I would if I could. Yet it appears to be one of my Oracle blessings to be attracted to the sex who make it their lives work to belittle and underestimate us."

Adira clicked their tongue. "'Tis a cruel world, my friend, but someone must do it. At least the prince is nice to look at."

Solveig had to fight away the visions of the prince's handsome face. The unruly mop of curls she wanted to rake her hands through and the glimpses of his powerful chest.

"So is Gabriel," she insisted.

"I haven't seen him in a long time, but if memory serves, he's all broody stares and icy words." Adira shivered. "That prince, however? He has flames in his eyes and on his tongue when he's around you, and it's not every day you find that."

"In another life perhaps, but in this one, going down that road will only lead to heartbreak. I survived it once, and believe me, that's enough for one lifetime." Solveig shuddered, thinking of the bone crushing fear she had felt at the sight of Prince Emmerich's prone body at the ball. How it had pushed long buried memories of Aldrik's death to the forefront of her mind.

"Take it from someone who knows Solveig. Nature is an unstoppable beast. You can fight it all you want, but all things succumb. It is the way of life. We hurtle toward it every day. Sometimes it's easier to just let go."

"If that were true, then nature would have stopped me a long time ago," Solveig countered.

"Maybe that's just it," Adira whispered solemnly.

"What is?"

"The weakness, the nosebleeds, coughing blood. Perhaps it's all nature's way of telling you that the power you wield goes against everything. That the more you use it, the more it feeds off you." They stared Solveig dead in the eyes, all semblance of humour gone. "Nature will have its prize, Solveig. That is something even you can't avoid."

Late into the evening, under the hazy blue flicker of elemental flame, Solveig jumped from her chair.

"What is it?" Adira demanded, muscles tensing, braced for an imminent attack.

"How do you have that book?" Solveig stammered.

"What are you talking about?" Adira leaned across the desk. The tome was old, the pages browned, ink fading. Still, they could make out the words of stories of old. Legends of the Seers of Vanahold who had long since deserted these shores.

"That book is blasphemous!" Solveig bit out, "And it was sitting out there for anyone to pick up. This text belongs in the vault."

Adira had to force a deep, steadying breath before picking up the book and moving it away from Solveig.

"Our kingdoms have a lot in common, but there is one way in which we differ."

"And that would be?"

"The Seers are our ancestors. Vanahold could once be seen across the Bay of Trivellian before they disappeared. We have never denied their existence, for we are their legacy."

Solveig staggered back in horror, blinking rapidly. "What you're saying right now is blasphemous."

"So," Adira hissed, "no one here is going to report me. Farrenhold is not Torrelin."

"This is insane."

"Do you remember my mother?" Adira said flatly, placing the book down on the table, dust moats flying in its wake.

"No."

"I do," they said with a wistful smile. "She used to tell me a story. A prophecy her family had passed down for generations."

"Adira..." Solveig warned, stepping backward.

"No Solveig, you need to hear this."

"I have no desire to."

"Too bad." Adira flicked out a hand, summoning rock from thin air to seal the door shut faster than Solveig could blink. "Now that I have your full attention." They gestured to the chair Solveig had vacated. Reluctantly, she returned to her seat, her eyes never leaving Adira.

"She would repeat this prophecy so often that the words burned into my memory, but never once did I utter them around you."

Solveig thought she saw a glimmer of guilt cross their face before it vanished completely. "You need to hear it now."

"Dark as night,

a dangerous might.

A kingdom torn.

Royal born,

to end our age-old plight."

Solveig sat stoic, as Adira looked on. "Don't you see? They knew something, were waiting for something, someone."

"To do what?" Solveig replied.

"I don't know."

"What plight?"

"I don't know."

"Which royal? When? What dangerous might?" she demanded; each word harsher as her anger grew.

"I..."

"Don't know," Solveig finished. "Only The Oracle has the power of foresight, Adira, you know that."

"Do I?" Adira's eyes narrowed.

"The Seers were frauds. They spoke in riddles so generic that anyone could claim any prophecy was about them."

"What would be the point of passing down a prophecy through generations if it were meaningless?"

"It may as well be a fairy tale."

Adira shook their head. "After all you've seen, all you've done in their name, you still believe The Oracle is all good?"

Solveig paused, because she knew, deep down, that Adira was right. She had seen it for herself, the darkest depths that The Oracle would go to, to root out those who were a threat to their rule.

"Well," Adira pressed.

"No ruler is all good."

"You're evading the question," Adira seethed, leaning across the table. "Do you think Malik hasn't told me about what goes on in that mine? About that, that *thing* that rips into your mind and allows The Oracle to see every thought you've ever had. Surely, you've asked yourself why it's even necessary. For a being who's supposedly omniscient, they shouldn't have to lower themselves to such violent deeds to see inside our heads."

"I came here for your help, Adira. If I wanted a lecture on all the cruel and terrible things The Oracle has done, I would have invited the prince and his commander along."

"If you want my help, you're going to have to stop accepting everything they tell you at face value and start recognising that which is staring you blind in the face."

"And what would that be?"

"That every single one of them is lying to us! Manipulating us, holding us hostage to their way of thinking, it's time, Solveig."

"To do what, exactly?"

"To bring their lies and misdeeds out of the shadows and into the light. You should know better than anyone the stain that lies beneath the surface of their rotted hierarchy."

"It's hopeless," Solveig sighed, thinking about all she had learned of her family. All the evidence she had of their misdeeds that she didn't know what to do with or if people would even listen to her, the Reaper.

"No, Solveig. It's necessary. How many more people must die before you'll see it? The Oracle is lying to us all. Whether indirectly or not, it doesn't matter at this point. It's time we uncovered all their darkest secrets."

CHAPTER SIXTY-ONE

Forbidden to Intervene

On their return to Farrowvale Palace, Solveig made straight for her guest chambers with nary a glance in Adira's direction. That evening she was woken from her restless slumber to the sound of someone pounding on her door, a deep, smooth voice shouting beyond it,

"Open the door, Princess."

She made no move to do so, having no desire to confront him now. Not when it felt as though her entire world was crashing down around her.

She spent hours locked away in that room. The servants of Farrowvale were the only ones allowed entry, as they carried fresh trays of food and drinks in every few hours. For a full night and day, she pondered everything that Adira had placed at her feet. Resigned to the fact that she had already considered most of it herself over the past month. Her bones chilled, as she stared the knowledge in the face that if another person could connect the dots in the same way, then it couldn't be by chance. It couldn't be a mistake. She had to accept the possibility that something more sinister than her family was spreading through Osvolta.

She would need reassurances, just as Adira had needed from her before she agreed to help her. This was the only way it could work. Solveig would not jeopardise everything now, not on a hunch that could cost them all their lives if they were wrong.

Still, she did not exit her rooms. Instead, enjoying the peace whilst she could. Lounging atop the chaise, drinking her coffee on the sun warmed balcony as the waves crashed against the palace walls, and the wind danced through the lush garden foliage. Farrenhold was a paradise to her, a beautiful salt kissed dreamscape she longed to hold on to forever, even as it rapidly slipped through her fingers.

The next evening, Solveig finally ventured beyond her closed door. Her footsteps echoing along the shining marble floors of the palace as she made her way out to the patio where a servant was attending her within seconds. Moments later, she had a bottle of chocolate spiked red wine and a spread of cured meats and aged cheeses alongside toasted bread on the table beside her. She watched the sky darkening across the ocean; the sun hanging low framed her body with its warm glow. She sipped her wine, savouring the warm chocolate notes, when a tall figure dressed all in black slid into the seat across from hers. She didn't have to look to know who it was. Could already feel the heat blooming over her skin from his presence, and the anger that poured off him in waves. Eyes still gazing toward the horizon, she murmured.

"Did you have something to say, or do you intend to annoy me by just existing?"

"You lied to me. Again," the prince's mahogany curls were already in complete disarray before the breeze even caught hold of them. She wondered how long he'd been stewing over this.

"Your point?"

"I thought we were in this together."

Solveig scoffed, gaze flicking across to him, "then you're more naïve than I thought."

"Perhaps." He leaned forward in his chair. "Or maybe I was hoping you wouldn't let me down again."

His words were meant to cut her, but she had drawn her walls back up so high they failed to lacerate. "Life is full of disappointments."

"Why did you tell me the wrong time?"

"For the same reasons, I didn't ask you to come to Farrenhold with me."

"Which are?"

Solveig slowly placed her glass back on the table. Facing the prince fully now, she whispered, "that I didn't want you here, that it's not safe for you."

"Not safe?" he questioned, ignoring the lie he'd sensed in her words. "And it's safe for you, the Reaper of Luxenal, to go swanning around a foreign city?"

"I can take care of myself."

"I know you can, but that doesn't stop me fucking worrying about you," he implored.

An eerie silence spread between them, almost choking the air as the last rays of the sun deserted them, and Farrenhold took on its usual nighttime blue haze.

"It's not your responsibility to worry about me."

"Like it or not, Princess," he said, gaze falling to her shaking hands with a knowing smile. "I've already seen inside those walls you've painstakingly constructed. I've seen what every kill has done and continues to do to you. I see your weaknesses, and your strengths and I know you can hold your own in a fight, but this is foreign territory. Do you have any idea what it's like to know you were out there wandering the streets? To know that anything could happen to you, and I wouldn't be there to stop it, or even help, because I'm trapped here under Adira's orders. First you lied, then you made me worry, and, to top it all off, you ignore me too."

Solveig's face betrayed no emotions. "I wasn't aware that I owed you anything."

"Owed me? No, you don't owe me anything, but I thought we were friends."

"We aren't friends," she laughed, eyes drifting skyward.

"Then what are we?"

"I don't know what we are, but friends is not it."

"Please," he whispered, voice as gentle as morning sea mist. "Stop shutting me out. This is not yours to bear alone."

Solveig finally glanced at the prince and saw the sincerity of his words in that flaming blue gaze. "If we do this together, there's no going back," she warned.

"I sailed halfway across the country to find you." Emmerich replied, staring at her, trying his best to not let the hope kindle within him, "I have no intentions of turning back."

"No one can know how close we're working together."

"Fine," he seethed through gritted teeth, prepared to take whatever she offered. "Tell me what you know."

As Solveig recounted the afternoon to the prince, he sat in rapt attention, focused solely on her. She, of course, left out a few choice details, mainly the conversation she and Adira had had about him. His ego was big enough already.

She divulged it all, right up to the prophecy, and the Seers, for that was not her secret to tell. Though she thought deep down that they could trust the prince with this information — given his blatant dislike for The Oracle — she wasn't willing to break Adira's trust.

But Emmerich caught her hesitation. "There's something you're holding back."

"It's not mine to tell."

"Then whose is it?"

Solveig looked at him with desperate, pleading eyes. She had never begged for anything in her life, and yet here she was, on the verge of doing so; to protect her still repairing friendship.

"Most likely mine," Adira said. Appearing as if from nowhere, they popped a grape into their mouth, chewing thoughtfully for a moment before continuing. "Am I correct, Solveig?"

The princess merely nodded.

"Make no mistake, Prince, I am not yet convinced that I can trust you with my kingdom's secrets." They paused, pouring their own glass of wine. "However, given that your country lies outside The Oracle's thrall, I will tell you this. My brothers and I come from a long line of Seers on our mother's side. She used to tell me a prophecy every night before bed."

"Which was?"

"Dark as night, a dangerous might. A kingdom torn. Royal born, to end our age-old plight."

"Adira believes the prophecy to be accurate," Solveig muttered, mostly into her own reclaimed glass of wine. "But as I told them in the library, the Seers were proven to be a race of charlatans. We cannot assume that the message is accurate. We don't even know when it was supposed to fruition."

Adira's eyes simmered with anger at Solveig's flippant remarks, and the implication that their deceased mother was a fraud.

The prince eyed them for a moment before taking a deep breath as he rubbed a hand down his face. His gaze fell to the floor.

"My grandmother was a Seer."

"Excuse me?" Solveig cried while Adira whispered, "Impossible."

Emmerich snatched the glass from Solveig's hand, drinking down the remaining liquid before continuing.

"You heard me, Princess," he said, burning her with his gaze, "and I assure you, Your Highness, it is possible."

"The Seers deserted Osvolta. They took refuge in their home of Vana-hold until it, too, disappeared. No one knows what became of them."

His gaze flicked to Adira then, "The Seers fled the mainland because The Oracle and its followers persecuted them. In Elithiend, they remained in their position as guardians of the future. We never abandoned them; you have my word on that."

"How many?" Adira whispered in awe, "how many of them are left?"

"Hundreds," Emmerich smiled, as tears threatened Adira's eyes at the prospect of a piece of their soul not being lost after all.

"I should like to meet them one day." They swallowed tightly. "My mother died when I was a child. I remember little of their ways beyond the prophecy she would tell me. That I would know when the time came to act, though I always found that statement odd."

"Why?" Solveig asked. Trying to find her feet in a conversation that was completely foreign to her.

"Seers were bound by their gifts, Sol." Adira smiled sadly, clutching her hand, "it is why their prophecies were vague. They could see the future, but were forbidden to intervene."

Solveig pulled her hand from their grip. "Sounds convenient if you ask me," she declared, snatching her glass back from the prince to refill it.

"You think knowing how your friends and family will die and being powerless to stop it is convenient?"

"They weren't powerless." Solveig shrugged, "if what you say is true, why can't they warn everyone when something bad is coming?"

Adira shook their head, "you need to pay attention Solveig, nature..."

"Is an unstoppable beast," she finished.

Adira nodded, "even if they went against their vow of secrecy. Nature would find a way. The journey to get there may change, but the destination is absolute."

CHAPTER SIXTY-TWO

Please. Stay.

Long after the sun had set, Solveig sat alone on the moss cushioned steps at the edge of Trivellian Bay. Icy water roiled and splashed to meet her as though it recognised the power that lay within her, however little it may be. The briny air was a calming force as it twined through her loose hair, braiding the ends together.

She didn't know how much time had passed. Only that the moon had tracked far across the sky, when the ocean's rhythmic waves met the soft melancholy strains of a piano melody drifting down from the palace. The sadness of the piece enraptured her. Without thinking, she rose to her feet. Silently padding her way up the slippery steps; along the cool stone of the patio in search of the soul responsible for creating such a heart wrenching melody.

She could see open balcony doors off to the right, where gauzy curtains danced as though the lyrical refrains blew them outward to tangle through the night. Hesitantly, she approached the entrance. When she saw who sat before the grand piano, her heart lurched to a sudden halt, before shocking to life again, beating double time.

She watched as the Prince of Elithiend poured his soul into the song. His eyes were closed, fingers deft as they flew across the keys. He'd dressed casually, in a loose cream night shirt, and dark trousers. The curled locks of his hair were in complete disarray, as though he had spent the entire evening running his hands through it. Cooped up in that room until he could stand it no longer, so he'd snuck down to the ballroom to unleash his anger in the most achingly beautiful way.

Solveig was used to harsh words on sharp tongues and raised fists to relieve anger. Not swaying hips and rolling shoulders as he pounded the keys.

She stood, mesmerised by the sight of him unguarded. Wondering if he'd wanted someone to find him. He hadn't chosen a private location or quiet outlet to vent his frustrations. Still, she worried she was intruding on something innately private. Had barged her way through a locked door to his mind and took up residence in the centre.

Yet she couldn't walk away, couldn't leave the prince to his thoughts. There was nowhere else she wanted to be than sitting beside him on that bench. With the warmth of his powerful body against hers, as his hips rocked and swayed to the beat of his own making. As he lost himself to the music, she'd sit silently, watching, because he would want her there as much as she longed to be there. For once, the wraith wanted nothing more than to step out from the shadows and bask in his light.

Reluctantly, she moved away, releasing the curtains, and stepping one bare foot back out on the patio when he spoke.

"Did you honestly believe that I couldn't feel your eyes on me?" His voice cracking as he continued to play, not missing a single note. Solveig spun to find his eyes on her.

"I'm sorry for intruding," she whispered as his gaze set her aflame from across the room.

"You weren't. I could've closed the door if I didn't want anyone to see me."

"Did you wish for me to find you?"

"You said that, Princess, not me."

"Then I shall leave you to your melancholy."

The music stopped abruptly at her words.

"Please." he breathed. "Stay."

Solveig stilled for a moment, swallowing softly before she whispered, "Okay." She turned on the spot, walking directly to him. His eyes glittered with humour as he studied her, a single brow raised. She could feel the flush creeping up her skin from his perusal.

"You can come closer, Princess. I don't bite."

"I don't want to be in the way," she reasoned, as she leaned against the piano, worrying her bottom lip between her teeth.

"You could never."

She had no answer for the raw honesty in his gaze. Nor the openness that frightened and electrified her all at once. She walked stiffly to sit beside him, as she had imagined moments earlier. In every place they connected, warmth radiated. The air crackled with sparks of tension as they sat in silence, staring at one another, their breaths the only sound.

"Any requests," he said after a minute, breaking the tension.

Solveig shook her head. "I used to play, too," she whispered, "before."

Emmerich didn't push, instead bringing his long fingers back atop the keys, resuming the melody. She watched in awe at the speed at which his fingers danced, feeling the vibrations of the piano in her bones. Matched with the fire that raged where they made contact, it had Solveig on the verge of forgetting her own name, as her blush deepened.

"How did you learn to play so fast?"

"My mother taught me as a boy, and I kept up the practice through school and into adulthood." He paused for a moment, letting his words sink in before drawing his gaze to her. "I could show you?"

Solveig sensed his eyes on her, burning her in the most delicious way as she nodded, too caught up in the moment to vocalise her assertion.

Swiftly, Emmerich rose to his feet, moving to stand behind her. He placed his hands back on the keys. In this position, with his arms encasing her, the warmth that radiated between them built into an inferno. His chest pressed flush to her back. She could feel his breath against her neck as he whispered in her ear.

"Place your hands atop mine." She did as he instructed, as though pleasing him was all she wanted to do. She felt his chuckle at her back, his whisky smooth voice sending shivers down her spine.

"Whatever you do, don't let go," he whispered as his hands flew across the keys, so fast she had to grip him tighter.

The music flowed around the room, softer now, without the pedals to dampen and stress the notes, but still spellbinding. How long they stayed in that position neither knew. The prince's arms strained from playing at such an awkward angle, though he had no desire to move.

They swayed and rolled together. Through every soul wrenching note, as the music built and built; faster and faster to an almost dizzying speed before crashing down around them in its crescendo. Leaving them both breathless. Still, neither of them moved. Content in the bubble of their own creation, a world where only they existed.

The prince reluctantly moved his hands to close the cover. Solveig's fell to her lap only for him to grasp them, unwilling to let her go.

"Trust me?" he whispered against her skin, nuzzling her neck. The scent of her filling his nose, ensnaring his senses as she nodded, as lost in the moment as he was.

The simple gesture was all he needed. He gripped her by the waist, lifting her until she perched atop the covered keys. He came to stand between her legs, their bodies flush together as he held her face in his hands. Brushing the dark strands of hair from her eyes as she clung to his waist, wrapping her legs around his hips, he brought their foreheads together.

"Tell me to stop," he whispered.

She didn't.

"Last chance, Princess. Tell me to stop, tell me you don't want me to kiss you, tell me how much you loathe me, tell me—"

Her lips slanted over his, silencing him.

"You talk too much," she whispered against his soft mouth.

His hands tunnelled into her hair, bringing her face back to his so he could fuse their mouths together once more.

The dark prince and the twisted princess burned together. With desperate moans and feverish kisses, they devoured each other. They moved to the silent orchestra of their hearts. Solveig's hands travelled beneath his shirt, skirting over the taut muscles of his abdomen. Fingers drifting with his quivering breaths as he tried to pull her closer. She gasped as she felt his hard length brush against her core. Stunned by the evidence of the raw effect she was having on him. Emmerich seized that opportunity to invade her mouth, nipping her lower lip, tangling their tongues together in more a dance than a war.

Beyond the open balcony doors, the sun lightened the sky in shades of soft blue and pale gold as it rose. The spell surrounding the two young royals didn't break, not until the first calls of the dawn chorus filled the surrounding air, and they pulled away in shock.

Solveig touched shaking fingers to her bruised lips as a small shiver wracked her body. Her eyes locked on the prince's smug smile when the sun shining through the windows caused something to sparkle on her hand.

Her engagement ring.

It was as though someone had dumped a bucket of ice water over her. Her eyes deserted the prince's gaze to stare unblinking at the ostentatious diamond upon her hand.

"Solveig?" Emmerich whispered, and she jumped, not at the sound of his voice but at her name on his tongue. The first time he'd ever said it to her. How she longed for it to have come in a different moment. A different time. When something other than shame wasn't pulling her away from him. She untangled herself from his embrace, even though it felt wrong to lose his touch, as though their bodies, their souls, belonged together.

"This was a mistake." She heard herself say, almost like her voice belonged to someone else, because how could she mean it when her heart sang an entirely different tune? Yet still, that damned voice continued to lie. "We shouldn't have done this," and it wouldn't stop.

Solveig moved to walk away, but Emmerich reached for her wrist, pulling her back to him. Cradling the side of her face with one hand, the other light at her waist, and the truth was laid bare for them both as she leaned into his touch.

"It wasn't a mistake," he bit out, "you can't tell me you don't feel that."

Before, there had been mere sparks of warmth from his touch. Now that she knew how he tasted, how his lips moved against hers, everything burned akin to an inferno ravishing her blood.

"I'm engaged," she whispered, not meeting his gaze, the first truth she had spoken since the sun rose.

"End it."

"I can't."

"Yes, you can," he reasoned, placing his other hand on her face, forcing her to look at him. "Come sailing with me," he whispered.

"Emmerich..." His name on her lips caused him to shudder.

He knew she was slipping through his fingers with every second that passed. "Get on my ship and never go back. You don't owe them anything. They don't need you."

"I can't simply leave. I have responsibilities..." She paused, tears brimming in her eyes. Remembering the death knell hanging over her head that she still hadn't confessed to him. How could she put him through what she had with Aldrik? How could she knowingly do that to another soul?

"They have manipulated you at every turn. They don't deserve you." His thumbs drifted across her cheeks. "Don't let them ruin you. You could be so much more, Solveig."

"Don't," she pleaded, "it's already too late. I'm already ruined. I've done too much I can't take back." Tears fell from her eyes then, "I need you to understand, please."

"I don't," he declared, catching her tears as they fell, "the only mistake is if I let you walk away now, you aren't ruined, you can still come back. You can make them pay for everything."

They stayed wrapped in each other's embrace, foreheads touching, hearts beating as one. When a new voice cleared their throat across the room. Solveig's face fell into the prince's neck, where he cradled her head softly as his gaze flew up to find Malik Etana watching from the threshold. His eyes flickered between them, gaze hard on where Solveig hid in the prince's neck.

"Adira has requested to speak to you, Solveig," Malik said through gritted teeth, his voice cold as ice.

"Very well," Solveig murmured, wiping the tears from her face as she pulled herself reluctantly from Emmerich's hold. But he gripped the hand he still held tighter, forcing her to turn and look at him once more, utter sorrow in her eyes, hurt in his.

"It wasn't a mistake," he repeated, so only she could hear, "for once in your life Solveig, be selfish."

It was the wrong thing to say to an utterly confused princess at that moment. She pulled her hand from his with a finality that stung as she straightened her back, her mask of indifference sliding into place. "I am a Princess of Torrelin. I can never be selfish. My people, my country, must always come first. I have made commitments I will honour. I'm sure you can understand that."

Solveig walked away with a broken heart, tears returning to her eyes once he could no longer see them.

"Did it have to be him?" Malik hissed as she approached him, nodding his head in Emmerich's direction.

"My life is none of your concern, Malik Etana," she skewered him with her red-rimmed gaze. "I thought I made that much clear the last time we saw each other."

"After everything we went through. Together." He implored. "It truly meant nothing to you?"

"I saved your life, Malik. You saved mine. We are even." The Reaper of Luxenal left two men with wounded hearts in her wake that day as she went in search of Adira Etana. One would recover with time, as he was recovering from his years in the mine. The other? He would give her space, as he tended his own wounds. But he had her taste on his tongue now, her fire in his blood. He knew how she felt in his arms. He would give her time, but he would not give up.

Emmerich returned to the chambers he was *technically* still forbidden from leaving without escort, coming face-to-face with his friend pacing the room.

"Where the hell have you been?" Wrenn Bleeker exclaimed in frustration.

"I need your help."

"And I'm afraid to ask why."

Emmerich grinned sheepishly at her as he rubbed the back of his neck. "I need to convince the princess to go sailing with me."

"And why would I help you get alone time with a woman who's as likely to slit your throat as she is kiss it?"

"I need her," he whispered; gaze clouded as the realisation hit him all at once.

"You barely know her."

"I can't let her go. Not yet."

Wrenn thought it over for a moment, resigned to the truth that, at the end of it all, he was her prince, friends or not. She was bound to his bidding.

"Fine, but don't blame me when she sends you to a watery grave. Better yet, write Valentina a letter so she doesn't kill me on sight when I return to Elithiend without you."

"Valentina won't kill you," Emmerich laughed, to which Wrenn raised a brow.

"Fine, I'll write the damn letter."

CHAPTER SIXTY-THREE

Wish for More

"What?" Solveig groaned in response to the knock at the door, from beneath the pile of feather pillows she was using to block the light.

The door to her room flew open. Adira strode in, a myriad of servants in tow carrying trays of food, drink, and pails of steaming hot water for the bath.

"Well, that's not a regal sight," Adira muttered as they leaned against a bedpost. Solveig pushed the pillows away from her face, clutching the blankets to her as she stared through the mess of dark hair tangled over her face.

"Is there a reason you've come barging into my chambers, or am I to guess until nightfall?"

"Don't mouth off at me. I brought you food and coffee. A bath is being readied for you. Now get out of that festering pit. My afternoon has cleared, so we're going to the library."

Solveig released a second dramatic groan as she rose from beneath her fort of pillows as if rising from the dead. "You couldn't have picked another day?" she griped, wiping the sleep from her eyes.

"The Harvest Festival starts tomorrow. I'll be far too busy. Besides, it's not my fault you stayed up with the gods, doing who only knows what." They chuckled with a knowing glance.

"I'm not even going to ask who told you," Solveig muttered as she pulled on a robe, heading for the bathing chamber.

"Well, it certainly wasn't you, though you had every opportunity to this morning!" Adira called.

"The more you needle me, the less I'm likely to tell you."

"I'm not sure I need you too," Adira smirked, and Solveig's head popped back around the door frame to the bathing chamber.

"What is that supposed to mean?"

"I had not one, but two unannounced visits after you left." Adira shrugged. "The first from the prince's commander demanding I keep the two of you apart." They paused. "You wouldn't know why they're concerned, would you?"

"Wrenn Bleeker has never been a fan of mine. I can only imagine the stories she's heard since arriving here."

"She hasn't left the palace since she arrived as per my orders."

"Who was the second? A gossiping servant?"

"Of course not. You'd have to give them a reason to do so, like say." They pursed their lips, an amused gleam in their eyes. "Giving the prince cause to ask me to stop you from running."

"I'm not sure that was a question, and if it was, I'm not answering." Solveig slammed the door to the bathing chamber shut.

"The more you protest Solveig, the more fantastical and scandalous my imagination is going to get," they called after her.

The door swung open with a billow of steam as Solveig strode out, freshly washed, and dressed. Dark hair hanging wet down her back, pausing when she spotted Adira sat at the table by the balcony snacking on chunks of melon and sipping on coffee.

"You're still here?" she muttered, walking over to take a seat.

"Had to make sure you didn't crawl back into that bed."

"I'm dressed, aren't I?" She poured herself a cup of coffee mixed with lavender and honey milk. Her favourite Farrenhold delicacy.

"Still." Adira shrugged.

Solveig sipped her coffee, sighing as she settled in her chair, allowing the sweet honey and calming lavender to wash over her. "You wouldn't happen to have an Aire Wender or Pyromancer in your employ, would you?" she asked, signalling to her wet hair dripping orange blossom scented water all over the marbled floor.

"Why don't I send for the prince?" Adira smirked. "I hear he's quite the adept Aire Wender. I'm sure he wouldn't mind assisting."

Solveig glowered at them, a faint growl rumbling in her throat that caused Adira to laugh.

"Oh, calm down, would you? I already sent for one. They'll be up after we've eaten." Adira's eyes never left her as they took bites of fresh fruit, followed by one last sip of their coffee, dabbing at their lips with a napkin.

"So," Adira stated.

"For Oracle's sake," Solveig muttered, her head falling back, "we kissed, okay?"

It was fortunate that Adira had already swallowed their coffee, or it would have sprayed across the food that still sat before them. Instead, they blinked a few times in shocked silence, before regaining their thoughts and smiling.

"How was it?"

Solveig rolled her eyes, setting her coffee down. "Does it matter? It was a moment of weakness in the stark loneliness of nighttime. It meant nothing."

"Spare me the false innocence," Adira smirked. "As long as I've known you, the dark has been your friend. You've never been alone in its embrace."

Solveig had to bite back a retort, "regardless, he's the future ruler of an enemy kingdom. We both know we can't go there."

"Not forever, no," Adira agreed, "but you can still have fun whilst he's here. It doesn't have to mean anything."

"Adira..." Solveig warned.

"You like him, don't you," they whispered, "as more than a friend."

"Don't be ridiculous, I hardly know him."

"Who says you must know him? How does he make you feel?"

"Free." Her mouth slammed shut, eyes growing wide.

"Free, huh?" Adira murmured, sitting back in their chair.

"No," Solveig insisted, "I didn't mean it that way."

"How did you mean it?"

She thought for a moment, all the while Adira studied her, watching for a lie. "He makes me believe I can be someone other than who I am," she whispered, "as though I can lead a life where I'm not this, one where I'm not a killer, one where I'm more."

Adira's eyes softened. "Solveig, that's a good thing." They reached across the table to take her hand.

"No." she snapped, pulling away. "It isn't, because it makes me dream and wish for something that isn't possible. I need to keep my distance from now on."

"That's one of the worst ideas you've ever had, and you've had plenty of them lately."

"Why?"

"There's life in you again, Solveig. Life that I did not see a month ago in North Watch, and I see it most when he's around."

"That's not possible," Solveig shook her head.

Adira sighed, "keep telling yourself that, but I know what I've seen. He merely enters a room and your entire demeanour changes. You light up brighter than the sun even when you're arguing. That man has lit a fire under you again, and I'd hate to see it go out."

"He asked me to go sailing with him," Solveig muttered, staring into her cooling coffee.

"Maybe you should."

"And then what?"

"Baby steps Solveig, get on the ship first. Figure out the rest later. Come back here, go back to Torrelin or..."

"Or?"

"Go to Elithiend with him, if he asks."

"If I go there, there's no way back."

"There's always a way, Solveig, and you'll always be welcome here."

"And the matter of my engagement?"

"A deal made on paper when you were still in such grief you weren't thinking straight," they said as though it were simple.

"Whatever you decide, Solveig, there will always be a place for you in my court. We can survive just fine without the alliance with Torrelin."

"Mere days ago, you were reluctant to even consider it."

"Things change."

"Would your father agree?"

"My father has been itching for an excuse to sever ties with your shithole kingdom for years. Whatever dirt you've got on them, he would be more than happy to hear it."

CHAPTER SIXTY-FOUR

Something in Common

The four of them made a striking group as they wended their way through the cobbled streets of Trivellian. All around, townsfolk were setting up for the festival the following day. Orange, green, and golden garlands were strung across the street from building to building. Stalls and stages lined the pathways, their signage promising a multitude of delicious food, drink, and entertainment.

"Tell me, Prince," Adira said, turning to walk backward so that they could watch him. "Do you celebrate any holidays across the Dead Strait?"

Emmerich's gaze flew to Adira from where it had been fixed on the woman stood as far from him as she could get. The same woman who had not once glanced in his direction, even though she had clung to him in the early hours.

"We celebrate the old holidays. Harvest, Solstice, some factions celebrate Hallows Eve and others the Spring Tides. To be honest, I'm more surprised that you still celebrate the old festivals."

"You'd be right too." They smiled. "Wouldn't he Solveig?"

Her eyes swung to Adira before flying across to the prince she had been determinedly ignoring. "Sorry I missed that."

Adira only smirked. "Emmerich expressed surprise that we celebrate the old festivals. I said he was correct to be."

"Oh, yes," Solveig swallowed, eyes narrowing. "Farrenhold's direct connection to the Vanahold Seers kept them stuck in the old ways." She said sharply, "Torrelin has celebrated none of them since the days of ascension."

Wrenn Bleeker stared at the princess dumbstruck, "then, what do you celebrate?"

"There used to be a monthly celebration for those who came of age. Each guild would host a banquet for the families of their newest members, but that stopped a few decades ago. The New Dawn, the day of The Oracles ascension, is the start of our new year and there's also The Anniversary."

"You mean the day an entire country perished?" Wrenn countered.

"The Oracle's ascension is a happy day. It granted Osvolta a peace and freedom we had never experienced before. A chance to live outside of Estrellyn's control." Solveig spat.

Wrenn stared at her plainly. "Innocent people had to die for your *freedom*? All for you to wear magic cuffs and watch your historic lines of power wither and die."

"That's enough, Commander," Emmerich declared, pulling her back. His and Solveig's eyes met for the first time since that morning, confusion and longing tangling between them.

"What's The Anniversary?" he said calmly, trying to douse the situation, but the commander's words had already hit their target.

"The date of my father's coronation. Families travel from across Torrelin to pay their respects and offer blessings."

Emmerich stepped closer to her, putting himself between Solveig and Wrenn. "Why did the monthly celebrations stop if you still hold the ceremonies?"

"We still have to register the elementals in our society. However, it was deemed poor taste to celebrate them when many had died or lost their power completely."

Emmerich nodded, as though he was truly trying to understand her world, as if it would make it easier for her to trust him, confide in him.

With the festival less than a day away, the Great Library of Farrenhold was quieter than it had been the last time.

"Was there something in particular we were supposed to be searching for?" Solveig asked, avoiding the prince's piercing gaze, that she sensed heating her blood from the entryway. The air between them crackling like the smouldering logs in the fireplace.

"We didn't finish our list of families," Adira said, blowing dust off a heavy tome that had been left sitting haphazardly on a lone table.

"I was hoping to do some research on the Seers," Emmerich replied.

Adira's eyes met his. "You claimed the Seers are still alive and well in your country. Surely, they can tell you all you need to know?"

"The Seers of Elithiend have imparted all knowledge passed down their many generations, but Farrenhold is as close to their homeland as any of us can get. Vanahold was once a part of your territory. I want to know if there are any gaps in my country's knowledge."

"He's got it in his head that the Seers knew more about The Oracle than they're saying." Solveig sighed, picking at her fingers to appear nonchalant. "It's a waste of time, if you ask me."

"I didn't," Emmerich muttered, growing impatient, "and what do you care if I waste my time?" His eyes alight as he sauntered across the room toward her. Standing so close, it forced her to step back against the wall until there was barely a breath of space between them.

"You were the one who declared us a team," she sniped.

"And you did your own research behind my back, Princess. I'm only giving you the space you obviously crave, unless you'd rather work together, read the same book... at the same time?" He reached up to tuck a strand of dark hair behind her ear as his own fell into his eyes. "You can hold one cover, and I'll hold the other."

Solveig let out a shaky exhale. That had he not been as close as he was, he may have missed. Instead, the warmth caressed his neck, sending gooseflesh across his skin. "Or maybe it's that after everything we've..." He paused again, searching for the right word, his eyes fixed on her mouth. "Shared. You still don't trust me."

"That's enough, Emmerich," Wrenn scolded as though he were a misbehaving child. Taking a step toward the smirking prince whose gaze flicked to her over his shoulder.

"Stand down, Commander, this is between me and the princess." His eyes met Solveig's again.

"What's it to be, Solveig?" He whispered her name as though it were illegal. Sending her heartbeat skittering, but his hold on her had shattered. That split second of reprieve he had granted her had allowed her the time to pull herself back together; shuttering the emotions he had all too easily pulled from her again.

"Do as you wish, Prince," she muttered, raising a hand to shove at his chest, forcing him to take a step back. "Waste your time reading old fairy tales. See if I care. Just take your friend with you." She flicked her gaze toward Wrenn. "Adira and I have real work to do."

Solveig shouldered past him down the nearest aisle, heading for the private room she had worked in previously. Throwing the door open and sitting down at the table. She propped her head up atop crossed arms, releasing the breath she had been holding so tightly she thought she might explode. The door to the room creaked open again. Solveig raised her head, ready to cuss out the prince for following her; but it was Adira who stood with their back against the door, arms folded.

"That was interesting."

"I'd rather not talk about it."

"Tough."

"You dragged me here, Adira. If all you wanted to do was gossip about my catastrophic love life, we could have done it at Farrowvale over a glass of wine and trays of food. So, whatever you have to say can wait. Work first, gossip later."

Adira shrugged. "I was going to say it's a good job that you have water magic flowing in your veins."

"And why is that?" Solveig sighed.

"Because you would have surely been set aflame with the way you were staring each other down. I thought I was going to have to lift the roof off this place to let some air in."

"Ever the dramatics."

"Still." Adira smirked. "If I had a connection like that with someone, I would have tasted every inch of them by now."

"Adira." Solveig slammed her fist on the table, rubbing at her brow with the other hand. "Enough, please."

Adira raised their arms in surrender. "For what it's worth, I'm sure the prince has long since wandered off to the alcove I sent them to. But out of the goodness of my heart, I'll even go fetch the books we were studying, and you can carry on hiding in here."

Solveig didn't respond at first. Her head once again lying atop her arms, a blistering headache rampaging its way through her skull, when she heard the door creak open again.

"Adira?"

"Yeah?"

"For the love of the blessed have them bring in some ale, wine, anything."

"You've got it, Solveig." They chuckled.

Up on the second floor, tucked away in an alcove that was so far from the central halls, the blue flames barely reached them. Where it smelled of old, musty books covered in dust that had sat untouched for centuries. The prince and commander got to work.

"What exactly are you hoping to find?" Wrenn asked from where she leaned against a precarious-looking bookcase.

"I'm not sure."

"Helpful."

"Sorry," he sighed, putting the book he had been reading down, "I can't shake the feeling that all of this is connected. The deaths and the loss of power aren't two separate events."

"And you think an ancient line of a dying race holds the key?"

"They foresaw almost everything."

"Yeah, foresaw and did nothing," she said, her voice laced with bitterness.

"We cannot blame them for holding true to their traditions and ideals, no more than you can blame the princess for hers."

"That's different,"

"How?" Emmerich glared at her.

"She's worse." Wrenn supplied.

"How did you reach that conclusion?"

"At least the Seers washed their hands of it all completely. She's been an active participant."

"There is only one to blame here," Emmerich snarled.

"And who's that?"

"The Oracle,"

"Careful Emmerich, Farrenhold may not be as pious as Torrelin, but they still worship that thing."

"Then we need to find proof."

Wrenn shook her head, still not moving to help. "Why? So you and the princess can work together to bring The Oracle down and walk off into the sunset?"

Emmerich merely shrugged.

"You know, at first I thought they'd drugged you," she said, stepping closer. "That maybe that witch queen of theirs was slipping something into that mystery tea you were drinking, but now I can see I gave them far too much credit."

"By all means, Commander, don't stop now."

Wrenn straightened her back. "You're being naïve, you are a prince, a guardian of an entire country."

"You think I've forgotten?"

"Then act like it!" Wrenn hissed. "Why do you care if she believes you? When did this become about proving to her that everything she has known is a lie? You came here to protect your people, to ensure that whatever was killing them stayed on these shores."

"Watch your tone, Commander."

Wrenn ignored him. "You brought me here for a reason, Emmerich. You need to decide what that is. If I am merely your commander, then I shall return to the ship and ensure it is ready for our departure. If I'm here as your friend, then I will stay and help you. But I cannot be both. As your friend, I want you to be happy. As your commander, I want my country to be happy. Those ideals clash horrifically, especially where that princess is concerned."

"You're here as my friend, of course," Emmerich swallowed, jaw tight.

"Then tell me what I'm missing," she pleaded. "Why is she important? Why her?"

"It's not just her, it's Adira too." He paused. "My grandmother told me once about a prophecy. She said that it was old, passed down for centuries, that no one was sure who the original Seer was, or who it was about."

"Okay," Wrenn whispered, trying her hardest to disguise her scepticism.

"Something is coming Wrenn, and I think now is the time that old prophecy may come true."

"How do Adira and Solveig tie into this?"

Emmerich paused again for a moment. "Adira told Solveig the same prophecy just days ago, when they did not know my ancestry."

"Which is?"

"Dark as night,

a dangerous might.

A kingdom torn.

Royal born,

to end our age-old plight."

"And we're giving it credence now because?"

"Two separate families of Seers, Wrenn. Passing down the same prophecy for centuries, word for word. If it were the discredited memories of a madman, it would have only one link to its origin."

"It could be any of you," Wrenn muttered, "but then you aren't the only ones born royal. It could be Valentina, or Adira's brothers, or maybe..."

"I don't think it's about one person, but a group. A representative of every element, all of them royal born."

"Then the three of you aren't enough. You need more."

"Now you're catching on."

"That's why you insisted on coming here? You needed Adira's power?" Emmerich nodded.

"But you don't have a representative of every element yet."

"Right again," Emmerich grimaced, "but I'll worry about that later. First, we find the proof."

"And then?"

"Then we convince everyone else."

"As your commander, I should tell you that you sound utterly ridiculous right now."

"And what does my friend Wrenn have to say?"

"She jumped off a cliff for you to practice your cushioning when we were in training so obviously, ridiculous or not, you know I'm with you."

CHAPTER SIXTY-FIVE

Find Proof

S olveig and Adira worked in tandem silence. Adira had brought Solveig a pitcher of ale to keep her happy, and it seemed to have done the trick. After hours of silent work, Solveig leaned back in her chair, pinching the bridge of her nose against the lingering headache.

"Everything okay?"

"Fine."

Adira's eyes narrowed on their friend at the sniped reply. "Find anything?"

One of Solveig's eyes opened then, landing on her friend across the room. With a sigh, she leaned forward again, her elbows meeting the wooden table.

"Only more evidence to back up our theory. Name after name, month after month," she flicked aimlessly through the pages, "they don't cross over."

Solveig herself wasn't sure which was worse. She had faced losing a loved one, had barely come out on the other side. Would she really miss her powers if they vanished? It had never been something she had relied on, always seen as more of a weakness than anything else. Her head flew up at the thought.

Weakness.

She jumped from the chair, scanning the spines of the books strewn across the table between them.

"What is it?" Adira asked, crossing the room to her.

"There are outliers," Solveig gasped, still searching.

Adira took a step back. "Do you need a break?"

"What?" Solveig asked absentmindedly, still searching for something that didn't want to be found.

"Not two minutes ago you said there was no crossover, and now you're claiming there're outliers?"

"Me," Solveig gritted, staring desperately at the books before her.

"What about you?"

"I'm an outlier. I come from two powerful family lines. According to the pattern, my family should lose members the way the Whitlock's have. But we haven't, we're weakening. Compared to the rest of them, I have virtually no power to speak of."

Adira bit their lip, as they took a deep breath, "Solveig..."

"What?" Her head swivelled to her friend.

"I'm not sure you are an outlier." They stepped closer, placing a hand atop hers on the desk. "You're already coughing blood from over exertion, Sol." Sorrow flooded their gaze as Adira regarded their friend, watching as the realisation dawned on her.

Solveig fell back into her chair, still holding Adira's hand. "It doesn't make sense. None of the other records list people weakening before their deaths. They just died."

She turned to face Adira fully then, "You said yourself perhaps my situation is different. Maybe mine is nature telling me to stop; that the twisting of my power is poisoning me the more I use it." The hope that lay in Solveig's gaze was enough to break Adira's heart in two.

"Solveig I... how bad is it?"

"I don't know. He never told me what was happening." Adira pulled her into a tight embrace then, feeling the bone deep shivers that wracked her body.

"I'm scared," Solveig whispered into their braids as she gripped on for dear life. "I should be ashamed that he thought he had to keep it from me. Guilty that even if he had said something, I would have failed him, anyway."

"None of this is your fault," Adira declared, pushing back to make sure that Solveig understood every word. "You did not do this to him. It was not for you to fix." They gripped her arms tightly. "Look at me Solveig."

It took a few moments, but eventually, she did, straight into Adira's steadfast silver gaze. "Somewhere here is an answer. I believe that. I will not stop searching for it, and neither will you. Aldrik's death is not your fault, do you hear me? It is not your burden to bear."

"I wish it were that simple."

"It is that simple. You were barely twenty-one when it happened, Solveig, a girl in love, with her whole life ahead of her. Why would you have feared the worst?"

When Solveig didn't respond, Adira moved to pile the books that were still splayed across the table. "Go get some air," they ordered. "I will tidy up here and when I'm finished, if you're up to it, we can delve into your outlier theory. If not, we'll find the others and head back to Farrowvale. Oracle knows we need a good night's sleep ahead of the festival tomorrow, anyway."

"I think I've skimmed about twenty of these damn books by now. They're all merging into one giant mess of doom." Wrenn groaned.

"If you need a break, go ahead," Emmerich muttered, his head still down, eyes scanning line after line.

Wrenn eyed him for a moment before closing her own book and leaning toward him, "at least tell me you found something."

"Maybe. It's hard to tell. The Seers could be tricky with their wordings."

Wrenn scoffed, "You mean how 'royal born' could mean one of you, or all of you damn head cases? Not to mention the lack of time frame."

Emmerich raised a brow, glancing over at her. "Your snarking is not helping, either."

"Just being honest." She shrugged. "I get they can't interfere, but surely they can be more specific with their doomsday tales."

Emmerich slammed the book shut with an exasperated sigh. "Did you find anything useful? Or did you spend the last few hours fanning yourself with the pages?"

"Not sure this musty old thing," she said, blowing dust off the tome, "would make a good fan."

"Wrenn," Emmerich warned, his patience wearing thin.

"Not one thing," she sighed, "but then I wasn't the one who grew up with a Seer for a grandparent, so what do I know about deciphering prophecies?"

"Remind me again why I put up with you?" Emmerich muttered, leaning back in his chair.

"Stop bitching and tell me what you found," she laughed, taking a seat next to him, "besides, you would have died of boredom by now without me around."

"Yeah, sure." He rolled his eyes.

"Focus, Em." Wrenn snapped her fingers in his face. "Research now, declarations of love for me later, okay?"

"It is a damn miracle I haven't thrown you overboard yet," he said, swatting her hand away from his face.

"I suppose it's lucky we're on land then, isn't it? You'll have to come up with a new murder fantasy for me."

Emmerich threw the heavy tome down before her, sending more dust flying, eliciting a coughing fit from the commander.

"Death by dust," she mused when she caught her breath. "That's a new one. Can you at least lie on my gravestone, make it sound cooler?"

"Read the page, would you?"

"Fine," she said, turning to the book. When she was done, she looked back up at the prince, confusion clear on her face. "Was I supposed to understand any of that?"

"Read it again," Emmerich pushed.

"Not sure how that will help, but fine," she said, doing as he asked, focusing now on each word individually, for altogether, it made little sense. Except for one part, a few lines that to most would be completely inconspicuous, and yet it gave her pause.

"You see it?"

"The darkest eruption,
half marked for expulsion.
A terrible arrival,
in a fight for survival.
blinded to loss by unwavering devotion."

"It's about The Oracle," she whispered. "It must be. A dark eruption? That's gotta be the Caldera." She paused for a moment. "Half marked for expulsion?" She turned to Emmerich.

"Could be Elithiend and Estrellyn, could be the dead families."

"Terrible arrival, obviously The Oracle itself," she muttered.

"A fight for survival?"

"Perhaps for those who didn't go along with The Oracle?"

"Maybe," she mused, unsure, "and the last line?"

"That's what I noticed first," Emmerich said grimly, "blinded to loss, it could be anything, loss of status, loss of friends."

"Loss of power." Wrenn supplied.

"And loss of life," Emmerich finished, "all for their unwavering devotion to a false god."

"Is it clear enough, though? Can it be explained another way?"

"Do you see any other meaning for this?"

"No, but then I barely saw this one, never mind a second option." She paused, thinking for a moment. "Have you found another record of this prophecy?"

"No," Emmerich sighed, "but I found the year it was recorded."

"Which was?"

"A century before Estrellyn fell."

Wrenn's face turned to stone at the implication, "if this is what we think it is," she gritted, "they had plenty of warning of what was to come."

"Put yourself in their shoes," Emmerich reasoned. "They were sworn to not interfere. They see only glimpses, not a complete picture."

"Still, you're gonna need more." Wrenn shrugged. "That princess is about as stubborn as you are. One record of a prophecy that gives you exactly the proof you need will not cut it with her. You'll need more accounts, and even then, it might not be enough."

"It has to be," Emmerich insisted.

"You're asking a woman who was raised to view The Oracle as a benevolent, omniscient deity. Someone who has had it spoon fed to them all their lives that the Seers were frauds." Wrenn paused, thinking for a moment.

"What is it?"

"Find proof."

"Didn't we already establish that?" Emmerich asked.

"Not of this." Wrenn shook her head.

"Find a prophecy that came true. Find as many as you can. The more Seer prophecies you can prove authentic, the harder it will be for her to deny this one."

Emmerich stared at his friend in shock. "That might be the most helpful thing you've said since we left Elithiend." He smiled. "Go grab a drink. We're in for a long night."

Wrenn groaned, slumping down in her chair. "Should've kept my fucking mouth shut."

"At least I'm making you do it now and not tomorrow." Her head perked up at that.

"Save the world tonight, celebrate tomorrow," she mulled it over, before thrusting out her hand between them. "Got yourself a deal, Prince."

CHAPTER SIXTY-SIX

Say Yes

Solveig wandered the halls of the library, searching for distraction from the wayward journey her thoughts had taken. She cleared the first floor, wandering up and up, looking for all the world as though she were searching for a particular book. Yet the names etched on cracked and aged spines didn't register. She hadn't been paying attention to her surroundings at all as she walked straight into a tall figure. Their broad back was draped with a fine silk blend jacket, the blue so dark it was almost black.

"Sorry, I wasn't..." she began as her eyes raised in the same moment the figure turned to her and she looked up into the blue-eyed gaze of the prince.

"By all means, continue that train of thought. It'll be twice in one day you've apologised to me." He smirked. Solveig continued to stare up at him for a moment, before thinking better of what she was about to say, moving to walk by him instead.

"Excuse me," she muttered.

But Emmerich was no fool. He'd spent the last month watching her every move, down to the twitch of her fingers, when she became aggravated. The woman before him, though, was as close to a ghost as he thought he would ever see. Without a second thought, he reached out gently to grab her arms, the familiar tingling warmth spreading through his fingers; along his palm and up his arm.

"What is it?" he whispered, as though she were a creature that was easy to startle as he gently tugged on her hand, pulling her toward him.

Solveig stared down at their joined hands, desperately trying to hide the reaction he wrought upon her.

"Don't insult me by pretending you care," she rushed, trying to tug her hand free.

His eyes darkened at her words, "when did I ever give you the impression that I didn't care," he seethed, growing tired of dancing around what he felt for her. Tired of her throwing accusations at him based solely on his reputation and not the man she knew. He wanted her to see him, as he had grown to see her. All the dark, gnarly, twisted roots that made her who she was. He hadn't turned away. Yet she continued to hold him back with every step.

Still, she would not meet his gaze, had no answer to voice, as he waited minute after minute, staring down at that maddeningly beautiful face. Her skin tinged with a soft glow from days spent in the Farrenhold sun, her dark as night hair had a few lighter strands running through it. On the outside, she was more approachable, and yet somehow, despite everything that had happened, she was more closed off than ever.

As time wore on, an exasperated growl ripped from his throat, jaw clenching. He gripped her hand tighter, pulling her deeper into the dark alcoves of the library for privacy, heartened at least because she hadn't objected.

Solveig followed his every step without fumble or hesitation. Once they were hidden away, he crowded her against the stacks; his arms raising to frame either side of her head, his body so close it stole all her senses.

That inexplicable pull thrummed between them, leaving Solveig no choice but to look up into his shadowed face, meeting his scorching gaze head on. Here in the dark, where she felt safest, he looked for all the world as if he could be any ordinary man, and she desperately wanted him to be. How was it fair that she had loved and lost in such a cruel and catastrophic way, only for her next chance to be forever out of reach?

"Talk to me," he whispered, lowering his mouth close to her ear. His breath against the side of her neck sent waves of gooseflesh across her skin.

"It's nothing," she gritted out. "I'm tired."

Emmerich brought one hand down to grip her waist, the other still shielding her face from view.

"Lean on me. I can handle it."

"Why? In the end, it would all be for nought."

"Stop fighting."

"It's not that simple. Fight is all I have done every day for the last four years."

"Then I'll teach you."

"You don't have that kind of time," she laughed, as a voice in her head whispered, *neither do you*.

"I'm a prince." He smiled. "I have all the time I want."

"You're a prince who has already been away from his kingdom for far too long."

"So, come sailing with me then. Let me show you the far reaches of Osvolta that I know you've longed to see."

She stared at him, eyes wide, mouth agape. "How did you?" Her words died on her tongue as he placed a soft, warm kiss, feather light against the spot on her neck where her pulse raced beneath her skin.

"I watched you when you thought no one was. In the darkest and quietest moments, searching the distant horizon. Staring out beyond the mountains and oceans. I've sailed the seas enough to know longing when I see it." He pressed another kiss, just below her ear this time; the tip of his nose grazing her cheek. "I can show you the pieces of Osvolta you're missing. From the towering black of the Ignis Mountains, to the treacherous passage of the Dead Strait, all the way to the glimmering beacon of my home shore." His head rose, so he could look her in the eyes once more, and she found only sincerity lying there. "If you'd let me, I'd take you to the edge of the known world and beyond."

A small, frustrated moan found its way out of the princess's lips as she immediately missed the warmth of his mouth on her neck.

"Say yes."

She longed to see the distant shores of Osvolta. But more than anything else, she wanted to see them with him, and that was a dangerous notion, a fool's hope. Her head fell back against the stacks he had her crowded up against, desperately trying to figure out a way through. She was at a crossroads, return to Torrelin and hope the answers to her plight lay there or see more of the world before nature called her home.

"I—" Emmerich brought one long finger up against her lips, halting her words, his eyes burning with mischievous fire. "Before you tell me no again, and wound my ego further, I have a proposition for you." He paused, waiting for her to object. Only continuing when she showed no signs of doing so.

"Spend the day with me tomorrow, no researching, no commitments, no titles, just Emmerich and Solveig. Two ordinary people enjoying the Harvest Festival and then you can decide." He stepped closer again. "Let me show you that you can lean on me."

Solveig stared into the endless depths of his eyes, emotion and sense warring within her. She wanted more than anything to throw caution to the wind and march straight onto his ship with him, sail away and never return.

"I'll go to the festival with you." A grin spread wide and bright across the prince's handsome face, and she couldn't help but smile back at him, at the quiet joy she beheld in his gaze.

"My dear Princess, one day you're going to realise that I will happily take whatever crumbs you deign to give me." His face drew closer to hers. Solveig's breathing hitched as she craved his lips on hers.

"Emmerich!" He froze, his mouth achingly close.

"Fuck," he whispered, bringing his forehead against hers instead, savouring the last few seconds of her touch, her scent, of her.

"Tomorrow," he whispered, eyes alight.

"Tomorrow," she whispered, and he tore himself away from her, heading back toward Wrenn. Solveig, dazed and breathless, found her way back down to the ground floor where Adira was waiting for her, worry marring their brow.

"Where have you been?"

"I think I agreed to go on a date," Solveig whispered. Adira's jaw practically hit the floor.

"With whom?"

"Emmerich," she forced out. "Tomorrow."

CHAPTER SIXTY-SEVEN

The Harvest Festival

Shimmering rays of pale gold sunlight pierced the sea mist surrounding The Bay of Trivellian as gulls chorused the imminent dawn, their cries despondent at the lack of seafood scraps to chase. For this dawn brought with it the Harvest Festival, a day of rest that saw even the fishermen leave their boats tied to the dock for the day. Everyone across Farrenhold would revel in the peace. Either lounging in their homes or on the lush golden beaches, watching the morning pass in quiet calm and building anticipation of the festival to come.

A soft knock woke Solveig at daybreak. The servant set a tray down on her table before scurrying away in silence. She dragged herself from the lusciously soft pile of pillows and blankets; donned a robe and slipped her feet into shearling slippers. There was a carafe of coffee, a bowl of steaming porridge with cinnamon and honeyed apples. Slices of toast with spreads ranging from marmalade to strawberry, and one she did not recognise. Sitting at the top of the tray was a glistening white rose, thorns trimmed, and a note tied to it with a thin ribbon of night black silk. She sat, pouring herself a cup of coffee before reaching for the note as she plucked a single slice of honey drenched apple from the bowl of oats.

Eat up and rest well, Princess. The day is yours to do as you please, for the evening is ours. Meet me in the square as the clock chimes five. Try the

blackberry spread, a delicacy from my home, and a small taste of the things
waiting for you should you agree to run away with me.

A smile lifted one corner of her mouth as she reached for the mystery
spread. Wondering what could make it special compared to any other? As
she bit into the crisp slice; she realised that the tart berries had been stewed
to create a spread that was a shrine to autumn itself. Sweet and spicy. It was
deliciously warm, and she ate every drop.

High noon passed by with little fanfare, those who had set up stalls in the
main square and the streets winding off it began loading them up with
their stock. Barrels of wine, ranging from sweet summer berry to autumnal
spice, ripe golden ales to the darkest of stouts. There were fresh fruits cut
into an array of designs kept from decay by the expert hands of an Aire
Wender sealing them from the elements. Musicians were setting up on the
main stage, checking the tuning of their instruments.

As the minutes ticked by, more people filtered into the bustling sandstone main square. Excited chatter filled the air as bakeries unloaded trays
of fresh goods. The scent of savoury pastries stuffed with garlic and cheese
wafted around the square, alongside mouth-watering meat pastry twists
with various dips and seasonings. There were sweet pastries too, cinnamon
sugared, fruit compote and honey cream filled. On the opposite side of the
square, a union of the kingdom's farmers and butchers took up the entire
row. There, they were turning slow roasted chicken, pork, and beef over
glowing hot coals; the steam rising and wafting along the wind.

Adira and Solveig arrived in the square together. The former dressed in
an immaculate turquoise gown; the neckline plunged a deep vee to their

navel; edges adorned in glimmering gold thread. They left their neck bare of jewels, long billowing sleeves skated down their arms. The gown was cinched at the waist with more golden thread. Except here it was inlaid with glimmering emeralds from the Evrosei mine, a homage to the power that lay in their veins. As the skirt of the dress danced in the sea breeze, it revealed a secret beneath. Flowing pants covered their legs, giving the illusion of a ball gown when stood. A golden circlet sat atop their braided head.

Solveig stood beside them, dressed in a gown as dark as night. It appeared to have been crafted from the same silk fabric as the ribbon that was tied around the rose the prince had gifted her that morning. Much like Adira's gown, it came with built in trousers. Only Solveig's were skin-tight. The flowing fabric, cinched at the waist also, but with a slate grey belt encrusted with sapphires. Solveig's hair was twisted back in a complicated braid design, created by Adira's deft hands. The neckline of her dress was a simple square shape that was in stark contrast to Adira's; yet each dress was in perfect balance, neither revealing too much.

Where Adira went mostly make up free, save a sweep of golden lustre across their eyes, in keeping with the softer lines and colours of their gown. Solveig was all drama. Smokey black kohl decorated her lids, darkening the green of her eyes to that of a twilight forest scape. She'd painted a deep red stain across her lips that would have been stark against her skin a month ago. Yet after spending days basking in the Farrenhold sun; she was less wraith and more woman. Still cold and deadly, but less likely to escort you to the land of the damned, with the faintest of touches.

Adira was due to give a speech before five. Intended to give thanks and declare the festival officially underway. Solveig secretly hoped that their speech wouldn't last too long; so that she could step down from the stage and position herself in the square as the clock tolled five.

When Adira finally ascended the stone steps, an Aire Wender moved into position, ready to project their voice across the square. Solveig ascended after them, choosing to stand back, so that all eyes would be on Adira and not her.

"Dearest Citizens of Farrenhold. On behalf of my father, our Sovereign, Warwick Etana, I thank you for joining us here in the blessed capital of Trivellian for our annual Harvest feasting." Adira smiled out at the crowd below them; a sea of colourful clothing and smiling faces. Some savouring food from the surrounding stalls, others sipping on wines and ales.

"May the will of The Oracle continue to bless us with ample light and water so we may feed our nation. May you, our citizens, continue to be safe and welcome in the home you have helped to build. My family and I are forever in your debt, for you are the vital cogs without which Farrenhold could not continue to thrive. May this night be a culmination of a year's hard work and sacrifice, eat, drink and dance on the fruits of your labour. For the night is young and the stars shall guide us along the eternal flame's light. Here we are safe, as long as we are one." Adira paused as a man rushed over to hand them a glass of the blush wine they favoured, tipping it to the sky. They saluted.

"To Farrenhold."

"Long may she soar," the crowd called back in unison as they each took a sip from their cups. Adira bowed, turning to take Solveig's hand, a radiant smile upon their face as they descended the steps together.

"Here." They smirked, handing Solveig the glass of wine. "You need to lighten up, and it's bad luck to not drink to a toast."

"I'm afraid I'm unaware of your meaning," Solveig simpered, seizing the perspiring glass, her hand trembling slightly as she took a small sip. Icy berry flavours exploded across her tongue, causing her to shiver. Her gaze fanned out across the square until it alighted on the clock tower, the minute hand inching ever closer to five. Her pulse skittered with every tick; breaths quickened with each tock.

Adira followed her gaze before it flicked back to Solveig. "I'm going to do the rounds with the vendors," they said with a knowing smile, prying the glass of wine from Solveig's white knuckled grasp. "Best of luck." They tenderly squeezed her hand before turning to wend their way through the jostling crowd, leaving Solveig alone in the melee.

Music picked up from the stage they had vacated, lilting and joyous; couples and groups of children danced in time. All around her, life and love blazed, glorious, and free. Solveig struggled to anchor herself, dizzy and nauseous at being so exposed as an icy dread spread through her stomach, her pulse quickening.

And then everything fell silent.

A warm, calloused hand slipped into hers. The music and chatter faded away. Replaced only by the sounds of their breathing; the delicious scents of food, overthrown by the warm amber of his skin. The icy dread in her stomach thawed as quickly as it had frozen, melting into a liquid heat that sent her pulse spinning for an entirely different reason.

"Dance with me?" Emmerich whispered, head bent to her ear so that his smooth voice warmed her skin like the burning heat of whisky.

CHAPTER SIXTY-EIGHT

Alive in the Shadows

Solveig's chin dipped, throat bobbing as she swallowed her nerves. Emmerich drew her closer. His moves were delicate and slow, as though he feared frightening her away. His other hand drifted over her hip as he lifted the hand he held and spun her until they stood face-to-face. Gazes colliding in the darkness.

"Hi," he whispered. Fingertips gliding down the side of her face, tucking a strand of hair behind her ear, and she leaned into the blood-searing heat of his touch.

"Hi."

"I wasn't sure you'd show," he murmured, eyes dropping to skate down her dress, sending shivers coursing through her body. "Then I saw you up there on that stage, hiding in the back under the dying light of the sun." His eyes drifted back to hers again. "And all I wanted was to drag you back into the shadows with me, where you come alive."

"You think you know me so well?" Her eyes were downcast as she drifted a hand up the front of his jacket.

"About as well as you know yourself."

"Then show me," she challenged. Meeting his gaze suddenly as her hand left his jacket and laid across his neck. His pulse thrummed beneath her touch, muscles tightening as he swallowed. He gripped her waist, a mischievous grin lighting his face; before dipping her backward in time with the music that Solveig had forgotten was playing.

"Challenge accepted, Princess," he laughed, pulling her back upright, their bodies flush as he led her through the dance.

Together, they spun, dipped, and swayed to the lilting melody. There wasn't an inch of space between them as they revelled in the warmth that flourished around them. Their last dance had been a twisting, sugar-coated dream. This was burning, all-consuming, as he lifted her in his arms, spinning her until the crowd became a daze of blurred faces. Her hands resting atop his shoulders. It was a move she remembered from before and revelled in further as he slowly lowered her once more, sliding every inch of her against him.

Their moves spoke of secrets and whispered kisses. Heat curled within her, as she stared only at him and his eyes that burned with desire. As though both were dreaming of a life, they wanted but couldn't grasp.

As the music slowed, Solveig could feel eyes on them as Emmerich continued to sway their bodies, moving them as one. The twin beats of their hearts were a song of their own making. It wasn't until their steps slowed; the sound of their ragged breaths in her ears, cheeks flushed, that the prince dipped her down once more. Right in the middle of the square.

Emmerich bent over her as though a predator holding its prey trapped. He pressed an open-mouthed kiss atop the silver scar at her neck, the chain of her necklace glinting under the firelight. Sparks blistered across her skin at the featherlight touch of his lips. A smile formed as he pulled back, bringing the gasping princess with him. Wrapping her tightly against his chest, she whispered.

"You make me want and hope for dangerous things, Emmerich."

"Remember your promise," he whispered into her hair, "that we focus only on tonight and nothing more."

"Then you'd better fetch me some food, or I won't last."

They stayed in the square for hours, sampling the various food and drinks on offer. Solveig returned to the wine and pastries more than a few times.

"Who knew the Princess of Shadows was powered by sugar and wine?" Emmerich joked from where he sat beside her on a perimeter wall. He sipped his own glass of ale, a tray of soft roasted beef and veggies laid atop a garlic butter toasted roll in hand.

"We all have our vices. Mine happen to be sweeter than most," she whispered, taking another bite of the flaky pastry that encased summer berries and cream. The sugar dust sprinkled onto the dark fabric of her pants like stars. Solveig leaned against his shoulder. A soft sigh escaping her as she tried not to think of how terrifying it was that she felt safe and calm beside the man who was supposed to be her sworn enemy.

"Hey," Emmerich nudged her lightly, his hand drifting down to grip hers again, "don't go sleeping on me."

"I'm not sleeping," she whispered with a smile, "only resting."

"If that's your story." He stood suddenly, moving to catch her from falling, "Come on, up you get." He laughed.

"That was rude."

"Rude would be if I let you fall, which I didn't. Now come along."

Solveig placed her glass down on the stone wall, taking his hand warily.

"Where are we going?"

"Back to the palace." He bent to pick up a bag of pastries and a bottle of the wine she had been sipping on all evening. "Don't worry, I gathered more supplies."

"Careful there, Prince," she whispered, eyes shining. "Keep tempting me with promises of sweets and wine, and you may never get rid of me."

"Maybe that's my plan." He grinned. "To give you everything you crave until you realise, I'm on that list too."

CHAPTER SIXTY-NINE

Taking Risks

They traversed the cobbled streets back to Farrowvale Palace, Emmerich holding her steady as her sharp heels caught in the grooves. Hand in hand, their gazes never leaving each other as though they were the only two people in the entire world. Even with Wrenn Bleeker keeping pace behind them, her gaze ever-watchful, as though every person who staggered past was a threat. Yet once the gates of the palace loomed, Solveig felt that carefree air evaporate around her. For two ordinary people wouldn't be returning to a palace.

"Don't run off on me yet," Emmerich whispered. "Let's go to the beach. It's too nice an evening to stay indoors."

Silently, Solveig let him pull her forward. The sounds of the crashing waves growing louder as she bent to slip off her shoes, the tiled patio somehow still warm against her feet. As she was about to step down onto the sand, Emmerich turned to grip her waist, lifting her gently down next to him.

A faint flush creeped across her cheeks that she tried to hide as she bent to pick up the wine bottle. But Emmerich brought a finger to her chin, lifting her face to his as the sea breeze blew tendrils of raven hair across her face.

"Don't hide from me."

"I'm not," she argued, tasting the lie on her tongue as surely as he heard it.

"Keep telling yourself that, love." He shook his head as he entwined their hands once more, leading her further out on the beach to where a blanket and basket already sat waiting for them.

"You planned this?"

"I set it up after you and Adira left."

Emmerich led her over to the blanket, where they sat, watching the waves; sipping on the wine from the party as they devoured the selection of treats he'd prepared. Time passed quickly as they enjoyed each other's company; chatting aimlessly, until they both grew quiet, a newfound tension springing up around them. Solveig sensed the nerves pouring off the prince but was afraid to ask, afraid to acknowledge that something had changed between them.

"What is it?" she whispered finally, watching as his throat bobbed.

"I keep waiting for you to say something," he forced out, rubbing a hand across his face. "Anything to let me know I'm not alone here."

"You said we'd forget about the rest for tonight."

"I can't keep ignoring it Solveig, can't pretend as though what I feel for you is nothing. I need you to be honest with me."

Emmerich pulled her gaze back to his so that he could see her desperately trying to rebuild her walls. "Look at me," he begged. "Let go. Stop worrying about the rest of them."

"I can't."

"Will you tell me about the locket?"

"Anything but that," she pleaded, hand gripping the collar of his shirt, as his drifted across her shoulder. The palace lanterns illuminated their faces.

"What are you hiding, Solveig? What hurt have you caged so tightly that you can't speak of it?"

"Please, Emmerich... I can't,"

His gaze became determined as he reached for the hand at his collar. "Come sailing with me," he pleaded, this thumb drifting across the back of her hand. "Leave all of this behind. The rumours, the legends, the pain, leave it here and run."

"I can't run. I've sworn a duty to my people, no matter the cost to me."

"Even if your soul is the price?"

"I traded my soul a long time ago. A twisted shadow is all that's left."

"You haven't lost your soul, Solveig."

She turned her face away as tears burned, staring out at the dark horizon. The crashing waves were an echo of her turmoil. "I wasn't always this way. They used to love me. I was happy. Then it all crumbled around me. I never wanted to become a legend, a monster. I wanted a simple life with my love, but that dream was stolen from me. So I sold what was left to survive my new reality. I revelled in the power I discovered in the darkest parts of myself until that was all I was. Darkness. Roiling, aching and monstrous."

"A monster wouldn't have saved Malik. A lost soul wouldn't have rescued Renit and her brothers. If you were truly all those things, you wouldn't have saved me. You would have watched my blood spill at your feet with glee. They have you convinced that you're the villain, but you aren't. Don't let them destroy you, Solveig. You've given them enough. Come sailing with me. Let me show you what true freedom feels like."

Emmerich was leaning back on his elbows now; giving her space as she bared her soul. He stared out toward the ocean that called him home, as the breeze played with the curls that spilled over his forehead.

Solveig copied his movement, laying down as she spoke. "You once told me your ship has but a solitary bed, in the captain's quarters. Your quarters." She eyed him, daring him to deny it. "So, unless you plan on sleeping out under the stars for the duration of that trip, you're shit out of luck."

Emmerich's head flew back suddenly, a full belly laugh escaping him. Solveig was too busy glaring at the dark waves that she realised too late as the prince went from lying beside her one moment. To hovering above her in the next.

The air fled from her lungs, mouth growing dry as a pleasant warmth tingled all over where his body was oh so close to touching hers. The despair that had twisted within her moments before fled, as the glow of his attention penetrated her shadows. She squirmed beneath his intense perusal as his gaze slowly raked up her body until their eyes met once more.

Emmerich lowered his head until his lips were at her ear. "I don't know why you're concerned, Princess. I would be the perfect gentleman."

Solveig turned her head to the side slightly, bringing their lips dangerously close to lining up as their breaths mingled in the slither of air between them. Slowly, she raised one hand to his side, the other gripping the back of his neck as though to close the distance between them. She smiled, venomous and sweet, before turning the tables on him entirely. Shifting one leg between his to gain enough leverage to flip him onto his back, their positions reversed.

In the flurry of movement, she slid one hand beneath her skirt to where a dagger lay hidden at the base of her spine; holding it to the prince's throat. Careful to not spill a single drop of blood.

"A perfect gentleman," she whispered, "wouldn't put a princess in a position where she may break her vow to another."

"A vow made under duress hardly counts."

"What if that's all that's stopping me from falling to the shadows completely? If I break it now, what will become of me?" She sighed, bending her head to bring her lips to the other side of his throat; feeling his heartbeat fluttering as she held the dagger resolutely still against him. Inhaling his warm scent.

"If only things were simpler," she murmured. "If we weren't who we are, if we weren't where we are from, if I hadn't made a vow to another. If. If. If."

"If what, Princess?" He gulped, attempting to control his movements, causing Solveig to smile slyly at him. Her green eyes darkening as she mirrored his previous manoeuvre, bringing her lips up to his ear as she whispered.

"If none of those things were true, I would have let you kiss me again in that library. Perhaps we would have stumbled our way to the archives and scandalised the ancient historians there. Maybe we would burn too bright and too hot, risking setting thousands of years of priceless history aflame."

Emmerich scoffed, raising a hand to where she held the dagger, and Solveig allowed him to lower it away from his neck. Pushing himself upward, holding her still in his lap, chest to chest. "There wouldn't be any stumbling Solveig," his voice commanded as the dagger fell to the blanket beside them. "I'd know exactly where to touch you to set you aflame."

Solveig sighed bitterly, wrenching her gaze from his again, "but we are who we are, and we cannot do this."

Emmerich loosened his grip, allowing her to pull herself free as she stood. Returning the dagger to its hiding spot, a chill skittered across her skin at the loss of his comforting warmth. Still, Solveig paused for a moment.

"I'll go sailing with you, Emmerich, but you will keep your hands to yourself."

As she turned to walk away, he jumped to his feet, grabbing hold of her wrist gently. "I will stay out of your bed for as long as you wish, but I make no promises to keep my hands to myself. Lest my manners force me to hold to it even after you renounce them." He brought a hand to her face, stroking her cheek softly. "All you have to do is say the word, Solveig. I'd see you burn this world to the ground and reign over its ashes a dark queen."

CHAPTER SEVENTY

Trust

They were worlds away from the frigid waters of Torrelin as the prince's ship flew across the Celestial Seas. A week, that was what they had agreed upon. Then he would return her to Farrenhold, but she already found herself not wanting to return at all.

Solveig stood against the wooden railing along the port side of the ship. Her raven hair hanging loose, the ends curling in the increasing humidity the further south the ship tread. She stared out at the distant shores of Osvolta; lost in thought when Emmerich's booted feet landed on the deck behind her from where he had swooped down on a line.

Being out on the open waters agreed with him, his mahogany curls tangling in the breeze, that deep bronze skin glowing beneath the sun. He was lighter. A faint smile decorated his features. His breaths coming easier as he took up space beside her; their shoulders brushing slightly. Fingers barely a dagger's width from touching as he raised his other hand to point out toward the curving coastline and looming mountains beyond.

"We're coming up to the border between Farrenhold and Estrellyn. Those peaks in the distance are the Ignis Mountains."

Solveig followed his gesture to where dark tumultuous clouds curled around the peaks; eyes narrowing as she watched them churn, changing shapes on a whim. When she spun suddenly, turning her back on Osvolta and Estrellyn. Hair whipping in the breeze, sending sea spray spattering across Emmerich's cheek; allowing him to breathe her in subtly. The scent of ocean salt mixing with her usual jasmine and lotus flower.

Solveig's voice pulled him out of his reverie. "Do you believe in fairy stories?"

Emmerich brought his eyes up to hers and saw that she was watching him. Her words sounded light, but her eyes had an edge to them.

"We live in a world with magic. It would be naïve to assume we're the only magical creatures."

"They say there used to be a terrible evil lurking in those mountains." Solveig picked at the weather worn wood of the railing as she spoke. "An evil only the most blessed of Estrellyn's pyromancers could contain."

"You mean the dragons," Emmerich supplied, seeing no reason to not name them.

"You know them?"

"No one knows them." Emmerich laughed, nudging Solveig with his arm, causing her to smile. "Even before Estrellyn fell, they were a dying race. What remained of them afterward died out with the rest of the kingdom." He paused, turning his gaze fully on her. "Nothing survived the Scorch."

"But a kingdom as vast and powerful as Estrellyn. You think it's possible they were *all* wiped out?"

"It wasn't just the eruption of the Caldera that ruined them. The surge wiped out everything. Isn't that the entire basis for the belief in your shadowed deity?"

"True." Solveig quirked a brow. "But that wasn't what I meant."

"Then what did you mean?" He turned to face her fully, leaning his elbow atop the rail as he studied her.

"Whether you truly believe that there is nothing left of them."

"I know you think I'm some all-knowing god, but there are some things even I don't know." He laughed, taking her hand in his with aching tenderness. "All I know of the High Kingdom is that the capital fell with the eruption. No one has seen a dragon since. No one has heard whispers of their being people left behind. So yes, I truly believe there is nothing left, because I have seen no proof otherwise."

Solveig spun around to face the shore again as she spoke. "That's interesting."

"What is?" Emmerich sighed, aware he'd walked into a trap now.

"I could have sworn I saw something flying around those peaks. I wonder if anyone in Farrenhold has seen anything like that before." She twisted her head around to study the prince again. She watched him, every tick, the flexing of his hands, the straightening of his back, and the bob of his stubbled throat as he swallowed deeply.

"It was likely a passing storm cloud, or flock of birds. They migrate this time of year."

Solveig shook her head, a disappointed smile on her face. "Seriously?"

"What other explanation could there be?" Emmerich said, his grip tightening on the wooden railing. "Hasn't Farrenhold had eyes on Estrellyn for centuries? Surely, they would have said something." He shrugged.

"Or maybe they're getting complacent."

"Or maybe you're focusing on all the wrong things."

"Such as?"

Emmerich leaned into her space, lips drifting beneath her ear. "You have me at your mercy here, sweet princess, and you'd rather have a history lesson? I'm wounded, truly."

Solveig's head spun. "You're trying to distract me."

"Is it working?"

"You wish to scandalise your crew?" she whispered, her eyes flicked behind him to where a pair of deckhands pretended to look anywhere but at them.

"Let them watch." His words were breathless as his eyes fell to her mouth, before flicking back up again, "I'm their captain. They follow my orders."

"Then can you order them to not throw me overboard at night? It might help me sleep better."

"If it's problems sleeping, you're having. I may have a few suggestions."

"If all of them involve you joining me, then you can keep them to yourself."

Emmerich ducked then, his lips whispering along the soft skin at the base of her ear, sending shivers skittering across her skin.

"I'll give the order, Solveig, if you make a deal with me."

She shivered at the sound of her name on his tongue. "What sort of deal?"

"That you come find me the moment you change your mind."

"Not likely."

"Humour me?"

"Fine." Solveig sighed. "If ever the day should come that I crave you warming the bed beside me, I promise you'll know."

"Good," Emmerich said, with a sincerity that almost shocked her. "I think we're beyond hiding from each other now, don't you?" He pulled back to hold her gaze once more as she nodded slowly, in a daze. The guilt of the secret she kept gnawed at her insides. She should tell him, she knew that, but something held her back.

"Think you'll be okay for a few hours whilst I go tend to my ship?" Emmerich asked suddenly, taking a step back to give her some breathing room.

"I kept myself entertained for years before you crashed into my life. I think I can handle a few hours."

"Good, I'd hate to bore you this early on." He smirked. "Keep your evening free, Princess. I have plans for you."

"It's not like I can run off," she called as he walked away slowly.

"That's what makes this so much more fun." He laughed before disappearing below deck, leaving Solveig alone with her thoughts.

Emmerich was in the deep stores, inspecting the inner beams of the hull for signs of cracks and wood rot. The Valdrych was an old ship, and as they approached the treacherous Wrecked Seas, he had to be sure she could withstand the pressure.

"Captain?" a quiet voice came from behind him as he inspected the large beam of the keel running through the mid-section of the ship. His head turned to find one of Wrenn's soldiers stood waiting.

"Is there a problem?" he asked, eyes wary. The soldier hesitated, appearing to think better of whatever it was they had come to say. "I'm waiting, soldier."

"Some of the crew, sir, are concerned about your guest."

Emmerich stiffened at his words.

"You've allowed her free rein of the ship. She has no one watching her. She could go anywhere, see anything." The Soldier rushed at seeing the prince's growing anger.

"We just—"

"Allow me to be plain. The princess is not to be touched. She is my guest and therefore under my protection. If you, or any of the others, lay a hand on her, you'll answer directly to me—" Emmerich paused, smirking to himself slightly. "If there's anything left of you after she's done, that is."

"Sir, if I may?" the soldier stuttered.

"No, you may not. Your orders are the same as always, to follow any direction I give you. Any further concerns, take them to Commander Bleeker. Is that clear?"

The soldier did not reply.

"Is that clear, soldier?" Emmerich repeated, punctuating each word.

"Aye, Captain." He grimaced.

"Good, then go have the dining room readied. The princess and I shall eat together tonight."

As the sun set over the distant horizon, Solveig watched the calm seas. A small voice, the one that yearned for freedom and adventure, urged her to hop up on to the railing of the ship. To feel the thrill of there being only one step between her and the waters below. Despite being a Hydromancer, she had never learned how to swim. The idea was foolish and utterly reckless. Yet the next thing she knew, she had one knee propped on the railing preparing to hoist herself up when a smooth voice called out from behind her.

"Running away from me already, Princess?"

Her knee slipped from the shock. "You nearly scared me half to death!" Solveig exclaimed, gripping the rail tighter as she righted herself. "I could've fallen overboard!"

"It's not my fault you tried out tightrope walking around the railing of a moving ship."

Solveig turned to find him leaning nonchalantly against the mast, arms crossed, a playful smile on his lips.

"Are you saying that you wouldn't have jumped in after me?"

"That's the game, is it? You're trying to get me to remove my clothes again?"

"I—that's not what I meant at all," Solveig spluttered, cheeks growing flushed.

He reached out to catch a piece of her hair that flew in front of her face in the breeze, tucking it behind her ear. The silence stretched between them for a few moments before he smiled again and turned. At first Solveig thought he was leaving, but he returned quickly with a line around his hand. Wordlessly, he held his free hand out to her. Solveig didn't move.

"We don't have all day, Princess. If you want to be reckless, at least do it before we lose all the light, so I stand a chance of plucking you from the water."

"Prick," Solveig muttered, causing him to laugh again.

"Such an elegant way with words." He paused. "Do you trust me?"

Solveig's eyes flicked down to his open palm. She gulped, trying to calm her erratic breathing before whispering, "yes." And placed her hand in his.

"Then hop on up, Princess."

"You can't be serious?"

"A moment ago, you were ready to jump up there all alone, now you have a safety net you aren't interested?"

"No, I—" She paused, her gaze drifting out to the sea once more. "Fine, let's do it." Emmerich grinned as he held her tightly, urging her up onto the rail. Still holding one hand, he moved to hand her the line.

"Whatever you do, don't let go of that rope. It's your lifeline. If you fall, don't panic. I'll slow it, and come in after you, I promise."

"Careful, Prince." Solveig smirked. "You wouldn't want anyone to think you're fraternising with the enemy now, would you?"

"Where we ever really enemies?" He questioned, but Solveig remained silent.

"Now get up there before I change my mind." He said after a beat, "I want to eat dinner at some point this evening and I'd prefer it if you joined me, and not the sharks."

CHAPTER SEVENTY-ONE

No Need to Beg

The only sounds were the clinking echoes of silverware; the faint crackle of candlelight and the aching groan of the ship's wooden hull as it moved through the water. With the absence of conversation, Solveig's mind wandered back to how it had felt to stand on the rail of the ship, staring out at the vast horizon. Nothing but a line of rope tethering her to the vessel. She remembered the power of the wind as it had whipped around her, ruffling her clothes and hair, threatening to push her off her perch with a wayward gust.

The Valdrych had been sailing smoothly since their departure from Trivellian, so when a rogue wave hit from the south; it blindsided her, causing her to lose her balance. She'd tried to regain her footing as her body pitched, not toward liquid death, but the unforgiving wooden planks of the ship's deck.

She braced herself for the smack and scrape of wooden boards, dreading the splinters she would have to dig free of her skin. When she fell upon powerful arms instead. One around her back and the other at the bend of her knees, drawing her toward a warm chest. True to his word, Emmerich had been there. Even when all the injuries she would have sustained were mere scratches.

She reached for the bottle of wine between them when Emmerich's gaze met hers. He swallowed a bite of lusciously soft, pink-toned beef, his face cast in flickering shadows from the candlelight.

"I'd forgo a third glass of wine if I were you," he stated, mischief in his gaze.

"Why is that?" Solveig leaned back on her plush velvet-covered chair, arms folded across her chest, drawing the prince's gaze lower.

When Emmerich didn't respond, she laughed. "Eyes up, Prince." A smirk lifted one side of her mouth, and the prince found he wanted to kiss that smirk right off her damned beautiful face. He couldn't get the image of her, stood upon the railing of his ship, out of his mind. It was a siren song straight to his heart. She was at home on his ship, as though she was born to be there, by his side.

"Emmerich?" at the sound of his name on her lips, his attention snapped back to her with a soft groan. What he wouldn't give to hear her say his name as he kissed her senseless. Laying her down on the bed in his quarters. Moving as one with the swaying of the waves as he rocked within her, and she took everything he gave as they raced toward their shared release.

"Emmerich?" she called again; her eyes were quizzical. "Where is your head at this evening?"

"Believe me," he muttered, taking a large swig of his drink, pulling at the collar of his shirt, as though his skin were overheating from his own damn imagination. "You don't want to know."

"Something tells me that's not entirely true."

"Don't rush to make promises your mind isn't ready to hold to."

"How do you know what I'm ready for?"

Emmerich eyed her across the table, hands clenched beneath it. "If you were truly ready, we wouldn't be having this discussion at all."

Solveig grew silent at that, and he quirked a brow in return. "You aren't ready, and that's fine. You'll find I can be patient..." He dropped his gaze to glide slowly across her body before rising to meet her eyes. "When I want something bad enough."

Silence yawned between them before Solveig doused it entirely. "Why should I skip the third glass of wine?" she backtracked, desperate to move away from the lingering attraction that simmered between them.

"We'll be dropping anchor early tomorrow and you'll need a clear head for what I have planned."

"Dropping anchor where? Elithiend?" Her eyes lit at the prospect of seeing the mysterious kingdom.

"Easy there." Emmerich smirked. "We'll technically be in Elithiend, but it's a more neutral territory. Tempest Cove."

Solveig sank back in her chair, her disappointment obvious at his words. "Alas, dear Princess, as you made clear on my arrival in Farrenhold, a foreign royal requires a direct invitation to enter another kingdom. I may be the future king, but my father still rules and that isn't a power he has handed off to me. We're lucky he granted permission for us to stop at Tempest at all."

"You said you'd show me all the corners of Osvolta that I longed to see."

"That I did," Emmerich shrugged. "I just didn't specify when."

"Why the cove?" she speared a piece of beef with her fork. "All our records say it's a barren wasteland."

"That's true. Its excess tidal activity makes it uninhabitable. But it also makes the perfect Hydromancer training ground."

Solveig's face paled at his words.

He placed his elbows on the table, leaning closer. "I'm curious to see how far your magic can actually go."

"It's a waste of time." Solveig rushed, shaking her head.

"I think we both know that's not true." he wiped his hands on a napkin as he stood, stalking like a predator. "I've watched you drain a body of every drop of fluid. That is no easy feat."

"You're—" Emmerich brought a finger to her lips, halting her words in their tracks, tracing the shape of her full, blush coloured mouth. Her lips parting slightly as chills covered her body. He leaned in close, and Solveig closed her eyes, anticipating his lips closing over hers again. This time she knew she wouldn't fight him, that she would claim him as thoroughly as he had claimed her with their last kiss.

The prince's eyes shone as he studied her flushed complexion, the slight movement at the base of her neck with her rapid heartbeat. "Eat up and sleep well, Princess. You're going to need all your strength tomorrow." He pressed a soft kiss on the hollow beneath her ear; her scent washing over him, far more intoxicating than even the sweetest wine in his stores. Solveig moaned in protest as he pulled away, her eyes shooting open in time to see his back as he exited the room without a backward glance.

The sensation of his closeness, of his lips grazing her skin, was a memory far too difficult to escape. Even as she lay in the warm comfort of his bed, sleep evaded her. His scent lingered all around her, so strong it was as though he were sleeping right beside her. It would be easy to go to him. To lead him up the stairs to share the bed with her. But would that be all they would do? Was she ready for what sharing a bed with the prince could mean?

She glanced at the cabinets across the room where a bunch of white roses, thorns trimmed, lay taunting her. Identical to the rose he'd bestowed her with the morning of the Harvest Festival. Sighing, she threw the sheets off, storming from the room and out on to the open deck above. The cool breeze clearing her senses with its briny scent as moonlight shone down from the heavens. She came to a stop against the rail, staring out into the endless inky black of the ocean. Alone with her thoughts, she listened to the soothing sound of the waves crashing and rolling against the side of the ship. Her eyes falling closed as the sound eased her racing mind.

Before long, footsteps sounded behind her, setting her pulse racing as the prince came up to stand beside her, the air between them charged with confusion and want.

"Can't sleep?" she whispered first.

"Once you get used to sleeping in a bed, it's hard to go back to the bunks," he muttered wryly. "You?"

"My mind is all tangled up over someone it shouldn't be, and it doesn't help when his scent is wrapped all around me."

"Guess we're both out of luck then," Emmerich smirked, nudging her shoulder playfully.

"Perhaps," she muttered, "or..."

"Or?"

Solveig turned to face him fully then, taking a deep breath. "Or you could come back to your bed with me," she whispered.

"Solveig." Her name ripped from his throat; hands clenched on the rail. "Are you sure?" He swallowed as she nodded. "I need to hear you say it. I won't do anything where you're concerned unless you voice exactly what you want from me."

The full moon cast them in silvery light as Solveig stared at him in thoughtful silence, gripping the rail tight as she dragged in a long salt-tinged breath.

"Emmerich, I want you to come and sleep in your own damn bed with me, so that I may finally get some rest." Her voice rang with a false bravado betrayed by the nervous shifting of her eyes.

"Fine," he chuckled, "there was no need to beg."

Solveig swatted his arm playfully, but he only grabbed it before she could pull away, rubbing his thumb lightly over the back of her hand.

"Come." He inclined his head. "If it's sleep you want, that's what you'll get."

Hand in hand, the prince led the princess back down to the captain's quarters. He slipped off his boots and belt, and she shrugged off her shawl and slippers before they climbed beneath the still warm sheets together.

Emmerich pulled Solveig tight against his chest, and she could feel his heartbeat against her back.

His face drifted to her neck, breathing in her scent, soft lips whispering across her skin as he spoke. "Next time we do this, I want to help."

"Help with what?" she laughed, burying her face in the pillows to hide her blush.

"Ever since the night of the ball," he whispered, fingertips skimming her thigh before stopping dead centre, his palm flush to her skin. "I've dreamed of being the one who gets to remove that holster from your thigh." He pressed another kiss to her nape, his fingers tapping her thigh gently as Solveig's breath caught in her throat, feeling her skin flush.

"I want to be the one who gets to strip your armour away, mentally and physically. Even if that's all we do." He paused, hand drifting away from her thigh, and she twisted to look at him.

"I want you to want me, Solveig." The words ripped from his throat, eyes falling shut.

She brought a hand to his jaw, drifting her thumb across his plush lower lip, remembering how it felt pressed to hers, "I.." she began, but stopped, words failing her. So she did the only thing she could think of to reassure him. Pushing herself up to press a kiss light as air over his mouth.

"I'm here with you," she whispered at last. Bringing their foreheads together.

"Sleep." Emmerich breathed. "I'll still be with you tomorrow."

They settled back into the bed, their hearts calming together. And with the added comfort and warmth of being wrapped in each other against the steady sway of the ship, they drifted off to sleep in quiet tandem. Consequences be damned.

CHAPTER SEVENTY-TWO

Tempest Cove

Through the lingering haze of a much-needed good night's sleep, Solveig realised two things. The first was that she was hot, unbearably so, as if she were sleeping beside a raging inferno. The second was that something was pressed up against her back.

Slowly, she cracked a single eye open. The ship rocked with the gentle swell of ocean waves. Beyond the portholes, where the sun had long since risen, she could see the barest hint of jagged grey land.

"So much for training at first light," she muttered as she moved to stand and found it to be a harder task than usual. Her eyes swept down to find a bronzed arm dusted with dark hair across her middle.

Everything came rushing back to her. Whispered words beneath the starry night. Walking hand in hand back to the captain's quarters. The kiss she gave him before they'd slipped into a dreamless sleep. Side by side, as though it was something they did every night, as if it wouldn't have lingering consequences in the harsh light of day.

Softly, she moved to lift the prince's arm from her waist to escape before he woke. As soon as she had garnered enough space to slide free; she was staring up into those incredible blue depths as he watched her.

"Going somewhere, Solveig?"

"I was promised a training session at first light. It appears my instructor has been waylaid."

"Hmm," Emmerich grunted, allowing his eyes to drift down her body. Covered by only a thin silk nightgown, he lowered slightly, allowing more of his body to lean into hers. The exquisite heat that bloomed extracted a small gasp from her lips, and his eyes flew back to hers as he smirked.

"I'm sure they have a damn fine excuse for the delay." His face lowered to hers, his intent to kiss her plain in his gaze, when she hurriedly whispered.

"I'm sure they're already up and looking for you."

"Let them," he whispered, touching his mouth to hers, and she yielded to his touch instantly. Felt his hands drift. One tangled in her hair, the other down lower, caressing the smooth skin of her thigh as he nudged her legs wider, settling atop her. He hooked her leg over the back of his and she allowed him to manipulate her without protest, erasing any space between them. Lost in the searing, blissful dream of his mouth on hers when he released her. Only for a moment. Allowing her a second to fill her lungs. She sighed, stretching her arms before lowering them around his neck, thinking of how this was her favourite dream.

"It's not a dream," he whispered, lips grazing hers as he spoke. Solveig's eyes opened slightly as she stared sleepily into his.

"I'm far too happy for it to be anything but."

"Then feel it, but don't forget that this is real." His mouth took hers again. Harder this time and she gasped slightly, allowing him entry as her hands slid through his tangled curls. The leg over his hip pulled him tighter to her. Desperate to get closer, and yet even through the haze, she felt his lips smirk against hers, as he moved to pull away and she fought to keep him close.

"We should stop." He laughed. The sound was music to her ears. "I promised you a training session, after all."

Solveig's eyes narrowed on him. "I can think of better ways you can help me exercise right now."

Emmerich's gaze darkened as his pulse throbbed at his neck. "You're the one who wanted to see all the sights the realm has to offer," he fought out.

"I think I'm enjoying the sights in this room far more right now."

Emmerich quirked a brow at her, eyes rolling playfully. "What am I going to do with you?" he muttered, shaking his head.

"I can think of a few ideas."

"Oh really? Well, so can I." He bent over her, lips at her ear. "In my head," he whispered, "I see you panting, eyes alive with wonder." He paused, pressing a kiss against her cheek, "soaking wet—"

Solveig gasped, gripping his arm tighter.

"As you learn how to control the waves of the Wrecked Seas." Emmerich laughed, pulling her from the bed with him as he stood.

"That doesn't sound anywhere near as much fun as my idea." She scowled.

"As long as you're here with me." He winked, "we can play your games later. But I promised you training, and that's what you'll get. Meet me on deck in thirty."

"Aye, aye Captain." She mock saluted, dropping back down onto the bed with a laugh as the door closed behind him.

If it hadn't been for the spray of the surrounding ocean, Solveig was convinced she would have melted on the spot. She was a princess used to lukewarm, rain-soaked summers and bleak frozen winters. She wiped a hand across her brow to collect the sweat that beaded there. A warm flush decorated her pale cheeks.

"Is it always this hot in Elithiend?" she shouted across the small dinghy to where the prince was busy rowing them to shore.

Emmerich burst into laughter. Barely breaking a sweat; despite the heat and back-breaking effort, he put in to fighting the stormy swells that grew more intense the closer they came to the shore.

"I suppose it helps that I grew up with it."

"It's autumn, and yet it's hot as summer."

"It'll be a few weeks yet before the humidity breaks and the heat dies off. That's the beauty of living in the south, Princess. Our winters are far kinder than yours."

"I'm not sure which I'd prefer," she muttered, drifting the tips of her fingers into the rippling waters. "Freezing to death or burning in a ring of fire."

"You'll soon be thankful for the heat. It'll dry you out when you inevitably get soaked." She raised a brow at the double entendre of his words.

"What's that look for?" He smirked. "I was merely referring to an incoming wave drenching you."

"Uh huh," she muttered, "sure, that's what you meant."

They fell into an easy silence as the prince focused on getting them safely to shore. Meanwhile, Solveig was more concerned with not losing the contents of her stomach over the side of the dinghy.

"Hold on," Emmerich said as the shore grew closer. "This could get bumpy." Solveig wasn't sure exactly what he expected her to hold on to. Except for the boat, that she was already gripping so tightly her knuckles had turned white.

Not a moment too soon, the dinghy came to a shuddering halt, but Solveig kept her eyes shut. Even as she heard the prince jump out, with the echo of his booted feet in the stony sand heading toward her.

"You can open your eyes now, Princess. We're safely on dry land." She cracked a single eye open to find his hand outstretched and waiting. She gripped onto him tightly as she rose to her feet on unsteady legs.

"If you ever try to get me out on this ridiculous thing again, you'll go mysteriously overboard."

"Not a fan of the dinghy?" He chuckled.

"Next time, take me somewhere your ship can dock."

"As you wish, my lady," he laughed, bowing dramatically at the waist. "This way, times a wasting and I heard a rumour that you were complaining about your trainer being delayed this morning."

"I'm wishing I kept my mouth shut now," she muttered, kicking at the pebbled shore.

"I bet you are."

Hand in hand, they travelled at a leisurely pace along the shore, gentle waves crashing around them until they reached a secluded cove. Dread taking over as she realised exactly how this small rocky outcrop had got its name.

Here the waves crashed impossibly high, sea spray flying out in all directions, spattering her face even from a distance. She turned to stare at the prince.

"You seriously mean for me to bring that raging beast under control?" she demanded, an arm flying out to where the water drew back and then surged again through the tight channel of jagged black rocks. The push and pull of the suction causing an almighty display. "It's not possible."

"In the months I've known you, I've never seen you walk away from a challenge. Don't tell me you plan to start now."

"This isn't a challenge, it's humiliation. My magic is not strong enough for this."

"Says who? You or your parents? How much training did you have before they gave up and decided you weren't worth the effort?"

Hot angry tears simmered at the edges of her eyes as he continued flinging all her deepest hurts in her face. "You are a manipulator. You cannot evaporate, but you can stop it in its tracks, even for a moment."

"Never with this amount."

"The amount doesn't matter, that's all in your head. You can do this. Deep down you know it too." He stepped in front of her, taking both her hands in his. Noticing for the first time that she was no longer wearing the engagement ring, a faint pale ring of skin was the only reminder it had been there. His thumb stroked gently across the naked finger as he drew his gaze back up to hers, one hand cradling her face with reverent care.

"If I succeed in anything on this trip, Princess? It will be that when the time comes that I am forced to leave you, you shine as bright in the light as you do in the shadows." He tipped her chin up, forcing her to look at him. "They have manipulated, belittled, and twisted you. Now it's time for you to prove them all wrong. Stop the wave Solveig. Control it, master it. Show them you're stronger than they know."

Hours ticked by, and the blinding blue of the sky and sparkling ocean darkened as tumultuous grey clouds roiled overhead. At the edge of the cliffs, the two young royals stood facing the oncoming storm.

"Again," the prince commanded, his clothes soaked through with sea spray. Beside him, Solveig stood on shaking legs, her brow drenched in sweat, clothes dripping with water from wave after wave that she had failed to stop.

"We've been at it for hours," she shouted through heaving breaths. "This is hopeless."

"Look at me, Solveig," She turned on the spot, anger, and bone deep tiredness clear in the slump of her shoulders and the clouded green of her eyes.

"You can do this. Focus your mind." He handed her a skin of water and an apple from the sack he'd brought with them. "Take five minutes and we'll go again."

He swept a hand out, stopping the next wave in its tracks with a dense shield of air, giving Solveig a few precious moments of reprieve from its onslaught.

As more waves continued to thrash against the prince's barrier, Solveig stared out at the vast ocean, as though it were mocking her and her inability to bring it under submission. Anger simmered in her blood. She bit back the bitter taste of overwhelming tiredness that threatened to drag her to the floor. Handing the prince his skin of water back, she turned back to the inky black ocean.

"Shut off everything but you and your power," Emmerich whispered at her back, fingertips stroking briefly across the nape of her neck before he stepped back. "Just you and the water."

Solveig closed her eyes, and sent her mind tumbling down on a slow, deep breath, searching for whatever dregs of power remained within her. Dragging, raking, and pulling all of it together for a final showdown. She would not let it defeat her.

When at last she could feel every drop of the ocean that raged toward her, she nodded. Opening her eyes to see Emmerich lowering the shield. Time slowed as she took in the swell of the fresh wave, barrelling closer and closer. She reached out with her power; forcing her will against the oncoming rage, and for a moment, it halted in its tracks. Churning and roiling in place. Solveig smiled in disbelief as she and the prince stared at the wave when it shook. Spurts flying free from her hold at the same time something wet dripped, thick, and hot from her nose.

CHAPTER SEVENTY-THREE

Friends with Death

"Solveig?" Emmerich's voice shook as he watched her body jerk, lost in the thrall of her power. The seduction of holding the might of the Wrecked Sea at her mercy.

"SOLVEIG!" He shouted this time, voice cracking with terror as blood flowed from her nose, her whole body shaking, breaths weak and ragged.

Time slowed as Emmerich watched from a step away as she fell. The wave she'd been controlling, now unleashed from its cage, came barrelling for them. He reached to catch her with one arm, narrowly shielding them with a barrier of Aire with the other.

Horrific, wet coughs rattled through Solveig's chest; Emmerich froze as warm wetness splattered across his face and neck, the scent of iron thick in the air. He stared down in fear at the sight of the princess's blood pooling from her nose and mouth. Her eyes greyed and unseeing as she fought to breathe through the blood coagulating in her throat.

Emmerich did the only thing he could think of before panic seized him, praying she would forgive him later. His eyes fell closed as he worked, stealing her air, leaving her in stasis. He used every drop of power that wasn't focused on protecting them from the raging sea to keep her organs fed with oxygen. Carefully he gathered her now still body in his arms and raced back to the dinghy as rain from the incoming storm began to fall.

A thread of calm filtered into the prince's racing mind as he powered along the pebbled shoreline; slick with rain, and saw the small boat finally come into view. He used all the strength he had left in his legs to race for it. Even as blood, thick and dark, continued to pool and fall from the princess's mouth and nose. It soaked the front of his shirt and trousers. Mercifully, the flow had slowed down, but he couldn't be sure how much she had lost or whether it was enough that she might never wake up again.

Once he reached the dinghy, he laid her down as gently as he could, using his pack to cushion her head against the wooden hull. Before pushing the boat out to sea, hopping in behind her once they were afloat again. He set a punishing pace back toward the Valdrych, where he hoped they would find help. They were too far from civilisation to search anywhere but within the limited crew at his side.

When they finally pulled up alongside the ship, a deckhand lowered the hooks toward them for Emmerich to attach, allowing the boat to rise from the water's grasp. Finally, they reached the gangway, where the prince found Wrenn waiting for them with towels and fresh water. Her smile dropped the moment she caught sight of the prince's blood-soaked shirt.

"What the fuck happened?"

"Don't just stand there. Grab her feet and help me bring her in." Wrenn's eyes fell on the still princess lying on the bottom of the boat.

"What..." she began again. Emmerich shot her a glare so dark that she promptly shut her mouth. Moving to grab the princess's feet as they hauled her from the dinghy and safely aboard the Valdrych.

"Ready the ship for immediate departure to Elithiend." Emmerich commanded, repositioning to take all the princess's weight now. "And send the healer to my quarters." he stalked away, but Wrenn followed.

"You're doing this aren't you," she demanded, "keeping her under, keeping her breathing." Emmerich ignored her.

Wrenn reached out a hand to grasp his arm. "What's it costing you?" she asked, concern clear in her eyes.

"She could die," he said simply.

"So could you if you keep this up!" she cried, halting him with a grasp on his elbow. "Tell me what happened."

"There's no time." He wrenched his arm free and carried on toward his chambers.

"Emmerich Ryker Anders, you tell me what we're up against. How are we supposed to help her without knowing what we're fighting?" she fired back, bringing him to a stop.

"I can't leave her," the prince whispered, staring down at her still form.

"I'm not asking you to," Wrenn said calmly. "I'm asking you to help us give her the best chance."

The prince's eyes closed as he warred with himself, "not here," he said finally. Knowing that if she ever woke up, she may one day forgive him for stealing her consciousness: her choices. But she was too proud to forgive him for spilling her weaknesses for his entire crew to hear.

The storm battered the Valdrych as the prince, his commander and the ship's healer worked to figure out the best way to heal the princess.

"You're sure there's nothing else?" Wrenn questioned; feeling her weak rapid pulse whilst the healer had their hands splayed over her unmoving, blood-stained chest; their magic unfurling to search for the hidden menace.

"Positive," Emmerich said. His tone bucked no arguments even as his shaking hands betrayed the blood curdling fear in his soul. "She was magnificent, halting the strongest wave we'd seen in its tracks. Then blood dripped from her nose. At first, I thought it was the strain, but then she collapsed. And the coughing started, and the blood wouldn't stop coming, it was like..." He paused, eyes blinking unseeing, face paling.

"Like what?" Wrenn pressed.

The prince's gaze fell upon the princess, hands fisted and shaking, "like how she described the Whitlock's deaths. Wet, chest rattling coughs, blood pooling and pouring unbidden from their noses and mouths." His hands flew to his face in frustration.

"Gods fucking damn it. Why wouldn't she tell me?"

Wrenn stared sheepishly at her prince as the night of the ball became clear in her mind.

"What?" Emmerich asked, eyes narrowed.

"The night of the ball when she saved you. Her nose was bleeding then. I thought little of it, but now? Maybe she didn't realise?" Wrenn tried.

"No. She knew," he cried, head falling into his hands again, this time to hide the tears that threatened. "It's why she agreed to work with me, because she knew her own clock was ticking, and I was her only chance of survival." He shook his head, staring at the floor, "I've been a fool, a blind, stubborn fool."

"It's not all bad," Wrenn shrugged.

"How do you figure that?"

"I thought she was stringing you along to uncover Elithiend's secrets. At least this is better."

"She had so many opportunities to tell me the truth. She let me push her, over and over. If I had known..."

Wrenn dropped the princess's arm, leaving the healer to their work. "You didn't," she whispered, pulling at his arms. "Ifs and buts are useless to you both now. What's done is done. You didn't know what danger she was in."

She seized her friend's face then. "Go clean yourself up. I'll stay here."

"But—"

"The princess will not wake up as soon as you leave the bloody room, Emmerich. Let me take over her oxygen. You're running on empty; I'll send for you the moment anything changes."

With one last glance at the princess lying still on his bed; Emmerich stalked from the room. Leaving Wrenn and the healer to focus on repairing her ravaged body.

As night fell, the Valdrych raced to outrun the storm that had descended on Tempest Cove. For now, the winds that raged as fierce as the despair in the prince's heart pushed the ship forward. Giving them a head start as they made their way toward Elithiend.

Emmerich stood alone in the crew bathing chamber, eyes lifeless with shock as he washed every drop of the princess's blood from his skin. He walked over to the saltwater bath, lowering down to soak his aching muscles in the mixture of ground lavender, Gabos leaf and peppermint root. He tried to close his eyes, to rest. To allow his mind and body to heal, but every time his lids fell shut; the terror of seeing the princess choking flashed before them, startling him awake. With nothing left to do, he dragged himself from the tub. Drying off the droplets with a wave of his hand. He dressed in fresh clothes and headed up onto the open deck, to where Commander Bleeker's second was at the helm.

"Report?" he commanded, voice harder than he intended, edged in lingering fear.

"We're out running the storm for now." Lieutenant Garrue stated. "We should arrive at the channel by sundown tomorrow if we keep this pace. How long the weather will hold for is anyone's guess," he said, staring up at the cloud drenched sky.

"Have someone on watch. We need to keep abreast of any changes. Rotate them every two hours to avoid any lapse in concentration."

"Aye, Captain."

"Take a break," Emmerich said finally. "I've got her for now. Go get some food and shut eye whilst you can. I'll need you at the helm again before daybreak."

"Aye, Captain," the Lieutenant repeated before heading below deck as ordered.

Emmerich ran a hand over the smoothed wood of the ship's wheel, feeling a wave of centred calm take over. This he could do. He could keep his ship and crew safe. Keep his mind occupied as his friend and the healer worked to keep the infuriating woman he had become dangerously attached to; from making friends with death.

Hours had passed whilst the prince followed the faint light of the stars through the thickening clouds toward home. Focused solely on his task. Desperate to keep the anxiety inducing thoughts of the dying princess from invading his mind. So much so that he didn't see the approaching figure until Lieutenant Garrue spoke from beside him.

"Commander Bleeker is asking for you, Captain." The prince's eyes flew to him, stuck to the spot for a moment.

"You have the helm?"

"Aye, Captain."

"Good, send for me if anything changes."

He nodded again, taking the helm. Emmerich flew as fast as his feet could carry him below deck to his quarters. Wrenn stood outside the door waiting for him, a forlorn look on her face.

"What is it?" Emmerich rushed.

"She's breathing on her own now. The healer mended everything they sensed to be injured. You should be there if she wakes up."

"When," Emmerich snapped.

"Right." Wrenn muttered, "When she wakes up."

Emmerich entered the deathly silent room where the woman who haunted his every waking thought slept soundly, as if she hadn't almost abandoned the mortal plane entirely. She lay still. The only movement was the rise and fall of her chest. Still in her waterlogged and blood-stained clothes, Emmerich sent for warm water and fresh garments and wiped away every reminder of the horror that had occurred. Until Solveig looked as though she was merely sleeping.

CHAPTER SEVENTY-FOUR

Missteps and Shattered Trust

There was a warm glow beyond Solveig's eyelids, and she felt as though she were swaying, floating through the clouds on a bright, sunny day. The temptation to let the sensation rock her back into sweet oblivion crept around the edges of her consciousness.

Her hand was warm, held in the tight grip of another's. A gentle heat coursed through her blood as the grip tightened and released, as though urging her to wake.

"Come on, open your eyes, Solveig," a whiskey smooth voice pleaded. She obeyed the command, but closed them instantly, as the harsh light of day burned.

"Easy," the voice whispered, so low it was almost drowned out by the incessant creaking and groaning all around them. "Take it slow." She did as instructed, blinking gently, slowly opening her lids little by little, until she could finally stand the full brightness of the room.

Solveig took in the arched wooden beams above her, the gauzy white curtains to the side and the lumpy bed covered by soft dark sheets. She was back aboard the Valdrych, though she had no memory of getting there.

She wracked her brain in search of the memories, standing atop the jagged cliffs of Tempest Cove. Looking out to the storm brewing on the horizon as another raging wave had barrelled toward her.

She'd stopped it. Halted it in its tracks. Remembered the power that had electrified her bloodstream. Recalling the pride in the prince's own gaze and then everything went utterly dark.

"You stopped it," the voice said from across the room. Having left her side in favour of perching on the edge of the desk opposite her; ankles crossed, arms folded atop his chest. His skin appeared more russet than usual, as though he had scrubbed it within an inch of his life. But it was his eyes that brought her to a halt. His usually warm blue flame was a swirling, angry maelstrom. "And then you stopped," he finished.

"What..." she began, moving to stand, but the single utterance caused an unbearable ache to pass through her ravaged throat, down through her abdomen. A gentle heaviness pushed her back down on the bed, and she looked to find one of Emmerich's hands extended in her direction. Hurt crossed her gaze as she thought of him using his power to trap her there, as though he had suddenly decided he could no longer trust her.

"You stopped breathing," he cursed, his hand dropping once she was laying down again. "Blood dripped from your nose and then you started coughing, rattling and wet."

What little colour had returned to her complexion drained instantly at his words, for she knew what the prince was about to say next. "It was a river, choking and unstoppable."

Solveig said nothing, so he filled the silence for her. "Just like Aldrik." She flinched at the mention of that name. Emmerich's gaze flared at the sight. "And Xanthe," he continued, standing to cross the room to sit beside her, just out of reach. His face was an emotionless mask. "And every other name we've read in countless books and reports."

Still, she said nothing, couldn't even meet his gaze.

"Why?" he demanded finally.

"Why what?"

"Why didn't you tell me?" he begged out of frustration, a palm slamming on the wall beside him. "How long have you known that death was knocking on your door? You let me push you to use more of your power. Knowing the danger it put you in." His voice broke, head falling to his hands. "Why didn't you trust me with this?"

"As you have trusted me with all your secrets?" she countered immediately on the defensive, guarding her heart. "If honesty is the game, let's not pretend like you've been playing by the rules any better than I."

"I didn't keep something that was a matter of life or death from you," he argued.

"How would I know? You belittled me, cursed, and judged. You formed an opinion of who you think I should be. Made up your mind and would see no other explanation."

"You didn't even try."

"Didn't I? How many times did I try to tell you that my power wasn't strong enough? How many times did you respond I could be more? You wouldn't hear me. You decided that my family had limited me and cast me aside." She twisted, leaning toward him, ignoring the pain in her stomach as she moved, the weakness in her arms as she struggled to hold herself up.

"You see, Prince, my master of hydromancy is that poor. My power is as weak and pitiful as they say. You made me want to believe I could be more, that there was something else lurking untapped within me." She shook her head, as though the idea was completely ridiculous now. "Dangerous thoughts from an untrustworthy prince of an enemy kingdom." Her eyes narrowed on him. "A kingdom known for celebrating the mastery of multiple elements, and yet their prince showcases only one." The accusation was plain.

"Maybe you wanted it to go this way," Solveig continued, "take us out one by one so you can conquer the known continent and remake it in your image?"

"You've got to be fucking joking," Emmerich sputtered, ignoring the barb about his power.

"Do I look like I am?" She stood in a single jerking motion; gritting her teeth against the pain that wracked her body, closing in on him, a single finger stabbing at the centre of his chest.

"If I wanted you dead, Princess, I wouldn't have raced back across Tempest Cove with you unconscious in my arms. My healer wouldn't have worked tirelessly for hours to help you. If I wanted you dead, I would have left you there to rot until the sea welcomed you into its depths."

"Or maybe you knew that my death on Elithiend soil would be an act of war that your kingdom isn't prepared for. I was foolish to trust any Elithiend, but you, you're the worst of them all, aren't you?"

Emmerich growled, grasping her arm; twisting so that her back pressed against the wall as he leaned into her space. "What the fuck is happening right now?"

"You tell me," she countered. Staring up at him, not backing down, as she tried to pry against the black hole in her memory. "You stole my consciousness, didn't you?" she accused, eyes turning black as her face twisted with anger. "Held me suspended between life and death."

Emmerich gulped, nervous now. "You would have died," he argued.

"You thought this was better, a black hole in my memory and you asking me to trust that your word is true."

"Why would I lie to you?"

She shrugged. "Same reason you'd sail me out to the middle of fucking nowhere with a limited crew aboard." She leaned into his space now, less than an inch separating them. "You planned to take me out, and you lost your nerve. Now you're covering your tracks."

"Why the kissing?" he countered, leaning his forehead against hers. "Why would I do any of that if I wanted to see you cold and lifeless?"

"A predator luring in its prey, and I happily swallowed every bite you fed me. They starved me for kindness, and you twisted that to your advantage."

Emmerich pulled back abruptly. "Fucking hell, are you even listening to yourself right now?" He almost laughed. "I'm flattered, Princess, truly, that you think I'm capable of such a wicked plan." There was only pity in his gaze now. "I'm afraid I'll have to disappoint you. That's more your style than mine."

Solveig's lips pulled back with an animalistic snarl. She reached behind her, feeling for a dagger that wasn't there, just as the door to the room swung open and Emmerich's head swivelled to face the intruder.

"What?" he snapped.

"Apologies, Captain," the boy stammered, "they're asking for you on deck."

"Close the door," he seethed. "I'll be out in a moment." The boy nodded, running from the scene before him.

"Where are you taking me?"

"Elithiend," he bit out. "As twisted as you interpret my actions to be, I set course for my home in case you needed further care. The last thing I wanted was to see you dead."

She ripped her arm free. "Take me home, Prince. I've no desire to be on this ship, or anywhere else with you any longer."

"For fuck's sake," Emmerich cursed, his head falling back. "Fine, if you want to go back to that filth, we'll go." He brought his gaze back to hers. "But you and I are far from finished here, Princess." He stalked from the room; the door slamming shut behind him.

CHAPTER SEVENTY-FIVE

The Dead Strait

"What was so important that you saw fit to go against orders and interrupt us?" Emmerich commanded as he stepped out on to the blustering deck.

"Apologies, Captain," Lieutenant Garrue said from where he stood at the helm, his stance weary, eyes glazing over, Commander Bleeker stood beside him.

"This idiot refused to stand down without your approval," Wrenn muttered. "He's been sailing us since before daybreak."

"Release the helm to Commander Bleeker, Lieutenant. Go get some rest. That's an order," Emmerich declared. The boy immediately stepped away from the wheel to head below deck.

"You know," Wrenn said, adjusting the ship's course slightly, "life would be much easier if you reminded the crew that my orders are to be followed in your stead."

"I'll try to remember that in the future. Now, what's going on?"

Wrenn glanced at him for a moment before refocusing on the horizon. "Storms catching up. We might outrun it for a while longer, but it'll be on us soon."

"We've had a course change anyway," Emmerich muttered over the wind that whipped his hair across his face.

"Where to?" Wrenn asked, concern marring her brow.

"Torrelin, back to Marrelin City."

Wrenn swung back to face him. "Tell me you're joking?" Emmerich shook his head. "You want to navigate The Dead Strait with a storm at our back? The Gate was bad enough, but the Strait?"

"You think I want to put the ship at risk? I've got an irate and armed princess below deck, and I don't particularly want to see what she will do if I refuse her now."

"Weddings off then?" Wrenn joked, earning a glare in return.

"You get us to the mouth of the Strait, and I'll sail us through."

"Aye, Captain," Wrenn saluted.

"And, Wrenn," Emmerich pressed, "save your jokes until tomorrow, if we live that long."

Jagged rocks lay scattered ahead as the sky darkened above them. The mouth of The Dead Strait lurked before them, shrouded slightly in the building darkness.

"We should drop anchor," Commander Bleeker said, from where she stood beside the prince. "Wait until morning."

"There's no time," Emmerich grimaced. "If we wait until morning, we risk navigating the Strait in even worse conditions."

"Sailing it at night is suicide, even for you."

"Have all hands on deck. We're going to need everyone to get through this night alive."

A dark head peaked above the deck. The wind caught her hair, sending it flying about her face and neck. She reached into a pocket, removing a black silk ribbon to tie it back at the nape. Emmerich watched on from the helm and Wrenn followed his gaze to where Solveig stood staring out at the passage ahead of them. The churning waters were littered with jagged rocks, many large enough to rip a gash in the hull that would founder the ship. Neither the coast of Elithiend nor Southern Torrelin were close enough to swim to in this weather, lest they risk being sucked under by an unseen current.

"I'll deal with her," Wrenn muttered, heading off before the prince could neither object nor agree.

Solveig heard the heavy booted approach of the commander but stayed staring at the siren call of The Dead Strait.

"I think perhaps it might be best if you returned below deck, Your Highness." Commander Bleeker intoned as she came to a stop beside her.

"And miss all the fun? I think not."

"The captain needs all his men focused. You may be a distraction."

"I can take care of myself."

"That's not what I meant."

Solveig turned to face her then. "Say that again."

"I meant no offence."

"Yet still you dared say it."

"We both know you wield your looks as expertly as any other weapon."

"And yet that still does not make me responsible for the reactions of your men." She flicked her gaze over the commander's shoulder to where the prince remained at the helm. "Or your captain. No, I think I'll stay and watch the game unfold front and centre."

"You truly have nothing better to do?"

"Believe me, there are many places I would rather be right now. Yet there is little I can do about it, and I refuse to cower below deck, wondering if the next sway of the ship will bring us to our doom. I prefer to face my fate head on."

"So be it." Commander Bleeker shrugged. "Just stay out of our way."

"Pull the sails," Emmerich called from the helm. "We don't want to give these winds any more control." The deck hands raced to the mast, pulling the lines to secure the sails as fast as they could. "Aire Wenders, block the gusts. Earth Breakers, do what you can to those rocks. Clear as large a path as possible and we may get through this."

A deathly silence fell upon the crew. Howling winds, slamming rain and the groaning ship were the only sounds as the sun fell below the horizon, plunging the world into darkness.

"PYROMANCERS," Emmerich called. "Light our way!" Solveig launched to her feet; the wind stealing her breath, as she raced to the edge, watching as each pyromancer sent their blue flames out into the darkness.

Strings of flickering blue light formed around each of the rocks; flying beneath the surface, allowing them to see every jagged edge that lurked below. It was a map. A way through The Dead Strait that only pyromancy could show. Giving the Earth Breakers time to break down any edges that came too close to the ship's hull, as they slowly entered the mouth of the Strait. It was the single most deadly passage surrounding the Osvoltan Continent; besides the whirlpool ridden gate on the southeast edge of Elithiend.

How it worked, Solveig wasn't sure. She didn't think volcanic rocks would have existed this far from the Caldera. Yet the only other explanation was too fanciful; that the citizens of Elithiend had painstakingly set charges along the Strait for this eventuality.

Their good fortune did not hold for long. As they approached the halfway point where the Strait narrowed slightly, the storm finally caught up. Aire

Wenders fought to keep the winds from sending the ship careening into the rocks and cliffs as they weaved slowly through the maze. But even from this distance, Solveig could see the prince's men were weakening. If they kept this up, they wouldn't survive the night.

Thunder rumbled overhead, angry and deafening. Pale blue lightning lit the sky as the rain hammered down. At the aft of the ship, Solveig could see the prince and his commander arguing, about what, she couldn't be sure. The winds stole their voices away into the night, far from her ears. Whatever it was, the prince appeared resigned, desperate. He didn't want to agree to the commander's demands, but with his crew growing weaker by the second, he was running out of options fast.

"Ma'am, the captain has asked that you go below deck now," a voice said from beside her.

"No."

"It wasn't a request, Your Highness."

"I don't answer to your captain. Unless he wants to drag me below deck himself, I'm staying right here. I'd hate to miss any other exciting revelations," she said gleefully, taking pleasure in seeing the uneasy glint in the boy's eye.

Solveig stood at the rail, sodden hair whipping around her face, as she reached out to touch the damp, moss covered rock before her as the ship crawled passed. Above the water it didn't appear dangerous, but she had seen the sharp jutting edges that lurked beneath the surface and felt a kinship with it.

She heard a faint command uttered along the wind; a command surely not meant for her ears. "Blind and bind," they said.

Her eyes flew up to the prince, meeting him glare for glare. She had known he wouldn't step away from the helm of his ship in their hour of greatest need. Thought she had beaten him at his own game but had failed to realise the extent of his resourcefulness. They seized her arms from behind, thrust a bag over her head and led her to the middle of the ship, where they tied her to the mast.

The wind kissed her cheek softly through the gaps in the weave, words drifting with it for her ears only. "I offered you the chance to go below deck and ride the rest of this out in comfort. You chose wrong. Now you can sit there, devoid of your senses, soaked to the bone, whilst we try to survive the mess you forced us into."

It was an Aire Wenders power, to send messages along the wind, one she hadn't seen him use until now. She struggled against her bonds as Emmerich's voice left her to be replaced by the howling wind. But the more she fought, the more the rope bit into her skin. Even blinded as she was, she could still see the flash of lightning through the bag.

Blinding lights: shouting voices, rolling thunder, crashing waves, and booted feet running across the deck. An orchestra of desperation surrounded her, and then there was nothing.

No crackle of lightning, no roll of thunder, not even a breeze to send chills over her sodden clothing. Even the rain had stopped. An eerie silence crept over the ship, but she could still feel the swaying as they moved along the current. Something had stopped the storm in its tracks, something the prince didn't want her to see. A secret more precious than how to navigate the Strait, something he had decided was worth severing their trust completely for.

Time passed unknowingly, seconds, minutes, hours. Try as she might, it was impossible to track them. Her mind raced through endless possibilities of what was happening beyond the blindfold that could have quenched the ferocious storm. What power medley had the Elithiend's uncovered in their years of separation from the rest of Osvolta? All questions her family would demand of her that she would have no answer for.

"HEAVE TO!" the prince called. His voice almost deafening now. Boots thundered across the deck once more as the hands raced to follow his orders.

But beyond their echoing footfalls, she heard another sound, one that chilled her to the bone. An ethereal, lyrical voice, unmistakably that of a woman's as it whispered, "You owe me."

For all the days Solveig had spent aboard the Valdrych, she had not come across another female crew member, other than Wrenn Bleeker. And the melody of the woman's voice that sang and echoed through her mind was not the commander's.

It was like a whip cracked. A sharp taste cut through the air as the noise of the storm was unleashed upon them once more, and they ripped the bag from her face. She stared up into the exhausted blue eyes of the prince.

"Time to go," he muttered, taking her by the arm to drag her along with him. Solveig twisted in his grip to see the Dead Strait now behind them. The ship was listing slightly to the port side.

"Who was she?" Solveig demanded.

"What are you talking about?"

"Don't treat me as a fool. I heard a woman's voice that was neither mine nor the commanders, so who was she? What happened? How did we make it through? How did you dampen the storm?"

"You needn't concern yourself with any of that."

"There you go again, keeping your secrets," she hissed.

"You know me, Princess, I hate to disappoint," he grumbled; leading her below deck, where he deposited her outside the door to the captain's quarters without another word.

CHAPTER SEVENTY-SIX

Making Plans

The Valdrych limped toward the deserted Solist Port on the south-eastern shore of Torrelin. Already the air felt cooler as the weak morning sun fought its way through a haze of sea mist. Solveig watched on from the porthole in the captain's quarters, where she had stayed since the prince left her there the previous evening. As the ship meandered up to the rotting dock, deckhands jumped from the Valdrych on unsteady feet as they made to moor the ship. Solveig gathered the rest of her belongings quickly before leaving the room for good.

Commander Bleeker was first down the gangplank, followed by the prince and a few of his men. Solveig lingered back, watching as those ahead of her stumbled across the uneven boards. She moved with a steady pace, as though she studied all the wrong moves those before her had made and somehow found the safest path across.

"State ye business or be on ye way," a grim voice called from up ahead.

Commander Bleeker spoke first. "The storm damaged our ship. We seek a place to rest whilst we shore her up to continue our journey."

"Who's we?" The man frowned, reaching for the weapon at his side, fingers flexing slightly.

"Solveig Aila Maleen, Princess of Torrelin," Solveig said. The crew cleared a path for her to step through as though she were the dark queen Emmerich had proclaimed to make her. She didn't even glance at him as she passed, though she could feel his heated gaze upon her every second that ticked by. "I was travelling with my companions on the king's orders. We'll be out of your hair within a day, though the ship may require longer mooring should they be unable to fix her today." She removed one glove, extending her hand toward the man in greeting. "I intend to continue on foot to Rialtus Keep."

The man stared at the princess's outstretched hand, his skin paling as she smirked, watching the nervous bob of his throat. Before his eyes rose, taking in her deadly form, dressed in all black, her multitude of weapons glittering in the silvery morning light.

"Your Highness," he stammered, "the pleasure is ours. Must be cautious, ye understand, what with our borders being close to unfriendly territory?" He cut a glance across the princess's companions, and she followed his gaze to where they had stalled on the prince.

"Of course, your diligence to our country's safety is to be praised." She smiled, a wicked gleam in her eyes as she replaced the glove on her unshaken hand.

"Taverns open, hot food served all day, ask for Mrs Tiansey, tell her Aboch sent ye. She might have a few rooms available t'any wishing to stay. Most of our establishments closed a long time ago, little traffic these days. It is only with the kindness of your family that we can continue our lives here." The man smiled now as if he was gazing upon the patron of some charitable god, and not the embodiment of death. "Without their yearly donations and generous tax cuts, we would've had to move on with the others a long time ago."

A grimace played its way across Solveig's face, for she knew it was not kindness that pushed the king to keep these people here. He needed eyes on the Strait, eyes on Elithiend. Without Solist as an outpost for the travelling King's Guard, the next closest was Rialtus Keep at the base of the mountains. Much too far away to spot an invasion in time. As long as Elithiend remained a threat, it benefited the king to keep these people here by any means, otherwise he would have flattened the place long ago.

Solveig took up a table in a far corner of Mrs Tiansey's Tavern. Borrowing a pencil and paper from the kindly lady behind the bar, she wrote a message to be sent to Rialtus ahead of her arrival. Once the messenger was on his way, with a pocketful of silver for his services, Solveig sat back and waited. Watching the ageing townsfolk as they huddled together around rickety tables clutching steaming mugs of broth to fight back the chill. All talk was of the mysterious ship that had arrived that morning, a ship that bore no markers of belonging to the Torrelinian Guard. It was the most excitement the port had seen since Estrellyn fell. Solveig consumed copious amounts of bland, overcooked food alongside hot bitter coffee and watered-down orange juice. But it filled a hole in her aching stomach and that was all she cared about.

Midday crept its way through the curtained windows as Mrs Tiansey placed yet another plate of food in front of the princess. Topping off her coffee, she asked.

"Will ye be spendin' the night, ma'am?" Just as the door swung open with an almighty clatter, and the prince entered, his hair in a windswept disarray, the commander at his side.

"No," Solveig said curtly, her eyes remaining on the prince in the doorway, "I'm merely waiting to see if any of my companions will join me."

The lady followed her gaze to where the new arrivals stood, a knowing smile on her face that Solveig wanted to bat away. "Of course, ma'am, I shall have as many rooms as possible made up should they require them."

As quickly as she left, Emmerich and Wrenn took her place, each dragging out a seat on the opposite side of the table from Solveig. She watched them with keen eyes over the cracked rim of her cup.

"The ship has significant damage to the hull," Emmerich began, filling the yawning silence. Solveig didn't reply as she set down her cup and dug into the fresh meal before her, a plate of mashed potatoes, onion gravy, soggy steamed vegetables, and bone-dry beef.

"Solist has been out of use for too long. They are no longer equipped with the supplies we need to fix her up."

Still, Solveig went on listening in silence, as Emmerich sighed, leaning back in his chair with arms folded across his chest. "Suddenly you have nothing to say?" he snapped.

"You talk enough for the both of us," she muttered, biting into a crust of bread, "I'm merely waiting for you to get to the point of why you interrupted my dinner."

The prince sighed again, rubbing at his eyes. "I'll be travelling to Rialtus with you." Solveig only nodded. "Commander Bleeker will remain here to watch over the ship and my men until I can return with supplies for her repair."

"Mrs Tiansey mentioned she would have some rooms available should you need them."

"They'll be living aboard the Valdrych. With orders to depart should they not hear from me within seven days." Solveig's eyes flicked up to his with an amused smirk.

"If you're that concerned about impending death, why wait seven days? There will be no saving you then."

"I care more about saving them than myself."

"So selfless, Prince." She smiled with a shake of her head. "So noble." Her smile dropped as she speared him with her gaze. "I see we're past pretending as though you had any interest in me."

"Who said I was pretending?" His hand fisted on the table, "this is who I am."

"Shame."

"What is?"

"I thought you might one day join me in the dark."

"The dark is yours, Solveig. I have no interest in joining you there."

"We'll see." She shrugged, drinking down the rest of her coffee. She wiped her mouth with a napkin that looked like it may have been white once upon a time, but had been stained and washed one too many times since then. Standing abruptly, she headed for the bar where Mrs Tiansey now stood, pretending to polish glasses that were already gleaming.

"How can I help, ma'am?" she asked cheerily. Solveig only slid a pouch of coins across the table that would more than cover her tab for the morning.

"For your time," she said simply. "I'll be journeying to Rialtus with my friend Anders." She pointed in the general direction of where the prince and commander still sat in their rickety chairs.

"The one with the curls?" Mrs Tiansey asked, that same knowing smile crossing her face again. "His gaze hasn't left you since he walked in here," she whispered, eyes shining with delight. Solveig knew as much. She had sensed the heat of his gaze every moment since the door had flung open. Even through their verbal sparring, she wanted to be close to him, touch him, to feel the warmth that caressed her veins with his nearness. But that door was all but closed to them now.

"There's something about him," the woman said, her eyes shadowed. "He's guarding a secret; one he's worried will push you away from him if you learn it."

"He's merely my escort," Solveig said coolly, tasting the lie on her tongue. "The king would not allow me to tour the kingdom without protection."

"Whatever he is," Mrs Tiansey whispered, patting Solveig's hand where it lay on the sticky countertop. "Keep your wits about you dear, I may be old, but I still have eyes, and that boy is the finest distraction there is."

Solveig tensed at her words. The secrets and half-truths the prince had kept and told in the weeks they had spent together built up in her mind like a fortress.

"He's no distraction. You've no cause for concern."

It was another lie, of course, and she thought the woman knew it too. Watching in silence as Solveig turned away, heading back to the deceitful prince, steeling herself to spend yet more time in his company. She wouldn't allow herself to fall under his spell again. He was as dangerous and secretive as she was. The sooner they made it to Rialtus, the sooner they could go their separate ways.

For good.

CHAPTER SEVENTY-SEVEN

No Friend to The Crown

The Elysian Caldera loomed to the west. A great hulking blackness at the end of the Rialtus ridge. Solveig and Emmerich crossed ancient wooden bridges that still allowed passage over the rushing Cuprum River. It was the largest river in Torrelin, flowing down from the mountains at East Watch.

They walked in silence. Emmerich lagging, having refused the food offered by Mrs Tiansey in favour of setting out for the Keep sooner. He followed Solveig as she weaved her way through the dense wood. She moved through the trees like the whisper of wind, no map in sight, simply following her nose to their destination.

Watching her here, he could see that even after everything she had done in the name of bettering her kingdom, it was still etched into her soul. A piece she could never carve out. She glided across the moss, twig, and leaf strewn passages where he stumbled and sidestepped the debris awkwardly. He was too used to the drier landscape of Elithiend and its vast meadows. They had little woodland like this in his home, except for Mistfall, the mysterious forest to the south that no one could explain. It had lingered there for as long as anyone could remember.

"The mountain passage is just beyond these trees," Solveig called back to him curtly, as though even giving him clues about where they were heading was a chore for her.

"And you can tell that how?" he questioned.

"I can feel it in my bones, like something is pulling me toward it."

It was more than that, he suspected, a power as old as the dirt they trod on. Something that had been twisted and warped five hundred years prior and yet, without setting eyes on a map, he couldn't be sure. It would have to be an old one, a map from before the fall of Estrellyn, something that most likely didn't exist within the borders of Torrelin anymore.

As promised, they soon stepped out of the thick dark of the forest to be greeted by the slate grey, snow-capped mountains of the Rialtus ridge. They stood before the perilously tight passage that had been blasted through it at the base. Solveig bent to grab a discarded branch from the edge of the forest floor. Emmerich followed her lead. They approached the arched passageway that was bedecked in copper lining, each side adorned with sconces lit with the blue flame of elemental making.

"Even in the brightest days, the tunnels remain dark," Solveig whispered, holding her branch up to the flickering blue flames. A faint breeze ruffled her hair, the chill raising gooseflesh across the prince's arms as she continued,

"Light your way or risk an end you cannot pay," she intoned, before ducking through the arch, disappearing into the blackness.

The prince felt as though a demon had stolen his sight as he stumbled on every fallen rock and unearthed root. The tunnel was endless, a terrible twisted place where one could be lost for eternity.

"You know," Solveig called from where she walked with ease a few steps ahead, "I swear I can hear the doomed direction of your thoughts from all the way up here."

Emmerich saw her glance back to him, her face glowing in the blue light like a phantom of his night terrors. "How can you see where you're headed?" he grumbled, gaze falling to the floor again in a hopeless attempt to see the hazards lying in wait for him.

"Torrelin is my home, Prince, or did you forget?" she murmured, falling silent for a moment, the only sounds the slight echo of their footsteps and the crackle of flame.

"When you become a weapon in the King's Guard, it becomes necessary to learn all the secrets of your land."

"You expect me to believe that you, a coddled princess, grew up traipsing through these caves?"

"Of course not. I spent my formative years in the plush comfort of Erynmar Academy. I did, however, spend two months mapping these caves for the king before he shipped me off to the mines. Even then, I'm not sure I discovered every passage, but the main ones are burned into my memory now."

Emmerich couldn't believe that this place would not have been mapped before. A ridiculous notion, too obvious, a weak link in their defences.

"They were destroyed," Solveig said, as though reading his thoughts.

"What was?"

"Most of our history before The Oracles ascension was burned, the maps of the tunnels included. Their creation harkened back to the..." She paused, swallowing. "The Seers," she bit out finally. "Legend said they were created on their orders."

"And in the centuries since then? No one thought it important enough to retrace them?"

Solveig scoffed at that. "Our enemies were burned, vanished, or trapped across the Strait. What need did we have to worry about hiding places for invaders?"

"Why now?"

"After my grandfather's death, the king spent too many years holed up in that rotting keep. It's made him paranoid." Solveig shrugged. "He's convinced your people infiltrated our communities and sort to shore up our defences."

Emmerich knew the story. The death of the previous king was as ingrained in his life as it was hers because it also resulted in the death of his grandfather. The party at fault changed depending on who told the story.

"If he's so paranoid, then why show me?" Emmerich questioned. "The enemy he desired to keep out?" Solveig's footsteps halted up ahead as he continued.

"What makes you think I won't run back to my king and spill my guts about this perfect place to hide weapons, an army even?" he pressed.

"This place would eat you alive," she muttered, still unmoving, as Emmerich caught up to her.

"What...?" he began when she swivelled suddenly, covering his mouth with her hand, pulling him to the ground. Her other hand drifted to the dirt, drawing up any liquid she could; extinguishing their torches.

In the darkness that descended around them, the prince's sight was completely cut off, heightening his other senses. He could smell the stench of mould ridden damp, and the soft floral of her. Could feel the wet earth soaking and staining his breeches and her skin so close to his as she moved nearer, bringing her mouth to his ear.

"Don't move, don't speak. If you must breathe, do it quietly and we may get out of here unseen," she cautioned and Emmerich only squeezed her hand in silent response.

Something had spooked her, and he knew better than to question her judgement. Before long, he heard soft, squelching footsteps approaching from the west. As they drifted closer, so too came the murmur of voices. Her hand remained over his mouth as though she worried he'd give them away. Yet he could feel the steady beat of her heart at his back, so calm in the face of danger, a stark contrast to the racing of his own,

They stayed huddled in the shadows, the prince silently praying they wouldn't be spotted. Solveig crouched with a hand already grasping the hilt of a dagger at her hip, ready to let it fly if necessary. Her eyes remained focused on the intersection she knew lay up ahead.

"You think it stretches all the way to the Caldera?" came one voice.

"Doubt it. Those demon worshippers wouldn't leave this place un-guarded if it led you straight to their heart." Replied another.

A third voice, that of a woman, with an accent Solveig couldn't quite place yet somehow sounded familiar, silenced the two men she travelled with. "We are here to survey and nothing more, you know the law."

"Oh, come on, imagine how easy it would be." The first said, "to bring this farce crashing down around them."

"Then you'd bring about destruction to us all. They aren't ready yet. We must continue to wait." The woman hissed.

"We have waited for centuries. When will it be enough?"

"The time will come before you meet your end, Silas, of that I am sure, but until then, you cannot interfere."

The voices faded to a whisper and finally silence as they passed by without ever sensing the two young royals lurking in the shadows. Solveig strained to hear more, anger simmering in her blood. Whoever these people were, they were no friend to the crown, the country, or The Oracle. She jumped to her feet as the anger continued to burn. It was the prince who pulled her to the ground this time, holding her tight against his warm, broad chest, whispering in her ear.

"I don't care how skilled you are with those blades. Even you would struggle three against one with unknown powers at play."

"I took down three guards in the sheeting rain escaping Luxenal," she hissed back.

"And if I remember right, you almost died doing so. Against guards who you'd seen train daily for two years."

"Would you be able to sit by as would be enemies to your way of life strolled on by?"

"I would play smarter, Princess. Whoever they are, they clearly pose no threat on their own." He loosened his hold on her. "Whatever you decide. If this is the life you wish to return to? You need only have your king guard every known entrance to these tunnels to keep your people safe. Going after them now helps no one."

Solveig slumped back against him, despite the loosening of his hold, still weak from her brush with death as the adrenaline fled her body. "If I live that long," she muttered, feeling the prince tense beneath her at the words.

"You won't die."

Solveig chuckled, a dark and desolate sound. "I'd be dead already if it weren't for your interference and we both know it." She pushed free of him, brushing the dirt from herself as she stood, holding out a hand to him.

"Come on, we keep going straight and we should be out of here soon." Once he was back on his feet, she turned to move forward, but the prince gripped her tighter. Pulling her back to him as they stood face-to-face in the dark. Close enough to see the other's eyes in the shadows.

"You will not die," he declared, bringing a hand to her face. "I won't allow it."

Solveig smiled, a forlorn expression as she leaned into his soothing touch, which held a promise she couldn't accept. "My time was chosen long before we met, Prince. There is little that can be done to save me now. I have accepted that, and now I can only use whatever time I have left to stop this from happening to anyone else."

Solveig pulled free from his grasp once more, shivering against the cold as the warmth of his touch fled her entirely. "Stay close," she whispered. "We've nothing to light our way now, and the last thing my country needs is a war started in your name because you lost your way beneath the mountains."

CHAPTER SEVENTY-EIGHT

Duke Whitlock

Night had long since fallen when they finally emerged from the tunnels. The moon and stars shone as bright as midday light after the long dark they had travelled through. Flat grasslands and streams lay before them, running off from the snow-capped mountains at their backs. To the east loomed a dark keep surrounded by a stone wall, topped with flickering blue torches, and patrolled by armed guards every few steps.

"Rialtus Keep was once the winter refuge of my family," Solveig murmured, her voice cracking audibly as she fought to get the words out. She stared up at the looming castle that had once held so much hope, warmth, and promise for her. Now it stood only as a stark reminder of everything she had lost.

"It was falling apart with disuse, and they sold it off to the Whitlock family, who then took over daily command of the southern villages and ports. Under our tight reins, of course."

"You came here a lot, didn't you?"

"I spent more time in the walls of the keep and Erynmar Academy than I ever did in High Tower Castle," she murmured, kicking at a tuft of grass. "That place was never a home to me."

"How long has it been?"

"I haven't been back since before his funeral."

Emmerich grasped her hand. The warmth comforting her weary soul. "With time and distance, you can lock away even the most painful of memories, but coming face-to-face with them? That breaks them open as surely as a key to its lock. Perhaps this is what you need, the last goodbye."

Solveig tore her hand from his. "I said my goodbyes," she seethed, turning to head toward the keep. "I'm here only because we have no other choice. Unless you wish to walk back to Marrelin City without food or rest, Rialtus Keep is the only warm bed we will find. If I had a choice, I would never step foot in these halls again."

Emmerich stared after her, confusion and longing cluttering his mind. "One day, Solveig Maleen, you're going to have to face every dark piece of your soul. The choice of whether you face it alone or with someone to help you from falling is yours and yours alone."

Solveig didn't acknowledge him as she walked to face the memories that lurked within the shadowed halls of the keep, leaving him to hurry after her. As they approached the locked gates, a voice called from above, echoing their greeting at the dock.

"State your business or be on your way."

"Princess Solveig Maleen, seeking an audience with Duke Whitlock, I sent word this morning."

The guard nodded, his gaze moving to the prince. "And you, boy?"

"I'm merely her highness's servant."

The guard stared down at them for a moment before waving a hand in a silent command that saw the gates groaning on their hinges as they swung open. Bidding them enter. Within the walls of the keep, a sense of foreboding peace fell, with the trickling sounds of water and flickering blue lights to chase away the shadows. Somehow, it was still home. Solveig fought back the emotions warring to the surface, the tears that threatened to clog her throat as the doors to the keep flew open. There at the top of the stone steps, a man raced down, pulling a surcoat over his shoulders.

Her resolve broke then as she raced into the arms of the Duke of Rialtus Keep. A kindly man of strong build, silvering blonde hair and creases around his ice-blue eyes.

"Never thought I'd see your face brighten these halls again," he whispered, pressing a kiss atop her hair, holding her in a tight embrace.

"I wish I could say this was a social call." She stepped back. "But I'm afraid I must ask for your help."

"Anything you need is yours." He smiled, pulling her into another hug. But as the duke's gaze drifted over to the prince, it hardened, the creases about his eyes and forehead deepening.

"Who might this be?"

"Prince Emmerich of Elithiend," Solveig answered, much to the prince's shock and dismay.

"You can wipe that look off your face," she said to Emmerich. "The duke is the one person in all of Torrelin you can trust."

Duke Whitlock released Solveig to approach Emmerich, shaking his hand in a grip that bordered on too tight. "Both of you are welcome to stay as long as you need, though I am afraid that despite your note, you have caught me unawares. Many of the rooms are locked up for the winter already and most that aren't are still being reinforced. You'll have to share."

"Not to worry," Solveig sang, "the prince is used to sleeping on the floor by now," she joked, eyeing Emmerich, daring him to argue.

"Right," he replied tightly, as though he wasn't already privy to the knowledge of how she felt curled against him in the night. Of the noises she made when his mouth was on hers.

Somehow, Solveig fell into a dreamless sleep despite the memories that plagued her thoughts. In every shadowed alcove, every lit hallway and every creak of floorboards, Aldrik's face, his laugh, and warmth invaded her consciousness. He was at the heart of this place, having spent many of his last years seeing it restored. A task the duke had kept up in his son's memory.

She feared the memories that daylight would bring. When she would walk the halls alone that they had once walked together. Would the portraits of their childhood, of every part of their lives, remain? Or had it been too painful for his parents to look upon day after day now that his laughter no longer filled the quiet halls?

The night deepened, and with it, nature spun her web. Wind howled through the mountains at the Keep's back. As though the storm had circled back to enact further suffering on their already exhausted bodies and frayed minds. Solveig tossed and turned. After a few hours of fitful rest, she woke surrounded by the darkness of midnight to a room black as pitch. The stars beyond the window veiled by a cloud drenched sky. The moon tried in vain to gild her surroundings in silver light, but succeeded in only adding further unease. Manifesting eerie shadows in the corners of the bedchamber.

She was frightfully hot beneath the heavy sheets, yet shivers still wracked her body, gooseflesh dancing up the pale length of her strong arms. With the wind creating its own cascading operatic masterpiece beyond the walls, Solveig decided it was useless trying to sleep further. She hopped down from the bed, careful not to trip over the prince whom she knew could sleep through the end of the world if he were so inclined. But he was nowhere to be seen. The floor was utterly devoid of life. An empty pallet dressed in fur rugs, thick sheets and feather stuffed pillows lay cold beside the bed.

Her blood turned to ice in her veins as all her worst fears echoed in her mind. She'd brought the enemy into the heart of her country. Though they were still miles from the capital. Rialtus Keep held secrets that could bring a nation to its knees. She knew her family had not been thorough when they abandoned the keep for ruin decades earlier. Many times, in her younger years, she had come across old tomes and documents containing pertinent secrets that belonged under lock and key.

She had to find him before he stuck his nose in something he had no business knowing. She had opened her arms and almost her heart to his treachery, but she would not surrender her kingdom to the might of his. No matter how she felt about the rulers, both living and metaphysical.

Every step sounded as though it would wake the entire keep. The groan of ancient floorboards echoed all around her. The usual silence of her steps was a distant memory in a place such as this. She would have had to fly to be silent and even then, she was sure the beat of wings would reverberate off the stone walls.

A lifetime spent running through these halls in search of privacy with her lover had its advantages. Even as she desperately tried to block out the distant memories, she could not deny the usefulness of knowing what waited at the end of every darkened hallway. She checked the kitchens first, hoping he had innocently awoken in the night, same as her, and had simply gone for a drink. But found only a servant against the far wall beside the stove, trying to stay warm beside the flame.

"They couldn't give you a blanket?" she asked, voice sharp as the crack of a bell, startling the boy to his feet, sending the stool he had been perched upon clattering to the floor.

"Your Highness, forgive me; I did not hear you enter," he stammered, wiping his hands on his breeches in a nervous tick.

"Don't trouble yourself. It is the middle of the night. You should rest instead of freezing to death down here."

"I do as my master commands," the boy shrugged.

"I don't remember your master being so exacting."

"Will you be joining them, miss? I can prepare you some food and drink too," he asked, changing tack.

"Joining who, where?" Solveig's eyes narrowed.

"The duke and your companion. They have been down in the library for the last hour. They were settling in for a long night."

Solveig spun, the skirts of her nightgown and robe rustling as she moved. Leaving the servant dumbstruck in her wake. She moved as fast and quiet as she could, but the keep did not aid her. Floorboards creaked with every other step, no doubt alerting the two men to her presence. The closer she got, the louder the hushed melody of arguing voices became. She watched, waiting, trying to catch words in the air, but it was fruitless. The two men had the power of Aire in their veins and could send messages along the wind meant solely for their ears if needed. Irritated with waiting, she grabbed a sconce from the wall, calling out to the two men sat within.

"Isn't it rude, gentleman, to whisper in the darkest places when you have other company around?" she said with a bored air. Emmerich's dark gaze skewered her, seeing straight through her nonchalance to the suspicion laced beneath it.

"The winds stole our sleep far sooner than yours. I was merely asking the prince tales of his kingdom to pace away the long dark." The duke smiled, his kind eyes warm and honest.

"Indeed." She clicked her tongue against the roof of her mouth, eyeing the men. "You won't mind if I join you?" she took a seat between them. "I am dying to hear tales of far-off places." Solveig met Emmerich's stare head on as she leaned toward him, her eyes never leaving his as she reached for the perspiring glass of untouched ale before him. Taking a long sip before settling back in her chair, not bothering to adjust her robe as it gaped open slightly at her chest. Neither did she miss his gaze, as it dropped for barely a second. A smirk crossing her face as his eyes lifted back to hers, fighting a silent battle that neither of them wanted to yield.

"Please don't stop on my account." She blinked with false innocence. Emmerich cleared his throat to continue his story, looking anywhere but at her.

"When I was younger, I used to run through the kingdom without care, as though nothing and no one could touch me. Until my grandmother sat me down and began spinning mystical tales of worlds and powerhouses. Of things that had been, and things that would be. She would tell stories of what she saw in my future. Warning of how even then, in the relative safety of Elithiend, there were still those who sought to do me harm. Cautioning that I would play a part in whether Elithiend would flourish or fall."

"No wonder your ego is so big, with a grandmother spinning grand tales of destiny. Such words are blasphemous in these lands. May I remind you, Prince?"

"My grandmother hails from an ancient line of Seers, Your Highness. I will not denounce her lineage just because you and yours have forgotten the old ways."

"The old ways were lies. Treachery meant to maintain the stronghold Estrellyn held over the kingdom."

"Ah yes, because life on the mainland has been bountiful since the fall."

The duke cleared his throat. "Now children, you could argue until the mountains thaw, but I doubt it would serve any good. We hail from lands of differing beliefs, but that does not mean we cannot get along despite them."

"I cannot accept his version of the world," Solveig declared.

"Only because you're too frightened to acknowledge the truth that's staring you in the face," Emmerich countered.

Solveig flew to her feet; chair clattering behind her, nightgown and robe swishing across the floor as she left. Only for the prince to grab her arm, pulling her back to him.

"Release me," she seethed through clenched teeth, eyes burning.

"What are you so afraid of?"

"I fear the fall of my kingdom. I fear the blood of innocents on my hands. I fear destroying everything for my own sake."

"Perhaps it needs to fall, for you cannot continue this way." Emmerich implored.

"Watch me." Solveig wrenched her arm free and stormed from the room, leaving the duke and the prince to finish putting their worlds to rights. She instead went in search of the one place she had been sure she would not enter, and yet now it was the only place she wanted to be.

She crossed echoing hallways; past archways and locked doors, racing up the spiral staircase of a towering turret on the eastern end of the keep, until she reached the top. She inhaled a long draw of air before reaching for the tarnished copper handle, twisting to find it unlocked. With another breath, she pushed it open. Coming face-to-face for the first time in four years, with every broken piece of her soul, kept like a history book in this one room.

CHAPTER SEVENTY-NINE

Revelations

Aldrik's chambers covered the entire top floor of the turret. Wooden support beams kept the ageing roof stable. The four-poster bed on the far side was still draped in lush velvet blankets and silken forest green sheets. All of it unchanged from the last time she had slept within it, her Lord beside her. The bookcases were untouched, still cluttered as he'd preferred. He'd run out of room for his ever-expanding collection, and never had the heart to part with any of them.

Solveig moved through the space, taking a seat by his desk. A book lay open beside a quill and a dried pot of ink, discarded as though in a hurry. The note he must have been writing was nowhere in sight.

This room was every piece of him. Of them. Of their lives. This would have been their home; had they taken the vows they had promised each other before she had held him as he took his last blood-soaked breath.

She continued to move around the room, as though she were living in a memory. Wandering over to a windowsill that held an array of framed flash powder images. Many already fading with time, ones they had planned to replace as the years of their lives passed by. Most of them she'd removed from her own chambers in High Tower Castle, no sooner than they had lowered his body into the hallowed earth. Hesitantly, she picked up a tarnished silver frame, tears in her eyes as she stared down at their smiling faces burned in time from the blackened flash powder.

They had taken the image at their engagement party. She had worn a dress of lightest ice-blue to match his eyes, and his suit matched the forest green of hers. It was her favourite image of them, but the more she stared at it, the more she noticed something was off. Where parts of it appeared faded by sun damage as was expected with flash powder, other areas did not. She brought it closer to her face, realising then that something lay beneath it.

Slowly and with shaking hands, she turned the frame around, loosened the fastenings, and removed the backing. She froze instantly as it revealed a folded square of paper. Solveig's shining eyes flicked back to the desk where the discarded ink and quill sat. Swallowing heavily, she lifted the paper with one hand and placed the frame back down.

Slowly, delicately, fingers still shaking, she unfolded the paper, almost falling to her knees as she saw the first line of his scrawl, addressed to her.

Dearest Sol,

If you're reading this, it means that which I feared has finally caught up to me. I know I should have told you, confided in you, but I didn't want you to worry. There was nothing you could have done, and I hoped to live out the rest of my days happily. Perhaps that makes me selfish, but I hope one day you will understand. That you will cherish the moments we had, and not those we lost.

Wherever life takes you, know that I will be with you. In this world and beyond. I was blessed to know you, to love you, and to be loved by you. You were the air I breathed, the blood in my veins, and every thought in my mind. My days started and ended with you, and if I am lucky, my life will come to its end with you as well.

To die with those you love around you is all that one can ask. Still the burden of knowing the pain I will leave in my wake grows almost too much to bear. Sol, you are the strongest person I know. The level of your power has never defined you and you must never let it. Who you are, and what you believe; your knowledge of that which is right and wrong; fighting for those who cannot fight for themselves. That makes you more deserving of the crown than that gold encased rot that looks down upon you. Never allow them to darken your spirit. You're more important than you could ever possibly know.

We deserved to see out our lives together, but I know now we will be robbed of that dream. One day I will fade to be but a memory to you, and you should not feel guilty for it. You were my whole life Sol, but I cannot be yours. Live Solveig, for both of us. My love will follow you endlessly. It will not fade, nor falter. Even in the darkest of places, and the bleakest of hours.

Yours, in this world, and the next.

-Aldrik

Tears clouded her vision as she held this gift, this last piece of Aldrik that she had not known existed, to her chest. It lifted and destroyed her, to understand, finally, why he hid it from her. Yet to stare the evidence in the face of just how thoroughly she had failed his memory, gnawed at her insides. She had allowed the golden rot to taint her, to darken her. To transform her into something that she was sure even Aldrik would turn away from, and she would not blame him.

Fight for those who cannot fight for themselves, he had written. Yet she had spent the last few years as a glorified executioner. She was the sword in the crown's golden hand, stained and dripping with blood. She had become the villain and saw no way of freeing herself from those bonds now. Aldrik had been her lifeline, her way out of the sickness, and after he was gone, it had all too easily infected her.

She had grown to find power in fear, freedom in blood. Who would she be without it? Nothing more than chattel to be sold off to the highest bidder. There was no place for the woman she had been. She had faced the unthinkable and fought to survive it.

Shattered tears fell unbidden down her sullen cheeks as she slipped the note into her pocket. Taking a deep shaking breath, she moved to piece the frame back together when her eyes caught on a larger one, hidden at the back. Its image severely faded. Older. A shot of Erynmar Academy, the school a foreboding presence in the background, the students lined up before it.

Solveig found herself easily toward the centre, Aldrik on one side, Adira on the other. This had been the end of her final year at Erynmar before they had summoned her back to Torrelin to face her manifestation ceremony. The last time her life had felt simple, through the eyes of a child, at least. She scanned the others, a sea of nameless faces, but paused. There, in the back row, a tall boy with a riotous mess of curls stared forward, smiling widely. He stood a step away from all the other children. How had she never noticed how odd his positioning and demeanour were before? Yet it was all too clear to her now as she stared into the fathomless eyes of the childhood version of the Prince of Elithiend.

CHAPTER EIGHTY

Betrayals

Every word had been a lie.
  Every.
Single.
Moment.

The Prince of Elithiend had been to the mainland before. He knew her; he knew them all. Was it all part of a long game? Had she allowed herself to be so easily fooled? She saw red, anger white-hot and aching dried her tears as she threw the picture at the wall, the glass shattering around her as it collided with the stones. Carefully, she lifted the picture free from the pile of glass before she stormed from the room and back down to the library to confront him. She couldn't allow this to stand. She had questions, and he was finally going to answer them, or she'd see him thrown into Luxenal with only the long dark for company.

His actions were already payable with his life, royals after all, needed permission to enter other countries. Luxenal would be a mercy that would prevent all-out war with Elithiend. The storm beyond the walls of the keep had finally roared its last, the silence that now descended upon them almost deafening. This time, as she approached, she removed her boots; footsteps light as possible as she listened for their voices from down the hall. They were louder now. Perhaps they had assumed she'd returned to bed, what with the quieting of the storm. Her steps grew even slower, desperate to not give herself away as she tried to listen for any snippets of information.

"You're outnumbered," the duke declared, accompanied by the sound of a fist hitting the table.

"You know nothing of Elithiend's resources."

"And you are not prepared for what Torrelin will unleash upon your people if given half a chance. You may have infiltrated their lands, but not their armies."

"They'd have to cross the Strait first, face the gate, or worse, the maelstrom."

"You just showed the most dangerous weapon in their arsenal exactly how to do it!"

"She wouldn't—"

"You don't know her. She was but a girl the last time you set foot on these lands, and you barely escaped with your life then. Things have changed in the years you've been stuck beyond the Strait. You have allies and spies but it's all for nought without eyes on the armies, on the king himself. Even Solveig has done unspeakable things in the crown's name. She seeks only to further her own ambitions. She wouldn't think twice about spilling your secrets if she believed it would somehow benefit her."

"Then it seems, Duke, that you don't know her that well either."

"You're being naïve, you spent the last decade sailing a free man. The prince of a thriving kingdom, she has spent the last two years becoming darkness. There is no light in her anymore. Whatever you hope to gain from her, you will not get it. You must leave before she entraps you."

"I'll take my chances."

"Then you are more a fool than I thought, and you would damn your people over misplaced lust. My family has protected you in every way we could, housed and hid you for years. I implore you to reconsider."

Solveig almost crushed the picture in her fist with the rage. Forget confronting him. She was still weak. If she confronted them now, they'd attempt to silence her. She had to ensure that both would get what's coming to them. Whatever was going on here, even the duke, was against her. He was familiar with Emmerich. What other secrets had he been keeping? Did she even know him at all? Did she even know either of them?

She was utterly alone. In a place that had once held warmth and freedom, now it suffocated her with secrets waiting to be laid bare.

She could do it. Could run home and spill her guts to her family, save her own neck by serving Emmerich's and the duke's up in her place.

But in doing so, she aided them. They who she had spent the last few weeks searching for a way to topple their reign. Had given the very documents to Adira for safe keeping.

There was only one choice remaining. One safe place, and no way to get there. She had to go back to Farrenhold, attack from the outside with the Etana's behind her.

Solveig hurried back up to the room she was supposed to be sharing with the prince. She dressed in a hurry, packing her things before leaving a note scrawled atop the haphazardly made sheets. The picture, she packed in her bag for safekeeping, valuable information for later.

The princess became the wraith once more, became that which stoked fear into the hearts of her people. The Reaper of Luxenal, dressed in all black, hood covering her head, scarf wrapped around the lower half of her face, daggers at her hips and sword down her back. She slipped out of the window, scaling the vine-covered trellis that adorned the outer walls before racing off into the shadows. She moved swiftly, silent as she approached the stables and freed the nearest horse. Walking out of the grounds, she paused, having been sure of her destination. Yet something called to her, and she turned, heading to the small graveyard to say goodbye to Aldrik for the last time.

She walked past aged and crumbling headstones before finally coming to a stop before a stark white one, infused with gold and copper threads, it read.

Here Lies
Lord Aldrik Torin of House Whitlock
Beloved Son and Betrothed.
Your Soul Burned Too Bright.
May You Find Endless Peace Amongst the Stars
At Home Within Their Light

There she sat, despite the chill of the rain-soaked ground that seeped into her skin and through to her bones, hands shaking as they held the Lord's last note.

"You were supposed to be the love of my life too," she whispered. "I have failed you in every regard. I allowed them to rot me, twist me," anger and sorrow laced her words, fogging the air as she spoke.

"After all, what was I to do? You left me with no explanation, no warning. I. Had. Nothing. Until this." She fisted the note as though he were sitting before her. "For years, your memory haunted me. I ran from every single reminder. Every piece of me you loved became a weakness I locked away, to protect myself, until I became that which you feared most. For years, I couldn't understand why. But now I do." She stared at his name etched into the cold stone.

"It seems keeping secrets was a talent of yours I never knew about. If you were here, would I be about to lock you in a cell alongside the rest of your family? Tried as traitors?"

"What else did you lie about? I wish there were some way that wherever you are, on the other side of the veil that you could speak. Someway that you could tell me that every happy memory isn't stained with lies and half-truths."

Tears glistened in her eyes, brows knitting together as she fought to keep her composure. "Tell me it's not true, tell me you didn't know, that all that time we spent planning for our freedom, you were also plotting our fall."

Her head fell against her knees as angry, ragged sobs racked her body. The night passed, clouds clearing to reveal the stars at last. The surrounding air grew colder, the damp ground freezing as she sat there, quiet in her grief. Hair prickled on the back of her neck as she heard a twig snap behind her, followed by the crunch of leaves.

"You should have stayed inside," she hissed over her shoulder, but no response came. "Come any closer and I'll take you down." Still, the footsteps advanced.

She reached back for a dagger, not knowing it was too late. Not realising that the person who had followed her was not the prince come to explain. And her manoeuvre had instead made their task only that much easier. As they grasped her arms, pulling her backward, an involuntary yelp escaped her. She kicked out. Tried to twist her way out of the person's grip as they placed a shackle around her wrist. A dark-coloured mesh bag was pulled over her head before they secured her other wrist at her back.

"Don't fight, Princess," General Anik sneered as she continued to struggle. "The king wants a word." Her breath was stolen from her and what little light had seeped through the dark fabric was snuffed out completely by her closing eyelids.

CHAPTER EIGHTY-ONE

Last Chance

She didn't know how much time had passed when she finally came to. Bile rose up her throat as the bag was ripped from her head. Eyes burning from the searing light and rush of colours, ears muddled as she heard voices and wheels and clanging metal. All she knew was utter confusion slithering through her mind as her lungs heaved for every desperate breath of fresh air.

"Welcome back, sister," Killian murmured from where he stood beside her prone form. Lightning quick, her senses focused. All it had taken was that snivelling voice to bring her back in alignment. She tried to move, not wanting to be laying at *his* mercy, but they'd strapped her down on a long examination table. The physical restraints bit into her skin as she struggled against them.

"Where am I?" she seethed, just as the damp stench of High Tower Castle filtered through her overloaded senses.

"Home," was all the prince said, her eyes tracking him as he nodded at someone behind her. She tried to twist, to see who else was there, but it was futile. Even her neck was caged to the table. She could only hear footsteps echoing, and the groaning rattle of something being brought toward her, but it was enough.

"No." Solveig whispered as the realisation hit. "I did everything you asked."

"Relax, and it will be over before you know it."

"You forget you've subjected me to this before. Your lies won't work on me."

"All we want is for the information you've collected to come straight from the source. We can't risk it being tainted by your own bias."

The fight drained from her; there was no way out. Killian had her at his mercy. She had but one option left. The thought alone made her ill, but this was a matter of survival, a game she knew all too well, and would do anything to win. Including, beg.

"Please. Killian." Her voice broke. "I'm on your side. Let me prove it."

"Oh, Sister." Killian smiled; blonde hair shining like gold in the light as he bent closer, eyes sparkling, lips twisting with a cruel smirk. "Begging won't save you now. We have spies everywhere. Or did you forget?"

No, she hadn't forgotten. How could she? She felt their eyes everywhere. "We saw every moment you grew far too close to that boy. Put yourself in our shoes. We can't risk you keeping any secrets to protect him."

"I have no desire to protect him," she spat, averting her gaze. He'd lied to her. Schemed and cheated his way into her heart. Saw her deep buried desire for connection and used it against her. And yet, even with all that, there was still a small part of her that cared what happened to him. She couldn't bring herself to hand him over to these people who had done so much to ruin her life.

"Come now, little Reaper," Killian smirked again. "You'll only hurt yourself more this way."

Solveig felt the familiar sting of the disks as their teeth bit into her head in the same spots; yet still she continued to fight. There was a faint red glow in her peripheral vision as Killian fired up the device at her back. White-hot pain pierced her skull. Her limbs painfully stiff, eyes rolling back in her head; mouth agape as though in a silent scream as The Oracle sliced into her consciousness.

Your choices put us all on the line.

Those words echoed through her mind as the icy presence of The Oracle stirred within her. It was as though every fibre of her mind was being picked apart as she saw flashes of memories that The Oracle ripped through. Visions of her and the prince, dancing, laughing. *Kissing*. Every moment over the last few weeks laid bare.

"Dangerous games, Princess," The Oracle tutted. *"Did I not warn you to be careful of your choices? Or did you simply not care?"*

"He's nothing."

"You can lie to yourself, but not to me. I see all, hear all, know all. Now you will show me what I require."

"Why?"

"This world belongs to me. Elithiend will bend or it shall fall."

"That isn't balance."

"That is where you are wrong. Having Elithiend on the outside, an unknowable threat? It destabilises us. We must bring them to heel, and you will either help me, or I will remove you from the board."

Solveig could smell salt air, taste it on her tongue. She could feel the wind and rain as though it lashed at her skin, memories consuming her, as The Oracle watched on with her.

The jagged rocks of the Dead Strait, glowing blue far below the darkened waves, lighting safe passage as Earth Breakers broke the edges of them down. Elithiend's most tightly kept secret, a major safeguard against invasion, was now in the hands of The Oracle.

Then the frigid air of the stormy seas abandoned her, to be replaced by the warmth of the library of Farrenhold, the scent of old tomes filling her senses.

"I see the insubordination runs deep. Have I been too lenient with you all? Do I need to remind you who is in charge?"

Pain seared Solveig's skull again as the memories of the books in Adira's library filled her mind's eye. The titles, the locations, all of it. She fought desperately to close her mind, to stop The Oracle from stealing anymore that would put her friends at risk. But a wicked laugh echoed through her, rattling her bones.

"Something to hide, Princess?"

She threw up walls to block them, but The Oracle tore through them with ease, as though every single one was made of paper and not brick. They pried further; Solveig's back bowed against her restraints as though The Oracle were truly ripping through her. Flashes of memories, weeks, months, years of them all in a rush.

Until they froze.

On a craggy storm scape. A raging sea and stony ground where the princess lay dying, drowning in her own blood.

Shifting again.

A circular room of lost hope and a picture that held one last truth. One that threatened to tear their world apart.

"You should have aided me willingly, Princess. Maybe then you could've kept some of your secrets." The Oracle laughed again. *"You're dying, and you know it, don't you? You're afraid."*

"I'm not afraid."

"Not of death, no. But afraid of what they will do to your friends should you be unable to warn them that you have spilled their secrets. How do you think they'll react to yet another betrayal? Do you think they will welcome you with open arms or throw you to the wolves as they should have the first time?"

Solveig's eyes flew open on The Oracle's command, clouded and unseeing as they took control. "Should you wish to invade Elithiend, Prince Killian, you will need an army of pyromancers at your side. They can light the way through the Dead Strait. Earth Breakers can temporarily break down the rocks that can't be avoided."

"Thank you, blessed Oracle." Killian bowed as though The Oracle were before him, and not his sister.

"I am not finished," they hissed through her. "The princess in Farrenhold is harbouring illegal knowledge in their library. Burn it down or I will deal with them and *you* personally."

The princess's eyes fell closed again, but The Oracle did not release her, feeding on her terror. Whatever was connecting them allowed the transfer of power, too. Even as a shadow in her own body, she could feel the power draining from her soul.

"Since you're unafraid of death, you won't mind meeting it sooner," The Oracle sneered, almost bored now. *"Your brother has a visitor in the castle, in the places so deep and dark that even the stars can't find it. This will be your last chance. Discover the truth of how the prince came here before, what waits for us in Elithiend, and I will restore your power. Fail, and I'll see you rotting beside your long dead lover before the snow sticks to the ground."*

Solveig was numb. Her skin clammy yet cold. Though her mind and body were her own again, she did not fight against her restraints. Blood, thick and hot, dripped from her mouth and nose as she coughed against the blockage. Even when Killian released her restraints, she made no move to stand. Staring only at the vaulted ceiling.

"The Oracle sees this as a failure, but I do not," he said calmly, completely unfazed by the sight of his limp and bleeding sister before him. "You have given us information we did not have before and to prove my generosity, I shall give payment in kind." Killian bent at her side, whispering in her ear.

"It was Gabriel who poisoned Prince Emmerich. What you do with that information is up to you." He shrugged and left the room. Left her there, prone and bleeding, her eyes barely moving to track him as she fell into unconsciousness. The pain, both physical and mental, consuming her.

They confined her to her chambers. Healers of both magical and natural abilities tried to fight whatever unseen malice pushed the sleeping princess to the brink. The wounds on her scalp were slow to heal, despite the best efforts of even the most talented Hydromancer.

She was undressed, bathed and redressed; fed and watered by Teris, supplied tea from her mother's kitchen in *all* varieties. Nevertheless, she would not wake. As the physical wounds healed, the mental ones remained. One's that only the princess could heal. Still, they tended to her, hoping one day she would wake up.

She was lost, trapped in a world of pain and memory. There, she relived her darkest moments in an endless loop. She saw every death, every face, every name. Every life she had snuffed out as easily as a candle flame, again and again.

There was Aldrik's death and Xanthe's too, drowning her in blood so thick and dark she would never be clean of it.

Time passed, trapped as she was, and slowly, agonisingly slow, she became aware of the outside world, of bustling bodies and whispered words. She fought to find her way free to no avail, still trapped in a time loop of The Oracles making. As though The Oracle didn't want her to complete her last task at all. The mere thought of it had The Oracle's voice shattering through her mind once more, impossible to tell if it was illusion or reality.

"I do not wish you to fail, Princess. I only need our visitor to be so broken down he may talk. He knows what you've done, knows you've spilled his secrets. We need him broken to the point of despair, and until then I shall keep reminding you of what is at stake, should you fail me again."

A week passed in the blink of an eye, with no sign of the princess regaining consciousness. The healers had long since given up, exhausted every remedy and therapy. All they could do now was wait.

For a flicker.

Wait.

For the flutter of breath.

Wait.

For the twitch of muscle.

Wait.

Only wait.

For the princess to open her eyes.

CHAPTER EIGHTY-TWO

A Threat or a Promise?

T he moon and stars were hiding. A whisper of a voice. One that was warm, not cold. Gentle, not eerie, slipped into the slumbering mind of the Princess of Torrelin.

Rise.

Open your eyes and rise.

The princess's eyelids flickered; her fingers twitched.

There are things at play in this world that you don't yet know.

Rise and stop the fall.

Rise and save us all.

Green eyes flew open to a dark room lit by a single blue flamed sconce. A red-haired woman slumbered on the chaise at the foot of the bed.

"Say that again." Her voice croaked, slicing through the quiet, causing the woman's head to fly up. Her own eyes were wide and blinking, mouth slack in utter disbelief. She pulled the blanket tighter around herself; rubbing the sleep from her eyes to see that the princess was indeed staring at her from the head of the bed.

"You're awake," Teris whispered.

"Say it again." Solveig repeated, harsher now.

"Say what?"

"Don't play games, I heard a voice."

"A voice?" Teris parroted, "There have been many voices, a cacophony over the past week that could have, should have, woken you but didn't. There was no voice tonight, it is just you and I here and both of us were sleeping."

"I know what I heard!" Solveig insisted, growing agitated.

"Perhaps," Teris stood, "but it was not me, I swear it. I have no reason to lie."

"Teris," Solveig whispered, eyes guarded as she took her in.

Teris beamed a gentle smile, taking a seat on the edge of the bed, clasping the princess's icy hands in hers. "It is a blessing to see you awake ma'am, how are you?"

Her voice, her words, seemed genuine, but Solveig knew, deep down, that this woman had every reason to lie, especially now. Still, she played along.

"I feel as though I have been run over by a fully loaded carriage, pounded into the ground by the horses' hooves." She pulled her hand free. "Why are you here, Teris?"

"It's my job, ma'am."

Solveig scoffed, trying to push her way out of the bed, struggling against her aching limbs and weakened heart.

"You should rest," Teris rushed, standing to help her lay back down, "the healers pulled you back from the brink of death." Solveig flinched away from her reach. Hurt flashed across Teris's face.

"Don't touch me."

"Ma'am?" Teris asked, taking a step back, confusion in her eyes.

"Do you think me blind?" Solveig questioned, wincing against the pain as she shifted her position. "That perhaps I am unaware of what goes on both within and without these walls?"

"Your Highness, I don't..."

"Silence!" Solveig commanded. "My brother never had a female servant, at least not by your name, that little piece of information I learned early on. I have kept a close eye on you ever since." Teris took another step back, closer to the door now. Solveig stood on shaking legs; an arm wrapped around her stomach as she grimaced through the pain.

"Tell me Teris, do you often slink off to the backwater taverns for a drink in the witching hours or was that meeting with the prince an accident? That pouch he gave you sure weighed you down on the journey home."

"I..." Teris stood completely still, only her eyes moved, flicking toward the door, judging her distance from escape.

"I have no desire for excuses. The next words out of your mouth better be the truth."

Teris bit back harsher words she longed to say, her eyes frosting over, the red of her hair somehow glowed brighter, fiercer.

"You're still a pawn." She shook her head, dropping the blanket as she reached for her wrists; easily removing the false cuffs encrusted in red gems that lay there. She dropped them to the ground with a thud before turning to leave.

"I did not dismiss you," Solveig ordered, still staring at the discarded cuffs in shock.

"And I will not stand here and wait for you to send me to the gallows."

"How do you know the prince?"

"I cannot answer that."

"Your life may depend on it."

"I swore my life to the secrecy of my kingdom—I will take my last breath before I reveal her to you."

"You are from Elithiend then?"

"Surely that much is obvious?"

Solveig shrugged. "There was always the possibility that you were a rebel, eager to earn coin as a spy."

"Elithiend is my home. They sent me here for a purpose that you may infer until the crow's sound, but I shall never confirm it. So, either arrest me and lock me up beside my prince. Or let me go so I may never have to wash the stench of this place from my soul again."

"The prince?" Solveig whispered, her turn to be confused now.

"Did you not know?" Teris sneered, shaking her head, "and I thought you knew it all, Princess."

A shard of pain scorched through the princess's mind; she stumbled forward for a moment as the cold eerie voice of The Oracle pierced her skull once more.

"Your brother has a visitor in the castle. In the places so deep and dark, even the stars can't find it."

The prince was the captive in the dungeons of High Tower Castle. The Oracle had threatened her life, pushed her to the brink, all for this moment.

Teris laughed, looking the weakened princess up and down with disdain. "Not quite fearsome these days, are you, Solveig?" she sneered. "It seems you have a decision to make."

"And that would be?"

"Free the prince and condemn yourself or send him to the gallows as one of your traitors risking a war you're not ready for."

"Is that a threat?"

"No, Solveig." Teris sighed. "It was a promise." She stalked from the room on a gust of wind as the sconce blew out at the door, leaving the princess in the same hellish dark as the prince.

CHAPTER EIGHTY-THREE

A Fair Fight

Solveig made the long descent from her tower. Down into the depths of the castle.

Every step she took on the slippery, moss ridden steps reverberated through the endless caverns below. The air grew close from the damp seeping through the walls. Water echoed as it dripped down through cracks in the floors above.

She gripped the dagger at her hip instinctively with every blind turn she made. Even the eternal blue flame she held could not eliminate the cold dark of the dungeons. It felt as though an age had passed before she finally reached the bottom. A central, circular chamber with a series of tunnels spanning every direction. She didn't know where most of them led, and she had no care to explore now. Instead, taking the first tunnel to her right, one she knew well. Walking past rows of empty cells to the end where she halted before the only cell with a locked door. The prince slumped against the far wall, barely visible in the darkness.

"To what do I owe the pleasure?" he spat, his usually warm whiskey voice bitter as it echoed around them. When she did not respond, Emmerich lifted his head, staring her dead in the eyes. His handsome face smeared with dirt was devoid of emotion. All his strength and warmth leeched by the damp confines.

"You came all the way down here and you aren't even going to speak? Is it finally my turn to endure the horror of your twisted power?"

"I was waylaid," was her only response.

"I never should have come after you."

"No, you should have fled when you had the chance, taken the duke with you."

He ignored her. "Are they bored with waiting? Sent you to torture the secrets out of me instead?"

Solveig took a step closer. The prince jumped to his feet, mirroring her.

"That's dramatic, even for you." She simpered, "You said it yourself Emmerich, I'm nothing more than an amateur Hydromancer and you? You're the formidable Prince of Elithiend. What could I do against you?"

Emmerich's gaze left hers, falling to the exposed cuffs at her wrists. "I've been wondering about that since the moment I watched you unleash that darkness for the first time." His eyes rose again, "such a curious use of power, a significant drain on you no doubt." He pursed his lips, angling his head to the side slightly. "Yet to use your magic in its natural form? You can barely hold back a wave for more than a second without me having to step in to save you from imploding."

They stared in silence; him waiting for a response, she, waiting for him to continue as she knew he longed to.

Emmerich shook his head, lips lifting on one side in a smug smirk, "You want something to blame for your lack of power? For all those elemental deaths?"

"I didn't come here to listen to you drone on," she snapped, not liking the direction his thoughts were heading. "Tell me how you came here as a child. How did you hide? How did no one know?"

"I gave you enough already, and you wasted no time feeding that to your king. I'd rather die than lay the secrets protecting my people at your feet."

"You're insane."

"No Solveig. Insanity is you making the same mistakes over and over and expecting a different outcome."

"Stop talking in bloody riddles. I'm trying to save your damn life!"

"My life is nothing if it comes at the cost of my people. Surely you realised that by now."

"No one loves a martyr."

"And yet I will make myself one if I must."

Solveig shook her head in defeat.

"Humour me, Princess. Have any of you fully removed those cuffs since the day they were welded to your wrists?"

"These cuffs give us balance, they allow us to honour The Oracle, to channel our magic to its highest potential."

"You're being naïve," he pressed, "even now, after all you've learned, after everything you've seen. You'll still stand there and spout their pious doctrine."

Emmerich moved forward, so slow his steps were near silent, until he stood before the bars of his cell, the hard lines of his face still neutral. His eyes bore into hers, pain meeting pain.

"Take them off Solveig. I dare you."

"You know I can't do that. And even if I could, what makes you think I want to?"

"You could be more than this, more than your brother's pet." He looked her up and down. "More than some pretty chattel ripe for sale to the highest bidder. You could burn it all down and start over if you were so inclined."

"What makes you think I have any interest in that?"

"Because if you don't." He stepped even closer, hands encircling the bars between them. "It won't be long until they're adding your name to the list of the dead."

White-hot rage tore through her, sick and tired of having her life threatened. She launched for him, her own hands colliding with the bars as she snarled in his handsome face.

"Bold of you to threaten me now, prince."

He moved so fast she almost missed it.

Within a blink, his hands had moved from the bars to wrap around her wrists. He yanked her closer until their breaths mingled. So close that had the bars not separated them, every inch of their bodies would have touched in all the ways they longed for but could not surrender to.

He'd played her again. Known exactly which weakness to push, which insecurities to inflict further wounds upon, as she stared down in shock at his unbound wrists.

It wasn't possible.

They cuffed prisoners with Elemental powers on arrest, using ones that were opposite to their known ability to stifle them. There was no way Killian would be so foolish as to let him wield magic freely down here.

"Oh, Solveig," Emmerich whispered in her ear, in that silken voice. The voice that had once driven her to insanity. Made her crave his mouth on hers, to taste him despite the mistrust and anger that raged between them now. "That wasn't a threat."

"Let go," she seethed, trying to pull free of his grip.

"Burn them down, Solveig. Because the next time we see each other," a strange warmth tingled where his hands held her, slowly growing hotter and hotter, yet somehow not burning. "I want a fair fight."

"I…" she was silenced, brows knitting together. The heat grew fierce. She looked down again and watched helplessly as the intricate copper of her cuffs slowly melted around her skin. Dripping to the ground between their feet, blue gems clattering against the metal bars as they fell to the dirt.

"What have you done?"

"I saved your life, and it's far more than you deserve."

Wind blasted from somewhere unseen. The air was warm, salt kissed and tropical. Solveig blinked as her vision shook and blurred. Through the haze, she could see sandstone and terracotta buildings beneath a glittering starry sky and then it all vanished, taking the prince with it. Leaving Solveig alone in the dark caverns of High Tower Castle.

With Emmerich no longer holding her in place, she fell backward to the floor, trying to scrape a coherent thought together. She stared at the space the prince had just occupied, then at the floor where molten copper solidified as it cooled.

They had let the wolf into their den without knowing the full extent of his might. Emmerich Ryker of House Anders, Prince of Elithiend, was no mere Aire Wender as they had thought. Nor was he duel powered with pyromancy, as she had suspected with the melting of her cuffs; that should've destroyed the skin and muscle of her arms beyond saving.

No, he was the one thing they feared the most, his kind supposedly extinct, defeated by the balance The Oracle had brought. As dead as the Seers were frauds. And yet there he had stood and vanished. Proof that wasn't true. They'd welcomed a living Aether into their midst. An Elemental with the power to walk between spaces, unseen and untracked, a master of all elements, uniquely capable of destroying everything.

CHAPTER EIGHTY-FOUR

Freefall

Shouts barrelled toward her, footsteps echoing as they raced down the stairs. Solveig jumped to her feet, mind still fogged as she tried to focus on whatever was coming, and how she was going to explain the missing prince.

"Who's down there?" called Prince Killian.

"It's Solveig," she answered, as the prince and two of his guards emerged. One Solveig knew, he'd mocked her in Farrenhold. Cuffed her on her return to Torrelin; and here he was again, beside his prince.

"What are you..." Killian's words died as his gaze moved from her to the empty cell she stood before.

"What have you done?" he seethed.

"I swear I didn't," she rushed.

"Shut the fuck up, Solveig. He was here an hour ago when they patrolled and now he's gone." He shook his head, thinking for a moment, before looking upon his sister with dead eyes, resigned.

"Arrest her."

The guards stepped forward; the prince's right-hand addressing her directly. "Your Highness, by order of Prince Killian, you are under arrest on suspicion of aiding the escape of a highly dangerous prisoner."

"Wait, you don't understand," she tried.

The guards advanced further, swords drawn, and she reached for her daggers. "Don't do this."

"Drop the weapons Solveig," Killian ordered. "You're only making this worse for yourself."

"Not until you listen."

"You'll answer to The Oracle for this crime."

"No..." Her blood chilled as though turning to ice as it ran in her veins. "No."

"You left us no other option."

They advanced further; this time joined by the prince. "Don't come any closer," she warned. They didn't halt, didn't falter, not even a single step. Holding their weapons high as they approached as if sensing the battle, knowing she would not go down without a fight.

"I said stay back!" Solveig screamed, throwing her hands up. A gust of wind materialised from nothing. So strong it threw the prince and his guards off their feet, sending them crashing against the walls of the caverns and the bars of the cells. Solveig's breath came in thick startled pants as she stared down at her hands; at the unseen power suddenly coursing through her, electrifying her blood.

Her own sense of self-preservation broken by the wonder of what she had done. Wasting precious minutes that she should have used to escape to stare at her cuff-less wrists and her hands that had summoned a wall of Aire. From nothing.

The groaning of a waking guard snapped her back to reality. She eyed the three figures. Scrapes marred them all, though the prince had fared worse. Blood poured from an open wound at his temple. Where his guards were waking, he remained still, save for the faint rise and fall of his chest that showed he had not yet passed beyond the veil.

One guard opened his eyes, whipping round to stare at her, reaching for his sword across the dirt.

"Don't move," he attempted to order through gritted teeth.

"You ought to choose your battles carefully." She shrugged. "What's worth more to you right now? Me, or the life of your prince?" She flicked her chin, feigning nonchalance in the still unconscious prince's direction.

"You tried to kill us."

"It was an accident."

"You aided a prisoner's escape."

"You talk as though it was my first time."

"You made an attempt on the heir's life. That carries the penalty of death."

"Try it," she sneered. "I dare you."

"You're unstable." He shook his head. "I can't allow you to leave here."

"No." she said, simply, "you can't allow your prince to die. So, I'll ask you again. What is worth more to you? I may have struck the blow, but your delay in helping him is aiding me in his murder."

The guard swallowed, hands shaking, before he finally lowered his sword; moving to run for the stairs, he stammered out, "You have however long I take to bring help. If you're still here when I return, I won't hesitate again."

Then he ran, every heavy panicked footfall echoing.

"That's more than enough time," Solveig whispered to herself, as she followed him, not sparing the remaining guard nor her brother another glance.

She raced for her tower and room, grabbing whatever she could carry, weapons, clothes, her cloak to help shield her from view before leaving her chambers. Out in the hall, more footsteps raced up the stairs toward her. She was out of options. Turning back, she headed for the window, flinging the shutters open to the moonless night as she stepped up to the ledge, glancing back toward the door. Either direction promised death, but she resigned herself to the hope that her fledgling Aire Wending powers may break her fall.

Breathing deep one last time, she launched herself over the edge as the door to her room flew open.

CHAPTER EIGHTY-FIVE

The Awakening

Her eyes watered as the air rushed past her, cold and deadly. It stole the breath from her lungs as she fell toward the frozen ground below and it rushed to meet her. Body aching as the wind assaulted her. Straining, she brought her arms forward, attempting to mirror the same movement she'd made in the dungeon. She slowed slightly, but the ground was still coming much too fast.

With as much strength as she could manage, she moved her arms back again, fighting against the rushing wind before repeating the manoeuvre. Closing her eyes as she did so, she was losing velocity, but it wasn't enough. She peeked one eye open and saw the ground still coming for her just before she collided with it. Slow enough to not die, but hard enough that she was sure she'd dislocated a shoulder at least, and possibly worse.

The air was still around her as she stared up at the sky, wincing through the pain in her left shoulder before forcing herself to stand. Her ankle was weak, grimacing as she put pressure on it, but it was mercifully still intact. The pain was worth it when they should have been scraping her splattered brains and disintegrated bones from the courtyard instead.

She raced as fast as her ankle would allow, cradling her damaged arm with the other as she headed for the gates. Shouts rang around the castle, sconce after sconce lighting in her wake. She pushed herself harder, ignoring the stomach-churning agony as time ran against her. The guard had been true to his word, and even worse, he set the entire castle to the task, too.

The gates finally came into view, mercifully still open. She saw a guard racing around the stone wall to the operator shouting as he went. The gate started to close, forcing Solveig to push harder, breathe faster.

Close.

She was so close.

Barely a metre from the ground, she threw herself down onto the gravel to slide beneath the sharp teeth. Knowing she'd have time to regret the move later once she was somewhere safe. She didn't look back. Even as more angry shouts came after her, the guards desperately trying to bring the gate back up to allow the rest of them to give chase.

Solveig disappeared into the night.

She cleared the hill, raced past the glistening façade of the Temple of The Oracle as it slumbered before vanishing into the town. She moved through the tangle of alleys, heading west toward Farrenhold. They would know it was her only chance and they would surely follow, still she had to try.

Her heart pounded in her ears as her vision blackened at the edges. It forced her to stop for a moment. Slumping in the shadows against a wall with closed eyes, she grimaced through the pain coursing down her entire left side. Fighting to slow her heart rate when a hand clamped down over her mouth, the point of a dagger pressed against her throat. She fought against their hold, screaming silently as it put pressure on her damaged shoulder. She would not go back to the castle alive.

"Stop fighting," a voice hissed. It was familiar to her, like an ethereal dream, though she couldn't place where she had heard it before. "If you want to live through this night, you'll come with me quickly. They'll be on us soon."

"Who are you?" Her voice was muffled by the hand over her mouth.

"Your last hope, now move."

They stopped only to steal a pair of horses that were left outside a run-down hovel masquerading as a tavern. Mounted them without a word and raced westward. Solveig lagged slightly, fighting to steady herself with only one hand strong enough to grip the reins. She prayed the horses would give them an advantage.

The mysterious rescuer kept a punishing pace, cutting northward as the dawn broke, heading straight for the port. There, a small boat waited, the guard's post mysteriously empty, though Solveig didn't care to wonder why.

The stranger dismounted their horse with ease, heading aboard without pause, but Solveig hesitated at the foot of the gangplank.

"Who are you?" she asked again, staring at the stranger as they busied themselves readying the boat for departure.

"We'll have time for questions once we're at sea. Now climb aboard."

"I'm not going anywhere until you tell me who you are," she insisted. The stranger paused, their back to her as they threw a line to the floor with a shrug.

"Suit yourself. I give you a day before those guards catch you, another before you're a spectacle at the gallows in front of the entire city. Choice is yours."

"Fine," Solveig grumbled, stalking aboard, where she leaned against the mast.

"You could help, you know?"

"I've never sailed a boat in my life. This is on you."

"Perhaps you could give those new Aire Wending abilities a stretch and help us get out of port faster."

"How did you..." Solveig didn't bother finishing her sentence, changing tack. "I doubt I'll be much use. I'm down a working arm at the moment."

"Anything is better than nothing. Channel some of that rage I know you still have coursing beneath the surface, or we're both dead. Is that enough motivation for you?"

Solveig closed her eyes, bringing every hurt to the surface; the prince's deceit, Teris's too, the revelation of her cuffs removal, the death knell The Oracle pushed her toward. A slight breeze picked up behind them. It wasn't much, but slowly the sails filled, and they finally got underway. It took all her concentration. Forcing her to keep her anger bubbling under the surface. Once they were clear of the secluded port. she let the wind drop, exchanging it for a dagger, tired of waiting for answers.

"Start talking," she hissed; blade pointed at the stranger.

They moved away from the helm without a word, instead reaching up to remove the hood that had been casting their face in shadows. Brown skin glowed in the early morning sun. Her braided hair had more silver than before but was still decorated with glittering charms, as stark, churning grey eyes stared back at her.

"You," Solveig gasped, taking a step back. "How?" The woman only pushed the sleeves of her cloak up, revealing cuff-less arms Solveig hadn't noticed before.

"You never did work for Luxenal, did you?" Solveig guessed, lowering her dagger.

"No."

"How did you know where to find me? How did you know I needed help?"

"I make it my business to know things."

"That isn't an answer."

"It's the only one you're getting."

"You said if a name is all I require that I could call you Viana, was that the truth?"

"Partially, though most people know me as Viviana, or even Seraphine."

"No," Solveig's head shook, eyes wide as she stumbled back a step.

"My true name, however, is Seraphine Viviana of House Etana, Queen of Farrenhold, Lady of the House of Seers."

"This is impossible," Solveig stammered, staggering back aimlessly, searching for something to give her purchase.

"Some would argue that the power you wield now is also impossible, yet here you stand."

"You died. I attended your funeral."

"A complicated explanation that's better saved for another time."

"Where are you taking me? To Farrenhold?"

"To Vanahold."

"That place is a myth," Solveig scoffed.

"It is no more a myth than your home is."

"We should go to Farrenhold," Solveig insisted. "I'll be safe there."

"Farrenhold has their own troubles brewing. It is best we steer clear."

"What of your children?"

"They will receive aid should they need it."

"How can you be so cold about all of this?"

"I cannot interfere more than I already have," Seraphine snapped. "We've waited decades for the awakening."

CHAPTER EIGHTY-SIX

Epilogue

Prince Emmerich stumbled as he landed on home soil for the first time in months. Safe in the courtyard of Valentia Palace under the early morning sun. Guards and servants rushed out to meet him, but he held up a hand to stop them.

"I'm fine," he declared, regaining his footing, walking without aid toward the entrance of his home. The doors flew open, and a rush of fire red hair flew down the steps, colliding with him with enough force to send him back a step.

"You're a fool, Emmerich Anders. We thought you were dead," Valentina cried into his neck.

The prince's arms circled around his sister. "I'm fine," he repeated.

"You're clearly not," she declared, pulling away, eyeing his frail body and paled skin. "You need medicine."

"I need to speak to the king."

"Food, medicine and rest first. Whatever it is, it can wait."

"No, Valentina, it can't," Emmerich implored as he made to push past her into the palace.

"What happened?" she called after him.

"They know," he stammered, "they kn—"

His voice halted as a shadow moved into place above them, blocking out the sun. A strange unnatural pattern of wind beat around them. The sound and sensation Emmerich had grown accustomed to in his youth. His eyes fell closed on a sigh as he steeled himself, but he did not turn around as the threat landed with a mighty crash. Dust careened into the air as the beating wind halted instantly.

Emmerich turned, as a long shining sword was levelled at his throat. He stared down the blade into sneering grey eyes; set in a pale face crowned with blonde hair, topped with an iron circlet, twisted through with intricate braids. At her back loomed a monster of myth and legend, sharp teeth gleaming. Its yellow eyes unblinking as the sun glinted off its reddish-brown scales.

TO BE CONTINUED.

Acknowledgements

To two weeks of isolation aboard a cruise ship, where the idea for TBKoO was first realised, as much as I'd like to forget that time, I'm not sure I'd be here with out it.

To my parents who sent me a picture from one of their dog walks shortly after this that inspired the first concrete scene that birthed Solveig and Emmerich's story. For those who don't know, it was the Tempest Cove scene, that started everything.

To the Fairies aboard the Disney Fantasy from 2021 – 2022, who listened as I talked about this book I was trying to write, and supported me as I bounced ideas off them, specifically Lorrayne and Mariah, you two are the real MVPs.

To Astrid, who practically held my hand the entire way, gave me advice when I spiralled and was the first person to ever read TBKoO in it's entirety, we wouldn't be here without you today! You were Emmerich's number one fan from day one and you helped me shape him into the ray of sunshine he is today.

To E. J. Lounsbury from EJL Editing, you're a true super hero! Taking my book and making it into what it is today, your advice was invaluable.

To David Gardias, my incredibly talented cover designer, thank you for giving this story the cover it deserved, it is truly beyond any of my wildest dreams.

To the people of BookTok, there are far too many of you to list but if you have ever once interacted with a single one of my videos, know that I'm directing this at you. Your support means EVERYTHING, when things felt hard. When I thought I would never reach this point, your likes, your comments and shares boosted me to keep going, I hope you enjoyed the beginning of Solveig's journey and are willing to join me on this ride to future books.

And lastly thank you to you, the reader, who took a chance on this authors debut novel. You're making my dreams come true.

About the author

Born and raised in Northern England she now resides on Ynys Mon (Isle of Anglesey) North Wales, with her two dogs (Fergus and Nova) and her parents... yes she is unfortunately (for all involved) one of those millennials as yet unable to afford to move out.

By day she answers medical queries, sign posting to appropriate services. By night she sleeps... she is after all thirty. But all other waking hours are spent, reading, writing, and aimlessly scrolling TikTok (she likes to call it 'market research').

Having spent years (decades) dreaming of writing and publishing her own novel the time has finally come. 'The Broken Kingdoms of Osvolta' is her debut novel.

TikTok: @AuthorRBretherton
Instagram: @AuthorRBretherton
Website: www.authorrebeccabretherton.com
Newsletter Available via the Website!

Milton Keynes UK
Ingram Content Group UK Ltd.
UKHW040702021124
450602UK00016B/196/J